Vengeance of Dragons

Also by Holly Lisle
in Victor Gollancz/Millennium

DIPLOMACY OF WOLVES
THE SECRET TEXTS BOOK 1

Vengeance of Dragons

HOLLY LISLE

VICTOR GOLLANCZ
LONDON

The right of Holly Lisle to be identified as the author
of this work has been asserted by her in accordance with
the Copyright, Designs and Patents Act 1988.

First published in Great Britain in 1999 by
Victor Gollancz
An imprint of Orion Books Ltd
Orion House, 5 Upper St Martin's Lane
London WC2H 9EA

To receive information on the Millennium list, e-mail us at:
smy@orionbooks.co.uk

A CIP catalogue record for this book
is available from the British Library

Printed in Great Britain by
Clays Ltd, St Ives plc

To Joe, with love and gratitude

Acknowledgments

.

Again, thanks to Peter James and Nick Thorpe, authors of *Ancient Inventions*, which has proved the most inspirational and useful book I've read in ages; to Betsy Mitchell, whose editing, recommendations, comments, and questions made the book far better than it would have otherwise been; to Russell Galen and Danny Baror, whose tireless work on my behalf made my first European sales happen, and made it possible for me to live off my writing income, and, in Russ's case, inspired the project in the first place; to Matthew, whose first-draft editing also resulted in major changes and major improvements, and whose encouragement keeps me going; and to Mark and Becky, who did all sorts of useful and kind things for me while I was writing that made my life easier, and who cheered me up when the work got hard. And finally, belated thanks to John 'JT' Tilden and Perry Ahern for cheerfully providing the bodies.

Vengeance of Dragons

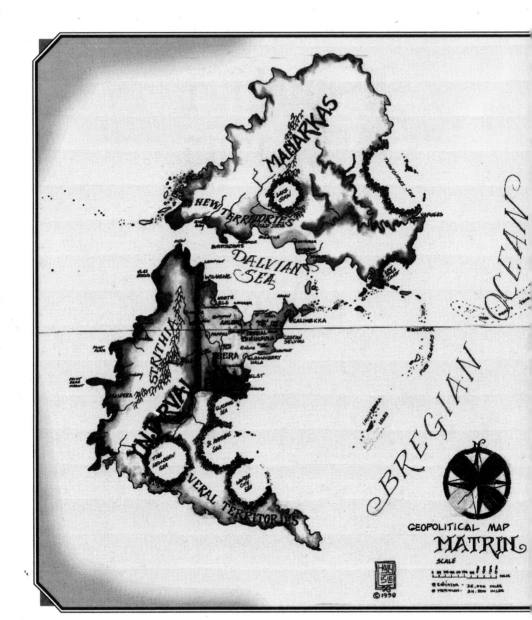

GEOPOLITICAL MAP
MATRIN
SCALE

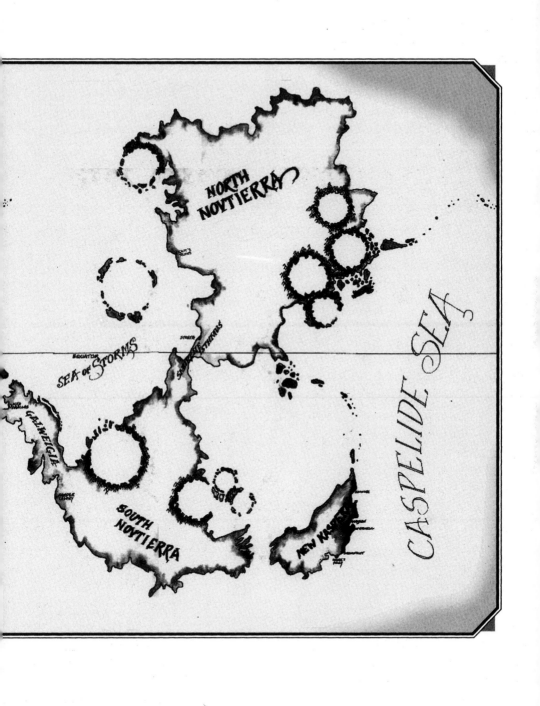

In Diplomacy of Wolves . . .

Magic, in the world of Matrin and especially in the Iberan lands where the last of the true humans live, has been a study both forbidden and reviled for a thousand years—but Kait Galweigh has survived to hide the secret Scars of old and dangerous magic. A daughter of the powerful Galweigh Family and a promising junior diplomat, Kait is Scarred. Her nature causes her to skinshift, a trait which would lead to her immediate execution even by members of her own Family. Chaperoning her cousin prior to the girl's wedding into the Dokteerak Family, Kait overhears a plot between the Dokteeraks and the Galweighs' longtime enemies, the Sabirs. The Families are planning to destroy the Galweighs at the upcoming wedding.

Kait survives a harrowing escape from Dokteerak House with her information, aided by a stranger who, like her, is Scarred by the skinshifting curse called *Karnee*. She is drawn to the stranger and is dismayed to discover that he is a son of the Sabir Family, her Family's oldest and worst enemy. She returns to the embassy, where she informs the Galweighs of the Dokteerak-Sabir treachery, and tries to put her attraction to the Sabir Karnee out of her mind. Her Family takes both military and illicit magical steps to foil the conspiracy and crush the conspirators. The Sabirs, though, never planned to share power with the Dokteeraks; instead, they use them to get the Galweigh military out in the open. Then, on two carefully managed fronts, they wipe out the Dokteerak and Galweigh armies and use both treachery and magic to capture Galweigh House back in the grand city of Calimekka.

However, magic used forcefully against another always rebounds. Both Families' wizards, who call themselves Wolves, expected to strike unprepared targets with their spells. But their attacks hit each other at the same time, and the magic rebounds, wiping out the majority of both Families' Wolves.

It simultaneously does two other things as well, both seemingly irrelevant. First, the magical blast wakes an artifact called the Mirror of Souls. A beautiful and complex creation designed by the Ancients before the end of the Wizards' War a thousand years earlier, the Mirror has been waiting for just such a powerful *rewhah*. It signals that the world has returned to the use of magic . . . and more importantly, magic of the right sort. The Mirror awakens the souls it holds within its Soulwell, and they reach out to people who might be able to help them.

Second, the *rewhah* horribly Scars a young girl named Danya Galweigh, a cousin of Kait's, who has been kidnapped by the Sabirs and used as a sacrifice by the Sabir Wolves when the Galweighs fail to meet the ransom. Danya is changed beyond recognition, and the baby she unknowingly carries, a baby conceived through rape and torture during her capture, is changed, too, but in more subtle ways. The force of the *rewhah* throws Danya into the icy southern wastes of the Veral Territories, where, were it not for the help of a mysterious spirit who calls himself Luercas, she would die.

Kait finds Galweigh House in Sabir hands and many members of her Family executed. She steals the Galweigh airible and flies for help to the nearby island of Goft, where the Galweigh Family has other holdings. However, the head of this lesser branch of the Galweigh Family sees the demise of the main branch as his chance to advance, and he orders Kait killed. A spirit voice claiming to be her long-dead ancestor warns her of the treachery, and she escapes again, this time after stealing money from the House treasury.

The spirit tells her another way she can aid her Family, even though it says they are now all dead. Following its advice, she hires a ship from the Goft harbor to take her across the ocean in search of the Mirror of Souls. The spirit tells her that this ancient artifact will allow her to reclaim her murdered Family from the dead. She enlists the aid of the captain, Ian Draclas, by telling him she is going in search of one of the Ancients' lost cities. Such a place would make any man's fortune.

Onboard the ship she runs into a man named Hasmal rann Dorchan, whom she once met briefly. Hasmal, a wizard of the sect known as the Falcons, had been trying to escape the doom that an oracle had warned would befall him if he associated with Kait. He is not pleased to see her.

Hasmal's oracle mocks him and warns him that to protect himself, he must teach Kait magic. She learns, but denies the existence of the doom-filled destiny he claims they share.

Kait is plagued by dreams of the Sabir Karnee; she becomes certain that he is following her across the sea. To break her obsession with him, she accepts the advances of the ship's captain, and she and Ian Draclas become lovers. But her obsession only worsens.

As the ship nears its destination, it sails into the heart of Wizards' Circle, a place where magical residue from the Wizards' War a thousand years before is still so strong that it can affect and control anyone moving within its reach. Hasmal works magic to free the ship, and Kait, in her skinshifted form, saves the life of the captain. In so doing, though, Kait is revealed as a monster and Hasmal as a wizard, and the crew turns against them. They reach the shore and discover the city, but while Kait, Hasmal, Ian, and two of his men set out to retrieve the Mirror of Souls from its distant hiding place, the crew mutinies and maroons them in the unexplored wilds of North Novtierra.

Book One

"Solander the Reborn will arrive
in the wind of the Dragons' breath.
Wanderers and Steaders joined
will slay the Dragons.
Born of blood and terror,
The opal city Paranne will rise at last."

FROM THE SECRET TEXTS, VOL. 2, SET 31
BY VINCALIS THE AGITATOR

Chapter 1

The scream was Kait Galweigh's first warning that something was wrong. The second, half an instant later, was the hard metallic stink of human blood mingled with the rank stench of predator.

"Run!" she heard Hasmal shout.

"The gap!"

"Slings!"

"Gods, I think he's dead!"

She heard running, and shouts, and animal howls. The smells and sounds and the terror hit her like a blow to the skull; her body responded before her mind could. Her blood began to boil and her skin and muscles flowed like liquid, and the human part of her, which had been hunting for edible plants in the forest, Shifted to embrace the monster that lived inside of her; she became the thing she both hated and needed. With the woman burned away, what remained was beast, furred, fanged, four-legged, hungry for the hunt. Karnee now, blood-mad, she raced toward trouble.

She came over the ridge at a dead run, and skidded to a stop at the sight laid out before her. The attackers had her people backed into a narrow crevice in the cliff that formed the north wall of their camp. Turben was down and bleeding heavily. The other three used the plentiful shale scree as their weapon; they were taking turns throwing volleys against the enemy with makeshift slings, timing their fire in such a way that a constant rain of the knifelike stone shards filled the air.

She couldn't see her attackers, but she knew where they were from the sound of them; they were using the ruin as their shield. They were better armed than the humans. She could hear the twang of bowstrings, the hiss of heavy arrows flying through the air, the rattle and clatter as the arrows rebounded off the cliff face and knocked loose more scree. Better armed and with their prey cornered, they couldn't help but win.

Unless she found a way to shift the odds in her favor.

She scrambled down the cliff, kicking loose scree as she did. But neither her friends nor her enemies would pay attention to her—four-legged, she moved differently than a human, and gave the impression she was moving away from the trouble.

Once into the valley and downwind of the attackers, she came in behind them, running through the underbrush with her belly to the ground. She was fast and quiet enough that they had no warning when she burst out of the brush to attack them.

She got her first clear look at them as she charged toward the nearest. They were taller than any man and gaunt as specters, and gray fur hung from their frames in ragged, moss-festooned hanks. She guessed they massed twenty to twenty-five stone—more than four times the weight and bulk of the average human. They ran on four legs but stood clumsily on two to fling rocks or shoot their arrows, and they called to each other in rough syllables that were not far removed from wordless grunts. Yet they did speak, and they did make weapons, and their faces, arranged in human fashion though larger and more heavily boned, bespoke their Wizards' War origins. They were Scarred—monsters whose ancestors a thousand years earlier had been men.

She was terrified. All her life, she'd heard horrible stories about Scarred monsters and what they were capable of—and she knew what *she* was capable of, which made her give the stories credence—but in the end it didn't matter. Her friends needed her.

She lunged in, keeping low to the ground and aiming straight for the rear leg of the nearest attacker, and before any of the four beasts could react to her, she'd sunk her fangs into the tendons of the monster's right leg and ripped through them.

The monster screamed, and blood gushed in her mouth. She bounded away, feeling the surge of the Karnee battle-lust boiling in her veins, fed by the raging river of her fear and determination.

The beast she'd hamstrung was on three legs, turning to face her as quickly as he could. She could read murder in his face. Another Scarred had turned, too, and nocked an arrow. She spun, darted from the cleared circle, and burst out at one of the two monsters still firing at the cornered humans. An arrow grazed her back and fire screamed through her body, but she kept going.

She launched herself upward at the creature's underbelly, her claws unsheathed and hooking forward, teeth bared. She ripped into the unprotected skin and the slippery, stinking weight of gut rolled down at her. The beast shrieked, its voice far too high-pitched for its size, and flailed at her. Her momentum carried her out of its reach, but into the path of the other two monsters.

One released an arrow in her direction; the other reached for her with dirt-crusted claws as long as her hands. The reaching monster hampered the aim of the shooting one, and the shooting one screamed at the grabbing one and startled him, and so both missed. She scrambled away before they could organize their attack, and ran out into the rain of shale.

"Don't hit me!" she yelled, and caught just a glimpse of the pale faces of her friends peering from the protection of the crevice. "I'm going to lead them away from camp. Hasmal—set a . . . a spellfire."

She heard them shout, "Kait!" Someone yelled, "Right!" and she hoped Hasmal had understood what she'd said. Her Shifted voice was deep and coarse, more the growling of an animal than the speech of a woman. Godsall, she hoped he could figure out what she planned, and that he would do what she wanted him to do.

The monster she'd disemboweled was down. But the others were after her, their long legs covering a hellish amount of ground.

She charged straight for the stream that fed into the bay and leaped it. On the other side, a game trail ran parallel to the water. Kait followed it; browsing animals had cleared much of the stream edge, so for something her size, it made easy running. The beasts that pursued her, much larger than she, struggled with branches and thickets over-hanging the trail at eye level. She could hear them crashing after her, falling behind. They started howling, and she could hear the frustra-tion in their calls.

She would make it. She was going to survive. She'd have time to get down to the beach, to swim into the bay—

Another monster appeared in front of her—another part of their hunting band, coming to assist its packmates. She shrieked, caught off guard, but it wasn't surprised to see her. It narrowed its eyes and lunged.

She barely evaded it; she was small and fast, it was large and slower. But not slow enough. It jumped sideways to block her escape, yelling as it did. From behind her, one of the others shouted back.

They talked to each other. It was too easy to think of them as ani-mals, but they weren't.

She shot straight up a solid tree, claws hooking into the bark. The monster stretched after her, its claws slashing into her haunch, and she felt a single instant of blinding pain along her spine. She dug harder with her hindquarters and pulled free. She clung to an upper branch, out of reach of the things, wishing for the safety of the bay. She was running out of time. She began the careful process of moving across the network of interfaced branches that would get her there.

She heard the flat twang of a bowstring, and an arrow buried itself in her flank. She screamed, feeling the hot gush of blood down her leg and the weight of the shaft throwing off her balance. The pain was an-other weight, sucking the fight from her. She stared down; one of them tracked her through the trees, waiting for another clear shot. She flung herself forward, and heard another of them crashing toward her from the side. The ones behind her were closing.

Hurry with the fire, Hasmal, she prayed. If he did, her friends would survive; they would find a way to get the Mirror to the Reborn even if she died. They had to succeed at that—Solander the Reborn had told her he had to have it. The Mirror, which was rumored to res-urrect the dead, would one day give her back her murdered Family, but even before it did that, it would serve Solander's purpose in creat-ing his world of peace and love—the world in which her kind would be accepted, not hunted down, tortured, and slaughtered.

She never thought she'd discover something worth dying for, but a world that would not murder little children for being born Scarred was such a thing. Her family's lives were such a thing. If her friends could live to get the Mirror to Solander . . .

She yanked the arrow from her flank with teeth and claws, and, fighting the agony, went scrambling on three legs along the branch. The Karnee Shift began closing the wound, but ate up her energy to do it. Her body would devour itself to heal; if she lived through this, she would have a hellish price to pay.

Then she heard fire crackling behind her and caught the first whiff of smoke. The spellfire wouldn't be stopped by rain, or by live, wet wood, or by unfavorable wind. It would burn everything burnable in its path, carving a perfect circle of destruction through the forest, stopping only when the energy with which Hasmal had fueled it ran out. It would burn faster than any normal fire, reducing a full-grown tree to ashes in mere moments. If she didn't get out of its way, it would burn her, too.

The stream ran below her, within reach. But the monsters held the game trails to either side of it. If she wanted to live, she had to get to the bay. She was out of time.

The monsters sniffed the air, smelling smoke—but they didn't know how fast the fire would come. She did. In desperation she threw herself into the center of the flooded, icy, boulder-studded stream. The water dragged at her legs as she scrabbled to touch bottom, lifted her off her feet, and flung her forward.

She fought to keep her head up. The current was fast, brutally fast, the normally negotiable water made deadly by days of rain. It slammed her into boulders as it dragged her downstream. With every bone-cracking collision she could only remind herself that worse was coming.

The current spun her backward for an instant before sucking her completely under the water. In that instant, she saw the world behind her lit up like a blast furnace, blue-white fire advancing in a wall faster than the fastest man could run.

She'd seen the monsters behind her outlined by the fire.

And then she was under the muddy water, caught in the fierce center of the current, dragged headfirst through blackness. She held her breath and kept her forelegs over her head, hoping to protect herself from rocks, but the current jerked her into one from the side, and when her head hit, the pain hammered her. She inhaled water and choked as the current flung her upward again, playing with her. She spewed water into the air and pulled smoke-poisoned, fire-heated air into her wet lungs.

Then everything got worse. The stream became a waterfall that plunged down the side of a cliff and poured into the bay. The current flung her over the precipice amid a torrent of pounding water. The sensation of floating seemed to last both forever and no time at all, ending abruptly in horrific pain. Her body crashed against rocks, water slammed her, and ribs and hips and legs all shattered and screamed agony at once.

She was with the pain, in the pain, made of pain for an instant that was an eternity, while her blood boiled and her skin burned and a fire erupted inside of her that was hotter than the spellfire that had destroyed the world around her.

Then . . .

Nothing.

Chapter 2

The Veil joins all the worlds—those that are, those that were, and those that will someday be; they exist simultaneously within its compass. It is no-time, no-place, no-thing; infinite, terrifying, unknowable. Its winds blow through the realities, its storms twist them, and even its silences cast long shadows.

Through the Veil, galaxies and souls travel as equals. In it, stars and gods and dreams are born, live out their spans, and die. It is neither a heaven nor a hell, though men of uncounted realities have named it one or the other or both, and have built stories and religions and civilizations around their error.

The Veil . . . is. Uncaring, unchanging, and unchangeable, it nonetheless offers much to those who know how to reach it and exploit it.

Within the Veil, the Star Council regrouped in answer to the summons of a single powerful soul, its members racing inward like stars in a tiny imploding galaxy—hundreds of brilliant points of light spiraling toward an ever-brightening center.

The soul that summoned the Council was named Dafril. Dafril yearned for the immortality of the Veil, the power of gods . . . and a body of flesh. When Dafril's soul had thought it would claim Kait Galweigh as its avatar, it had begun forming its thought patterns in female mode. Now things were changing. Kait's compliance was ever more in doubt, so it began to shape itself toward a male existence. A thousand years earlier, it, or rather he, and his friends had devised a plan that they hoped would bring them all they yearned for. At last they were close to achieving their dreams.

We have two orders of business, Dafril announced when all the councillors save one—a missing soul named Luercas—were gathered. *First, we must prepare our avatars, for the hour of our return draws near. Second, we must decide how we will deal with the forces that have risen against us in our absence.*

We've spent a thousand years in the planning of our return, Mellayne said quietly. *If we don't know what we hope to do now, will we ever?*

At the last moment things change, Dafril said. *And this has become the last moment. We could only speculate before now about the kind of world we'd find when we returned—now we know what we face. We could only guess what sort of people would inhabit it. And we never expected betrayal by one of our own—yet we must assume, since Luercas has disappeared, he has done so in order to oppose us.*

I thought the Mirror would only wake us when they'd rebuilt a real civilization, Shamenar said. *I cannot believe the primitive conditions we face. The filth of even their greatest city stuns the mind. Raw sewage in the gutters; animal waste in the streets; slaughtered animals hanging in open-air markets; rooms lit only by fire. And the sicknesses of the people . . . worms and boils and rickets and yaws, influenza and diabetes and rat plague and things I haven't even heard names for before.*

They're ignorant, Tahirin added. *Superstitious, cruel, violent, dishonest—and as brutal as their short, uncomprehending lives, most of them. How can we work with these people?*

Dafril drew energy from the Veil and grew more luminous, to give his people courage. *This is the world we come into. This is the lot we've drawn. They've built what they could—now we make it better. Only we can return civilization to our home. We can cure their diseases; we can improve their city; we can teach them and set them on a new path. The white cities will rise again, and we will ride through their streets in skycarts and breathe perfumed air and feast on wondrous food. The wind will once more play the White Chimes, and a hundred thousand fountains will sing and cool the breezes, and coldlamps will illuminate the darkest corners. Remember. Remember what we did before, and know that we can do it again.*

I wish I could be so sure, Werris said.

Dafril felt their fear. A thousand years of passive waiting lay behind them, and that time had weight. In it, his people had grown accustomed to the limitations of bodilessness and fearful of change, challenge, and danger. Now they faced all three, and he sensed in many of his followers a desire to continue as they were, to cling to the known. He felt the same fear and in some small way tasted the same desire, but he also recalled the hunger he'd brought with him from life.

Life was the only game worth playing.

More than a million people inhabit Calimekka, he reminded them. *And the city grows daily. You can bring civilization to a million souls far more easily than you can to a hundred, because you have more people to work with. We shall . . . tax them. We'll apply a fair tax equally to every soul in the city. With that little tax, we give them the good things they haven't the talent or the intelligence or the imagination or the ambition to give themselves. We will have our civilized city, and they will live healthy lives protected from violence in a world that no longer knows war, famine, or pestilence. What could be more reasonable?*

Well. Yes. Why would anyone object to our making their lives better? Except Solander, of course, Sartrig said. *And his Falcons. And evidently Luercas.*

Dafril felt the stab of truth there. Solander, who had fouled their work so completely a thousand years earlier, had somehow come back. He'd found himself a body, an incredible body subtly shaped by magic, hardened by magic the way fire hardened steel—a body worthy of immortality. He was not yet born, but he and that wondrous body were waiting for them, already watchful, already planning to oppose them again, standing as ever on the side of dirt and disorder and chaos. They would have to deal quickly with Solander. And Luercas . . .

Luercas had been Dafril's closest and most powerful ally a thousand years earlier. He'd been a friend and a companion; he had shared Dafril's dreams of their shining white city and of immortality spent amid beauty, luxury, and art; he had struggled with Dafril to save their fellow dreamers when everything went bad at the end. But when the Mirror of Souls finally woke the hundreds it held within its Soulwell and set them free within the Veil, Luercas had vanished. And Dafril was left wondering what his absence meant—whether the cold and twisted things that preyed between the worlds had devoured his soul, or whether some unsuspected bitterness or treachery had turned it against the Star Council. He could not believe that Luercas, ever the most careful and patient of souls, would carelessly allow himself to be devoured. Which left . . . betrayal.

Sartrig's spirit-light darkened as the senior councillor brought himself to the fore. *I have a problem. I have chosen a marvelous avatar— a young Wolf named Ry Sabir—a powerful, well-bred man with training in magic and a body shaped by magic. But he has some knowledge of blocking and shielding, and he fights my direct influence at every turn. As long as he believes me to be the spirit of his dead brother, he at least considers my council. But he is most intractable and strong. When the moment comes, I don't know that I will be able to penetrate his magic to . . . lead him.*

Dafril felt the fear behind Sartrig's remark and its echoes shivered through his own soul. Men and women in this new time and new place were not all purely human—an interesting result of fallout from the last weapons in the final exchange between his people and the Falcons. He and his companions had just barely missed seeing the first fruits of that fallout, he suspected. A thousand years had honed the changed people—the people the Calimekkans called the Scarred— into a host of lovely species; some of the specimens in this new time offered options he had never imagined a thousand years earlier. *His* preferred avatar was a young woman named Kait Galweigh, a strong, beautiful girl of high birth with an interesting twist. She was a skin-shifter, thereby possessing a talent he found irresistible. She was well thought of, had the necessary connections to Calimekka's ruling factions, and had for some time been willing—even eager—to listen to his advice, believing that she heard a long-deceased ancestor when he spoke to her.

But she had become increasingly suspicious in the last weeks, after falling in with unfortunate companions who had introduced her to magical training which allowed her to block out his presence.

He had therefore chosen a backup for his preferred avatar. Exquisite little beast though Kait was, he had accepted the fact that she might be out of his reach when the great moment arrived. So his second choice was another of those marvelous skinshifters—a powerful wizard who had friends in useful places, and who was as beautiful as Kait. To his detriment, he was not as young. He wasn't female, either, and Dafril had been fascinated by the idea of femaleness. He was also cruel, and known for perversions of a sort that Dafril found disgusting. And he had enemies. But Dafril had decided that he could cope with Crispin Sabir's drawbacks if Kait failed to work out.

Another fact made Crispin interesting to Dafril, though it wasn't something he yet knew how to use. Crispin was father to the body that Solander inhabited. Dafril could feel the faint resonance created by the link of paternity. He knew that if he found a way to use it, his enemy could also use the link against him . . . if he knew of it. If he didn't, well . . . it was, for the moment, something to keep in mind.

Meanwhile, the avatar Sartrig had been drawn to was also one of the world's few skinshifters. Those flexible bodies were so tempting, but offered special problems as well as opportunities.

Prepare an alternate, he said. *For that matter, each of you should have at least one alternate. We will have only the one moment to reach our avatars once the Mirror draws us through the Soulwell into the world. If your avatar is beyond the Mirror's reach at that moment, or is in any way closed to you, you'll be tossed back into the Veil without an anchor, and lost to us forever.*

The silence that greeted this statement echoed with fear.

Someone from far in the back of the Council's cluster finally broke the silence by changing the subject. *Which leaves us with the problems of Luercas and of Solander and his minions.*

Dafril considered that for a moment. *Serious problems, both, though I think Solander is the lesser. We have already defeated him once, and though he is already embodied, and the body is truly his, in order to acquire it he is being born. He will be an infant, and then a child, and while he is helpless, we will have time to prepare. We know of his presence and that of his followers; they should pose little danger to us.*

Luercas is another matter. We must accept that with every moment he ignores our calls and hides himself, the likelihood of his plotting against us increases. Nor am I comforted by the fact that he is one and we are many, for though we have the strength of numbers, we cannot assume that he is alone—he has always had a talent for finding allies in unlikely places.

We'd thought to show him mercy, to give him a chance to rejoin us, Dafril continued, *as suits those we love and would call friends; but though I am loath to admit it, I must now concede that those of you who advocated his destruction were right. When you search for him, search in groups large enough that you can overcome him if you find him. He is old, and clever, and he survived things in the Old World that most of you cannot imagine. When you find him, don't try to reason with him, don't warn him of your presence. Annihilate him. For if you do not, I fear he will annihilate you.*

Chapter 3

The *Wind Treasure* cut through rough seas, heading south along uncharted North Novtierran coastline. Ry Sabir leaned against the curved bulkhead of the cabin and frowned out the porthole at the ragged black line of land that lay on the horizon to the east, feeling sick dread in his belly. Kait was in trouble. The link that bound them, whatever it was and wherever it came from, had sent him fear, rage, pain . . . and now nothing. Nothing was the worst thing of all.

He turned back to his lieutenants and said, "I haven't discussed it because there hasn't been any need."

All five of his lieutenants, who were also his best friends, had gathered in the small room. They'd locked and barred the cabin door and now sat crowded on the two bottom bunks.

Yanth, dressed for high drama in black silk breeches and a black silk shirt, with his long blond hair braided with black cord, said, "I'm afraid there is a need. Each time one of us has mentioned what we'll do when we get back home, you fall silent. Or you look away, or change the subject, or make some mock of the idea of returning to Calimekka. And not once have you told us how you expect to show up with a bride who's a Galweigh. Surely that seems to us to require some planning, or at least some thought."

Trev, Jaim, Valard, and Karyl all nodded.

Yanth continued, "You're hiding a problem from us, and the

problem you're hiding concerns us. We're determined to have the truth out of you, no matter what we have to do to get it." He flushed as he finished speaking, and the vertical scars on his cheeks stood out like two stripes of white paint.

This was the moment Ry had dreaded, the moment when his friends would no longer be turned aside from asking their questions, the moment when he would have to face the truth. He pushed his worries about Kait to the back of his mind—they would still be there later. He had immediate problems.

"Doesn't matter that you're first-line Family and we aren't," Jaim said. "Doesn't matter that Trev's not Family at all. We're going to know what you're hiding from us before we leave here, or we won't leave here."

Yanth would speak out of anger. It was his way. And he could cool down as quickly as he heated up. Had it been only Yanth in the room with Ry, he felt sure he could have avoided the confrontation his friends sought.

But Jaim arrived at no decision quickly. He weighed and considered and argued with himself until everyone was certain he would never say either yea or nay . . . and then without warning he would come to his conclusions. When he did, nothing could sway him. If Jaim had decided he must know the truth, he would starve to death waiting to find it out. And keep Ry starving with him. When Jaim spoke, Ry saw all his options fly out the door.

They were his friends, had been for many years—but when he looked into their eyes, he saw no warmth, no willingness to laugh and be turned from their questions. He smelled on them the beginnings of anger and fear, and he knew he would finally have to face what he had done to them. He simply wasn't sure how to go about it.

"My mother . . ." he began, and stopped.

They looked at him, expectant.

He swallowed, tasting shame.

"The day we sailed, I went to tell her I was leaving. All of you were already on the ship, waiting for me. But she refused to give me her leave. After all the deaths . . ." He closed his eyes, remembering that horrible confrontation with his once-beautiful mother, who lay in her sickbed, Scarred beyond recognition by the fallout of his Family's abortive war against the Galweigh Family. "She didn't want to hear anything I had to say. She insisted that since my father was dead, I take over leadership of the Wolves. I refused, telling her that I was coming after Kait. She was furious with me, and asked if you were all accompanying me. I told her that I sailed alone—that all of you were dead." He heard their indrawn breaths, saw the shock and horror on their faces, and he looked down, unable to meet their eyes.

"You told her we were *dead*?" Karyl, Ry's cousin, fell back onto the bunk and covered his face with both hands. "Dead? You . . . *idiot!*"

"I feared her reprisals against your families if she knew you were helping me defy her."

Yanth had gone so pale his scars disappeared. "Dead. So what advantages did you feel you got for us by our being dead?"

"I told her that you died heroes . . . fighting the Galweighs in Galweigh House." He shrugged. "It seemed like a good idea at the time."

He saw them wince at those words.

They had the right, he thought. He didn't even dare recall the number of times he'd said those words before. So many of his disasters had seemed like good ideas at the time.

In his defense, he told them, "Your families are now in high favor. *High* favor. Trev, your sisters will be presented to first-rank Sabirs when they are of marriageable age and will be eligible to carry title all the way up to paraglesa. Valard, your brother and father will have already been given the title of parat. You other three—your families were already parats. But they won't be dead . . . and if my mother had any idea that you were helping me defy her, they would have been, with their heads on the city walls."

Valard crossed his arms over his chest and glowered at Ry, green eyes blazing. "That seems exaggerated. How much trouble could you have been in? Meanwhile, while we're dead and will never be able to go home without destroying our families, you'll go back a hero, eh?" He had always been willing to do anything for Ry, but at that moment he looked like he'd reconsidered.

"Either we go back heroes together or none of us goes back at all. As far as everyone knows, I'm as dead as you are."

That gave them pause.

"They think you're dead, too?" Karyl asked. "So how did you accomplish that? And why?"

"I made it look as if the Hellspawn Trinity killed me, because they knew I was going to make my bid to lead the Wolves. That was as much to convince my mother that I intended to comply with her demands as to get out of the House without breaking my word to her. You see, she told me if I didn't stay and fight for leadership of the Wolves, she'd declare me *barzanne*. But she failed to consider that if I stayed and made a real bid for power, the Trinity would have killed me for real. And being 'dead' legally was better than being dead in fact. And far better than being *barzanne*."

His friends were stunned.

"Your own mother was going to declare—"

"*Barzanne*—"

"By my own soul—"

"Had she known you were alive and helping me, I have no doubt she would have declared you *barzanne* as well." He looked into their eyes. "Your families would not have fared so well then."

"No."

They were nodding, agreeing, ready to forgive.

"I'm sorry," Ry said. "I never intended to involve you in such trouble. I never thought going after Kait Galweigh would be such a mistake."

His friends looked at each other, shrugged, looked at him.

Jaim said, "The man who knows the future makes no mistakes. But such a man isn't a man. He's a god."

Yanth shook his head slowly, then grinned. "True. And you just *think* you're a god."

"You don't hate me?" Ry asked.

Valard sighed. "Not yet. Figure out a way for us to be heroes, and to go home again, and we'll forgive everything."

Karyl leaned back on one elbow and smiled slowly. "At the least find us an island inhabited by beautiful girls we can take as wives, and set us up like parats. With a beautiful young wife, my own land, and decent weather, I'll forgive and forget almost anything."

"At the least, you say?" Now Ry was smiling. "It isn't enough for the five of you that all of us are alive and healthy?"

Yanth tugged at the front of his shirt, smoothing the silk. He didn't bother to look up as he said, "Ah, but we know you. You'll do everything you can between now and the time we find a safe harbor to get us all killed. Yourself included." Now he did look up, and his eyes were full of laughter. "All we want is moderate compensation for the hell you're sure to put us through."

Ry decided to tell them what he knew, though not precisely how he'd learned it. If his dead brother's spirit had crossed the Veil to offer him counsel and beg his help, surely that was a secret the two of them could keep. "I've discovered through magic that Kait is going after an artifact that returns the dead to life. I'm going to take her home as my wife—but all of *us* are going to carry home that artifact, and any other wonders we find in the Ancients' city she's discovered. With a ship full of such riches, my mother will be able to resurrect my father to lead the Wolves again, and be able to have my older brother back. And we'll be heroes."

And he would be freed from the cloistered life of dark magic and intrigue his mother had planned for him.

Yanth frowned. "I would think you would have said something before this, if only to let us know we had as much stake in reaching Kait as you do."

"I didn't know if she would find her city, or if she would find the Mirror of Souls—and why give you hope when there was none? Or, for that matter, why let you know how bad things were when we might yet hope for a chance of reprieve? Lately when I've looked through her eyes I've seen both ruins and an artifact that I believe is the Mirror—so now you can find out about the trouble we're in and find out that we might hope to get ourselves out of it at the same time. Meanwhile, as we try, your families are safe."

What he didn't know and would not tell them was whether Kait still lived. Perhaps he'd brought all of them to the other side of the world for nothing—that inexplicable link that bound him to Kait was as silent as if it had never existed. He had followed her across half a world, a madness he still could not explain even to himself. He had thrown away his name, his Family, and his future for a stranger who was the born enemy of the Sabirs, a woman he had met in the flesh once, and that in a dark alley in front of the corpses of the men who would have killed her. He did not know if she could love him. He did know she had every reason to distrust him, and perhaps even to hate him.

And now he could no longer tell if she still lived.

He stared out the porthole. She was ahead of him somewhere. And he would give anything to find her still alive.

Chapter 4

Imogene Sabir had placed her chair carefully beneath the beam of sunlight that poured through the high window of her study. Though she couldn't see the sunlight, she could feel it; ever since the attack on the Galweighs, when the *rewhah*—the magical backlash that came from using magic as force—nearly destroyed her, her bones craved its heat.

Finder Malloren stood before her, but not in the attitude of profound obeisance required when one of his station faced one of hers. He mistook her blindness for lack of ability to *see*, which was his error, and one for which she would eventually make him pay. With her heightened Karnee and magical senses, she could not only determine his physical position, but also his mental impressions of her, while her sense of smell picked up a secret he thought he kept from everyone that she could, at some time in the future, threaten to expose. She thought doing so would make him virtually her slave.

When she had time for such amusements, she decided she would play with the Finder a bit.

Meanwhile, however, she listened to his presentation of his latest hunt.

". . . This long after the fact, it was hard to find anyone around the docks who remembered anything. I had to pay a lot of money to people who *might* be able to put me in touch with people who *might* have been there. It was difficult—"

"But if you'd failed," she interrupted, "you wouldn't be standing here right now, expecting to be paid. I already know my *son* is alive. That humiliating scene Crispin orchestrated proved that clearly enough. I just want to know the rest of the story."

"W-w-well . . . yes . . . but I wanted you to know how hard—"

"Your personal difficulties don't interest me. Your results do. I pay you for the results, and for the costs you incur in getting them. If you want to be paid for the dramatic way you tell your story, I suggest you change to a different line of work."

She felt him flush—from humiliation at being spoken to thus, and from having to take it, and finally from anger at being denied telling his tale the way he chose. She sensed in him frustration, too. He had no doubt expected her to offer him a bonus when she heard how much work he'd had to do to bring her his findings.

She smiled, and felt him recoil. That amused her, too. She wished she could see what she had become in the wake of the disaster. She could guess from touching her face and from the reactions of others that little of the human was left of her. She supposed she had become hideous, but she could not see her own reflection—in her mind she was still as beautiful as she had been the day she lost the last of her sight. She didn't mind being hideous. Being beautiful had worked for her, but that was gone. She had discovered, however, that terror peeled as much cooperation out of people as beauty ever had.

He said, "Yes. Of course. I cannot verify names—the people I have located were careful to keep their names from any records. Or from even having them spoken. Ironically, it was that care which finally allowed me to find them.

"On the night your son disappeared and was presumed murdered, five young men spent the better part of the stations of Dard and Telt in a dockside tavern called The Fire-eater's Ease, passing the time drinking, playing hawks and hounds, and dicing and betting at fortuna. They were obviously of the upper classes—four wore swords prominently displayed and the fifth wore two long daggers. All dressed well. From eyewitness accounts, I have that one was tall and slender with blond hair and scars on his face; he was reported as being a boaster and a dandy, dressed entirely in silk. Another, somewhat shorter, wore brown hair pulled back in a long braid, and seemed to those who saw him to be quiet. Thoughtful. A doxy who works there says she sat on his lap and tried to talk him into going upstairs with her, but he refused even though he was interested. She says he said he was waiting for a friend, and that when the friend arrived, he would have to be ready to leave immediately. He refused to tell her anything about the friend or where he had to go—refused so adamantly that she remembered him. He called himself Parat Beyjer."

"Parat Beyjer, eh?" Imogene chuckled, delighted in spite of herself. "Parat *Beyjer*? And tell me, were his friends named Soin, Gyjer, Torhet, and, perhaps . . . Farge?"

She'd shocked him. "How did you *know*? I mean, none of them was named Torhet, but there was a Gyjer. A Farge, too. Another was named Rubjyat."

"The boys had classical educations. *Beyjer* was the 'god of green' in the classical mythos of ancient Ibera, when Ibera was still called Veys Traroin and included much of what is now Strithia, back when it was a member nation of the Empire of Kasree. Gyjer was the 'god of purple' in the same mythos. Farge was the 'god of blue,' and Rubjyat the 'god of no color'—I wouldn't have expected one of the boys to pick him."

Imogene could tell the Finder was interested in spite of himself. She sensed him leaning toward her, heard a slight quickening in his pulse and breath. "Why not?"

"The god of no color was associated with disasters. I would have thought that the boys would have saved that name for my son when he arrived. Disasters are, after all, his specialty."

"Then you're sure these are the right men?"

"I'd bet your life on it." She felt him tense as he caught the wording of her little joke, and she smiled again. "But just so I don't make any irrevocable mistakes, tell me the rest of what you found out."

She heard him swallow. "As you wish. The one who appeared oldest to the witnesses wore his hair short—the doxy recalled him as well. Said that she thought he was balding, and had shaved his head to make the fact less obvious. He apparently was rude to her, telling her he had no interest in women of her sort. Another was remarkably pale, and had, two male witnesses said, a face like a moon. He was apparently adept with fortuna—won a great deal of money from them before he finally left the tavern. And the last no one recalled until I asked if they were sure there weren't five men together instead of four. Then various witness recalled a fifth man who had occupied a chair at the same table."

"That would have been Jaim," Imogene said. "He has the most remarkable ability to be unremarkable. It's a gift."

"It would be," the Finder agreed.

"Well, then." She rubbed the silk hem of her tunic between her fingers, a nervous habit she'd acquired since she lost the last of her sight. She considered her options. "You've found them. I have no doubts of that. So what became of them? Where are they now?"

"The men who lost so much money followed them to the harbor, where the five men boarded a ship. No one recalled the name of the ship. So I checked the harbor records. Several ships sailed that night—the tides and winds were favorable. None would seem to be the ship they sailed in, for each listed a cargo and a destination, and none noted passengers, but one, the *Wind Treasure,* claimed to be sailing for the colonies with a cargo of fruit and wood. The log was signed out by one C. Pethelley. Merchant Registry lists no Pethelleys, Sea-Captains' Registry lists two Pethelleys living but both are accounted for, and the *Wind Treasure* had never received a cargo, and never arrived in the colonies. It is a Sabir registry, a secondary ship that had been in dry dock for repairs, had just been returned to the water and recrewed, but was well-known to have had empty holds. I still cannot prove a connection between your son and his friends and this ship, but every other deep-sea vessel that sailed that night—and for the next week, in fact—I can account for. They went where they said they were going, and did what they said they would do."

Imogene snorted. "Oh, I doubt you can account for *every* ship. Piracy being what it is in these waters, I would expect there are dozens of ships he and his friends *could* have left on. So, tell me. Where did they go?"

"I don't know. The *Wind Treasure* has not signed in to any harbor whose records I could obtain. I'm waiting to hear from Kander Colony, Finder's Folly, and the settlement in the Sabirene Isthmus, but

I don't expect the results will be positive. All I can tell you for sure is where they aren't."

"I see. You can't tell me what I most wish to know." She let him fidget for a long moment, considering possible outcomes for her displeasure. At last she said, "Still, you've been laudably thorough."

The Finder exhaled softly. "Then you're satisfied?"

She leaned back in her chair and sighed. "I'm *convinced*. All I requested of you was that you bring me enough information to convince me. Satisfied . . . well . . . my satisfaction lies outside your influence." She twisted the silk hem, imagining it as her son's face, wanting to shred it. "Do go. I need to be alone to think. My secretary will pay you before you leave."

"Will you be needing anything else?"

"If I do," Imogene said softly, "I know where to find you." She made sure that sounded like the threat it was.

Finder Malloren scuttled from her study like a bug whose rock had been lifted away, exposing him to the light.

Imogene waited until she felt him leave the House, a matter of only a few moments. She stayed cautious around Finders—men and women who collected information for a living could collect it for many buyers, and Imogene knew Calimekka was full of enemies who would pay well for anything that could weaken or destroy her.

Once she heard the outer door close, though, she rang the bell that summoned her secretary.

When he entered the room, she said, "Porth, I'm going to require a talented assassin. The best you can locate. Not one already contracted to the Family, however. I want an independent."

Porth waited, saying nothing.

"I have a bit of punishment to exact." The Sabir paraglese—for the first time in two hundred years—had removed the Wolves' right of self-governance by naming Crispin head of the Wolves and creating assistant positions for Anwyn and Andrew. This elevation of the Hellspawn Trinity to power over Imogene she could attribute directly to her son Ry's actions. Because of him, she was shut off in a marginal corner of the House and relegated to near-powerlessness in the affairs of the Family. Now she found his friends far from being the heroes she'd believed them to be—heroes who'd died for the Sabirs at

Galweigh House, as Ry had claimed on the day he was "killed"—his best friends had aped his lies and betrayals. They had abetted him in fleeing the city and her orders. "Ry and his five dearest friends have been having a joke. At my expense."

"They are alive, then?"

"All *six* of them are very much alive. And apparently very much out of my reach."

"But you know where they went? You're sending the assassin after them?"

"Not at all. For now, at least, I cannot touch them. But they have thoughtfully left their relatives behind, and put me in a position where I have come to know them. After all, as family of these 'heroes,' I have given them every courtesy."

Imogene chuckled, and felt her secretary shudder.

"Then the assassin . . ."

"I want to play a little game. I want this assassin to kill off Ry's friends' families, person by person, in creative ways. Let's see how many of them we can annihilate before the boys get back home. Don't you think that will be amusing?"

Porth said nothing.

Imogene let the silence run for a while, then said, "Porth?"

"Yes, Parata. Amusing."

He didn't sound amused at all. Poor Porth—he lied so badly.

Chapter 5

The water simultaneously weighed her down and buoyed her up as she slipped through a world marked by shifting, fluid light. Water flowed in through her mouth and out through the sides of her neck, and though something about that seemed wrong, she didn't know what it was. She heard the pounding of the tide in her bones and felt the movement of prey through her skin, as if her entire body had become her eyes. Pain lay behind her; ahead of her lay uncertainty. In her present, she knew only hunger, a hunger so immense that it devoured her. She knew she was more than appetite, but she could not reach the part of her that insisted this. She knew that breathing water was somehow wrong, but she didn't knew how she knew, and for the moment she didn't care.

She rolled, shifting fins to arch her body around, and caught sight of a cloud of silver shimmering before her. With a flick of her tail she was gliding toward it, hardly disturbing the water through which she moved. She slammed into the center of the cloud and devoured a dozen of the fish before the school erupted, then followed the largest group that broke away, pushing after it with three hard thrusts of her tail, conserving energy. She hunted, and fed. When the school of silver fish scattered beyond convenient reach, she moved into a smaller school of large red and yellow ones, and then another, and another sort of fish. She avoided anything that created a bigger pressure line while moving than she did, and when she tasted blood in the water, she stayed away.

She refused to question her existence, avoiding her mind's nagging insistence that she was not what she seemed to be. She fed, because she had been weak and damaged and near death; and as she fed, she grew stronger.

And when she was strong enough, her mind forced her body to acknowledge its presence. It named her to herself, and with remembrance of her name came the flood of other memories.

She was Kait.

She had friends who would need her help.

She had a task she had to accomplish.

And trouble was coming.

Shifted into human form, exhausted, waterlogged, naked, freezing, and with her senses dulled and slowed, Kait dragged herself back to the camp. She could not guess how long she had been gone, and she could only hope that she would find her friends alive when she returned. The burned wasteland through which she'd come had been nothing but a sodden stew of ash, with the ruins of the Ancients' city suddenly standing as clear and obvious as if they'd been abandoned only the day before.

In that sea of ash, the perfect circle of ground that Hasmal had been able to protect from the spellfire stood like a vision of Paranne: heavy with evergreens, laced with the fine sculptures of deciduous trees picked out in black against the gray winter sky, carpeted with leaves that still retained some of their autumn color and that lay like gemstones carelessly tossed upon the ground. The castaways' camp lay within the center of that circle. Kait heard voices inside the ruin they used as their base. She also smelled decay and death. She knew that when she stepped into the shelter, she was going to get bad news, but her nose refused to tell her how bad it could be. Post-Shift depression, post-Shift dullness.

She went in.

Her bad news greeted her by the door. Turben lay to the right in the first room, his body pulled under the intact portion of the roof.

She knelt at his side and touched him. His corpse was cold and rigid. He'd been dead for a while.

A soft groan from the back room caught her attention next, and she hurried in. Ian and Hasmal crouched at either side of Jayti's bedroll. Jayti twisted and groaned again.

"Not Jayti," she whispered. She'd come to admire the crewman, who had impressed her with his loyalty, his common sense, and his courage. "What happened?"

Jayti looked at her with pain-fogged eyes, and managed a smile. "You're back," he said. "Gives me hope that the captain's prayers for me will be heard, too."

"Kait!" Hasmal shouted. "You're alive!"

Ian leaped to his feet and ran over to her. He picked her up and swung her around, holding her close, unmindful of her nakedness. He kissed her passionately, then pressed his cheek to hers. "Ah, Kait," he whispered. "I thought I'd lost you." He pushed her back from him briefly, studied her, then pulled her into his arms again. "You're nothing but bones, girl," he said. And then, when he let her go, "How'd you get through it? And where have you been? I . . . we . . . I gave up on you yesterday."

"How long have I been gone?"

Hasmal had been digging through her bags; he handed her spare breeches and tunic to her as he said, "Three days, two nights."

"That long?" She frowned, surprised that she'd stayed in Shift longer than a day. "I was . . . under the water. Lost." She tugged on the clothing. "Lost inside my head. I was in the bay, but I'd forgotten who I was. I jumped into the stream to get away from those . . . the beasts, and to escape the spellfire. I remember that well enough. And after I went over the waterfall, I just barely remember hitting those boulders at the bottom. And then I don't remember anything else until this morning, when I suddenly recalled my name and remembered that I wasn't supposed to be a fish. Or whatever I was. My body Shifted me into a form that would let me heal and eat, and I guess that's all I've been doing since I disappeared."

They looked awed. "You can do that?"

"I've only done it one other time," she said. "And that for less time than the passing of a single station. When I jumped into the bay in

Maracada, the night I met you"—she looked at Ian—"I hit the water so hard it stunned me, and I nearly drowned. My body Shifted me then, too—partly. Left me human, but gave me gills so that I could breathe in the water. Until that happened, I didn't know I could take any form but the four-legged one."

Hasmal looked thoughtful. "To answer *your* question, Jayti walked past the corpse of the beast you disembowled after the spell-fire stopped burning," he said. "Except it wasn't truly dead. It grabbed him by one leg, mangled the leg. We got him away from it and finally managed to kill it, but . . ."

"Hasmal took the leg off for me. Did a good job of it. I'll be back t' myself soon enough." He said it, and he might have believed it, but Kait knew it wasn't true. She smelled the stink of blood-rot—faintly, perhaps faintly enough that human noses couldn't detect it. Jayti wasn't going to get better. She looked quickly at Hasmal and saw the bleakness in his eyes. He knew, then.

Ian said, "Jayti will be helping us build our boat before you can blink." The pain was in his eyes, too. They were keeping it from him, the fact of his impending death. Keeping it from him as long as they could.

She turned back to Jayti, and knelt by his side. She looked into his eyes, and willed him to fight off the blood sickness. "We need you," she said in a voice pitched only for his ears. "Especially Ian. He's lost his ship, his crew, everyone he thought he could count on except for you. Don't let him lose you, too."

Jayti, face gray and waxy, smiled a little, and in a voice even softer than hers, said, "I smell it. I know—but they're happier thinking I don't. So we play this game." He patted her arm. "But even when I'm gone, the captain hasn't lost everything. He still has you."

She returned his smile with a false sincerity that hid the pained awkwardness of the truth. Ian *would* need Jayti. He would need a friend from his past to stand by him in the days to come. And sitting in the back of the room they all occupied was the one thing she could think of that might save Jayti's life, and spare Ian's friend.

The Mirror of Souls glowed softly, its light rising up through the center of the tripod pedestal and shimmering into a lake of radiance that pooled within the ring resting on the pedestal. She had crossed the uncharted vastness of the Bregian Ocean to this abandoned continent to obtain it. It was an artifact from the long-gone Ancients, the people who had once ruled all the world, and with it, she was supposed to be able to resurrect her slaughtered family. The spirit of her long-dead ancestor, Amalee Kehshara Rohannan Draclas, had insisted that her dead parents, her dead brothers and sisters and nieces and nephews, were not entirely beyond her reach. That they could come back; that they could be brought back; that she could resurrect them with this artifact, which she had obtained with terrible struggle and at terrible cost.

But Kait did not know what to do with the Mirror now that she had it—and she had been unable to find Amalee's spirit since she'd made the decision to take the Mirror to the Reborn. When the *Peregrine* marooned her and her companions on the western shore of North Novtierra, she'd been sure Amalee would return, full of advice on what she had to do to get home. But that yattering voice had fallen silent, and the sick feeling grew in Kait that she'd made a mistake somewhere.

Had she been wrong to trust her ancestor's spirit in getting the Mirror, or had she been wrong in ignoring Amalee's assertion that if Kait got the Mirror and took it to Calimekka, the Reborn and his needs would not figure into her future? She couldn't know, and Amalee wouldn't answer her silent call for help.

Amalee could have told Kait how to use the artifact to resurrect dead Turben and save dying Jayti. Instead, the Mirror sat there useless because Kait didn't dare touch the glowing inscriptions that curved around the front quarter of its rim. Magical artifacts could be deadly. Without instructions, Kait feared she would unleash destruction on the survivors instead of salvation on the lost. Raised in Galweigh House amid its deadly mysteries, she'd learned that caution was the first and best of virtues.

"Hang on," she told Jayti again, and took his hand in hers. "Please."

He smiled, and she rose and turned away.

Ian pulled her aside. "I need to talk to you. Alone."

She nodded and followed him out of the ruin.

When they were out of sight of the others, he embraced her again, pulling her close and stroking her damp hair. "I thought I'd lost you forever," he told her. "I don't want to lose you again."

"We may not survive this," she said.

"I know. We probably won't. But I know that I want to be with you for the rest of my life. I love you, Kait. With all my heart and soul, I love you. I'd do anything for you—"

She pressed her fingers to his lips and said, "Hush," and pulled him close, praying that he wouldn't say anything else. She stroked his hair and closed her eyes tight, and wished with everything in her that she could make him *not* love her. She cared about him, but whatever magic it took to create the sort of love he professed to feel for her did not exist inside of her. Not for him. Not, perhaps, for anyone.

He held her close to him, rocking from side to side. She remembered her father rocking her like that, and for a moment she felt both small and safe. Then he pulled away from her and looked into her eyes, and said, "Marry me," and all feelings of safety fled. He said, "I have nothing but myself to offer you, but I'll find a way to win back all that I've lost. We'll get back to Calimekka, and you'll want for nothing."

She closed her eyes, trying desperately to think of the acceptable excuse, the one that would let her refuse him without hurting him. It came, and she thanked whichever god watched over such things. "I know we'll make it back somehow. That's why I cannot accept a proposal of marriage without knowing if either of my parents still live."

She saw him consider that and see the reason in it; if her mother or father still lived, a suitor would have to ask permission before broaching the subject with Kait. This was the way things were done among Families. So she bought herself time, but did nothing to solve the problem—her answer led him to believe she would find his proposal acceptable if her parents did.

She turned away—and in that instant she felt a delicate touch in her mind, and eyes looked out through hers, seeing the devastation before her. Ry Sabir. Her heart raced; she felt his elation, his relief . . . and his nearness.

She snapped a magical shield around herself—one of the few bits of magic Hasmal had been completely successful in teaching her so far—and the sensation of being watched, even *inhabited,* vanished. She turned to face Ian and said, "Trouble's coming."

He laughed bitterly. "We're stranded on the far side of the world, probably the only humans on the continent, down to four survivors and"—he nodded back toward the ruin—"perhaps soon to be three. We have no food stores, we had to burn our ground, winter won't be over for months, and will surely get harsher before it gets better." Ian leaned against a tree and rubbed at his eyes with his knuckles. Kait realized how exhausted he looked. "I'd say trouble is already here."

"A ship will reach us soon."

Ian stared at her, his immediate disbelief clear on his face. She met his eyes, and saw that disbelief become hope. "A ship. Bad news? Please tell me you have more bad news."

"This ship doesn't intend to rescue us. My Family's enemy followed me across the ocean, using a . . . a link that the two of us share. Something related to the fact that we are both Karnee, I think. This enemy intends to take me prisoner. But you and Hasmal and Jayti . . ." She frowned. "I expect he and his men will try to kill the three of you. You aren't the reason that he's coming here, and if you aren't his friends, you're unknown, and unknown is often the same as enemy."

Ian turned away from her and stared at the blackened ridge before him. "Perhaps we can negotiate with them. Perhaps we can work our passage. Perhaps we can do something to help you, and in helping you, help ourselves." He glanced over his shoulder at her. "So which of your Family's enemies are we talking about? Dokteerak? Masschanka?"

"Sabir," Kait said.

Ian winced. "Ah. Sabir. That's bad, or at least it *could* be bad. I have an unfortunate history with the Sabirs. Clever as I might be at offering my services as a navigator, or helmsman, or whatever the ship might need, if I'm recognized the Sabirs aren't likely to want my help." He sighed and looked back at the burned ground. "I wish we'd known earlier that Sabirs were coming. We could have been preparing. We could have had ramparts in place, made some sort of weapons . . ." He frowned and shrugged. "Well, that can't be helped." He licked his lips. "You don't know exactly which Sabirs are following you, do you?" he asked. He put the question to her casually enough, but Kait heard the tension hidden below the surface.

"I only know of one for sure. Ry Sabir. There may be others, but he's the only one who's"—every bit of color had drained from Ian's face as she spoke—"linked to me. Ian? What's the matter?"

"Ry?" he whispered. "Ry Sabir?"

Kait nodded. "You know him?"

For a long time he said nothing. Then he glanced at her, and he was a changed man. Cold. Deadly. Full of hate. "I know him," he said. "We have things to do. We're going to have to get his ship, and we're going to have to beat *him* to do it."

"Three of us against a ship's crew? We can't take the ship by force."

Ian rested both hands on Kait's shoulders and stared into her eyes. "If Ry and I meet, one of us is going to die. I know my chances of killing him aren't good. But if I have to die, I'll die fighting."

He stalked away from her, heading for the bay.

She looked after him and considered the trouble that was to come, and what she might do to prevent it. She ran through her head all the histories she could recall where smaller forces had defeated greater ones. Somewhere in the past, someone she'd studied about had found himself in a similar situation, and had managed to survive. In most of the cases, like the Brejmen defeat of the Cathomartic hordes or the Marepori repelling the Jast invaders, the smaller force was better-armed and better-disciplined.

With the right terrain and the right weapons and plenty of time to prepare, Kait thought the three of them might have had similar success. But without those advantages . . .

There is always a way to win, General Talismartea had written in his masterwork, *The Warrior's Book. If you are willing to redefine winning.*

Ian had defined winning as taking over Ry's ship and forcing the crew to sail back to Calimekka. But she knew that even if she and her friends could wrest control from the captain, they'd have a hellish time keeping it—and if they lost it, they were dead. But what if they didn't need to be in charge to win?

She had to redefine winning. They won if all of them got back to Ibera alive and free, with the Mirror of Souls in their possession. That was the only thing they had to have.

If they didn't have to take over the ship and control it for months, they were free to consider any form of safe passage as winning. They couldn't hope to have safe passage given to them. But they might hope to demand it.

How?

An idea came to her. She'd have to get Hasmal and Ian on her side, though she suspected from his reaction to Ry's name that Ian wouldn't like her proposal. Then she'd need subterfuge and negotiating skill and a bit of Hasmal's magic and more than a touch of luck to make it work. She found herself wondering if her years of diplomatic studies would serve her as well as even a day's worth of real experience. She closed her eyes and breathed in the ash-scented air, and hoped she'd learned as much as she thought she had.

Chapter 6

After three days in which Ry had become more and more certain that Kait was dead, the tiny flashes of energy that linked him to her suddenly reappeared. He couldn't guess what had happened to her to make her disappear, and he wouldn't try. He was satisfied to discover that she was still alive, and better yet, that she was close. Incredibly close.

When the *Peregrine* marooned her, he'd seen through her eyes that she was not alone, but he didn't know if any of those who had been with her had survived. He wished he could get another glimpse through her eyes, so that he could see what he was heading into, but she was wary, holding her magical shields as tight around herself as a woman would hold her cloak in a blizzard. Only flickers broke through to guide him to her; he suspected that she hid herself as much from the dangers around her as from him, but he couldn't touch her mind, so he wasn't sure.

At the moment when the tug he felt from her ceased to be "ahead" and became "beside," he was standing at the prow of the *Wind Treasure,* anxiously watching the coastline that ran by off the port side of the ship. He wouldn't have been able to explain to the captain or any of his friends how he knew that the ocean had brought him as close to her as it could, but he did know. So he shouted, "Here! This is the place. Go inland here!"

The captain sailed through smoke-laced fog into the bay and dropped anchor.

For the first time, Ry saw the place where Kait hid. Rain-washed ruins dotted the burned hills and cliffs that rose out of the bay on all three sides. Not a single tree, not a single blade of grass or scrawny shrub, offered reprieve from the sea of black ash that covered the ground. In his travels, Ry had seen the aftermath of a volcanic eruption; what he saw before him reminded him of that.

He stared at the bleak panorama and smiled slowly. Kait's city of the Ancients lay before him. Such cities existed in Ibera, as well. But an Ancients' city that had not been known for at least a hundred years— that had not been pillaged and plundered by a century's treasure-seekers—a city like that could exist nowhere but in the Novtierras. This city had been visited by one ship alone. Even after the fire, it would house wonders; ruins that had survived the Wizards' War and the Thousand Years of Darkness would survive fire.

Hidden within those ruined buildings lay pieces of knowledge lost to humankind for the last thousand years, pieces of knowledge that had waited for him and his men. With such treasures in hand, he could return to Calimekka in triumph, reconcile with his Family and the Wolves, and reinstate his friends. He could force his Family to accept his Galweigh parata.

Once he rescued Kait, he would have time to explore, but first he had to get her to safety. She waited somewhere within those burned hills. She was so near, he could almost smell her. The passion—the obsession—that had driven him to pursue her across half a world, through storm and disaster, across uncharted ocean to unmapped land, burned higher than ever. His blood, his bones, his very soul sang with her nearness.

"Kait," he whispered, "be safe. We're almost together."

A hand dropped onto his shoulder and he jumped. "The men want to go ashore to search the ruins." The captain stood behind him, and Ry hadn't even heard the man approach. Ry didn't think anyone had ever successfully approached him without his being aware of it before. His mind was too taken by Kait and too full of excitement. He needed to reach her, to have her—then he thought he would be able to concentrate again.

"No. I go ashore alone first," he said, and heard the growl in his voice. That growl worried him. He was near Shift, close to becoming the beast. The one time Kait had seen him, they had met Karnee to Karnee, in a back alley in Halles over the bodies of seven murderers. This time he wanted to be human. He wanted to be *with* her as human—to first taste her mouth in human form, to have the pleasure of undressing her, of hearing her whisper his name in the silken tones of her human voice. . . .

He breathed deeply, and fought to find the peace that would calm his racing pulse. He didn't try to cage his excitement by sheer force of will, for such an attempt would only set the Karnee part of him to beating wildly against the bars of its cage, and when it broke free, it would run out of control and take him with it. Instead, he acknowledged his desire, his hunger, the pumping of his lungs, and the shiver in his spine, and said to them, *Later.* Later, he would fulfill all his hopes and desires.

"I'll go ashore alone," he repeated. "I don't want to frighten Kait away—if I take men with me, she might flee."

"And if she isn't alone?"

Ry was staring back at that hideous burned shoreline again, at those blackened hills. "I can take care of anyone she might have with her."

As two sailors readied one of the longboats for him, Yanth strode up to him, for the first time in a long time wearing sailors' roughspun rather than dramatic silk and leather. "The captain said you intended to go ashore alone."

"I'm going alone."

"You aren't. I know you think you'll find your true love there, but you have no idea what else you'll find. And I won't chance you getting yourself killed. I owe you better than that."

Ry glared at him. "You owe me the loyalty of respecting my wishes. I *wish* to go ashore alone."

"No." Yanth rested a hand on the hilt of his sword and smiled, but the smile was without warmth. "Friends never owe each other complicity in suicide. Do you hear me? I'll follow you ashore, and I'll guard your back."

Ry turned away from Yanth and gripped the rail. "There's only one first time," he said. "This is it for us. The first time we'll see each other as a man and a woman. The first time we'll touch. The first time we'll . . ." He closed his eyes, conjuring up the image of Kait standing atop a tower, her long black hair blowing in the breeze. He'd conjured that image of her to show his lieutenants. It was still the way he saw her—chin lifted, eyes fierce, the blue silk of her dress barely able to contain her vitality, her passion, her beauty. After coming so far, he refused to share their first moments together with anyone.

"We knew you'd fight having *all* of us going," Yanth was saying, "so we made a concession for you. We drew straws, and I won the draw." He smiled and said softly, "I cheated in order to win, but you needn't tell the others that. I suspect that they cheated, too. I had to win, though. I trust my skills at sword and knife more than theirs, and I was determined that if only one of us went with you, I would be the best. So. You may not want me, but you'll by the gods have me."

Yanth had cheated, had he? Probably broke his straw, palmed the longer part of it, then glared down the rest of them when they'd challenged him—Yanth would do that. Well, Ry could cheat, too. He could keep the peace, get off the ship without argument, and then do what he wanted to do anyway.

So Ry sighed and said, "You'll get in my way if I don't agree, won't you?"

"Yes."

"Then get in."

They rowed ashore in silence, and dragged the boat up onto the beach. Five cairns above the tide line marked five graves. One of them was new. Ry glanced at the graves and said, "You'd best stay with the boat, so that something doesn't come along and take it. I want to make sure we have a way to get back."

"You're a liar." A half-smile twisted across Yanth's face, then vanished. "If something takes the damned boat, our friends can row here in one of the other ones. If you get killed while I'm here watching the boat, though, we can't undo that. Can we?"

Ry sniffed; though the atmosphere was redolent of charcoal and raw wet earth, one swirl of clean air blew from somewhere back of the hills, carrying the faint and wistful promise of green and growing things. And . . . he breathed deeper . . . and the mouthwatering smell of food cooking. The cookfire scents mingled with the burned-charcoal stink and so were almost hidden, but when he closed his eyes he could catch the faintest whiff of boiling greens spiced with pepper and *rath,* and meat braising slowly on a stake, the juices dripping into the flames. The scent lay in the same direction as the strengthening tug of the magic that drew him toward Kait. And she had loosened her shields a little. She felt receptive.

He smiled slowly. Perhaps she wanted this moment as much as he did. He turned to Yanth. "Well enough. You can come with me, then. If you can keep up."

He took off up the hill at a dead run, dodging between the gutted ruins of the dead city, putting them between him and Yanth. He was Karnee, faster and more agile than any human, and with inhuman stamina. By the time Ry dropped over the first rise and caught a stronger draft of the cook-scents, Yanth floundered far behind.

Yanth would follow his tracks, of course. But by the time he caught up, Ry would have found Kait. And a well-hidden place to be alone with her.

He ran easily through the ruins and leaped over a muddied, swollen stream, all his senses focused toward Kait. He ran along the face of a cliff and around a corner to find a perfect half-sphere of un-burned forest awaiting him. And in the center of the half-sphere a ruin less ruined than most. And in the doorway of the ruin, a woman of average height and lean build, her hair black as a jungle river, her dark eyes flashing, her white teeth bared in an unsettling smile. Kait. As he had seen her in his mind, and in his magic, but never in person.

She was—as he had dreamed, imagined, hoped—alone. His heart thrummed against the inside of his chest like an animal caught in a trap, and he slowed to a walk. There could be only one first time. He wanted this moment to be something that both of them would look back on in years to come—for the rest of their lives together—and remember with joy. With passion. He wanted perfection.

He stopped outside the circle of greenery. Standing in the muddy ash, he said, "*Vetromè elada,* Kait," addressing her with the intimate greeting reserved for lovers, though the two of them had never truly met.

Vetromè elada. It meant, *Our souls kiss.*

Kait had known he was coming. She was braced; she told herself she was ready. But when Ry Sabir moved into view and she saw him as a man for the first time, she almost wept. He was beautiful—golden-haired, tall and lean and tightly muscled. His pale eyes transported her into the past, into the alley in Halles where they had met as Karnee. His scent caught her by surprise, as it had the first time she crossed paths with him. That scent was a drug to her, shooting straight past logic and upbringing and all her knowledge of her Family's rules and her place within the Family and her determination to do what was right, driving into her heart and her gut. She smelled the animal hunger in him, the nearness to Shift; she breathed his desire and felt matching desire flood her veins.

He spoke to her, and his voice was the voice of her dreams, rich and deep and smooth on the surface, with a raw edge that lay beneath, just at the limits of her perception. He said, *Vetromè elada.* If she could have picked the words that came from his mouth, she would have picked those words. *Our souls kiss.* Her mind, her body, and her spirit all told her he was the man she had dreamed of, the one she had hoped to find, and the one she had believed did not exist. He was the love she had believed she would never have. He was everything she had ever wanted.

And she was going to betray him.

She had to—for the Reborn, for her Family, and for her friends, she had to. She said, "You are Sabir, and I am Galweigh. We are enemies. Our souls can never touch." She lied, and knew it was a lie when the words were forming in her mind, before they ever passed her lips, and determined that she would make the lie a truth because the lie was right and good, and her desire was wrong. She put distaste in her voice. Loathing. She found the distaste and the loathing easily, but though he wouldn't know it, they had nothing to do with him. She had never hated herself as much as she did at that moment. She hated her weakness, her desire, and her hunger for him; she hated the fact that she could want a Sabir with the overwhelming desire that raged through her body . . . and she hated herself because she was cold enough, hard enough, callous enough that she could betray him, when all she wanted to do in the world was run to him and lose herself in his embrace.

She saw his pain reflected in his eyes, and noted his body's change in posture. He denied what she said with rigid shoulders and clenched fists before he denied what she said with his words. He told her, "I came for you," and in those words he put his longing, and his passion.

Tears burned in the corners of her eyes. She hungered for him as much as he hungered for her; their obsessions were equal, if not identical. "I know. I wish—" she said, the words blurting out before she could stop them. But she got control. She had not survived to adulthood—Karnee in a world where Karnee meant death—by giving in to her impulses. She straightened her shoulders and swung her hair out of her face and glared at him, forcing herself to remember that he was Sabir, and that her family had died at the hands of Sabirs. She remembered the burning bodies, she remembered Sabir soldiers standing around the pyre laughing to each other, and she forced herself to put him with those men in her mind. "What I wish doesn't matter. I knew you were coming. I knew from that night in Halles that you would be coming for me."

"You want me as much as I want you," he said.

He took a step forward, toward her green haven, and she lifted her chin and crossed her arms over her chest. "I don't want you," she told him. "The Karnee part of me doesn't control me, and I don't want you."

She saw the ghost of a smile flicker at the corners of his lips; she realized that she had as much as admitted that the Karnee part of her did want him.

He took another step toward her, and a third.

She did want him, gods forgive her. She didn't want to hurt him. She didn't want to make him her enemy.

He said, "You're more beautiful in real life than you were in my visions."

She licked her lips. "You are, too," she whispered.

The rational part of her mind looked at the two of them standing there and screamed insanity. The other part of her—the part that accepted magic, however unwillingly—knew that what was happening between them fell within the realms of wizardry. She had felt lust, and this was not it. She had felt love, too, if only for her family . . . and this was not love, either. The world had narrowed down to her and him, and to the blood pounding in her ears and the tingling in her skin and the sudden hollowness in her gut.

He came to her then, hurrying, and for an instant she forgot herself in her hunger for his touch. For an instant, she forgot what she was about to do to him.

He rested his hands on her shoulders and she exhaled once. She could never have found the words to describe the perfection of his touch, the rightness of their bodies together. She would have been lost there, and all of her ideals and aspirations with her.

But the knife materialized out of nothingness at Ry's throat, and behind the knife, Hasmal. She pressed the palm of one hand flat against his chest and said, "Be still."

His eyes went wide, and he froze. She felt the tremor that jolted through his body.

"Be still," she said softly, "or you will die. This is not you and me, Ry. This is Galweigh and Sabir, and Wolves and Falcons; this is the way things have to be."

Ian stepped out of the other half of the shield Hasmal had spun for the two of them, sword drawn, smiling. Kait could see Ian's hatred; she could smell it. Hasmal's magic had hidden everything about them—scent and form and mass and movement and shadow, the sounds of breath and heartbeat and nervous movement—but it could never have worked so well if she had not offered herself as bait. They had been truly invisible only because Ry had all of his attention focused on her. They had become completely invisible to her only when she lost herself in her desire for him.

"How—?" Ry started to ask, but Ian snarled, "Silence, you bastard," and Hasmal, more calmly, said, "Down on your knees."

Kait saw the shock and dismay and the hurt in his eyes, and steeled herself to do what she had to do. She told him, "Don't Shift. The blade is poisoned with *refaille*—you'll die before you can complete your transformation." She gritted her teeth and willed away the tears building in her eyes.

We all decide what we will have in our lives, she thought. We decide what we will do; we decide what we will say. And when we decide, then we pay the price. He is the price I must pay to get the

Mirror to the Reborn, to save my friends' lives, to resurrect my parents, my bothers and sisters, and my Family.

Ry kept his eyes on hers, and she made herself watch what Hasmal and Ian did to him. They forced him to his knees, and bound his hands and his ankles. She told them how to tie him so that the rope would hold even if he Shifted. She never looked away from him. She would not be a coward. She would watch the consequences of her action, the end result of her plan. She would not hide herself from the price she paid.

He did not look away from her, either. With his eyes he told her *I love you, even though you betrayed me;* the look she gave him in return said, *I love you, too, but love doesn't matter.*

Something in the air caught her attention, and she turned away. She parted her lips and took in one slow, careful breath. Coming along the ridge . . . being careful to make no noise . . . yes. She said, "Someone followed him. He's trying to circle behind us." She could smell him—a man who let himself get upwind because he wasn't used to thinking about people with senses more acute than his own.

She looked back to Ry. "What's his name?"

She could see him toy with the idea of lying. But his eyes flicked downward, to the poisoned blade at his throat, and he told her.

She shouted, "Yanth! Stop where you are!"

Hasmal said to Ry, "No words. We'll do the talking for you."

Ian added, "Or for your corpse if you give us reason. Please . . . give us a reason."

Ry twisted his head slowly, fractionally, until he could look upward out of the corner of his left eye. Kait saw the initial bewilderment in his face give way to shock.

"Ian?"

"At least you remember me. And now the situation is reversed, isn't it? After all these years, your life is in my hands." Ian kept his voice low and said, "And I've sworn to have your life . . . brother. So will you die today?"

Kait stared from one to the other. Brother? Ian was Ry's *brother?* She closed her eyes for just an instant. What were the odds that she could love the brother that she couldn't have, and have the brother she didn't love, all the while not knowing they were brothers? She would have screamed at the coincidence, but it wouldn't be a coincidence, would it? The gods had their sticky fingers deep in her life, and they were toying with her. Having fun at her expense. Planning traps for her as carefully as she'd planned this trap for Ry.

"What in the hells did I ever do to you?" Ry muttered.

"Pretend you don't know and watch how fast I kill you." Ian kicked him in the ribs.

Kait grabbed Ian and snarled, "Stop it."

From the top of the ridge, Ry's friend called down, "Let him go. We'll kill all of you to get him if we have to."

Kait reluctantly turned her attention from Ry and Ian and the strange drama enacting itself between them. "Don't waste your breath. First, I know you're there alone. Second, the blade at his throat has been dipped in *refaille*. If we don't like the way you blink your eyes, he'll die before you can do it twice."

Yanth, after a moment's pause, apparently came to the conclusion that he didn't have the upper hand. "Don't hurt him. I'm listening. Tell me what you want."

Kait said, "Go back to your ship. Bring the captain and your parnissa back to shore, and wait for us by the graves. We'll meet you there."

"What guarantee do I have that you won't kill Ry if I leave him here with you?"

Kait said, "If he's dead, we'll have no hope of negotiating with your people, nor any hope of surviving a confrontation. As long as he obeys us he'll come to no harm."

Under his breath, Ian muttered, "Not today, in any case."

The negotiators stood on the beach with the rolling pulse of the incoming tide growling behind them. Kait studied the parnissa, a cold-eyed young man who looked as though he spent every spare moment in the study of the warrior arts, and the captain, who looked to Kait both sensible and patient. The parnissa's robes were of bright silk, in greens and golds, heavily embroidered with the sacred symbols of Iberism: the eye of watchfulness, the hand of industriousness, the sword of truth, the scales of justice, the nine-petaled flower of wisdom. The captain, too, had dressed to show his status: the green and silver silks of the Sabir Family but cut in the traditional Rophetian fashion, a heavy silver chain around his neck stamped with the insignia of the god Tonn, and silver beads braided into his beard and shoulder-length hair. Yanth stood behind both of them, his silk shirt and leather breeches both black as an executioner's. He kept his hand on his sword and glared at her.

Kait knew how she looked to them—a waif-thin woman in the worn and patched rags of the lowliest of sailors, wearing a dead man's too-large boots. She rested her hand on the pommel of her own sword, with its Galweigh crest and inlaid ruby and onyx cabochons, and pulled her shoulders back and lifted her chin high. She was no impostor. She walked forward, leaving Ian, Hasmal, and the kneeling Ry behind her. "I declare myself Kait-ayarenne daughter of Grace Draclas by Strahan Galweigh. By virtue of my training in diplomacy, where I have reached the position of *yanar* in the Galweigh Family, I will state our case for my people. They are agreed, and my word is binding, sworn to the gods of Calimekka and Ibera."

The captain raised one eyebrow in quickly suppressed surprise that she knew the formulas of negotiation, then nodded. "I declare myself Madloo Sleroal. By virtue of my captaincy of the *Wind Treasure,* which I have achieved by Tonn's choice and grace, and in the honorable service of the Sabir Family, I state the case for my people. My word is binding, and sworn before Tonn and Tonn alone."

That was typically Rophetian. They wouldn't swear on the gods of Iberism, only on the single Rophetian god of the sea. Kait would accept that, though—a Rophetian captain with a whole ocean lying between him and home would never forswear himself in front of Tonn.

The cold-eyed parnissa glanced from the captain to Kait, undid the cord that belted his robe, and held out the black silk rope. He said, "I stand between the disputing parties. I serve only the gods, without loyalty to one party or the other, and the gods oversee through my eyes all covenants, pacts, and bonds made this day. All words spoken before me are spoken before the gods, and carry the force of soul-oath." Kait held out her right wrist, the captain held out his right wrist, and the parnissa bound them together with the cord, carefully tying the negotiators' knot. "Bound together, you swear before me to deal honestly with each other for the good of all. Should either of you break the bond, your life will be forfeit." He stepped back. "Men act and gods attend."

"Men act and gods attend," the captain said.

"Men act and gods attend." Kait inhaled slowly and let the breath out even slower, trying to calm the shuddery feeling in her belly. This, her first negotiation, was for her life and the lives of her friends, and that alone would have made it terrifying. But it was also to negotiate safe passage for the Mirror of Souls, and as such, what she did or failed to do would affect the future of the world. She wondered how many other untried junior diplomats had been faced with such high stakes and decided that she was alone.

The captain said, "Since you have"—he glanced behind her at Ry, kneeling in the ashes with a knife at his throat—"called this negotiation, why don't you tell me what you want."

"My needs are simple. First, the services of your physick. Second, guaranteed safe passage and freedom aboard your ship for myself, my three colleagues, and our possessions and cargo, to our chosen destination."

"Which is . . . ?"

"Southern Ibera. The harbor at Brelst will do." She did not know how far south her cousin Danya was, but where Danya was, the Reborn was—and that was where Kait and the Mirror had to be, too. From Brelst, she could get the Mirror wherever it needed to go.

"You ask a great deal of us: the diversion of our ship from its intended destination; the disruption of our crewmen's lives; and an increased chance of encounters with pirates, storms, monsters, and reefs. What do you offer in return?"

"Ry Sabir's life."

The captain smiled at her. "He came across the sea to rescue you. Had he not come with your good in mind, you would not now have his life to use as a bargaining chip."

"And if he had come to rescue all of us, I would not be forced to use it."

"And you can be so certain that we would not have rescued all of you?"

"Never mind that you assume I knew you came to rescue me. Galweighs and Sabirs don't share a happy past—knowing a Sabir ship sailed into our harbor, how could I assume that my friends would be your friends? And indeed, I've discovered that your Sabir and our captain are enemies." She did not elaborate—the gods had drawn her to both Ian and Ry, the gods had brought the two brothers together, and now she was sure the gods had their bets placed on what would happen next. She, however, saw no reason to complicate her negotiations with that information.

"Fair enough," the captain said evenly. "What is your cargo?"

She shrugged. "Bedrolls, the few possessions that the mutineers didn't steal, a single artifact that we came here to get."

"The Mirror of Souls," Ry said. Kait heard the slap that followed, and Ian's voice saying, "Another word from you and you're dead—and if we die with you, we'll at least send your friends to the grave first."

The captain snorted, clearly disbelieving what Ry had said, but the parnissa was staring at her with wide eyes. "The Mirror of Souls?"

She could not lie—not bound in negotiation, with the gods her witnesses and her life forfeit if she failed. She said, "Yes. We found the Mirror of Souls."

She thought for an instant that the parnissa was going to drop to his knees before her, but then he steadied himself. "Captain," he said, and she heard the trembling in his voice, "the Mirror cannot be allowed to go anywhere but to Calimekka. It is . . . it belongs to . . ." He swallowed so hard she watched the head of his windpipe bob. "Only the parnissas should be permitted anywhere near it. In the wrong hands it would be enormously dangerous—it is the most magical of the old Dragon artifacts."

The captain looked from the parnissa to Kait. "Hmmm," he said. "We seem to have a problem."

Kait stared at the parnissa, disbelieving. She said to the captain, "The parnissa's *neutral*. By suggesting courses of action to you or interfering in any way with the negotiations, he voids the process and eliminates himself as the arbiter. Without an arbiter, we cannot negotiate. And if we cannot negotiate, we will have to kill Ry. You cannot use anything he's told you. You have to forget all of it."

The captain closed his eyes for a moment, thinking. Then he sighed. "I hate diplomats." He looked over at the parnissa. "Just be quiet and observe, Loelas. The girl and I will work this out without any help from you. This is—this *has* to be—between the two of us."

She caught something that surprised her then. The faintest ghost of a smile passed across the captain's lips, and the slightest scent of admiration reached her sensitive nose.

"Let's dicker, girl," he said.

She nodded.

"You want safe passage for your people, medical help for one of 'em—I'm guessing one that isn't here."

"Yes."

"Fair enough. I'll give you that right away, for Ry's life. Agreed?'

"Let me hear the rest first."

"The rest? Well, yes, there is more." His smile was plainer now. He was enjoying something about this—he'd thought of some trick, or perhaps some loophole that would let him go back on his word. "You want us to take you to Brelst. I cannot do that. By the time we get back there, the Wizards' Circle storms will be at their worst, and Brelst gets the blow from four circles."

Kait considered that, then nodded. "We'll negotiate for another port, then."

He pursed his lips and blew out his cheeks until he looked like a puff-fish. "Phah! The port isn't the biggest problem. The Mirror of Souls is the problem. What I've heard about that is . . . frightening. To take it on board my ship, I'm going to need something extra."

"I understand your position," she said. "But I cannot permit the Mirror of Souls to stay with the parnissa or to go to Calimekka. If that's your demand, we all die here."

He chuckled. "I wouldn't expect you to agree to giving the parnissa your prize, girl. You came all the way across the ocean and braved terrible dangers to get it."

She nodded. And waited.

"Something you've gone through so much to get, you deserve to have, don't you agree?"

She nodded again, slowly sensing a trap closing around her but not able to see where it was coming from.

"Good." The captain smiled a tiny smile. "Because everything you went through to get your prize, our parat went through to rescue you.

And if you deserve to keep your prize, you must agree that he deserves to keep his."

Click. The trap snapped shut around her, and she had already
agreed with the captain that its bars were solid and its use acceptable.
"You want me to . . . give myself to him?"

"No. I insist only that you share his quarters and remain his companion throughout the return trip. Meanwhile, I will sail you and your
friends and Ry and his friends and your Mirror of Souls to a neutral
harbor: neither Brelst nor Calimekka. I think Glaswherry Hala might
serve. Once you're on land, all of you may go where you please.
Should he decide to go with you, he may. Should he decide to return
to Calimekka with me, he may. In that way, I will fulfill my duty to
him and meet your needs as well."

"You *can't* let her have the Mirror!" the parnissa wailed.

"You *can't* force Kait into Ry's company!" Ian snapped.

The captain glanced first at the parnissa, and for a moment Kait
saw the hint of disdain that every captain she'd ever known held toward the parnissery. It was the look that men who were truly free and
in charge of their own domains held toward those who chose the path
of bureaucracy. "I can and I have." He turned to Ian. "And you . . . you
are not a captain on my ship. You are less than nothing—you and the
rest of your people will be the parolees of this woman. As long as she
speaks for you, I'll see you're treated with courtesy. But you have no
voice of your own. You understand?"

Kait watched Ian from the corner of her eye. He blanched and
nodded.

She wanted to refuse. Ry and his men would surely choose to "accompany" them once they were on land, and she and Ian and Hasmal
and Jayti would be outnumbered, and would lose the Mirror of Souls
to the Sabir Family anyway. They would simply lose it closer to home.
Meanwhile, she would have to share quarters with Ry, when sharing a
continent with him already seemed too intimate.

She could not demand that the captain guarantee she and her
people would keep the Mirror once they were on land again; Captain's
Law began and ended on the sea, and he could offer nothing that
would bind Ry and his men beyond the decks of his ship. Further, she
had chosen to negotiate with him—she could not now state that she

wanted to negotiate with Ry, too. If she tried to demand too much, she'd lose everything.

She wanted to spit in the captain's face and tell him she'd sooner see him in hell. But she had defined winning as getting her people and the Mirror safely across the sea to the Reborn. The captain's bargain would let her win, at least temporarily—and she would have the whole voyage in which to figure out a way to win permanently.

She stared into the captain's eyes. "You swear to protect my friends' lives as if they were the lives of your own family or crew, protect our cargo as if it were your own, get us safely to a harbor that isn't Calimekka, and let all of us leave when we get there, permitting us to take the Mirror of Souls with us?"

"I swear."

She saw honesty in his eyes, and smelled sincerity in his breath.

"And you will be satisfied that I have carried out my portion of the bargain if I share a room with Ry Sabir and attend him as a companion during the day; you do not stipulate that I become his mistress or his *eylayn*."

"Correct."

"I'll kill you if you touch her, you bastard," she heard Ian mutter to Ry, but that oath was spoken far too softly for the others to hear.

Kait sighed. "Then I accept your terms for my people."

The captain now asked her, "And you will hold parole for your people, and submit yourself to my judgment without question or argument if they violate that parole?"

Kait turned and gave Ian a look that clearly stated, *Put me in his hands and I'll make you pay for the rest of your life,* and said, "I will."

"Then I accept your terms for my people."

The parnissa glowered at both of them, but stood between them and tapped the knot in the center of the cord that bound them. "Gods attend these actions of men, for these two have acted for the best interests of all, in the spirit of fairness, dealing honestly one with another," he said in a flat, angry voice. The words came out as hurried rote, the recitation of a furious schoolchild made to perform against his will. "They are now made law and subject to the penalties of the laws of Matrin and the Veil." He tapped the knot again. "I witness, remember, and record." When his finger tapped the knot for the third time, it undid itself as if by magic, but Kait could see that it had only been cleverly tied.

Kait turned to Ian and Hasmal. "Untie Ry and release him."

Neither man was happy about it, but both complied.

Ry got to his feet, brushed the ashes from his face, and rubbed his chafed wrists. He looked at Ian, and the hatred that passed between the two of them was visible. She had sworn that she would keep Ian under control, at forfeit of her life if the captain so chose; she wondered if Ian's love for her would be enough to make him obey the parole, or if he would sacrifice her to get at Ry.

Ry's eyes held Ian's death in them, too. He smiled—a tight, ugly grimace of barely controlled rage—and strode across the beach to join Yanth and the parnissa.

The captain said, "Would you prefer to go to the ship first, parata?"

Kait was afraid to leave any of her people alone, protected by the captain's sworn word or not. She glanced up at the ridge behind her and said, "I'd rather get our injured man on board first. The Mirror can travel with Hasmal and Ian and me."

The captain smiled. "As you choose."

Kait led her people and Ry's back through the hills, toward Jayti and the Mirror of Souls, and wondered how much of an ordeal the trip ahead of her would be.

Chapter 7

Shaid Galweigh, pretender to the Galweigh paraglesiat, ushered his contingent of diplomats, traders, and Wolves into the magnificent Palm Hall of the Sabirs. He was the first Galweigh to step within the walls of Sabir House as a guest in over four hundred years, and if he did not represent Calimekka's great Galweigh House, but only Cherian House in the city of Maracada on the island of Goft, that was a fact that both he and his Sabir hosts were willing to overlook.

He took his seat in the enormous gilded ivory chair at one end of the long table and nodded toward the two men who sat at the other end, in chairs of matching magnificence. One was the Sabir Family paraglese, Grasmir Sabir, old and leonine and majestic; the other was a handsome young man named Crispin Sabir, who had beautiful golden hair and a warm and ready smile that Shaid instinctively liked. The two Sabirs had personally greeted each member of the delegation before anyone moved into the Palm Hall; now, finally, Grasmir gave a signal and the meeting began.

"We have both old and new business to discuss," Grasmir said with a wry smile. "The old stretches back over four hundred fifty years; I think perhaps we ought to settle that before we move on to those things which immediately interest us."

Around the table, various Galweighs and Sabirs chuckled.

"As acting head of the Galweigh Family, I have to say it's about time we got around to that."

"Very well, then. *Old* business. Family records tell of an argument between Arathmad Karnee and his partner Perthan Sabir over the dowry of Arathmad's daughter. The daughter was to marry the Sabir son when both came of age—at the time they were still small children. Perthan accused Arathmad of belittling his son by offering such a small dowry; Arathmad said Perthan's son was ugly and spindly and that the only reason he offered his daughter was because he was Perthan's only friend, and Perthan's son would never find a suitable bride otherwise. The dispute became bitter, the partners separated their business, which from all evidence was in the practice of black market magic, and—though history is vague on this point—one partner cast a spell on the other partner. The Sabirs have always held that the caster of the spell was Arathmad Karnee."

Shaid nodded. "And the Galweighs have always said the spell was cast by Perthan Sabir."

Around the table, those who were hearing the story for the first time shook their heads.

"That's what brought about four hundred fifty years of inter-Family war?" someone asked.

Shaid and Grasmir looked at each other from opposite ends of the table and smiled. Grasmir gave the nod to Shaid, who said, "Not entirely. Both Perthan and Arathmad died from the effects of the spell— one from the spell itself, and one from what the histories refer to as *rewhah,* which is apparently some sort of magical backlash that comes from using magic." He knew more about it than that, and he assumed that Grasmir did, too—one didn't command the Family's Wolves for long without knowing what their strengths and weaknesses were. Susceptibility to *rewhah* was a big weakness. But one had to maintain appearances at all times, and the appearance of being free from any taint of magic had saved more than one man's life.

One of the junior members of the Sabir Family asked "Then if the two principals in the dispute died, why did the dispute continue?"

Grasmir said, "Because both children were also hit by the spell— not visibly, though. The effects didn't become apparent until each of them took mates and had children. Their children were Scarred.

Someone called the Scarring the Karnee Curse. The children were skinshifters. Dangerous, deadly, unpredictable creatures. Calimekka already celebrated Gaerwanday—the Day of Infants—and of course all Scarred children were sacrificed. Except the parents of the Sabir children and the parents of the Karnee children (the Family line that joined with and was subsumed by the Galweighs) neglected their duties as citizens. They hid their children, and the monsters were permitted to grow and breed." Grasmir Sabir sighed and shook his head sadly. "Both Families still carry a taint of this Scarring in their blood. It was over the Scarred children that the long-term war between the Families broke out."

The faces around the table had grown more somber at that; a thousand years after the horrible Wizards' War, its magical fallout remained clearly visible to anyone who ventured to the docks and saw the Scarred slaves at work on the ships, or watched the executions of those foolish monsters who dared to pretend to humanity and who ventured within Ibera's borders. No true human ever forgot that the Scarred had, after the war, hunted down humans and destroyed as many of them as they could get. Just thinking about citizens in their own Family lines who had permitted abominations to live, rather than sacrifice them, horrified all of them.

Grasmir looked from face to face, and finally sighed. "Both Families carry guilt in the matter, though at this late date we cannot hope to unravel which of the two principals, if either, might have been the more guilty." He managed a faint, weary smile. "And I say it no longer matters. Call the matter settled, forgive the stupidities of the past, and move on."

Shaid waited, just a beat, to make his impact greater. Then he stood and applauded. Around the table, other members of the Galweigh delegation followed his lead, leaping to their feet and clapping vigorously. The Sabirs rose, too. Grasmir's smile grew broad, and when the applause finally died down, he dropped into his chair with an air of satisfaction.

"I take it as agreed, then, that the Sabir and Galweigh Families have put the past behind them."

More applause greeted that statement. Without making it obvious that he was doing so, Shaid glanced around the room, looking for any dissenters. He saw none. Excellent.

He rose in the silence that followed the applause and said, "Then perhaps now is the time to move on to the new business that brings us here today." He waited until he noted nods of affirmation from around the room. Clasping his hands in front of his chest, he said, "Well, then. The Sabirs and the Goft Galweighs face both a problem and an opportunity, and as our Families are resolved to put past differences behind us, we can perhaps work together to leap on the opportunity, and eliminate the problem." He cleared his throat, suddenly unsure about how to continue.

He glanced around the room. The faces that looked back at him were those of friends and of associates, and also of men and women who just the day before had been sworn to work toward his ruin. Now each of them looked at him with some variation on the same theme—curiosity mixed with a tinge of avarice and a hint of excitement . . . and a pinch of fear. He especially noticed Crispin Sabir's eyes—eager, fascinated, watchful. The eyes of a man ready to grasp any advantage and make it work for him.

Best play to the excitement first.

"About our opportunity . . . well, no one has discovered a new city of the Ancients in any of our lifetimes. Until now. A member of the Calimekkan branch of the Galweigh Family chartered a ship with money she stole from the Goft treasury, and acting on information that she stole from archives in the Goft House, sailed east. She was successful in locating the city she sought." He leaned forward, resting his palms on the table.

One young Sabir woman looked stunned that he would admit to the discovery of such a treasure by his own Family, even if by Family acting without official sanction. Had he kept secret the fact that Kait had gone off on her own, the Galweighs would have had unquestioned claim. A few members of Shaid's own delegation appeared surprised and uneasy that he was being so forthright. After all, with those few words he'd abolished the Galweigh rights to the claim, leaving it solely Kait's if she lived and throwing it into the hands of the strongest taker if she died.

He had also, however, shown himself willing to be brutally honest. He thought an appearance of absolute honesty made for the best negotiating, and had long ago learned that giving an enemy a concession up front so often shocked him that he thereafter was less cautious in his dealings.

"We have . . . spies . . . who have been watching this young woman's movements closely. She's found an artifact of enormous importance. We suspect, though we cannot be absolutely certain, that it is the Mirror of Souls."

He heard a gratifying number of gasps. Not from either Crispin or Grasmir Sabir. Of course not. Their Wolves would keep them as well informed of the situation as Shaid's Wolves kept him.

"From what we can determine in our archives, the Mirror of Souls would be an excellent tool in the hands of friends, but a devastating weapon in the hands of enemies. Kait Galweigh, the finder of this artifact, has made herself the enemy of Goft House. Because she stole both money and information from us to acquire the Mirror, we can make a strong claim to it, and to the ruins in which she found it. We want that Mirror. For your assistance in the Mirror's recovery and for an uncontested claim to it, we offer you half the ruins. Further, we offer our expertise and assistance in getting the one thing the Sabir Family most desires."

Crispin Sabir laughed softly and asked, "What exactly do the Goft Galweighs imagine the Calimekkan Sabirs want most in the world?"

Shaid stood up straight and met the question with a calm smile. "Galweigh House. Controlling it would give the Sabir Family the entire city of Calimekka. The Goft Galweighs will give you uncontested claim to the House and its contents. Of course, we'll expect you to . . . ah, clear your claim by eliminating any members of the Calimekkan Galweighs who survived your last attempt to win the House."

For one long moment, the silence in the room weighed enough to crack the stone walls of the great hall. Then all around the table, Sabirs exploded with questions.

"That went well, I think," Veshre Galweigh said. She was head of the Goft Wolves, a wizard of tremendous talent and deceptive ferocity who disguised that ferocity behind a jovial manner and a pleasantly plump facade.

Shaid pulled his attention from the enchanting view of the countryside that slid beneath the airible, and leaned back on the cushioned seat. "Probably less well than it seemed; nevertheless, I'm pleased."

"You should be ecstatic." Veshre snorted. "They agreed to supply their troops to assist us in our attack on one of *their* ships, to give us undisputed claim to the Mirror of Souls, and to destroy that bitch, Kait. And they also agreed to kill off the only people who stand between you and Galweigh House. Meanwhile, you already have the Dokteeraks lined up to wipe out the surviving Sabirs after they clear out Galweigh House but before they can claim it. That was the most brilliant bit of negotiating I've ever seen."

Shaid sighed. "Perowin, the greatest of the Ancients' diplomats, once said, 'Diplomacy is the art of getting your enemy to cut his own throat for you, convincing him to do it outside where he won't leave a mess, and making him believe he's getting the best end of the bargain while he does it.' I aspire to make that very bargain someday, but in the meantime . . ." He thought for a moment, then grinned broadly, and finally began to laugh. "In the meantime, by the gods, I came pretty close, didn't I?"

In the courtyard beside the Palm Hall, three black fawns strolled between the fountain and the waterfall, grazing on hibiscus flowers. On a rotunda well away from the falls, a band of Rophetian musicians played *dool dlarmas*—traditional Rophetian dancing airs—for the entertainment of the Family. Crispin Sabir sat on the windowsill in the room above the hall and watched the deer and the dancers and listened to the cheerful music, which suited his mood.

His brother Anwyn, rummaging around the shelves along the inner wall of the room, said, "The last bastard that was in here finished off the *paurel* and didn't replace the bottle."

Crispin laughed. "I think that bastard was you. You're the only one in the Family who'll drink the vile stuff, and you get so drunk when you do that you don't remember having done it."

Anwyn squatted on his hocks, balancing delicately on his cloven hooves, and rubbed absently at the horns that curled from his forehead. After a moment he said, "You might be right, come to think of it. I brought a girl in here only a week ago. I might have drunk it then."

After years of Scarring induced by the constant practice of *dar-sharen*—the sacrifice-magic of the Wolves—nothing human remained of Anwyn's body. Besides the horns and the hooves, spikes protruded from his spine and joints, scales covered what had once been smooth skin, and talons curved from his fingertips. Crispin's body had taken as much of the *rewhah,* the rebound magic, as Anwyn's had, but because Crispin was Karnee, his body had absorbed it and fought off the changes the same way it reverted to human form after a Shift. Anwyn, without the benefits of the Curse, had been trapped in an increasingly hideous form.

Crispin raised an eyebrow. Girls were never with Anwyn by choice. "A girl?"

Anwyn was going through the shelves again, looking for something that would suit him as well as the thick, bitter tuber beer that he liked best. He took his time answering. "Andrew found her for me—a street urchin with a bit of size to her, and an attitude. She thought she could handle anything."

"Until she met you."

"Until then, yes." Anwyn chuckled.

"And when you were done with her, Andrew . . . borrowed her?"

Anwyn pulled a dark green bottle out of the back of the bottom shelf and said, "Hah! I thought I'd put this away for later." It was *lakkar,* green mango beer, and to Crispin it was as unpalatable as *paurel.* Anwyn uncorked the bottle and strolled over to the window, his hooves clipping sharply on the marble floor. He dropped into a seat opposite Crispin, took a swig of his drink, and sighed. "She wasn't young enough to interest Andrew. You know his tastes." He shrugged. "I played with her until I broke her. Then I put her in the Wind Garden. The bellshrubs were going gray and dropping their flowers before they could set their seeds; I thought they could use some fertilizer."

"I'm glad you were paying attention. I've been too busy lately to notice any of the plants, but I'd hate to lose the bellshrubs. They're charming when they're fruiting. I'll take a look at them the next time I'm in the West Wing—make sure the fertilizer did enough." Crispin sipped his own drink and leaned back against the cool, smooth marble of the window frame. "At least I haven't been neglecting them for nothing. All that work looks like it's going to pay off. The meeting went well, don't you think?"

"Hard to believe it could have gone better. I wish I could have been there in person—I would have loved seeing those faces up close when your Galweighs were setting out their bargain." Anwyn took another gulp of his drink and shook his head. "They didn't see a problem with their plan at all?"

"If they saw a problem, they certainly didn't mention it."

"Amazing. They're ready to commit two of their airibles to the attack against Ry and that bitch of theirs? And troops? And they'll send in their troops against their own Family?" Anwyn chortled. "The question then becomes: Are they genuinely naive, or do they think they're being clever?"

"I read their paraglese this way: He's a small-time, double-dealing manipulator, but he sees himself as the future head of a great Galweigh empire. He certainly doesn't intend to hand over Galweigh House without a fight—I think he closes his eyes and sees himself at the head of the table there, commanding armies and armadas across the known world with the twitch of a finger. He may take us for fools, but perhaps he believes whatever double-cross he's set up will be sufficient to get us out of the way."

"Then you don't think he intends to honor his word."

Someone rapped at the door.

"To Sabirs? Of course not." Crispin rose to unlock it, and found his cousin Andrew waiting on the other side. "I was wondering where you'd got to," he said. The scent of blood still clung to Andrew, as did the smell of child. Crispin wrinkled his nose and, disgusted, turned back to his brother. "Would you honor the word you gave to a Galweigh?"

own in the belly of the *Wind Treasure*, Kait and Hasmal crouched beside the Mirror of Souls, padding the bulkhead behind it with rags and roping it in among the ship's other cargo. Ian and the ship's physick were tending to Jayti, and most of the crew were searching the ruins for prizes to take home. Those on board the ship were sleeping or carrying out necessary repairs.

So the two of them were alone, though Kait felt sure someone would come checking on them sooner or later.

"They'll never let us take this to the Reborn," Hasmal whispered.

"Not willingly." Kait twisted her end of the rope around the silver-white metal of the base. "I know that. I knew it when I agreed to their deal. What they won't permit, we'll have to achieve by force."

Hasmal looked at her and rolled his eyes. "Force? We'll still be outnumbered when we cross the sea. Vodor's bones! The captain or Ry Sabir could send pigeons days in advance of our arrival and have the whole of the Sabir army waiting for us on the shore when we arrive, no matter where the captain puts us in."

"Well, not force, perhaps. Maybe by guile."

Hasmal tipped his head and gave her a long, thoughtful look. "Ah. Planning on winning the Sabir to your side by love, Kait? You think he won't take it back to his Family if he's passionate enough about you and you don't want him to?" Hasmal shrugged. "That might work, though I don't like the idea of the future of the world depending on it."

Kait stared at him, momentarily lost for words. Finally she said, "You . . . think I'd bed him to keep control of the Mirror?"

Hasmal frowned. "I'd *hoped*. It isn't as if he's diseased or repugnant. You'll have the opportunity—the captain's seen to that. And the Reborn needs the Mirror; what matters to him matters to us and the whole of the world. Women have futtered men they didn't want for lesser reasons than the fate of the world."

At that moment she didn't like Hasmal, though she could understand that in his eyes the idea must seem practical. She called on her diplomatic training and didn't say what she was thinking about him. Instead, she tempered her response. "It wouldn't work. If I loved him more than all the world, I'd still demand that the Mirror go to the Reborn, then to my Family. He's the same. He was raised to duty. No matter how infatuated he was with me, he'd still demand that the Mirror go back to his Family, either exclusively, or else first—and once it was in Sabir hands, his Family would make sure it never went to my Family, no matter what his arrangement with me or mine with him. My Family would do the same. That's the way Families are—they take care of their own, and they never let private agreements between individuals override the good of the Family as a whole. Never." The Calimekkan Galweighs wouldn't, anyway. Goft Galweighs might be another matter, but she never intended to deal with those traitors again.

"So anything you swear to him or he swears to you is already meaningless if the Galweighs or the Sabirs won't eventually approve of it?"

Kait started to deny that.

Then she thought about what he'd asked her, and what she'd said.

She'd always considered her word a thing of value, and her honor as solid as the rock on which Galweigh House was built. But she realized at that moment that no matter how honest she was, no matter how hard she worked to keep her promises, her Family could make a liar of her with a single command. And if that was true, what value had her word to anyone? She stared down at the rope in her hands and said, "Yes."

She shook her head. People struck bargains with the Galweighs all the time. She'd always thought it was because of the Galweigh reputation for honor. Now she reconsidered. The Galweighs ruled half of Calimekka and much of the world—only a fool would dare refuse Galweigh business, and only a fool would renege on a contract with a Galweigh. But did the men and women who marked wax with the Galweighs consider the Family's mark worthless? If so, no wonder the streets stank of fear when she walked down them. No wonder she smelled such hatred from strangers. No wonder women pulled their children from the streets, and little shops had often just closed their doors for the day, when she strode by them.

There had to be a better way. There had to be a way to protect honor and the Family at the same time.

Hasmal said, "Then we're going to have to learn to use it before we reach land."

Kait, still thinking about her Family and the problem of honor, didn't know what he was talking about for an instant. Then she stared at the Mirror of Souls, and shivered. Learn to use it? "I can't read the glyphs inscribed on the buttons," she told him. "Any of the Ancients' artifacts can be deadly if misused. The Mirror of Souls . . ." Her voice trailed off to silence, and in her mind the bodies of dead legions scrabbled from their graves and shambled across the darkened face of the world, seeking revenge against the fools who had trapped their souls in foul-fleshed husks without restoring those husks to healthy life. She dreaded the idea of a mistake, even a small one.

"I've dealt with the Ancients' work before. I know the dangers."

"Have you learned to read the glyphs since I found this?"

"No. But if Ry Sabir won't come around to our side, we have no other choice."

There were always choices. "If Amalee would speak to me again . . ."

"No. Don't welcome her back." Hasmal's eyes stared faraway at nothing, unfocused. "Something was wrong about her," he said after a moment's thought. "She told you that the magic that destroyed your Family released her soul from captivity. But a soul held captive would race to the Veil, wouldn't it? Beyond the Veil she could have claimed a new birth, a new life, all the things from which she'd been deprived for so long. Instead, she satisfied herself with seeing things through your eyes, hearing things through your ears, and existing as a power-less, disembodied voice that meddled in affairs hundreds of years after her death as if they affected her personally."

"She hoped the Mirror would raise her from the dead, I'm sure."

"Why?"

She wondered if he was intentionally stupid sometimes. "So that she wouldn't be dead anymore."

Hasmal shook his head. "That would make sense for your broth-ers and sisters and parents, Kait—they have you here, and everything from the life they've left behind. But if you raised her from the dead, your ancestor would have no one and nothing familiar in the world. Everything has changed. Why wouldn't she choose to find the souls who shared her other lifetimes with her and rebirth with them? Why wouldn't she want to return to her rightful existence?"

Kait considered that. "I don't know, really. She talked about help-ing me, about having her revenge on the Sabirs, about, well . . . She was interested in my life, in what it was like to be me. She thought it would be exciting to be Karnee—she talked about that a lot. I don't know why she was more interested in me and now than in going on. I didn't think about it." She rocked back on her heels. Perhaps she'd been stupid. "I was so grateful to know there might be a way for me to get my family back, I didn't worry about what Amalee would get out of the deal."

"Don't do anything to call her back, Kait. I don't know where she's gone, but I think we're better off without her. Even if she returns to you, don't ask her to help you work the Mirror. I think she's danger-ous."

"She's the reason I came after the Mirror."

"I know." He rubbed his head. "That's just one of my many night-mares."

"Nightmares?"

When he looked over at her, she noticed the dark circles under his eyes and the tension in his face and realized that the serenity that had molded his features the first time they'd met was gone. "I haven't forgotten the prophecy that sent me running from you after we first met: If I allowed myself to be entangled in your life, I faced a horrible death. Now I am indubitably enmeshed in your affairs, and the two of us are custodians of nothing less than the Mirror of Souls. And you're haunted by a ghost, and we're in the company of Sabirs. And I am and shall always be a coward. I sleep poorly these days."

"You're still alive."

"That's less comfort than you might think."

Heavy footsteps thundered overhead, and Hasmal rose. Kait stayed crouched, untying a knot and beginning to retie it. Several of the crew came down the gangway, arms laden with the toys and tools of the Ancients. They were laughing to each other, but they stopped when they saw Kait and Hasmal. "Up you go, both of you," one man said. "We have work to do down here."

Kait nodded. "We've just finished."

Hasmal met her eyes. "The rest of what we have to do will wait."

Chapter 9

A hundred awkwardnesses, a thousand embarrassments: Kait carried her few belongings into the tiny cabin she would share with Ry, conscious of the stares of the crew, his men, and her own comrades, and stopped just at the door. Ry stood beside the bunk beds, the expression on his face carefully neutral.

"Don't just stand there," he said. "Bring your things and come in."

She nodded and took the extra step that carried her across the threshold. The hatchway closed behind her with a muffled thud—a sound that echoed the beating of her heart.

She looked around the cabin. Ry hadn't been there long—the little room lacked his scent, and his belongings were all in his chest or a bag on the bottom bunk. "Where shall I put my belongings?"

"You don't have much, do you?"

"Not much." She was still looking around the room because it was easier than looking at him. Well-done woodwork, a washbasin built into the starboard wall with a pitcher beneath it, a tiny skylight, the two narrow bunks one on top of the other (and she was relieved that they were so narrow—two people couldn't hope to sleep side by side in them with any comfort), a built-in armoire, a tiny table hinged to the wall and stowed at the moment, two small plank benches also hinged to the wall on one end, also stowed. The floor was clean and polished, the walls smelled of citrus and wax, the linens were clean and tucked neatly into place at the corners and smelled only of soap and sunlight and fresh air.

"You can have the drawers beneath the bottom bunk." He moved away from the bunks.

She didn't want to step any closer to him, but she couldn't just stand there holding her bag until he left. So she took a deep breath, walked over to the bunk bed, and knelt on the floor. She gave the drawer a tug and it slid out smoothly; she was so tense she pulled it clear to the end of its run, and only the fact that the carpenter who'd built it had included stops kept it from landing in her lap. He was behind her, so close she could feel the warmth of his body, so close his scent became a drug, and her vision grayed at the edges and narrowed into a tunnel and she could hear only the rushing of her blood in her veins and the quick, sharp pace of his breathing.

She stiffened her back, dreading his touch and half-expecting it at the same time. But he kept his distance. She shoved the bag into the drawer, not bothering to unpack it, shoved the door closed, and moved away as fast as she could.

Through the wall, she heard someone begin to pluck the strings of a guitarra. "My cousin Karyl," Ry offered, noting her shift in posture as she listened to the music.

His playing was sweet, his voice a mournful tenor as he began to sing.

No, I'll not for lads nor lasses.
My dancing days are done.
The bitter tide
Is my final ride
To the sea I am now gone.

 And I follow the rush of the water
 For the water flows to the shore
 And I have cried
 Where the pale tides died
 And wept to weep no more.

I lost my faithless lover
To the sea, my faithless friend—

For the one devoured the other
Leaving nothing but pain at the end.
Now I hear her song in the wave
And her voice in the water deep.
She is gone but her music lives on
And it's all that I can keep.

> And I follow the rush of the water
> For the water flows to the shore
> And I have cried
> Where the pale tides died
> And wept to weep no more.

When that song was finished, the unseen singer paused for a moment, then launched into another one, equally mournful.

"Sad songs," Kait said, not wanting to listen to any more wistful, yearning ballads.

"If he knows another sort, he's never shown it."

"I've never heard that one before."

"You won't have heard any of them before. He only plays the songs he writes himself. A hundred variations on the theme of grief."

Kait had no wish to discuss love, or longing, or grief. She said nothing, and the stilted conversation died there, and the two of them were left looking at each other.

The silence was becoming unbearable when Ry said, "I have some things for you—I picked them up when we took on supplies in the Fire Islands." He unlatched the doors of the armoire and pulled them open. Opulent, gauzy silks and fine linens in rainbow colors hung on the rack to the left and lay folded on the shelves to the right. She caught a glimpse of tabards and blouses and skirts and dresses, soft robes and dressing gowns, nightshirts, leg wrappings, and stockings . . . even delicate underthings. The people of the Fire Islands were famous for their fine fabrics and remarkable stitchery— and it appeared that Ry had picked only the finest of what the island markets offered.

Kait felt her face grow hot. She could not imagine allowing herself to wear any of those things—to let the silk undergarments that he'd picked out for her touch her skin, or to pull on one of those filmy nightshirts before climbing into her bunk for the night. "No," she said. "I have my own clothes."

Ry arched an eyebrow. "You have hardly anything. You're wearing a sailor's work clothes. A woman of your birth should wear fine silk dresses, not cotton shirts and roughspun breeches." He smiled, and she shivered. He was too close to her, and too near Shift; from across the room his body heat was a pressure against her skin, simultaneously drawing the Karnee part of her forward and pushing the human part of her toward the door and flight and the dubious safety of the deck.

"I have enough." Her voice sounded husky in her own ears. She was responding to him even though she didn't want to.

Shield, she thought. Magic drawn close and held in place will make a wall between us. Magic will give me control.

She offered her own energy and strength to Vodor Imrish, and with the power she gained from that quick, bloodless offering, drew the shield around herself. Instantly she could breathe easier. Although his scent remained seductive in her nostrils and his heat still touched her skin, a calm silence blanketed her racing thoughts.

He was staring at her, astonishment evident in his eyes. "What did you do?" he asked.

She shrugged. For the moment—for as long as her strength fed the shield, anyway—she would have peace. "Doesn't matter. I want to sleep. Which bunk will be mine?"

"The top one." He moved toward her. "You seem . . . gone . . ." he whispered. "Don't do that. Come back to me."

With her courage supported by the shield, she was able to say, "We are going to be nothing but roommates, Ry. Not friends. Certainly not lovers. I'll obey the conditions of my agreement with the captain, but . . . that's all."

"I came so far to find you. I gave up so much. . . ."

She nodded. "And for the rescue, I thank you. Truly, I'm grateful. My Family will certainly reward you. But I cannot forget—and neither can you—that I am Galweigh and you are Sabir. We have our duties."

His face twisted with bitterness, and for the first time since she'd used herself as bait to allow Ian and Hasmal to take him prisoner, she saw both pain and anger slip across his face. "Ah, duty. The cage of cowards afraid to live. You may have your duty—I have already taken a different road."

He moved past her, still angry, and left the room. When he was gone she sagged against the wall and closed her eyes. She wondered how long her obligations to duty would keep her from touching him, from stroking his hair or kissing his lips.

She built her shield stronger and, removing only her boots, climbed into her bed. Then she lay staring up at the plank ceiling and listening to the slow creaking of the ship. Sleep would be long in coming.

Interlude

From the eighth chapter of the Seventh Text of the Secret Texts of Vincalis:

[13]Solander sat in the Hall of Wizardry and taught the apprentices, saying, "These are the Ten Great Laws of Magic, known from old.

[14]"The First Law—the Law of Magical Reaction—states: Every action has an equal and opposite, but aligned, reaction.

[15]"The Second Law—the Law of Magical Inertia—states: Inertia holds; spells in force remain in force unless acted on by an opposite force. Latent spells remain latent unless acted on by an opposite force.

[16]"The Third Law, which you know as the Law of Magical Conservation, states: Magic, mass, and energy all conserve.

[17]"The first iteration of the Fourth Law—the Law of Magical Attraction—says: Aligned spells attract, [18]while the second iteration of the Fourth Law—the Law of Magical Repulsion—says: Unaligned spells repel.

[19]"The first iteration of the Fifth Law—the Law of Spellcasting—says: The force of the spell cast will be equal to the energy used multiplied by the number of casting magicians, minus conversion energy, [20]while the second iteration of the Fifth Law, which is the Law of Spellshielding, says: The damage done to the

casting magicians by a spell or spell recoil—*rewhah*—will equal the energy sent minus the capacity of the buffer or sacrifice, divided by the number of spellcasters.

[21]"The Sixth Law, the Law of Alignment, tells us: Negative magic begets negative reactions. Positive magic begets positive reactions.

[22]"The Seventh Law, which is the Law of Compulsion, says: Every spell used to compel the behavior of any living creature against its will carries a negative alignment.

[23]"The Eighth Law, or Law of Harm, says: Every spell used to inflict harm, damage, pain, or death, no matter the nature of the target, carries a negative charge.

[24]"The Ninth Law, the Law of Souls, states: The mortal representative of an immortal soul carries the charge of the soul, whether positive, negative, or neutral.

[25]"The Tenth Law, or Law of Neutrality, says: Anything that carries a neutral charge will be drawn to the strongest force around it, whether that force be positive or negative, for neutrality is a position of weakness, not of strength.

[26]"These are the Ten Great Laws, which are the laws of the nature of magic, and which nature enforces. [27]But I give you another law, and this is a law of the nature of man and of the nature of Falconry, enforceable only by yourselves. [28]This law is: Pay for your magic with nothing but that which is yours to give.

[29]"*Ka-erea, ka-ashura, ka-amia, ka-enadda,* and *ka-obbea*: your will, your blood, your flesh, your breath, and your soul. These are the five acceptable sacrifices, and acceptable only if offered freely. [30]Magic drawn from your life-force, from these five acceptable sacrifices, will be pure, and free of *rewhah,* and will not scar lives or land. [31]That you offer only these sacrifices is the Law of Ka, the Offering of Self, and I declare it the highest law of the Falcon, and the law by which Falcons will be known.

[32]"For the Law of Ka is the Law of Love—love of humanity and love of life—and my greatest requirement of you is that you love all living things, and live your lives in demonstration of your love."

olander the Reborn waited in the belly of his mother for his time of birth to arrive, but already the faithful reached out to him, and he reached back. From hidden rooms in forest houses, from scholarly studies, from the decks of fishing boats and the ever-moving wagons of the peripatetic Gyru-nalles, faithful Falcons drew a few drops of their own blood to form the link that let them touch him, and he reached into their souls, and gave them acceptance, and gave them love.

He spent the stations of darkness and growth in the deep meditation of the soul, focusing not on the future, when he would at last give the people he loved a world worthy of them, nor on the past, wherein lay the pain of torture and his magical escape from his enemies at the moment of his physical death: Those were memories and thoughts that gave back nothing. He could not plan for what would come, and he could not change what had already been. But from the warm safety of the womb, he could begin his work, reaching into the souls of those he had left so reluctantly a thousand years before and showing them that hope existed, that their lives could be better, and that the secret that would bring about the new and brighter world was a simple one: Accept each others' faults, be kind, and love one another.

But he did draw himself from the peace and the joy of that long gestation to touch his sword, his Falcon Dùghall Draclas.

* * *

Dùghall.

The voice came from all around Dùghall Draclas as he knelt by the embroidered silk *zanda,* preparing to throw his future with a handful of silver coins. The quadrants of House, Life, Spirit, Pleasure, Duty, Wealth, Health, Goals, Dreams, Past, Present, and Future lay empty, awaiting the patterns that the *zanda* coins would make within them.

Dùghall.

He put down the coins and took a deep breath. His heart knew that voice.

"Reborn?" he whispered.

My faithful Falcon—you have listened with your heart and with your soul. You've gathered allies for me, you've readied them, and I can see that they're strong and courageous. Send them to me now, in secret.

"I'll bring them to you," Dùghall said.

No. You've gathered good men and you've trained them well, but you aren't a soldier, Dùghall. Wait where you are.

The Reborn's dismissal crushed him. He'd thought that he would accompany the army that he'd gathered for the Reborn—in fact, he'd thought that he would lead it. Now he was being told to send the men—many of them his sons—off alone, while he waited in the middle of this nowhere he'd chosen as a training ground.

He was a sword unsheathed and hungry for the blood of the Reborn's enemy, and he'd been waiting for this call from the moment he left Galweigh House in secret to follow the dictates of a throw of the *zanda.* He'd suffered deprivation and hardship, pain and fear; he'd served with his whole heart, he'd offered everything he had. He was an old sword, he knew, and one with rust on the blade—but that Solander the Reborn would call the men he'd gathered and not call him . . .

Solander's soft voice whispered in his mind and heart, *Dùghall, I have other plans for you than to have you die on a battlefield. The Dragons are returning. They move among the Calimekkans already, preparing a place for themselves there. You will wait where you are, for I foresee a disaster, and I also see that your presence can overcome it. But only if you wait where you are.*

"What disaster? What can I do here? There's nothing here but a fishing village."

If I were a god I could tell you the future, but I'm only a man. The future is as opaque to me as it is to you. I know only that if you wait where you are, you will avert the destruction of everything the Falcons have worked for in the last thousand years.

Dùghall said, "Then I will wait. I serve as you desire—I ask only that you use me."

You are my sword, Dùghall. Without you, I am lost.

Then the Reborn was gone. The warmth that had surrounded Dùghall vanished, and with it the cocoon of joy and love and hope. He rose, his knees creaking as he did, and walked to the window of the grass hut in which he'd been living, and stared up at the smoking cone of the volcano to the north. Life was like that volcano—calm on the outside, while underneath it was seething and deadly and able to explode with unimaginable violence at any instant. What could destroy a thousand years of planning? What could go wrong with Solander's triumphant return?

In the field to the north of the village, the men he'd gathered drilled together, preparing for a battle that he'd convinced them was coming. He needed to send them to the Reborn. The little fleet of islander longships he'd gathered would need to sail away without him to the south, to the edge of Ibera, where the Veral Territories met the Iberan border. His magic had pinpointed that place as their eventual destination. From there, they would meet the Reborn, and he would take them to fight against the Dragons in Calimekka.

And when his troops were gone, Dùghall would wait in this little fishing village until a sign told him that his moment had come. He would fast. He would prepare himself physically, as he had been doing. He would study the throws of the *zanda,* and summon Speakers to tell him what they saw moving within the Veil. He would serve.

He only wished he had some idea what sort of disaster was coming.

Chapter 11

Hasmal crouched in the aft bilge, dabbing filched oil of wintergreen beneath his nostrils and trying to ignore both the stink of the bilge and the rolling of the ship. He'd have a hard time controlling his magic if he were retching all the time he cast his spell.

He felt lucky he'd found a place where he could work unwatched. The *Wind Treasure* boasted three separate bulkheads in her bilge—an aft bulkhead, a middle one, and one at the fore. All three had access hatches, but the aft one had a hatch that lay just beyond the head. He could go to the head without raising suspicions, especially now that the ship had sailed and the crew had seen him both seasick and gripped with bowel flux. If he bolted toward them, a pained, half-panicked expression on his face, they scattered, clearing his path.

He could be gone as much as a station after such an act, and no one would come looking.

Kait crouched beside him. "We aren't going to have long. Just because your spell got me in here without being seen doesn't mean *he* won't notice I'm missing."

"He's with his friends. He won't look for you for a while."

"We can hope." She refused the oil of wintergreen when he offered it to her, wrinkling her nose. "I'd rather smell the bilge," she said. "I hate perfumes."

"Sorry." He got out his magic bag and pulled out a hand mirror, blood-bowl, thorn needle, and herbs. "I have everything you need. You're going to have to link to the Reborn and get him to tell you how to work the Mirror of Souls."

Her eyebrows went up and she shook her head. "You said you needed my help . . . but I'm no wizard, Hasmal. I'm just now getting a feel for the simple magics. Linking . . . that's big."

"Not as big as directing a shield around as much of your spell as I can, and watching over you to make sure that no other wizard notices the movement of magic, and holding a spell ready to protect you if you're attacked. You *or* I could link to Solander, but only I can make sure you don't die while you're doing it."

She looked queasy. "Isn't there some other way?"

"I've tried the other ways. I've summoned Speakers, I've spirit-walked the past, I've gone through the Texts looking for anything that might tell how the damned Mirror works or what Solander intended the Falcons to do with it. I'm not strong enough or talented enough to reach the place in the past where the Mirror was last used, the Texts are mute about the Mirror, and the Speakers just laugh at me. I'm out of options."

She shivered and nodded. "Then give me the thorn and the blood-bowl and help me through this."

"You have to ask Solander how to use the Mirror—exact steps, exact words, what we should expect it to do. . . ."

Kait nodded again. "I'll get everything."

He waited while she stabbed her finger with the thorn and dropped her blood into the blood-bowl. He coached her through the ceremony that would link her to the Reborn. She was afraid, and he could understand that—but she had a courage that he envied. She did what she had to do.

He started casting his own spells even before he saw the change come over her body; by the time the blissful smile spread across her face, he'd formed the shield that surrounded her, a sphere of energy flawed only at the point where Kait's life force curled out from her in a thin tendril that connected her across uncounted leagues to the soul of the Reborn. He set it so that if anything attacked that delicate connection, the shield would snap shut on its own. Kait would lose her connection to Solander, but she'd survive.

With that set, he opened himself to the ship. He loosed his conscious self from the confines of his body and connected himself to the boards upon which he sat; his mind traced the connections of each board to the next, flowing outward, stretching, cautiously touching each new structure and noting the presence of each living thing until the ship became his body, with his human body only a tiny appendage. He "knew" the ship the way he knew his own body—felt its movement, saw the water stretching away from him and beneath him, heard and followed every conversation going on in the ship simultaneously.

Such openness put him in tremendous danger—he could not shield or protect himself in any way while his soul stretched outside of the confines of his flesh—but in no other way could he be sure that his and Kait's activities had aroused no curiosity.

In one of the forward cabins, Ry and his lieutenants played cards. The crew did their work. Ian stood on the aft deck, staring back toward Novtierra. Hasmal watched his eyes—Ian looked like he contemplated murder. Not at that moment, however. The ship was quiet . . . the activities of its passengers safe for the present . . . and yet . . .

He felt something wrong. Some*thing* marked the ship; some*one* tracked it from a distance. He felt around blindly, as a man would feel for a door in a dark room. A link lay within the ship's wooden body— a physical focus for distant magic. Before he could find out who watched the ship, he had to find that link.

Welcome, Kait.

Reborn. . . . In the wordless exchange that followed, Solander's touch filled her soul. Again she felt his complete acceptance of her, his unconditional love for her. For a long and blissful moment, she asked nothing of him, feeding herself instead from the simple joy of being in his presence.

Her task couldn't wait forever, though, and at last she forced herself to the unpleasantness of her reality. *We're in trouble,* she told the unborn infant. *We've been taken by the enemy, and we have every reason to believe that when we reach the shores of Ibera, the Sabirs will take the Mirror from us. If we have any hope of getting it to you, we have to know how to use it now.*

No, Solander said. Kait felt fear suffuse featureless light in which she floated. *Do nothing with the Mirror of Souls except bring it to me. It is the vehicle through which the Dragons will return to Matrin.*

Kait felt the chill of his words. *If we can't get it to you, then we should destroy it.*

No. A failed attempt to destroy it could well free the Dragons through you. And even if you could manage a successful attempt, you would do so at the price of the destruction of your own soul.

Why?

Because you would be destroying the souls of those within it. Those who destroy immortality pay an eternal price.

Kait thought of the smooth platinum-bright curves of the artifact, of the warm light that spiraled up through its center, of the feeling of comfort she got from being near it. She had been sure it was something good in spite of the faintly unpleasant scent that emanated from it. And that, she thought, made sense. The Dragons wouldn't find any advantage in creating something that *looked* evil; people would be far too willing to destroy something like that. But things that looked valuable, that gave off pleasant sensations . . .

And that brought to mind Amalee, who had suggested to Kait that she cross the ocean to retrieve the Mirror.

The soul you know as Amalee is one of the wakened Dragons, the Reborn told her. *But she set you to a task as important to me as it is to her. When I have the Mirror, I can release the souls it holds directly into the Veil, where they will be judged by the souls of their peers. Then I can destroy the Mirror, so that the Dragons' evil will not return to Matrin in any form*

Kait started to ask him if he could offer her some help, some advice, on getting the Mirror safely to him, but without warning, she was torn away from the warmth of the Reborn's presence. His light vanished and for an instant she hung in the absolute darkness of void, her body consumed by pain so fierce she felt certain she was being ripped apart.

Then she was in her body again, in the bilge, racked by nausea, blinded by pain, with Hasmal shaking her and slapping her face and whispering, "Kait! Kait? Wake up! Are you hurt? Kait?"

His face was right against hers when she came around enough to look at him, and she could see stark terror in his eyes.

"What happened?" She groaned and held her belly; the pain receded slowly but the nausea remained.

"The shield I set around you snapped shut," he told her.

She shook her head, not understanding.

"You were attacked. Someone was watching you—watching the whole ship—and when you reached for the Reborn, whoever it was attacked."

"Ry attacked me?" she asked.

"No. The attack didn't come from anyone on the ship."

"Are we in danger now?"

"Not for the moment. I've shielded both of us. We'll be safe for a while yet."

"So who found us? Who tried to get me?"

"I'm not certain. I managed to trace the trail of the wizard who was spying on us as far as Calimekka, but when I got too close, something about my presence alerted him. He came after me fast; I had to break off my connection with the ship. I barely shielded myself in time—and while I did, he attacked you."

She noticed that Hasmal's hands were shaking. Even in the darkness of the bilge she could see his pallor, and even over the stench of stale water, dead rats, and refuse she could smell his fear.

He added, "I'd guess Wolves were watching the ship."

"Then they may know about the Reborn. And the Mirror."

"Almost certainly."

She pressed her fingers to her temples to ease her aching head. "Oh, gods. Then what do we do?"

"We use the information you got from the Reborn to activate the Mirror. We—" He saw her shaking her head and stopped. "What's wrong?"

"We don't touch the Mirror of Souls," she said. She quickly gave him the rest of Solander's bad news. When she finished, Hasmal buried his face in his hands.

"Then what *do* we do?"

Kait took a deep breath and let it out slowly. "We keep our eyes open. We do what we can to win Ry over to our side. If we see that things are going badly, we steal one of the longboats in the dead of night and row ourselves and the Mirror to an island, or trust ourselves to the currents." She leaned forward and rested a hand on his knee. "We are going to do what we have to do, Has. The Mirror is going to reach the Reborn. The Wolves are *not* going to get it."

He looked into her eyes and saw calm in them. A ferocity that he lacked. A determination that he thought he could find within himself. He felt answering echoes of it already. He put his hand over hers. "You're right. We will. And they won't."

Chapter 12

Ian stopped Kait as she stepped out of the ship's shower, having just finished rinsing the stink of the bilge off of herself. "Jayti's been asking to see you."

Kait felt a quick, sharp anxiety, and after an instant's concentration, understood why. Ian carried the smell of death on his skin and in his clothing. "He's gotten worse?"

Ian met her gaze angrily. "He's dying. All the physick's promises to do his best are come to nothing."

Kait said, "He was dying before we boarded the *Wind Treasure*; we didn't think he was going to live. If anything, the physick has given him time and eased the pain of his last days."

"You can be satisfied with that. You seem satisfied with everything right now." He turned away from her, every motion he made and every line of his body charged with his pent-up rage.

"I'm doing what I have to do to get us all to safety."

He stalked toward the gangway, turning only before he ascended to the top deck. "Of *course* you are. Well, do whatever you're going to do for Jayti soon. He'll be dead before the day is out."

Then he was gone. His anger hung in the air like a poison cloud.

Kait twisted the ends of her hair to wring out the water and stared after him. He was trouble waiting to happen.

* * *

"You look worse than me," Jayti said. He lay in the bed, his skin white as bleached linen, his dark hair sweat-drenched and plastered to his skull. His eyes, sunken in their sockets, burned with feverish brightness. The smell of blood-rot and decomposition in the room overwhelmed her. Greenish stains marred the sheets where the stump of his leg lay. Ian had been right. He wouldn't survive much longer.

"I haven't been sleeping well," Kait told him. It was true. Her dreams in Ry's cabin became far too seductive, and bled over into her waking moments with maddening constancy. So she fought sleep.

She didn't comment on Jayti's appearance. Instead she said, "I was . . . surprised . . . that you wanted to talk to me."

"Because I'm afraid of you?"

"Because I don't think you like me much."

Jayti managed a twisted smile. "You're right. I don't. Skin-shifters . . ." He shrugged, and even that tiny movement seemed to suck a bit of the remaining life out of him. "You can change, disappear, pretend to be normal, but inside you're hiding the monster. . . ." He sighed. "But what I think about you doesn't matter. The captain loves you."

Kait cringed, hearing those words presented so baldly. "I know."

"You don't love him," he offered as a statement, not a question.

She considered lying, telling the dying man something to make him think better of her for whatever time he had left. He already knew the truth, though. "No. Ian is . . . ah, well, I . . . I want good things for him. But I'm not sure that I *can* love. Not him . . . not anyone." She considered her obsession with Ry, and again wondered if anything so consuming and so painful could be love. She sometimes felt it could only be the early stages of madness. "I wish I could. It would make everything . . . easier."

Jayti grinned briefly, a death's-head smile that only accented his gauntness. "Life doesn't give you easy. Honor only makes things harder. But for the sake of honor, and if you really care what happens to him, you have to tell him. He talks about getting you away from Ry, making you see that he's the one who's best for you. He thinks he has a chance to win your heart. I don't."

Kait considered that.

When she said nothing, Jayti added, "It's eating him inside. As long as he believes he has a chance to have you, he won't think of anything else. He talks about finding a way to throw Ry overboard when no one is around, or of running him through with a sword and claiming it was an accident. He's . . . obsessed."

Kait knew what he said was true. When she looked in Ian's eyes, she saw a feverish brightness not that different from what she saw in Jayti's, and a fixity of gaze she'd seen in the steady stares of hunting wolves evaluating their prey.

"Telling him I don't love him won't change the way he feels."

"It won't. But if he knows he has no hope, it might keep him from doing something that will get him killed."

She sighed.

Jayti said, "He's my friend. He lost everything else that mattered to him—his ship, his crew, his treasure. He doesn't know it, but he's lost you as well. If he dies trying to win you, and you could prevent it by telling him now that he has no hope . . ." Jayti looked away and fell silent. Kait, not knowing what to say, said nothing.

The dying man finally looked at her again. "If he dies because you let him think he still might win you, my ghost will haunt every instant of the rest of your life. I swear it on Brethwan's eternal soul."

The hair on Kait's arms stood on end, and a shiver crawled down her spine. She looked into those eyes, so near death, and wondered if he could already see the Veil before him. "I'll tell him," she whispered.

"Swear it."

"I swear it." *On my word as a Galweigh,* she almost said, but stopped. "On my own soul," she said, "I swear I'll tell him."

Chapter 13

Kait stood on the deck of the *Wind Treasure,* staring out at the endless ocean. The ship rocked with the waves, its sails for the moment furled. Sunlight illuminated everything with a haze of gold; the water sparkled, the brass fittings gleamed, the soapstoned deck shone like polished ivory. The crew wore their best clothing and stood in lines along the port and starboard sides of the foredeck, and one of them played a soft drumroll.

Loelas, the *Wind Treasure*'s parnissa, led the small procession that stepped out of the aft cabins. Hasmal and Ian and four of Ry's men followed, the black-shrouded form carried between them. She watched Ian closely without turning her head. She would have to talk with him soon. The weight of her oath bore down on her, and she felt Jayti's ghost watching her.

"The gods are smiling on his spirit, to give him such a fine day for a funeral," Ry said. He stood to her right, dressed in his Sabir green and silver, with his black boots polished until they mirrored the sun and his sword unsheathed and raised before him in a salute.

Kait held her own sword in the same attitude. For this occasion, she'd finally put on some of the clothing that Ry had brought along for her. She wore a heavy cream silk tunic that reached to her knees, embroidered in blackstitch at each hem and layered over a black silk underblouse; a wide black braided leather sash as soft as a summer

breeze that held the folds of the outer tunic precisely in place; a narrow black silk skirt; embroidered cream silk leg wrappings; and soft
split-suede shoes. The clothing was as fine as any she had ever worn,
and she wore it to honor Jayti. When the funeral was over, she would
rid herself of it and go back to coarse sailors' breeches, tunics, and
deck shoes. Wearing those was a barrier between her and Ry, however
thin. She needed every layer of separation she could get.

She kept her gaze fixed on the funeral procession and under her
breath murmured, "Fine as the day is, I think he'd rather be alive for
it."

Out of the corner of her eye, she saw Ry turn toward her for just
an instant, annoyance clearly marked on his face. She almost smiled at
having goaded him into a social error. But the smile would be as inap-
propriate as his gesture of inattentiveness had been. She kept her eyes
forward, her face blank, and her sword steady in front of her.

The procession came to a halt in the center of the foredeck, and
the parnissa turned and knelt, and unfolded a deep green cloth, its
edges weighted with lead, across the white boards. The men carrying
Jayti's body lowered it carefully to the center of the cloth.

The parnissa stood, and one of the cabin boys hurried to his side,
carrying the censer and the lamp. Loelas took the censer and crossed
it over the body five times. "Jayti of Pappas, called Cousin Fox, you
have left the realm of the living this day to traverse the Veil. I commend your spirit to Lodan, she who rules both Love and Loss, and to
Brethwan her consort, he who rules Pain and Pleasure, Health and Ill-
ness, Life and Death. Release your last hold on the flesh, follow
through the Veil, and find peace and new life."

He would not, she thought. Not until she had kept her promise.

He handed the censer back to the cabin boy and took the lamp.
He crossed it five times over the corpse, and when he had finished,
rested it on the cloth above the head. "Jayti of Pappas, called Cousin
Fox, you have left the realm of the living this day, and your flesh lies
empty. It has served for your good, but now must nourish all those
who follow. As you served the sea in life, so you will serve the sea in
death. I commend your flesh to Joshan, she who rules Silence and
Loneliness and Solitude, for the sea is vast and lonely, and all return at

last to its embrace. May she light your flesh through the darkness to its best service, that a human body will await your spirit on its return."

Loelas picked up the lamp and handed it to the cabin boy. He stepped back, and Hasmal and Ian knelt and folded the green cloth over Jayti's shrouded body, tying the ties sewn along the back when they'd finished.

The parnissa turned and looked at the men and Kait gathered on the deck and said, "This same passage each of us will one day take. Contemplate your mortality, and thank the gods for each moment of each station, living neither in the past nor the future, for the moment of *now* is the only moment you will ever have. Contemplate the value of your life in its service to gods and humankind, and serve now in whatever form you would, knowing that you cannot serve tomorrow. Hold Jayti, our fallen brother, in your heart and thoughts, and find a lesson in his death, for in this final way you can assist him in serving his fellow humans, and finding his humanity in another life."

The parnissa nodded, and the six men picked up the corpse again and carried it to the starboard side of the foredeck, walking between Kait and Ry. Kait and Ry turned to present their swords as the body moved past them and finished their quarter turns facing each other, swords forming an arch.

"You came from the sea; return to the sea," Loelas said.

The men dropped Jayti's body over the side. The body splashed, throwing sparkling beads of water into the air, and the green lead-weighted shroud pulled it down; out of the corner of her eye Kait could see the way that the sunlight illuminated the stream of bubbles that trailed like silver coins behind it.

Ian wouldn't look at her. He strode past her off the foredeck, followed by the crew, the parnissa, and the captain, and finally Hasmal.

As the last man save Ry walked off the foredeck, Kait gave Ry a cold nod and resheathed her sword. She had done her duty to the deceased, honoring his spirit with Family steel since he had died fighting with her. Ry slid his sword back into its scabbard, too, though still not bothering to explain why he chose to pay tribute to the dead man in that formal way, and rested a hand on her shoulder as she turned to go to their shared cabin.

"Wait," he said.

She turned back to him, tensing at his touch. He had kept his distance in the cabin, and after a few attempts to speak to her, had accepted her silence. The heat of his hand through the soft silk seemed to brand her.

"I don't want to talk to you now."

"I know," he said, his voice calm and reasonable. "I can see that you would choose to never speak to me, never look at me, and never touch me, in spite of what you really want."

"What I really want? I'd love to know what you think you know about that." She glared at him, wanting to hate him, despising herself for wanting him. The wind ruffled his hair, and the sun burnished the dark gold strands until they matched the heavy gold hoops in his ears. His pale blue eyes with their black-ringed irises seemed to pull her toward him, as if they exuded their own gravity. He was fiercely beautiful, as a wolf in his prime or a stooping falcon was beautiful—the air of barely leashed ferocity about him only made him more compelling to her.

She held her magical shields tight around herself as Hasmal had taught her and willed herself to hate him, to see him as the destroyer of her parents, her siblings, and her Family, and the enemy of everything she believed in.

He watched her closely for a long, silent moment. Then he shook his head. "We have a long way to go, and a lot to accomplish. If you won't follow your heart—and your dreams—at least talk to me when we're alone. I've done nothing to deserve the unending silence."

She wanted to believe him. Gods all forgive her, she did. "You had nothing to do with the slaughter of the Galweighs."

"No." He sighed. "I went into your House with my men, but that was to rescue you. I believed you would be there. I knew the attack was planned, but I had no part in the planning."

"And it was sheer coincidence that you and I crossed paths at the Theramisday party in Halles?"

"Of course not." He shrugged. "I was my Family's messenger to Paraglese Dokteerak."

"Then you *were* involved in my Family's destruction."

"I was the *messenger*. I served the Sabirs as they directed me. I was of minor importance—the son of the head Wolf, in training for bigger things, but still too young and inexperienced to be anything but a go-between."

Kait arched an eyebrow. "Messengers are never chosen for their lack of experience."

Guilt flashed across Ry's face, quick as a bolt of lightning. She could have imagined that she saw it there, it vanished so rapidly. But it hadn't been her imagination.

Ry held out his hands palm up—a gesture both placating and confessional. "You're right, and we both know it. Kait, I can't claim to be completely blameless. I had no more love for the Galweighs than you had for the Sabirs. You and I spent much of our lives learning to work against each other. But that changed when we met." He paused and leaned against the rail and studied her. The sun hit him full in the face, making him squint. "At least it changed for me."

She thought, It all changed for me, too. But she didn't say that. She couldn't.

He waited a long time for her to respond, and when he finally realized that she wouldn't no matter how long he waited, he nodded again. "Well enough. Your feelings for the Sabirs haven't changed. But consider this: I've been cut off from the Sabirs. If I return home now, with things unchanged between me and my Family, my mother will declare me *barzanne*. That sentence will rest on my head because I chose to come after you instead of staying with my Family and taking my father's place as head of the Wolves when he died. No matter what I once was, I am not a Sabir any longer." He turned his face away from her, either wearying of the sun in his eyes or wanting the small measure of privacy that turning away afforded him. "I won't beg you to find room for me in your heart, Kait. Begging isn't in me. If that's the only way you could accept me, then you aren't the woman I think you are. I *will* appeal to your reason. Consider what a team the two of us could make. Both Family, both magic-trained . . . both Karnee. Imagine what we could do together."

Kait had done nothing but that since she'd come aboard the ship.

"I dream of you," she said quietly.

He turned back to her, looking at her sharply. "And I, you."

"We're dancing," she added.

He flushed. Nodded. "In the air."

"In the darkness."

Naked.

Neither of them said that word, but that was only because they didn't have to. The image from those nightly dreams hung between the two of them, as real and vivid as life. Kait felt the heat in her cheeks and the racing of her pulse. She smelled Ry's excitement, sensed his arousal, felt her own breath coming faster.

"I don't think they're dreams," Ry said. His voice dropped to a rough murmur. "I think our souls give us what our bodies will not."

Kait felt herself moving toward something irrevocable. She took a step back from him, needing physical distance and some reassurance that she was still in control of herself. "Why did you come after me?" she asked him. "If you had duty to your Family, if you knew you would be declared *barzanne,* why did you not stay and carry out your duty?"

His hands balled into quick fists, the knuckles whitening before he took a breath and stared out at the sea. He was forcing himself to relax. Pushing back the hunger that had been there an instant before. So control did not come easy to him, either. She had wondered about that, lying in the darkness every night staring up at the cabin ceiling, listening to him breathe. After a moment, when neither his stance nor his scent betrayed anything of his emotions, he said, "I have no good answer. Not for you, not for myself. I can tell you only that from the moment that you and I crossed paths, something about you compelled me. Or maybe it was something about *us.*" He shrugged. "Until then, I always believed I could control everything about myself." She caught a glimpse of the rueful curve of his smile at the corner of his mouth.

They shared their dreams. They affected each other in ways she couldn't understand. She wanted him.

And her Family was gone. From what she'd learned, so was most of his. Perhaps that meant that the battle between the Sabirs and the Galweighs could end.

"I'll . . . I'll think about what you've said." She smoothed the tunic. "I'll promise nothing, except that I'll . . . consider . . ." She tested the word, and found that it offered only as much as she wished to offer. "Yes. I'll consider . . . a truce." She turned before he could say anything in response and hurried toward their quarters. Halfway there, she turned back, and saw that he still stared out at the endless, hypnotic sea. "I think . . . I'd like to talk."

Chapter **14**

*T*he Mirror has almost reached us, Dafril said. *But my chosen avatar has been led to direct it toward the south—toward the cold lands. Solander has called it to him there.*

Only the heads of the Star Council gathered in the cold infinity beyond the Veil—Dafril hadn't wanted to deal with the panic that would ensue with the younger members if they realized Solander had returned.

We've already taken steps to deal with the Mirror, Mellayne said. *It will reach Calimekka.*

Yes. Unfortunately, Solander won't be so easy to take care of. He nears the time of his birth, and he has already started gathering his Falcons together.

But if Solander returns in the body of a babe—memories or not—we'll have years before he can stand against us.

Dafril sighed. Solander had nearly destroyed them once. He couldn't believe the bastard found a way to get himself embodied without having his memories scrambled yet had failed to take into account the time it would take for that body to reach usable age. *We cannot count on that. I have to suspect that Solander has a plan. He always knew what he was doing.*

I wish we did.

So do I, Mellayne, Dafril said. *So do I.*

Chapter 15

Kait woke to darkness, to the sound of Ry's steady breathing in the bunk beneath hers and to his scent in the room. Shreds of the nightmare that had awakened her still clung to her, twisting in her gut.

She'd been dancing with Ry. That same maddening, tempting, passionate dance—the embraces, the kisses, the touching. And then someone else had been there with them, watching. Waiting.

She sat up, not soothed by the steady rocking of the ship, or the rhythmic creaks and murmurs of boards and sails. "Ry?"

He was already awake—had, in fact, awakened just an instant after she did. After she left the dream, she realized. She heard his breathing catch, and smelled wariness about him . . . and anticipation. "Yes?"

"Someone is hunting for you. Wanting to kill you."

"Why do you say that?"

"We were being watched. In the dream. In the dance. The watcher was . . . malevolent."

"I felt nothing of the sort."

"He was shielded from you, but some sort of current runs between the two of you—either a blood tie or something magical. I could see the current. A tiny black stream. I followed it back to its source, and when I did, I saw his eyes looking out at you through the darkness. I don't . . . I'm not sure, but I don't think he knew I was there. He wasn't shielded from me."

Ry was silent for a moment. "What could you tell of him?"

"That he hates you. That he wants to see you dead. That he's waiting for you to move within his reach."

"Sounds like Ian," Ry said, and chuckled.

"But it wasn't." Kait had actually considered that. "The stream that binds the two of you—it runs back to Calimekka."

"It can't." She heard Ry moving in the bunk below, and an instant later, his head and shoulders popped up at the side of her bunk. "Everyone who has reason to want me dead in Calimekka already thinks I am." Except the Trinity, of course, he thought. But surely they had been executed already for murdering him. He told her about how he had faked his own murder and the disappearance of his body.

"Someone knows," she said when he finished. "Someone knows, Ry." She wondered if the one watching Ry was the same one who had nearly caught her and Hasmal when they communed with the Reborn. That the one who hunted Ry also hunted the Mirror seemed at least possible. She couldn't say anything to Ry about that, though.

He pressed his lips into a thin line. "That would be . . . Brethwan's soul! That would be a disaster. Because if someone knows of my survival, he could know I left by sea. We were careful, but we assumed no one would look for us. Someone who was looking would discover that I left with my friends. My enemies would pay for that information. Hells-all—my *mother* would pay for that information. She thinks my friends died in service to the Sabirs. Their families have been honored because of their sacrifices."

"Your mother honors your friends' families? The woman who would declare you *barzanne*?"

"If she knows I'm alive, then I'm already *barzanne*. And my friends' families . . . are doomed." He looked at Kait with haunted eyes. "This dream of yours—it had to be just a dream."

Kait couldn't manage much of a smile. "Our spirits dance while we sleep, Ry. Is that a dream?"

He didn't answer her. He didn't need to. The stricken expression on his face told her more than she wanted to know.

"So what are you going to tell them?"

He winced. Thought a moment. "Nothing. Even if what you dreamed is true, we can't do anything to protect the people we left behind in Calimekka. But if I tell them, I could cause my friends endless unresolvable fear, and I could chance them throwing their own lives away."

"How so?"

"We'll pass close to Calimekka on the run toward Glaswherry Hala. We'll sail through the Thousand Dancers, turn south just off the point of Goft, and follow the coast down. They might jump ship in Goft to get home; if they reach Calimekka, they'll be executed for sure."

Kait considered that. She had once held some hope of seeing her own dead relatives again; now she knew that would never happen. Her beloved family was dead, all of them lost to her as surely as they would have been to anyone else. Their souls had already crossed through the Veil, their bodies fed the earth, and she would never see them again in this life. That was the hard truth.

She said, "I hope for their sakes that whoever pursues you knows nothing of them."

Ry nodded. He dropped into his own bunk again, and she heard him adjusting his covers. He said nothing for so long that she thought he wouldn't say anything else, and she let herself drift toward the hazy borders of sleep. So when he did speak, it surprised her.

"I owe them my life several times over," he said. "I *owe* them the safety of their families. If I've betrayed them, even unknowingly—if I've cost them the people I promised I kept safe . . . how then do I pay them what I owe?"

Chapter 16

Long weeks passed, and storms followed fair days, and winter winds filled the sails, but little changed aboard the *Wind Treasure*. Kait had not yet found the words to say to Ian, and since he avoided her, even refusing to look at her, she let herself accept his distance.

Nor had she made peace with her close proximity to Ry. She had hoped at the beginning of the voyage home that she would become used to his presence, and that familiarity would breed, if not contempt, at least indifference. But her desire for him only grew stronger with every passing day, and the effort she had to put into maintaining magical shields to buffer his effect on her doubled, then tripled, then quadrupled. She'd spent two full Shifts hiding out in the bilge, subsisting on rats; she had made Hasmal lock her in because she knew that, in Ry's presence and in Karnee form, she would not have the self-control to avoid him. She became thin, then gaunt, and her eyes hollowed and shadowed until the image that looked back at her in the cabin's brass mirror might have been Jayti's specter.

Finally Hasmal said, "You can't live like this any longer." He was sitting on his bunk, restitching the seams in his boots. "You're killing yourself fighting against him this hard."

But she shrugged. "We're almost to Ibera. We'll leave the ship with the Mirror before it makes landfall, and I'll never see him again. Once I'm away from him, I'll be better."

His fingers looped the gut cord around themselves skillfully, worked the needle through the holes where the old seams had been, and tugged firmly, and the cord disappeared into the boot like a snake down a rat hole. "I wish I knew that were true. But I don't think distance will have any effect on this thing between the two of you. It's magic, Kait. Part of a spell that is bigger than both of you, and as powerful as any spell I've ever seen. And it's growing stronger. I noticed the first edges of the spell even before he . . . ah, before he *rescued* us. For lack of a better word. Now it binds the two of you together like a rope—visible to magic-sight, and so thick and strong that there are moments when I imagine I can see it with my eyes."

"Ropes can be cut."

"So can arteries, but you die when you sever them. This seems to me to be something that will kill you before it lets you go."

"No one lives forever. I have my Family to remember," she said quietly. "Ry admitted to having a part in their destruction, though he claims to have only been a messenger. I don't entirely believe him, and even if I did, how will I explain to their spirits that I have chosen *him* as my lifemate? How could I so dishonor my dead as to love a Sabir?"

Hasmal shrugged. "Life is for the living," he said. "The dead made their choices and had their say while they still lived. Once they're dead, both their tongues and their edicts fall silent."

She glanced at him and raised her eyebrows. "That isn't what Iberism teaches."

"Pah! Iberism is a government religion created by those already in power—men who intended to have the gods keep them in power. Of course it's going to support the idea that your dead ancestors have a say in your actions. What better way to stifle change and command the future from the grave?"

The breathtaking sweep of his heresy left her speechless for a moment. Then she hid her face in her hands and tried to muffle the laugh that burst from her. "You're right," she said when she had herself under control. "Godsall, but you're right. My Family used Iberism as a tool, and the parnissas as their spokesmen. The Sabirs, the Masschankas, the Dokteeraks, and the Kairns all did the same. No matter how much we hated each other, we all worked through Iberism—and the gods spoke in favor of the Families time and time and time again.

Though you could be beaten in Punishment Square for saying such a thing."

The tight smile he gave her and the fleeting, pained expression that crossed his face—an expression he hid quickly—made her wonder what truth she had inadvertently uncovered, but he didn't give her the chance to ask him any questions. He said, "Right. So if you know the truth, face it. Apply it to your life. Don't kill yourself over what the dead will think. I can't say that I have any great love for Ry, but the two of you were made for each other. Truly."

Kait rested a hand on his chest and leaned forward to peer into his eyes. "Matchmaking? You? So a heart does beat inside that armored breast after all. I'd thought you immune to the pull of passion."

He smiled. "Why? Because I didn't fall for you?"

"Perhaps. Most people do." She shrugged. "The Karnee Curse pulls them all to me, you know."

"I do know. I see the effect you have on the men aboard the ship. I saw what you did to the crew of the *Peregrine,* too. And Ry shares with you the same sort of all-encompassing appeal—his friends will be his friends forever, and women will flock around him like gulls around a fisherman's catch." He smiled. "I've often wondered what that would be like—to be able to have any woman just for the asking."

"When you know it isn't *you* they desire, the appeal dies quickly enough."

"I suppose you're right. Though, if someone offered me the chance to find out, I'm not sure I'd be man enough to refuse. Anyway, your curse doesn't affect me. My shields make me immune . . . which is why you and I can be such good friends. You don't compel me"—he paused and grinned impishly—"and you don't attract me. You aren't my sort. You're too young, and too uncertain, and . . . please don't take this wrong, but . . . too unfinished."

Kait snorted. "Ouch. Unfinished? You wound me. But now I'm curious. What is your sort? I've imagined you losing your heart to some tiny, delicate girl with birdlike bones and a diffident manner."

"Thank Vodor Imrish you aren't in charge of picking out a mate for me. No. My taste has always run toward . . . ahhhh . . . *interesting* women. I met the one I could love forever when I was escaping from Halles . . . trying to get away from you. She . . . well, her people were the ones who bought me from the thieves who robbed me and were going to hang me. The Gyrus were going to sell me as a slave, but she came to see me. Like me, she was a Falcon. Gorgeous. Older than me by a few years. Long red hair. Fantastic legs, a strong, lean back. She . . . ah—" he blushed, and his voice went soft—"liked to bite. Damnall, but I'd give the world to be with her again."

"She liked to bite?" Kait was intrigued. "Sounds like a difficult sort of thing to explain to your mother."

"Which is probably why men don't tell their mothers about their sex lives." He stared off into space, his eyes wistful. "Alarista knew *all* about sex."

Kait snorted. "So does a cat, but that doesn't make it an ideal partner."

Hasmal leaned back and put the boot on the bunk beside him. He looked into her eyes and said in an even voice, "When you aren't killing yourself avoiding the one man in the world you think you can love, feel free to comment on my romantic life. In the meantime, I'll trust my own judgment on who's right for me and who isn't."

Ry paced the deck, Trev at his side. Trev said, "I'm worried about our route."

"Why? It's the safest one this time of year. Most of the pirates are going to be harbored along the Manarkan coast riding out the last of the storms, and running close in will give us harbors against the squalls that come up."

"I have to tell you, Yanth and I have been checking omens the way you showed us. We've seen things that make this seem a bad time to be near Calimekka. Even the harbor in Goft seems dangerous."

Ry stared at him, startled. He'd taught them as much simple magic as he dared, but he hadn't considered the possibility that they might be using it without his supervision. Sailing out from the Thousand Dancers toward deep water would be dangerous, but it would keep them away from Calimekka and Goft. And from any temptation any of his friends might have to send word to their families. Families which might well be dead.

"We were still going to go to Calimekka," he said.

"I . . . we . . . all of us think you should reconsider trying to take her and her artifact to the city when we land. We think all of us should go with her where she wants to go. Brelst. Or even farther south. The omens seem to point that way."

Ry was startled. Weren't you counting on seeing your families? he wondered. But he didn't say that, of course. The odds were too good that his friends' families were dead. "I had a reason for wanting to go to Calimekka," he admitted. He never looked up. He didn't think he could meet Trev's eyes and still say what he had to say.

Trev waited. And waited. Finally he said, "You've been acting so distant lately, I wondered if you didn't have some secret you were keeping."

All sorts of secrets, Ry thought. "I was going take the Mirror to the Potter's Field outside the South Wall. My brother is buried there—my brother Cadell. You never met him. His ghost came to me the night we left Calimekka. He died when I was a boy." Ry fingered the medallion he wore, which had been a final, posthumous gift from his much older brother. "He was my hero, and my friend, and he was Karnee like me. The day he died, he had been found in beast form out in the streets of the city. I still believe my cousins Crispin, Anwyn, and An- drew betrayed him. City guards captured him, and dragged him to Punishment Square, and tortured him publicly. He never confessed his family; never said anything. So the parnissa passed immediate sen- tence and had him drawn and quartered right then. Had he admitted anything about us, I don't doubt but that my mother and father and my sisters and I would have been sacrificed, too. But no one claimed to know him, and . . . he had no identifying jewelry or insignia on him. . . ." Ry touched the medallion again, and felt the lump rise in his throat. "He left this with my mother, as he did every time he Shifted, telling her that if anything happened to him, she was to give it to me."

He swallowed hard, and Trev rested a hand on his shoulder. "You don't have to tell me."

"I don't. But if I don't tell someone, I think I'll go mad." Ry took a deep breath, then continued. "Anyway, his ghost came to me in my room the night all of us sailed from Calimekka. He told me Kait's name, and that she was searching for the Mirror of Souls. Later, he told me that if I could get the Mirror from her, and take it to his grave—it's unmarked, but I know where it is—I would be able to bring him back. Give him life again." Ry clenched his fists and blinked back the tears he refused to cry. "I could have my brother back."

Trev was silent for so long that Ry finally did look up. He was surprised to see his friend, wetness glistening on his cheeks, staring out at the sea.

"Trev. . . ?"

"I'm fine," Trev said. "I didn't know about your brother. Didn't even know you had anyone but your two sisters, and I know you were never close to either of them. I . . . didn't know what you'd lost."

Ry said softly, "But that's just it. If I could take the Mirror and go back, I wouldn't have lost anything. Time . . . of course I would have lost that. He would be . . ." Ry stood and shook his head, startled. "He would be younger than me now, instead of my older brother. He was . . . twenty when he died."

"He must have been very brave, to keep from revealing who his family was."

"He was the bravest and best person I've ever known."

Trev said quietly, "I'm going to tell you something you aren't going to want to hear, Ry. I'm going to say it because I'm your friend, and you can make of it what you will. There's an old saying that keeps running through my head as you tell me this, and I can't silence it, even though I have sisters who are my world, and if I put myself in your place, I can understand why you feel the way you do."

Ry waited.

"It's, *Let the dead stay buried.* I know you want your brother back, but something about this feels wrong to me. I can't point to the wrongness in what you tell me and say, 'There, that's the problem,' but my gut says something is wrong." He turned to face Ry, and looked up at him. "I'm your friend. I will help you in every way I can, with anything you need; if you need me to die for you, I will. But please, Ry, for me, consider what I'm saying. I don't know why this is so important, but I believe it is. Let the dead stay buried."

Ry watched the waves falling away behind them. Calimekka drew closer every day, every station, every moment, and Cadell drew closer, too. Once the Mirror was in the hands of the Reborn Kait spoke about, his chance to get his brother back would be gone forever. He would have this one opportunity. Cadell's ghostly voice still sometimes whispered in his mind, begging for rescue from his beggar's grave.

And the hidden enemy still watched Ry as he slept.

His mind said, *Only a coward would leave his brother in the grave.*

His gut said, *Let the dead stay buried.*

He turned to Trev. Would he advise me this way if he knew his sisters were probably dead? he wondered. If we could take the Mirror and bring them back to life as well? Probably not.

Which changed nothing. The omens said he should avoid Calimekka. Kait said danger waited for them there. His gut said he should head south as quickly as he could. What he *wanted* to do probably wasn't what he *needed* to do.

He gripped the brass rail with both hands and gritted his teeth. "I'll tell the captain to run for deep water," he said.

The captain shrugged. "We can avoid the resupply in Goft; I have no problem with that. We can turn out of the Thousand Dancers early if you wish, and run farther from the coast. If you truly wish to take the girl and her friends to Brelst instead of Glaswherry Hala, I can do that, too. We can resupply farther on and we'll be fine. But we can't turn south now. You see the horizon?"

Ry looked to the south, where the captain was pointing. A dull greenish haze blurred the line between water and sky to invisibility. "Yes."

"That's a storm brewing. The mercury is falling in the glass—we'll outrun it easily enough if we keep heading west for now, but I'll not sail us straight into it."

Ry let out a slow breath. He might be Family, but the captain was a captain—in his ship he was powerful as a paraglese, subject to the orders of no man, and answerable only to his god, Tonn. If he would not take them through the deep water by choice, Ry could not compel him by force, threat, or cajolery.

And he wasn't fool enough to try.

"Well enough. Then just keep us as far from Goft and Calimekka as you can, and keep us on the shortest path to Brelst that you can manage."

The captain tipped his head and stroked one side of his beaded, braided mustache thoughtfully. "Any particular thing you wish to avoid?"

"Only that I don't want to find out in person why the omens are bad."

"That's a good enough reason for me."

Ry had to leave it at that, and hope it would be enough.

Chapter 17

For two days the storm lashed them, a mad and screaming thing that kept them anchored to the lee side of one of the tiny islands of the Thousand Dancers. When it passed, though, it passed completely, leaving the sky clear as crystal, the breezes cool and clean, and the sailing smooth. Kait stood on the starboard deck of the *Wind Treasure,* watching islands slipping by.

Ry joined her, and because she couldn't think of a good excuse to leave, and because there were plenty of other people on the deck, she stayed where she was. He said, "This is the beginning of the Thousand Dancers. The chain runs all the way in to Goft, but the captain says we'll turn out of it and bear south long before then. You see the tall island with smoke spilling from the top?"

Kait nodded.

"That's Falea. She was supposed to be the daughter of one of the local goddesses, back before Ibera claimed these islands. Thrown to earth and sentenced to burn from the inside out forever in punishment for some sin or other. Seducing the lover of another goddess, I think." He shrugged.

Kait stared out at the water, without warning as sick as if she were trapped on a storm-tossed ship. "How much longer until we turn out of the islands?"

Ry didn't seem to notice her distress. "Captain said if the wind keeps up like this and he runs the sails the way he is right now, he could reach Merrabrack by late tomorrow. That's the best place to head south."

Late tomorrow. Kait hadn't realized they were so close to Goft. To Calimekka. To the danger that had been plaguing her dreams.

By tomorrow, they would reach the turning point, they would begin to increase the distance between themselves and the faceless danger that waited in Calimekka, and the sick feeling in her stomach would leave. Perhaps she would be able to sleep nights again without being haunted by the hunter who watched Ry through her eyes.

She sighed and leaned against the ship's rail and stared out at the islands. She turned forward, to catch the wind full in her face and to look at where they were heading. It was then that she saw the airibles.

They were two round white circles on the western horizon. If they'd been running north-south, she would have seen them as two long ellipsoids. Since she saw them as circles, they ran east-west, their course parallel to that of the *Wind Treasure*.

Her heart skipped a beat and her breath caught in her throat. Airibles. Airibles were Galweigh devices, massive lighter-than-air airships built from designs patiently and laboriously culled from the records of the Ancients. She had flown in them, had flown them herself, had known many of the Family pilots, had been friends with one of them. She thought wistfully of Aouel, now certainly dead.

And what of the other pilots she had known? What of the Family's fleet?

The circles of the airible envelopes were getting bigger, which meant they were heading east. Toward her.

She bit her lip, staring at the oncoming airibles. When Galweigh House fell, what had become of the airible fleet? Had the Sabirs claimed it, or had the corollary branches of the Galweigh Family managed to keep it within their possession? Were those aboard the two great airships friends? Enemies?

The airibles rarely ran to the east of the Iberan coast. Kait did not know of any instances where they flew through the Thousand Dancers—the easiest way to reach the colonies in Manarkas was to fly due north across the Dalvian Sea, and no one but a madman would try to take one across the Bregian Ocean to the Galweigh colony in South Novtierra. They weren't yet reliable enough.

So what were these two doing, coming to the end of the Thousand Dancers, beyond the edge of the civilized world?

Kait's nerves jangled at the sight of them, and fear crawled beneath her skin.

"Ry. . . ," she said, "do you see those?"

He glanced in the direction that she pointed and froze. He didn't answer. He didn't have to.

Kait could make out the gondolas strung beneath the huge envelopes, and the catch-ropes trailing like a hundred spider legs beneath. "They shouldn't be out this far, or headed this way," she said.

"I know. But we still have leagues until they come level with us."

Ian, standing on the other side of the deck with Hasmal, had noticed what they were looking at. He squinted, frowned, and after a moment's hesitation, came over to them. "Airibles?" he asked.

The advantage of Karnee eyesight. They were perfectly clear to Kait. "Yes."

Ian nodded. "You think they're a threat?"

"I don't know," Ry looked at Kait, a worry crease furrowing his brow. "They're making straight for us. If it's coincidence, and we take evasive action, we're a few stations behind schedule, and we make Merrabrack Island the day after tomorrow. If they are coming for us and we don't try to escape—we give them what they're after without a fight."

Ian closed his eyes and it seemed to Kait he turned inward. He stood that way for a long moment, his arms crossed over his chest, his body swaying with the movement of the ship. Finally he drew a deep breath, straightened his shoulders, and opened his eyes. Kait could tell he'd come to some sort of decision; the anger that had been in his eyes since she'd accepted the captain's bargain was either gone or well hidden, and some of the tension had left his face. He said, "If we turn south now, we'll be pushing straight against the Deep Current. This time of year it runs close to the continent. We have to get to Merrabrack before we can catch the shelf countercurrent. If it were a few months on . . ." He shrugged. "It isn't a few months on. We try to run south now and we'll be as good as sitting still, and those airships will have their way with us. And if the airships aren't here for us—and why would they be?—we've run for nothing, cost the *Wind Treasure* stores and time, and put ourselves right into the path of seasonal storms."

Ry and Ian both locked at Kait. Ry said, "Your Family, your nightmares. Your call."

Kait thought for only an instant. "I say we get out of their way."

Ry left them without another word. Within moments, the sailors were scurrying in the rigging giving the ship more sheets, and the captain at the wheel was taking the *Wind Treasure* hard north, straight into the heart of the Thousand Dancers.

Kait, Ian, and Ry moved to port and stared west again, watching the airibles. After a few moments, Hasmal joined them.

The four of them were silent, waiting and watching. The airibles maintained their swift, majestic course, heading due east.

"We'll be out of their path soon," Ry said. "We'll skirt a few of the islands and when they've gone past us, we'll resume our previous course. The captain wasn't thrilled, but like you, he couldn't think of a time when he'd seen airibles this far east."

"Thank you," Kait said. She leaned against the rail, weak-kneed with relief. She wouldn't have to face the doom Hasmal had warned her about. She would, perhaps, survive the adventure, give Solander his Mirror of Souls, and then . . .

And then, find a way to return to whatever might remain of her Family and resume her life.

They stood that way for a long time, watching the islands growing larger off the ship's bow, and the airibles growing larger off its port side. The airibles kept their course, running due east, giving no notice to the *Wind Treasure*.

Finally Kait let out her breath, only then realizing that she'd been holding it, only taking the air in scared little sips since she first saw the dots on the horizon.

Hasmal to that point had said nothing. Now, however, Kait heard him whisper, "I thought so."

The dismay in his voice was warning enough. She turned to the southwest.

Both airibles were turning. Northeast. A course designed to intercept the *Wind Treasure*.

"Not our shadows after all," Kait whispered.

"Ah, Brethwan," Ry muttered, at the moment that Hasmal said, "Help us, Vodor Imrish."

Ry turned to Kait. "Do you know anything about those ships that might help us survive what's coming? Can you even tell us what's coming?"

"I recognize both airibles," Kait said. "Those are the Galweigh greatships. *Galweigh's Eagle* and *Heart of Fire*. Each holds fifty armored men plus armaments, a captain, a first mate, and eight engine crew. I might even know the captains and crews—or I would have before the Sabirs attacked our House. In any case, they'll be carrying fire pitch and quicklights, and they'll have stones in the ballast that they can drop on us to hole us. They can take those ships higher than this ship's catapults can fire, and they can destroy us from that height." She looked at one island not too distant, where umbrella trees grew down to the shore and their canopy overhung the bay, forming an arboreal cave. She pointed. "They couldn't get in among the trees. . . ." She looked at the *Wind Treasure's* three masts and forest of yards, sails, and rigging. "But then, if we got into them, we probably wouldn't be able to get out. But we can't outrun the airibles."

"You know a lot about them," Hasmal said.

Kait nodded, still watching the approaching ships. "I've flown smaller ships. There's nothing we can do to them that they can't do to us first. And worse."

Ry laughed—a dry, humorless sound. "Then what *do* we do?"

The airibles could cover as much as three times the distance of the fastest sailing ship running flat out in open water, and the *Wind Treasure* wasn't going to get to go flat out. She was already in the nest of islands, and having to watch her channel closely.

"Die?" Kait sighed. "Make it a little harder for them to kill us? The best we can do is get in under the trees—force them to come at us from the side to board. If they have to do that—get within our reach—we can hurt them with our catapults. Maybe shoot the envelopes with fire arrows—though the cloth has been treated to keep it from burning. I'm guessing that they know we have the Mirror of

Souls. That fact should keep them from sinking us until they can get it." She'd kept her eyes on the airibles while she talked, but now she turned to Ry. "I'm also guessing that once they get the Mirror, they'll want us dead, so anything we do to them, we have to do before they board us. We can't fight them once we have nothing they want."

Ry ran to talk with the captain. After a moment, the ship changed course and nosed in toward the island Kait had pointed out.

Hasmal was at her shoulder again. "Kait? Would a hard wind dispel them?"

"It might."

"Well, I *might* be able to conjure a wind. The way I did on the *Peregrine,* when we were trapped in the Wizards' Circle. Perhaps."

Kait turned to stare at him, feeling a sudden, impossible hope. "I'd forgotten about that."

"Yes. Then, I offered my blood and my flesh and my life and my soul in exchange for getting us out of the Wizards' Circle, and Vodor Imrish got us out. But there's a problem. I can sacrifice my blood again, but he already owns my life and my soul. So perhaps he'll feel that I'm already in debt to him with everything I have, and he may choose to collect rather than let me go even deeper into debt. What else do I have to offer him?"

Kait frowned thoughtfully. "I don't know. He's your god. What does he like?"

"Mostly, he likes to be left alone."

"Then I suppose all of us had better hope he likes you." She put a hand on his arm. "Will you summon him?"

Hasmal said, "I'll try."

"I'll go with you. Last time, you almost bled yourself to death making your offering. I'm still surprised you lived."

"He wasn't done with me yet."

The airibles were close, close enough that it would be a race to see whether they could get above the ship before the ship could get under that tangle of umbrella trees that grew down to the water's edge and arched far over it.

"Let's hope he still isn't," Kait said as they ran for the hatchway and their cabin.

Chapter 18

Ry stared at the oncoming airibles, and tried to think of what he could do to turn them around. They were Galweigh ships, true, and within them he felt the touch of Galweigh magic—but with it, he felt the touch of the Sabir Wolves as well. That mix felt foul . . . greasy . . . tainted. What sort of alliance had sprung up in his absence . . . and why did it stink of the Hellspawn Trinity? He could *feel* the influence of his second cousins, the brothers Crispin and Anwyn and their cousin Andrew, dripping through the spellcastings like poison.

They knew he was aboard the *Wind Treasure*. Perhaps one of them was the hidden watcher who had haunted Kait's sleep.

He joined his lieutenants, who had been assisting the crew, and said, "There are Wolves aboard those ships. Some of them are Sabir Wolves, and some are Galweigh Wolves, but we are going to shield the *Wind Treasure* from their attack. All of you to the foredeck now."

Ian Draclas had been a ship's captain too long to avoid the action; the fact that his ship had been stolen from him and that he found himself virtually a prisoner aboard the ship his half-brother had chartered mattered not at all to him. He knew how to fight, and he knew how to survive, and he intended to survive this encounter.

He hammered volley shields into place beside the catapults along with the crew, and when that was finished, went to stand beside Captain Sleroal, who held his place at the ship's great wheel.

"They'll be overflying us soon," he said. "We aren't going to make the trees before they get off their first volley."

"I can see that," the Rophetian said quietly. "You got anything you can do besides tell me the obvious?"

Ian kept his temper. Sleroal flew the Sabir flag on his topmast; a flag that would ward off most enemies before they even attacked. The Sabir reputation for retribution protected them as surely as if they rode protected by an armada. Ian, who had been both attacked and attacker throughout his years captaining the *Peregrine,* figured himself to have much more experience in actual battle than the older man.

He said, "They'll most likely hit us with burning pitch first. But if you have your men fill the scrub buckets with seawater while there's still time and soak our stores of canvas in the sea, we'll be able to put out the worst of the fires before they can spread."

The captain glanced at him. "Decided to join our side, eh?"

"I'd prefer to live through the day."

"I, too." Sleroal shouted at several of his sailors, "You . . . and you . . . fill every bucket on the ship with seawater. You and you . . . below for the stores of canvas and soak all of it. Ready it for the fires. Everyone, stand ready to run for buckets."

Both Ian and the captain looked up at the airibles. They blocked off what seemed like half the sky. One had moved itself neatly behind the other; he assumed this was so one flying ship could pour fire and arrows down on them and then move to reposition while the second took its place.

"You have any other ideas, I'll be more than happy to hear them now," Sleroal said.

"Not until I see what they do." The *Wind Treasure* couldn't hope to win. Ian didn't give himself much chance of survival, either. But he was determined to give the bastards as much fight as he could muster. "They'll be over us in just an instant," he said.

"Aye." The captain stared around his ship and grimaced. "Best get under the volley shields." He locked the wheel and shouted, "Men! Under cover!"

Like a school of fish in front of a shark, the sailors poured into the hatches and beneath the volley shields. Ian and the captain were last under. Ian peeked out from beneath the shield's edge and watched as the leading airible's gondola moved toward the *Wind Treasure*. Anytime now. . . . He braced himself for the burning pitch that would come pouring out of the base of the gondola, or for the stream of rocks that would begin to pound the ship's frame.

The airible sailed gracefully overhead, dropping nothing.

A sailor next to him growled, "Y' mean t' tell me we did all this scramblin' an' worryin' an the damn things were na' after us at all?"

Someone laughed, and then someone else. Everyone still waited under the shields, watching, because caution only made sense. But the second airible soared overhead, doing nothing more than the first had, and the laughter got louder.

The sailors poured out from beneath the shields and started for their stations, and the captain murmured, "I told him it was just coincidence them being here when we were." He returned to his helm.

Ian felt like a fool, and figured Kait felt twice the fool, since she was the one who had finally declared the airibles a threat. She deserved to feel a fool. She was a paranoid, a freak, not even human.

He wished he didn't love her. He wished he could excise her from his mind.

The first airible reached the island to which the *Wind Treasure* had been running. The ship changed speed, so that it hung over the canopy of trees that would have sheltered the ship. Hatches in the rear of the gondola opened, and dark streams of liquid began to pour out. It spread as it fell, turning into a faintly green cloud that covered the area—they weren't pouring unlit burning pitch, then, but something else. Ian wondered what it was and what it did.

The torrent of liquid stopped abruptly, and an instant later the single flaming arrow launched toward the trees from the front of the gondola answered his questions. The air itself caught fire, that one arrow spreading flames through the deadly rain faster than anything Ian had ever seen. In an instant, the entire island forest was alight, and their hope of sheltering there gone.

Bastards. Filthy bastards. Not just attacking, but cutting off the *Wind Treasure*'s only escape route first.

"About!" the captain screamed. "Give me mains and forecourses. Fly, you whoresons! Fly, or we're dead men!"

The *Wind Treasure* hove hard to port, her bow digging into the choppy strait, turning back the way she'd come. The men on the rat-lines unfurled sails with frantic speed, and the sails dropped and caught and filled, bellying out with a wind that hadn't been there a moment earlier. A hard wind.

By the gods, a hard wind couldn't have come at a better time. Ian stared up at the airibles—they were taking a hellish buffeting. One had been caught sideways; the wind tore at its envelope, and he saw the side ripple as if punched by an invisible first. The sailors cheered, and Ian cheered with them. The other airible managed to keep its nose into the wind, but the sudden gale pushed it off course, away from the *Wind Treasure*.

Sleroal saw what was happening and reversed himself. "Furl sails and drop anchor," he bellowed, and as quickly as the sails had appeared, they disappeared. The anchors splashed into the strait, and in an instant the *Wind Treasure* was tugging at them, fighting the rising waves, but watching the two airibles blowing away.

Every man on the deck screamed defiance at the airibles, and they cheered their fantastic luck . . . and then a flash of brilliant green light in one of the airible gondolas shot out of a near-side port, lobbed gently through the air, and struck the center of the *Wind Treasure*. Fire blossomed, an eerie, silent, green chrysanthemum in the center of the deck. It consumed the mainmast and the men on its riggings, the captain and the wheel, and a perfect circle of deck in one burst of light. The stricken men hadn't even had time to scream before they ceased to exist. The fire didn't spread, it didn't die out slowly, it didn't leave embers in its wake. As quickly as it appeared, it was gone. The sailors were too stunned to react. Ian stared at the airibles, where another flash warned him that another volley of the deadly fire was on its way.

"Cover," he screamed. "Take cover! Incoming!"

Men fell off the ratlines in their hurry, and lay stunned on the deck. Others, more graceful or else just luckier, pounded over and around their fallen comrades and flung themselves down the ship's hatches as the second green fireball descended. Ian judged arc and trajectory and guessed the thing would hit the foremast; he raced aft and was under cover in time to see foremast, forecastle, yards, sails, ratlines, part of the cabins, and another circle of deck disappear as if they'd never been. But the gale kept blowing, and the next fireball one of the airibles launched fell into the sea short of its target . . . and the next fell even farther away.

The ship hadn't been holed. That was a mercy—or else planning on the part of the attackers. Boring clean through it with that green fire of theirs could have destroyed the thing Ian was certain they had come to get: Kait's artifact. They wouldn't risk that. They'd just disabled the ship.

But they hadn't counted on that lovely, sudden, wonderful wind. The airibles blew out of range of their target and, while the sailors watched, almost out of sight. That was a hellish wind. Ian would have cheered, and certainly felt that his own survival deserved a cheer, but the survivors had much to do. The *Wind Treasure* was a wreck. They might manage to limp the ship to a safe port on just spritsails and mizzens, but they'd have to shore up the bowsprit to do it. They'd lost all but their aft square sails, all their jibs, and even the top spritsail, and they'd have to rig a tiller to the rudder since the ship's wheel was gone. Nevertheless, with sufficient time, Ian thought he could get them to safety. To do it, the wind would have to remain in his favor and keep the airibles at bay.

A wave of nausea overcame him suddenly. It felt like it had rolled over him from outside, and when it left him, he was weaker, and plagued by a nagging feeling of sickness that hadn't been there before.

But he'd no more than gotten control of that strange malaise than the wind died, cut off as if it had been the breath of a giant who had ceased to find amusement in blowing his toys around. Ian prayed that the stillness was just a pause between gusts, but before his eyes, the chop in the strait died away, leaving the water smooth as rolled glass. The *Wind Treasure* quit tugging at her anchor. The air took on a hush of expectancy. And in the far distance, tiny as minnows but graceful as eels swimming through the sky, the airibles got themselves under control and slowly turned back toward the *Wind Treasure*.

The battle was as good as lost. With the captain gone and the first mate nowhere to be seen, Ian declared himself temporary captain of the doomed ship and the lost fight and shouted, "All hands on deck!

All hands on deck! Prepare to abandon ship! Prepare to abandon ship!"

They came running then, streaming from the hatches like mice from a flooded burrow. The sailors were first, and they swung the longboats free from their tie-downs and moved them over the ship's rails with amazing alacrity. Behind them came Kait, dragging Hasmal, who—bleached white as death, and with his eyes rolled back in his head—looked like he'd already fought the losing half of a war. Ry came next, sword already in hand, with four of his five lieutenants carrying the halved, bloodless body of the fifth. They, too, looked drained, though not as near death as Hasmal—and they looked terrified.

"What happened?" Kait yelled as she dragged Hasmal toward the nearest of the three longboats. "Hasmal sacrificed to his god and raised a wind, and the airibles were out of range. We'd beaten them, and then suddenly the spell snapped like an overstretched cord. It whipped back on him and knocked him out—I thought he was going to die on me." She looked at Ian and growled, "He still might."

Ry stopped and stared at her. "The two of you *summoned* that wind? Ah, gods' balls. . . . We set up a shield that blocked their spellfire. But we shielded the whole ship, so of course it broke your spell. We thought the wind was natural—I couldn't feel the magic."

"Damned fools."

Ry and his lieutenants claimed one of the longboats and swung it over the side of the ship into the glass-still sea. "Get in here," he told her. "We're going to have to run for it."

Ian looked at the corpse they started to ship into the boat and said, "Leave your dead behind. The smell of death will have the gorrahs on us before we can commend his soul to the gods." He couldn't bear to look at the body. It had been sliced in half, the right side of the head, the right shoulder, right chest, and a portion of the outer right thigh removed neatly and bloodlessly, and the wound had been cauterized black and hard and shiny.

The sickness in Ian's gut twisted tighter as he looked at the body and he turned away. The man had been Karyl—Ry's cousin, so his as well, the player of the guitarra, the writer of insipid love songs. He'd been decent enough to Ian when they were children, and he'd been decent enough to him aboard the ship.

Ian felt only relief, though, that *Karyl* was dead and he still lived.

Kait said, "I can't get aboard yet. Take Has. I have to go back and get the Mirror of Souls."

Ry grabbed her arm. "They're coming. *Coming.* And the thing they want—at least as much as they want to see you and me dead—is the Mirror. If we take it, everything they want is in one neat package. They get it, they kill us . . . and one, two, three, everything is tied up pretty as a Ganjaday present."

"If we leave it, they'll have it."

Ry picked her up and flung her over his shoulder. "I have as much reason as you to want to keep the Mirror with us. But if we take it, they'll *still* have it, only none of us will be alive to try to get it back."

Kait twisted, braced her feet against Ry's stomach, and shoved free. She landed on the deck on her back, but sprang to her feet faster than a cat could have. "We'll *take* it. We'll shield it, and us with it. But I'm not leaving without it."

The two of them glared at each other, deadlocked.

"We'll get it," Ian said. "The three of us. But we have to hurry."

While Ry's surviving men lowered the unconscious Hasmal into the longboat and lowered the Allus ladder over the side into it, Ian, Ry, and Kait raced down into the hold and cut the bindings that held the Mirror of Souls to the bulkhead. They hauled it up the gangway and out onto the deck, careful to avoid touching the column of light that flowed upward through the center and also the jeweled controls on the rim. They ran a rope around the base and lowered it into the long-boat. Then they scrambled down the Allus ladder. Both other long-boats, and all of the *Wind Treasure*'s crew, were already gone.

By the time Ian cast them off from the *Wind Treasure*, Hasmal lay on the bottom of the boat in front of the thwarts, the Mirror of Souls beside him. Ry's lieutenants had already unshipped the long, two-man oars—the sweeps—and fitted them into the oarlocks. Ry, who had clambered down the Allus ladder before him, had taken the seat at the tiller; he glanced up at Ian as he dropped into the boat, then back at the sky.

Ian was the only sailor in the bunch, and the others' inexperience

showed. There were eight of them in a longboat that could have ac-
commodated twenty; it had thwarts and sweeps for twelve—three
sweeps on each side—and the escapees had readied all of the sweeps
and sat facing the front of the boat. The empty sweep waited for him.

Ian snapped, "Face the rear, not the front—you can put your back
into your stroke that way. The sweeps were made to be pulled by
two—you'll have Brethwan's own time pulling one alone, much less
trying to do it facing forward." His eyes locked with Ry's. "You're going
to take the last sweep. I'll take the tiller."

Ry said, "I'm already here, and I understand how a tiller works."

"I'll take the tiller because I know these islands," Ian said. "I know
where to hide in them, and where to get help and find friends. I sailed
along these waters all those years that you were conniving in your little rat hole in our father's House."

Ry held his position for a moment and Ian began to think that
they were going to have to fight each other right there. Then Ry nodded and took a seat at the sweep.

Ian gripped the tiller with both hands and said, "You'll row on my
count—"

Kait, at the middle port sweep, said, "Hasmal had a spell that
might keep us unnoticed. Not that he'll be able to do anything for us
now . . . in his condition." Hasmal's eyes had opened, and his head
lolled from side to side, but he still showed no sign that he understood anything that was happening around him.

"I can't do anything that will make us disappear," Ry said. "I can
only create an energy wall to shield us from the magic they throw . . .
and I don't know who we'd ask to take the *rewhah*. We spread it out
among everyone on the ship before."

Ian, like most Iberans, had spent his life thinking that magic was
dead—a banished perversion of the past. He didn't know what *rewhah*
was, and he didn't want to know.

Kait said, "That's why we all feel so sick, then," and glared at Ry's
back again, and Ian's nausea reminded him that it was not yet gone. So
rewhah was something that made people sick. It figured.

Kait continued, "I was going to say, I know his spell, though not
well. If you'll give me a moment, I'll do what I can to cast it for us,
though I can't promise it will work."

Ian considered only for an instant. "We won't reach cover before the airibles have us in sight. As we stand now, we'll only survive if they pursue the other two longboats before us. If you can do something to change our chances, do it."

Ry twisted to look over his shoulder. He said, "I don't know *farhullen,* but if you'll tell me how to help you, whatever I can do, I will."

"I'll need a *peth*—a blood-gift." Kait hurried to Hasmal's side, took his pouch from him, and from it extracted a wooden bowl with its interior surface plated in silver. "You can only give what is yours to give," she said, working her way back to her oar. "Hasmal told me the Wolves always draw their magic from the lives of the people and things around them."

Ry nodded. "That's the essence of magic. If we drew only from ourselves, we'd deplete ourselves—"

He stopped at the vehement shake of Kait's head. "If you do that, we will have to fight the *rewhah,* and we might all die anyway. *Farhullen* has no backlash—part of the reason that you can't see it, I suspect—but we'll avoid the *rewhah* only if you do as I tell you. Give me only what is yours to give. *Your* blood, *your* will, *your* willing life-force. Nothing more. If any of your men know how to draw energy from themselves, I can use that, too. But only what belongs to you, and only what you give freely."

Ian saw every other head on the boat nod in understanding. How could he be the only person aboard the boat who was ignorant of this forbidden spellcasting she spoke of? It was as if he was the only one present who knew one vast sea, and the only one who knew nothing of another.

Kait had drawn her ornate Galweigh dagger. She sliced the side of one of her fingers lightly, and let three drops of her blood fall into the bowl. She whispered something, and Ry, turned around on his thwart, watched her intently. When she finished, he drew his own dagger. She passed him the bowl and he followed her lead. Each of Ry's men cut a finger and contributed to the little puddle of blood in the bowl, and to the whispered words. Trev, the last to hold the bowl, nodded toward Ian, but Kait said, "No. Ian sees only the outward form of what we've done. If he gave, he would not know what he gave, or how to limit his gift. Pass the bowl back to me."

Ian thought briefly of protesting, of insisting that he could give his blood, too. He didn't want to be seen as a coward, even if he hated the idea of magic. But she was right; he'd seen them drip their blood into a bowl, but he had the feeling they'd done much more than that just beneath the surface of perception. He couldn't duplicate what they did, so he couldn't offer them any help. He could only sit and watch and hope that the airibles would not spot their longboat before Kait finished whatever she had to do. He could now hear the steady *thupp, thupp, thupp* of the approaching engines, and the shouts of the men in the other two longboats.

Kait sprinkled some sort of pale powder into the blood, and began to chant:

We offer what we have—
Purity of intent,
Willingness to serve,
Desire to survive.

We ask what we need—
A shield with no shadow,
A wall with no window,
A road unseen.

So we say,
So shall this be.

Light sparkled up out of the blood-bowl and spun itself into a ball; the ball expanded like a bubble blown by a child. The light dimmed as the ball expanded, and as it reached out to cover the whole of the boat and its crew, the bubble vanished completely.

Ian looked at the boat, at the people in it, at the water outside of it. He glanced behind him at the *Wind Treasure,* and at the white curve of the first airible, rising over the edge of the hull. He couldn't deny that she had done *something*, but it seemed to have failed. Nothing looked any different to him.

"Did it work?" Ry asked. "I can't feel anything."

Kait's face was tight with worry. "I'm not sure. I think I can feel the edge of the shield around us, but if it's there, it's thin. I don't know if it will do what we need it to do."

Ian's mouth went dry.

Ah, gods. They'd lost the little lead they had, and meanwhile the other two longboats, fully crewed with experienced men, were shooting across the water toward cover.

"Man your sweeps," Ian snapped. Everyone gripped their oars. He shouted, "Row! Back to my count; oars in the water. Ready! Pull . . . and lift . . . and forward . . . and dip . . . and PULL! . . . and LIFT! . . . and FORWARD! . . . and DIP!"

He leaned into the tiller and swung the boat back toward the west, angling their path until the anchored *Wind Treasure* blocked out all sight of the oncoming airibles.

"Pull . . . and lift . . . and forward . . . and . . ."

Behind him, the great engines of the airibles thundered. He alone would not see them when they rose over the false horizon of the *Wind Treasure*. But he wouldn't need to. Six pairs of eyes stared over his shoulders at the scene behind him, while six backs pulled the longboat across the strait. He saw where he took them, but the faces before him would tell him all he needed to know about where they had been.

haid Galweigh, from his velvet-covered chair in the *Galweigh's Eagle,* surveyed with deep satisfaction the wreckage of the Sabir ship and the wild rowing of the men in the longboat the *Eagle* pursued. The Sabirs looked like they were going to go through with their half of the agreement. Their job had been to locate their ship, take it over, find the Mirror of Souls, and bring it on board one of the two airibles. When they did that, the Galweighs were to be responsible for getting them all back to the city and for attacking Galweigh House.

Of course Shaid had no intention of following through on the second half of that bargain. Once he had the Mirror of Souls in hand, everything was in his favor. The airibles were his, and the crew that worked on them, and the pilots who flew them. The Sabirs' sole contribution had been that they knew how to find the Mirror and Shaid didn't.

His Wolves were already primed to kill their Sabir counterparts the instant the Mirror came aboard the *Eagle.* His soldiers would take care of Crispin and Andrew and that monster Anwyn. And he, being Galweigh, would land in the great yard of Galweigh House in Calimekka with men and Mirror and claim it for himself. By the end of the day, he intended to be a god.

And so you shall, the reassuring voice whispered inside his skull. *I*

*have promised you the immortality that the Mirror can confer . . . and you
shall have it.*

Crispin Sabir leaned against the gondola window and watched
the airible drop down to the *Wind Treasure*. He noted with pleasure
the leadsman's facility with the catchropes, which he latched onto the
ship's bowsprit and mizzenmast with only one throw apiece. Another
toss to attach the ridewire, and then a few moments' wait while the
leadsman rode a pulley down the ridewire to the ship and attached
the anchor ropes. Once the man finished and signaled, the airible's
motors fell silent, and the great ship hung in the air over its captive, a
spider above downed prey.

Competent crew—Crispin already thought of the ships and the
men as his own. The one thing the Galweighs had that the Sabirs
needed in order to take Galweigh House: Galweigh airibles. By the
end of the day, Crispin would have *everything* he needed.

Ladders unrolled from the gondola, and the soldiers waiting in
the *Heart of Fire* swarmed down them. They'd search for any crew or
passengers who hadn't taken to the longboats, question them, then
kill them. The other airible and her crew and complement of soldiers
would take care of those who had chosen to abandon ship rather than
stand and fight.

Crispin grinned down at the wreck of the *Wind Treasure*. He was
always fond of an unfair fight in his favor. He wondered how his
young cousin Ry was feeling at that moment.

Crispin didn't think he'd find Ry aboard the ship. The lying, ma-
nipulative bitchson would have done the sensible, cowardly thing: He
would have run, just as he ran from Calimekka. Crispin's people
would find him, of course—provided the gorrahs didn't devour him
first. Those longboats were slow and awkward. And Crispin had time.
Even if Ry managed to elude the first roundup, he wouldn't escape.
Once they'd taken the Mirror of Souls aboard the airible, Crispin
could afford to spend a few days thoroughly searching the area. He'd
make sure Ry went back with him—Crispin had a ceremony planned
in the Punishment Square that would make the one he'd pulled off
with Ry's brother seem like an afternoon's chat with friends.

Meanwhile, though, the *Galweigh's Eagle* chased down the second

longboat. Let Andrew giggle and squirm over the spectacle of the gorrahs' feeding frenzy while they devoured the capsized crew on the first
longboat; Crispin had things he could be doing.

He went forward to the pilot's cabin, and followed the last of the
soldiers down the ladder to the deck of the *Wind Treasure*. He had a
few bad moments—he didn't like heights, and he discovered that
being inside the *Heart of Fire* was much less disturbing than dangling
on a rope ladder halfway to heaven, with that crazed pack of feeding
gorrahs beneath him and nothing between him and his death but the
tiny, distant deck of a damaged ship.

He almost climbed back up the ladder, but he didn't trust soldiers
to be able to find what he was looking for and transport it to the *Heart
of Fire*. So he steadied his breathing, dried his palms—one at a time—
on his shirtfront, and worked his way down the ladder one wobbly
step after another.

"Had a bit of trouble with the ladder, eh?" a Galweigh soldier
asked, grinning. "Most do that first time."

Crispin memorized the boy's face. Dark-haired, dark-eyed, dusky-
skinned: typical Zaith. They all looked alike to Crispin, except when
they were screaming and dying. Still, he noted the gap between the
front teeth, and the mole at the corner of the mouth. He would make
a point of remembering that face. He said, "The soles of my boots are
plain leather, and too thin and slick for such a climb. Unlike yours,
which have rubber soles." He turned and walked away, thinking of
ways that he could be sure the soldier would meet his death before the
crew returned to the airible. He hated having people laugh at him.

When the boy went back to his duty, Crispin closed his eyes and
smelled the air. Honeysuckle and rot, the scent that his silent partner
told him was the scent of the Mirror of Souls. It was close. The scent
permeated the ship.

The voice said, *If they'd taken it with them, the scent would be
stronger over the water. You could follow it straight to them. But the smell of
its magic ends here.*

He walked aft, following that compelling odor. He closed his eyes,
tasting the air with Karnee senses. If he Shifted, he thought he would
be able to track it down faster. In Karnee form, his nose was a thousand times as sensitive as it was in human form—though it was good

when he was human. But if he Shifted, he would show what he was to the watching Galweighs—and he didn't wish to give them that much information about him, even if he did intend to see them all dead at the end of the mission. People had a nasty habit of surviving no matter how carefully one planned; he always kept that in mind and acted accordingly.

He smelled its presence faintly in one of the cabins, but only faintly. So in human form he followed his nose to the hatch, and down the gangway, then through the crew areas and at last into the cargo holds. His eyes lit up and he laughed out loud at the sight that greeted him there. Row after row and shelf after shelf of artifacts from the Ancients. In the first two rows alone, he recognized a distance viewer that didn't look too far from serviceable, an eavesdropper, a marvelous matched set of transmuters, and half a spell amplifier that would at least serve as a source of repair parts for the broken one he had back home. Of course there were plenty of things he recognized as useless or merely decorative, and another, larger mass of things he couldn't recognize at all.

"Mine," he whispered. A wondrous trove all in itself, he thought—worth a paraglesiat, worth a House, worth power and more power, and all of it was his. But the trove was nothing compared to the single final treasure he sought. The Mirror of Souls might rest in such an obvious hiding place, though he doubted it. The scent of it lay strongly in the hold, but he felt certain Ry would have hidden it before he abandoned the ship.

He cast around the room, and on the far forward bulkhead he found proof that his instincts were good. The scent of the Mirror of Souls was strongest there, but the ropes that scent permeated had been hastily cut, and lay in a tangle on the decking.

Crispin smiled. He would have to backtrail. He smelled Ry's touch on the ropes, and that of another Karnee—this one a stranger to him—and a third person. Human. He decided to trail the Mirror first, and to focus on the people second.

Then he had a thought that both startled and amused him. Suppose Ry knew that he, Crispin, was the one who would come after him. Recently Ry had seemed to be aware that Crispin spied on him while he slept. If he knew that, and if he were trying to be clever again, he would hide the artifact someplace where Crispin would have an especially difficult time finding it.

Ry hunted with his nose, and he knew Crispin did, too. He'd use that. He would hide the Mirror down farther. In the bilge.

Crispin wrinkled his nose just thinking about it; his exquisite sense of smell came with a few drawbacks. It would be almost useless in the conflicting sea of stinks that would fill a ship's bilge. And he was fastidious, having nearly conquered his animal nature; he was proud of that fact. But he could, when necessary, get a bit dirty. He sighed and headed for the stinking bilge.

A third of a station later, soaked in fetid, slimy water, his fine clothes ruined, he had to admit that the Mirror of Souls wasn't in any of the three bilge compartments.

He climbed onto the deck, sent the crewman with the mole and the smirk up the ladder to the airible to fetch him clean clothing, and retired to the ship's bath to clean off. When he was alone, he asked the voice that traveled with him in his mind. "So where is it?"

It isn't on the ship, the voice said.

Crispin snarled out loud, "It must be. You said I'd smell its trail leading across the water if they'd taken it with them."

You would. And I would clearly see it. The Mirror . . . calls to me.

"But I've checked the cabins, the holds, and even the bilge. It isn't here."

No. It isn't. I already said that.

"Then where is it?"

If they didn't take it with them and it isn't aboard, there's only one place it can be.

And Crispin saw the truth and hated it in the same instant.

"They threw it overboard." He stood against a bulkhead and leaned his head against a stanchion as realization hit him. "Damn them," he said softly. "Damn them, damn them, damn them."

He threw his clothes on and raced upward through the ship until he reached the main deck. There he called to attention the Galweigh soldiers on loan from the Goft Galweighs, and said, "The one thing that we must have from this ship our enemies have thrown overboard. You are going to go out in boats with a grappling hook and get it back."

And of course they asked what it was, and how they would know when they'd found it. They pointed out that they didn't have a boat, since the ship's crew had taken the longboats. They complained bitterly about the gorrahs that circled in the water below the *Wind Treasure* hoping prey would fall within their reach.

Crispin accepted no excuses, and put a quick end to complaints by assigning complainers to the first shift. He pointed out that the other airible would be bringing back its boatload of captives soon, and with them the boat. He smiled.

And then he assigned the Zaith boy who'd taken such pleasure in his awkwardness on the ladder to handle the grappling hook. He watched the dark forms of the gorrahs circling in the water beneath the ship and thought they would make the boy's chances of seeing his home in Calimekka again slim ones.

With his orders given, he climbed back up the ladder into the airible—an easier task than climbing down. There he sat down to a pleasant meal with the airible's pilot and Andrew and the contingent of Galweigh Wolves who had insisted on accompanying the expedition.

"Did you find Ry?" Andrew asked as the servant passed out plates. The men and women loaded them from dishes of chilled cubed monkey and dipping sauce, fingerling trout, sweetmeats, and fried goldbeetles over strips of jellied mango.

"No one stayed aboard the ship." Crispin took a sip of iced wine and tried the goldbeetles. Deliciously crunchy, and not too salty—a tricky balance to get right. He would have liked to keep the Galweigh cook—easy enough to do once the Galweighs were dead. But cooks did taste their cooking, didn't they? Such a waste. "So either he's already been eaten by the gorrahs, or Anwyn's crew is picking him up now."

Shaid Galweigh took a few of the goldbeetles and sampled them, then settled on the monkey and sauce. "Disconcerting that they've hidden the Mirror so far."

"We'll have it in our hands before the end of the day," Crispin said.

Andrew said, "When we overflew them, I thought I saw three longboats on their aftercastle. But after the wind, I've only seen the boat the gorrahs destroyed and the one the *Eagle* is chasing. So what happened to the third?"

Crispin put down his knife and pick and stared at his cousin. "*Three* longboats. No. I'm sure there were only two."

Andrew grinned. "That's the funny thing about you, Crispin. You're always so sure about everything—even the things you're wrong about. That ship is a Rophetian galleon. They carry more than forty people, and the Rophetian longboats're built to hold twenty. If you look at the aftercastle, you'll see the tie-downs and the spaces for three boats. And three places where the wood isn't bleached as light—all three in the shape of longboats."

Crispin looked down at the back of the ship, at the broad deck where a mast had once risen, and where, clearly, three boats had once rested. Three.

Andrew tugged at the long black braid over his left ear, the only hair on his otherwise shaved skull, and said, "Remember, I *earned* this braid."

"You skulked around docks with a bunch of illiterate bums," Crispin said, forgetting for the moment the Galweighs who sat observing the two of them.

"I sailed with the Sloebenes. We pirated any number of Rophetian galleons, and they had one longboat for every mast."

Crispin leaned toward his cousin, meal forgotten. "Then you tell me, you who know everything about ships and the sea: If there were three boats, why are there only two now? Eh? You have an answer for that?"

Andrew shrugged his massive shoulders and giggled. "Me, I just figured some of the people got away."

"We would have seen them, you mare-dick. Look down. We can see everything that happens in the whole region—that's the advantage of approaching by air. We can't miss things." He rolled his eyes and leaned back on his couch.

Andrew had proven time and again that he was an idiot—useful as brute muscle, with the occasional moment of cleverness. But he was never reliable. Never. The *streune*-bolt that had disintegrated the mast and part of the decking had destroyed one of the three boats as well; that seemed obvious enough to Crispin. Ry was in the boat that had been taken captive, or he was in the one that had been capsized by gorrahs. Either way, he was dead. Dead already or dead in the Punishment Square, and Crispin was willing to consider either a happy outcome.

Wasn't he?

"We disintegrated the third boat with magic," he said.

Andrew giggled. "Did we, did we, did we? Are you so sure that you'd bet your place as head Wolf? Eh? Are you that sure, cousin? Because if you're wrong, it'll come to that ere long."

The Galweighs were making a show of eating their food and ignoring him and Andrew, but they were, Crispin knew, hanging on every word. Dissension between Sabirs could only work to their good. And Sabir failures in carrying off the joint mission would only make them look better when they got home. Their smiles were hidden, but Crispin knew they were there.

So he ignored Andrew's question, instead asking one of his own. "Why don't you think we destroyed the third boat?"

Andrew's grin grew broader. "Don't want to bet me, eh? Don't want to take a little chance that stupid Andrew might know something you don't know? Smart of you, Cris. Smart, smart, smart."

"Why, Andrew?" He spent a moment imagining Andrew in the Punishment Square, the four horses ready to leap toward each of the four points of the world. That calmed his temper enough that he could say, "I'm willing to concede you might be right."

"How generous." For just an instant, Andrew's dark eyes looked at him with unnerving intelligence—but that penetrating gaze vanished, shattered by another idiotic giggle. "I know we didn't get one of the three ships because no one would have tried to swim to safety through all those gorrahs. And there were no people on board when you got down there—you said as much yourself."

Andrew was right. That was something new.

"But perhaps the ship didn't carry a full complement of crew. Perhaps there were only forty people on board. Or less."

"Rophetians have no trouble keeping crew," Andrew said. "No trouble, no trouble, none at all. Lads sign with 'em when they're juicy boys, and die with 'em as old, old men. Rophetians don't run ships light—they figure long shifts make the men unhappy, and unhappy men get careless. They might be light on crew if they ran into trouble across the sea, and you could bet that way and maybe you'd win. But me . . . I'm betting the third boat is out there. I am, I am." He took a huge bite of fingerling trout, chewed it, and grinned around the food at Crispin. "I'm betting Ry got away."

Crispin studied his cousin from the corner of his eye, and considered what a problem he was becoming. He wasn't reliable, but Crispin began to believe that the perverted bastard wasn't as stupid as he usually seemed, either. He might be smart enough to double-cross Anwyn or Crispin.

Before long, perhaps Andrew needed to have an accident.

Meanwhile, Crispin could enjoy the predicament the Galweighs were finding themselves in. Their eyes drooped—he knew they would feel like they had eaten too much, like their bellies were full and their heads were stuffed with rags. He felt a mild version of those symptoms himself. Already Shaid yawned and murmured something about having eaten too much, and one of his Wolves chuckled and said she felt like she could sleep for a week.

Crispin grinned and said, "Don't leave this marvelous food uneaten. Your cook deserves a reward for his magnificent repast." It would probably have to be posthumous, of course.

Veburral tasted almost pleasant—nutty, in fact. It stood up well to heat. Unlike some poisons, it remained deadly after frying, baking, or boiling. Unlike some venoms, it did not have to be injected into the bloodstream to be effective—a man eating it in moderate quantities would die nicely. Best of all, however, *veburral,* derived from the venom of the copper flying viper whose range was to the Sabir settlements on the Sabirene Isthmus, could be taken in increasing doses over a period of months or years, and the taker could build up a complete immunity to it. Most of the Sabirs took regular doses as a matter of course—and since the Galweighs didn't have access to the snakes, they didn't have access to the poison.

They would drift off to sleep one by one, and Crispin and Andrew would carry them off to the sleeping quarters and tuck them in. Alone in their darkened rooms, they would die quietly, without alerting the Galweigh loyalists, who wouldn't suspect that anything was wrong until the Sabir loyalists and those Galweighs who could be bought killed them.

Their impending deaths had already cost Crispin a small fortune. A double agent deep under cover in the Galweigh household had placed a bottle of *veburral*-laced nut oil into the cook's traveling supplies just before he boarded the airible, replacing the bottle that should have been there. The agent had been in place in the household of the Goft Galweighs for five years, and this was the only service he had rendered. He had been worth his price, though. When Crispin and the Sabir army flew the Galweigh airibles into the landing field behind Galweigh House without challenge, and swarmed out to claim the House and everything in it, the Galweighs would fall and the Sabirs would hold Calimekka alone.

Chapter 20

Night buried the escaping longboat beneath its cloak, and Ian's voice, long since reduced to a croak, called out the beat of the sweeps in slower and slower measure. Kait's palms wore blisters beneath blisters, the skin ragged and weeping. The muscles in her back burned, her thighs ached, her calves cramped, even her gut felt like it had been set afire by a sadist.

Ian called, "Ship sweeps and rest. Trev, drop anchor."

The chain rattled out of the front of the boat; it tugged as it bit into the sea bottom, and the boat drifted lazily with the unseen current until it swung around to point them all back in the direction from which they'd just come.

Kait sat panting, her head between her knees. "I'm starving, but I can't swear that I wouldn't be too sick to eat if we had food," she said.

"I could eat," Yanth said. "If I puked it up, I'd just eat more. I feel like I'm dying right now."

"I want water more than anything," Trev moaned.

Water. Everyone agreed with that. The boat had a small barrel of water on board for emergencies, of course, but it hadn't been changed in a long time, and it tasted as bad as bilgewater smelled. Clear, cold, fresh water from a spring . . . that, everyone agreed, would be the true gift of the gods.

"We're half a station's hard rowing from our destination," Ian said.

"All the sweet water there that you could drink in a lifetime. But I think we can afford to rest just a bit before we go on. The airibles haven't come after us in spite of the fact that we were in clear sight for more than a station. So I suppose we're safe to assume the spell worked."

Hasmal spoke up from behind Kait. "There's a solid enough spell around the boat right now."

She sat up in spite of the agony in her back and turned around to look at him. He lay with his head propped against the forward bulwark, taking a careful sip of water from the barrel.

Ry twisted toward the front of the boat, too. "You can . . . see . . . the shield?"

Hasmal shrugged. "No. It isn't like your kind of magic, which leaves marks everywhere. *Farhullen* doesn't even leave marks that those of us who practice it can see. But I can, um, see what isn't there."

"And what would that be?" Ry asked.

Kait was curious about the answer, too.

Hasmal said, "Look at the glow the Mirror of Souls gives off—but don't look with your eyes. Look with your magic." He waited. Kait closed her eyes and focused on the artifact as Hasmal had taught her. After a moment of concentration, she thought she saw what he meant. The faint, warm light that she could "see" with her magical senses glowed around the boat in a perfect sphere. And ended abruptly, which she knew, after months of sailing with it, was unusual. The soft glow had always spread to fill most of the *Wind Treasure,* fading as it neared the periphery—but there had never been a clear line between where the magic was and where it wasn't.

"You see?" Hasmal said.

Kait nodded, as did Ry. The others who'd tried to look only shook their heads. "Seeing" magic was a matter of practice, and Kait had only recently reached the point where she could do it with any certainty.

"If you hadn't put that shield up, the Mirror would leave a trail behind us that any of Ry's Wolves could follow." He studied Ry and said, "And if she'd done it with *darsharen*—Wolf magic—the *rewhah* would have marked us so that they would still have seen us anywhere in the Thousand Dancers."

Ry said, "You know *darsharen*?"

"Of it—its strengths, its limitations, the ways it works. I know many of the same things about *kaiboten*."

"*Kaiboten?*" Kait asked.

"Dragon magic."

"What is that like?" Kait asked.

Hasmal shrugged. "It's best explained in comparison. *Farhullen* is the magic of the individual. It draws its strength from the resources of the practitioner alone, though wizards can band together to cast stronger spells. It is entirely defensive, and because of this, doesn't create *rewhah* or leave trails. *Darsharen* is the magic of contained groups. It draws its strength from sacrifices held within a spell circle, and is more powerful than *farhullen*. Wolves have found ways to use the blood, the flesh, and the life energy of their sacrifices, and can create either offensive or defensive spells with that energy. *Darsharen*, though, always leaves a trail and almost always creates *rewhah*."

He took another sip out of the water barrel and propped himself against one of the curved ribs of the longboat. "And then there is *kaiboten*. It's the magic of uncontained groups, and the most powerful of all. The Dragons discovered ways to use everyone around them as unknowing sacrifices, at any time, without needing to prepare their victims or even identify them. They could sacrifice entire populations of cities, and according to histories and brief references in the Secret Texts, toward the end of the Wizards' War, they did. Further, *kaiboten* offers access to something no other magic has ever touched."

"Which is?" Ry asked.

"According to Solander, the Dragons learned how to harvest souls for their sacrifices. They didn't satisfy themselves with stealing blood and flesh and life energy, but stole the energy of immortality itself."

Kait frowned. "*Farhullen* uses the soul energy, too."

Hasmal shook his head wearily. "In *farhullen*, you may offer your own soul to the service of Vodor Imrish, and he may accept your offering, or not, as he chooses. But even if he accepts your sacrifice, he doesn't destroy your soul. The Dragons were crueler than the gods in this respect. *Kaiboten* uses the souls of its sacrifices the way a fire uses wood. It burns them for the energy they give off, and destroys them utterly in the process."

Kait considered that. She had always believed in the immortality of the soul, and in its sanctity. She had faced the ever-present fear of her own death when she was a child by consoling herself with the knowledge that her soul would go on, and with the hope that in another life she would be found worthy to be a true human, and not a Cursed Karnee. She had believed then—in fact had always believed—that the soul was safe from all assaults.

And now Hasmal told her that the Dragons destroyed their victims both body and soul.

Ian cleared his throat and rasped, "Hasmal, you've been talking about the Dragons returning. Your religion—it knows this is going to happen?"

Hasmal nodded. "I believe it's already happened. They're back, and trying to get the Mirror of Souls to Calimekka. We're trying to get it to Solander, because Solander and the Falcons will stand against the Dragons, as they did in the Wizards' War."

Kait turned to look at Ian—she'd never heard a sound from a human throat like the one he'd made right then. He was staring at the Mirror of Souls. "That thing—it burns souls?"

Hasmal shrugged. "I don't think so, but I don't know what it does. All I know is that Solander says he needs it, and Solander and the Falcons are all that stand between humanity and a return of the Dragon Empire."

Ry had been silent while Hasmal talked, but now he said, "Hasmal, when we're safely out of this, I want you to teach me *farhullen*."

Hasmal's mouth twitched in the faintest of smiles. "A Wolf approaching a Falcon for help. These are surely the latter days of the world." He closed his eyes wearily; in the dim light he still looked pale as death.

"We're already safely out of it, aren't we?" she asked. "We're shielded, we're well away from the airibles and hidden from them now by islands, and we have the Mirror."

Ian looked at the setting sun and frowned. "I don't know that I'll ever feel safe again. I liked the world better when magic was dead, and swords and speed and cunning made a man."

Hasmal said, "That world has never existed—but I'm sure it was comforting to believe it did."

Kait closed her eyes and leaned forward, letting her head drop down over her knees and her arms and shoulders hang loose. Her spine popped in a dozen places, and for a moment burned with fresh pain. She sympathized with Ian. She, too, had preferred the world when she hadn't known that magic still ran beneath its surface like thick poison in the bottom of a glass of wine.

Ian said, "We need to get moving again. I don't like being on the water any longer than we have to. Since my hands aren't blistered, if you'll give me your shirts, I'll tear them into rags for you. You can wrap your hands with them. It will ease the pain and keep you from breaking any more blisters."

Kait groaned. "Why didn't you think of that earlier?"

"I did. But all of you had two choices—blisters on your hands or sunburn and blisters on your shoulders and backs and faces. And with the sunburn, you'd have gotten sun poisoning, and you'd have been sick and feverish, and have slowed us up when we reached our destination. I know your hands hurt, but at least you don't have to walk on them."

He tore strips for them. Trev told Kait, "You don't need to use *your* shirt for strips. I'll give you some of the cloth from mine."

She smiled at him. He had always been pleasant to her, where the others among Ry's lieutenants limited themselves to being cautiously polite.

"Thank you," she said.

"I'd want someone to do the same for one of my sisters," he told her.

She managed to smile. "Me, too," she said, trying not to think of her own sisters. They were gone, and the part of her life that had contained them was gone, and nothing she could do would change that.

Valard asked Ian, "Where are we headed?"

Ian said, "There's a village on the island of Falea, right at the base of the volcano. It's called Z'tatne, which my friends there tell me means 'good mangoes.' It's a hard place to reach, easy to defend, and my friends will be happy to take us in and help us on our way. They're fishermen, hunters, sailors, and farmers most of the time, and pirates when the crops aren't good or the fish aren't running."

Kait was wrapping strips of linen around her hands when the hair on the nape of her neck started to stand on end. Her gut tightened, and the air around her seemed to get thicker. And she felt a greasiness she hadn't felt since . . . since . . . She closed her eyes. When?

Then it hit her. She'd felt that precise sensation in the airible on the way home to Calimekka. Right before the magic attack that heralded the onset of her Family's destruction. She looked at Ry, and found he was staring at her, his face marked with fear.

"Not you?" she asked him, and he shook his head. They both looked at Hasmal.

He wasn't creating the feeling, either; he was staring at the Mirror of Souls.

Yes. That was where the magic originated. The air grew thicker, and filled with the stink of rotting meat, the stench sweetened by honeysuckle, but only slightly. "What's it doing?" Kait asked.

Hasmal shrugged. "I don't know. Nothing good."

"What did you do to it?" Ry stood, and began making his way back to the back of the boat.

"I didn't do anything to it. I was sitting beside it, and Ian was talking about where we were going, and I felt it start to . . . to *hum,* after a fashion. Like a cat purring with its side pressed against my skin. And now . . ." He frowned and rose, and stood staring down at it. "It isn't humming anymore. I don't know what it's doing now, but I don't like it."

"We need to figure out how to turn it off," Ry said. "I don't trust an artifact that starts working on its own."

"It's *been* working," Kait said. "The column of light in its center already glowed when I found it. I just don't know what it's been doing."

Ian said, "You're sure your Reborn needs it?"

"Yes," Hasmal said, and Kait echoed him with a soft, "Yes. He told me so, too."

"Because I'd be for throwing it over the side and leaving it to the gorrahs," Ian continued.

"We have to take it," Hasmal said.

"It was waiting for something," Ian insisted. "As if it wanted to know where we were going, and once it knew that . . ." His voice trailed off into silence and he stared at the glowing Mirror.

"We have to take it," Kait said.

"Shang!" Ian clenched a fist tight and stared out at the dark hulks of the islands that rose around them. "Then let's get going before it does something else."

Everyone turned to the sweeps, and gripped the sturdy oak with wrapped hands. Hasmal pulled in the anchor, then settled himself beside Trev on the front thwart and gripped the oar. "Forward . . . ," Ian said. "And down . . . and pull . . . and lift. . . ."

Her back was an agony, and fire lanced through her palms, partially healed though they already were. She tried to think about pulling her sweep, about finding safety. But Kait shivered. She had a premonition that they were doing the wrong thing by moving on instead of staying and finding out what had gone wrong with the Mirror of Souls.

She started to say something, but the air changed again. It filled with crackling energy, with a current so powerful that it constricted her chest and made each breath feel as if she was sucking through a narrow straw.

"Motherless Brethwan!" Ry swore. "We have to stop that thing."

If they had ever had the chance to stop it, that time had passed. The light in the center column of the Mirror of Souls—that lovely golden light that had poured silently upward to pool in the center of the ring—turned the red of blood, and burst out through the top like a whale leaping from a puddle. It hit the shield that all of them had created with their wills, blood, and magic, and for an instant strained against it. Everyone could see the fiery light filling up the invisible sphere Kait had crafted. But that shield had been created to keep things out, not to keep them in—so when the crimson light finished filling the space around them, it grew brighter, and then brighter yet . . . and then it shattered the shield and erupted into the clouds, a beacon in the blackness more brilliant than a pillar of fire.

"They'll find us fast enough now," Valard growled. "I knew all along we wouldn't get away."

"Throw the thing overboard," Yanth said.

Kait and Hasmal stared at each other. Hasmal said, "If we lose it, all the souls on Matrin and in the Veil stand forfeit."

A long way away, she could hear the engines of the airibles starting up. The wizards aboard them would have felt the magic bursting free of the shield, and everyone would have seen the beacon.

Kait said, "They're coming. We have to decide fast."

Lit from below in bloody hues, Hasmal looked like a fiend from the nightmare realm. He frowned and stared back the way they had come. "If we could save it, it would be worth dying for. But they'll come, and we'll die and lose it to them anyway." He shook his head. He buried his face in his hands, and sat that way for a long moment. Kait heard him sigh, heard him mutter something she couldn't make out—not because she couldn't hear it, but because she didn't recognize the language—and finally saw him shrug. He looked at all of them. "We have to throw it into the water. Deep water, if we can find some. Tricky currents would be best, a reef would be good, and if you know of such a place within our reach, someplace where the gorrahs are especially dangerous . . . maybe we can keep our pursuers from retrieving it."

Ian said, "And while we're trying to find the perfect place to throw it overboard, the airibles are closing on us. No. Pitch it over the side here. It will have to do."

Kait half-rose from her seat. "No, Ian. We have to do what we can to keep them from getting it—"

Ry cut her short. "We have to save our own skins. If we live, we can, perhaps, get the damned thing back from them before they figure out how to use it. We'll have some time," he said. "You've had the thing for—how long?—and you have no more idea how to use it than you had the day you found it. Am I right?"

Kait didn't know if he was right or not. But the sounds of the airibles were becoming clearer, and there was an undeniable sweetness in the logic of dumping it into the sea and hoping her enemies wouldn't find it, or that if they did find it, they wouldn't know how to use it.

But that hope didn't hold water. The ghost of a Dragon had masqueraded as her ancestor, and had told her how to find the thing. That ancestor could tell whoever retrieved the Mirror how to use it.

Ry, Yanth, and Valard had moved to the front of the boat. Valard pushed his way between Hasmal and the Mirror. Ry and Yanth grabbed the Mirror.

"One, two, heave!" Ry said.

The Mirror arced through the air, tumbling, the blood-red beacon cutting a swath through the sky and through the water like a sword.

It splashed into the glass-smooth strait, the water hissed and boiled, the light illuminated a spinning path as it dropped toward the sea floor far below. Hideous, hideous, that light—as if the islands were bleeding. Kait couldn't take her eyes off of it. It burned through the murky water below and set the surface ablaze.

"Man your sweeps!" Ian shouted. "Now! And row! And maybe we'll live to see the sun rise."

Kait stared at the cold fire that burned across the surface of the sea while she pulled her sweep. It was as if the Mirror had *chosen* to betray them all, she thought. As if, having gotten what it wanted from them, it had chosen to rid itself of them and summon new allies.

Her heart was hollow, and her bones ached with dread. They might live out the night, she thought. They might reach Ian's island. But even if they did, her enemies—and the Reborn's enemies—would have the Mirror of Souls.

And then what price would the world pay for her survival?

Chapter 21

The sun beat down on the Thousand Dancers, hot as rage and heavy as sin. Crispin stood at the front of the *Heart of Fire's* gondola and stared at the red blaze that called out to him from beneath the water, and swore against Ry's soul that he would make his devious cousin pay for throwing the Mirror into the sea. He could see its light down there, even in daylight, as brilliant as a sun. He just couldn't reach it.

Three of his own men had died in trying to raise it, along with seven Galweigh soldiers. The gorrahs schooled above the thing, circling . . . circling . . . and every time one of the crewmen tried to grapple it up from the bottom, one of *them* would grab the chain and pull, and about half the time the monster would drag the man into the sea. One dead gorrah floated belly-up in testament to the fact that the monsters didn't win every round; it was a small one as such creatures went, which meant that it ran the length of ten men laid end to end, and the sea vultures and gulls and blackbeaks covered it like larger cousins of the flies that swarmed around it in clouds. Its mouth-talons hung limp to either side of its huge maw; its bony, armored body stank in the oppressive heat; and its two spine-tipped, clawed forearms floated above its head in a gesture of surrender. That one had caught its jaw on the grappling hook, and the crew had locked down the chain, and the pilot, thinking fast, had taken the *Heart of Fire* straight up and, when it was as high as it would go, they'd snapped the chain free and the bastard had fallen back into the sea and smashed itself flat when it hit the water.

Which hadn't been as satisfying as it should have been. They'd lost the first of two grappling hooks then. The second—the one they'd salvaged from the *Wind Treasure,* along with the replacement chain— they lost when one of the big gorrahs hooked onto it and nearly pulled the *Heart of Fire* into the sea. They'd had to cut that monster loose.

So Crispin had sent the *Galweigh's Eagle,* which had been trying to find Ry's boat and its occupants, back to Goft to get replacement grappling hooks, and more chain, and a grappling boom to mount on the front of the gondola, and more soldiers to work the equipment. He'd spent the better part of the day waiting while Anwyn loaded the supplies and came back. Anwyn had been in a foul mood when he returned, too—the pilot had tried to alert the Galweighs to the fact that the airibles had fallen under the command of the Sabirs, and Anwyn had to hurt him. Crispin thought he was lucky he didn't have to kill the man; that, unfortunately, would probably be necessary at the end of this work.

For now, he concentrated on the job at hand. The Mirror of Souls called to him. He could smell it, he could taste it, he could see its radiant light; it knew his name and it sang a song that only he could hear. If not for the dark shadows of the gorrahs circling it, he would have Shifted and dived into the water to bring it up himself.

As it was, he stared down at it and sweated and slapped at seaflies and bloodflies, and he worried. He suffered doubts. He didn't mind that he'd lost men—most of them had been crew belonging to the Goft Galweighs anyway, and men were easier to replace than grappling hooks or chains. What worried him was that perhaps he would never get his hands on the Mirror—that maybe nothing he tried would successfully bring it to the surface. Or that if he did, it would no longer work. Or that if it worked, it would not work as the voice had promised.

But, oh, if it worked the way the voice had sworn it would . . . then he would be a god. Power, immortality, more magic than he'd ever controlled before: He could tolerate huge discomforts and worries with those images to sustain him.

From the boom, two of the crew began to shout. "We have something, Parat! We've latched on and we're bringing it up."

The gorrahs were everywhere. They were following the line as if they were bait on the hook. The chain clanked on the winch; the grappling boom swung left and left and harder left, dragged by a great weight; the nose of the airible swung to follow the boom; the men on the deck strained at the crank, and sweated, and swore.

The brilliant red light rose through the depths, eclipsed by the schools of gorrahs. Crispin moved closer to the ship's rails and looked down into the water, squinting against glare and waves and clouds of stirred sediment to see what he had. His gut writhed and his heart began to race. The smell of honeysuckle grew stronger, and with it the reek of death that underlay it.

For a long moment he fought back the urge to puke. His stomach heaved against the stink. He shuddered, and his instincts told him to cut the thing loose—that he would regret claiming it. His heart told him to turn away, to go home content with the treasures from the *Wind Treasure*'s hold, to forget about the Mirror of Souls.

Crispin wasn't in the habit of listening to his gut or his heart. If men were meant to listen to them, they wouldn't have minds. His mind told him that with the Mirror of Souls, he would be a god, and without it, he would be mortal, and would someday die. He yelled, "Keep at it! Haul it! Haul it!"

His skin felt tight, his muscles ached, a chill ran down his spine, and his pulse raced. Magic unlike any the world had known in a thousand years, unlike anything it would ever know again without his efforts, was about to become his. He grinned and shouted as he saw the first light in the depths begin to grow brighter. "That's it! Bring it up faster! Faster, damn you!"

He could begin to make out its shape. Big as a horse . . . no, big as a house, and black as moonless night, with a ring of fire around it. Almost alive, with tendrils trailing out from all around it like a—

Gorrah! he thought, and leaped back from the rail of the gondola's catwalk.

The gorrah came up out of the water ahead of the Mirror of Souls, twisting its whip-lean body as it rose to gain more altitude. Its red eyes focused on Crispin, the fingers of its mouth-talons spread wide to embrace him, the wreath of tentacles it wore behind its head whipped upward to the place where he had stood only instants before, and easily half of them curled around the rail. The airible gondola creaked, the rail cracked, Crispin scrabbled uphill along the catwalk as it started to peel away, with the metal bending and screaming beneath the monster's immense weight.

Crispin reached the back edge of the gondola and stared down at the thing. Its maw, big enough to swallow a tall man standing up, snapped and opened, snapped and opened, and it thrashed and glared at him.

A sign, he thought. Danger from the depths.

Then he grinned again, because if it was a sign, it was one that would turn to his benefit quickly enough.

The rail broke away at last—mere moments that had seemed like entire stations passing—and the living nightmare corkscrewed back into the sea.

The crew cheered . . . though Crispin suspected they would have cheered twice as loudly if the beast had devoured him.

It had followed the chain up to the ship, blocking out Crispin's view of the Mirror of Souls. Now, though, when he looked over the edge, the men on the winch seemed to be raising a small sun. Other gorrahs circled the artifact, all lesser kin of that great monster who'd burst from the sea. Crispin, who hated the sea and everything in it, watched them with loathing. Giant sharks circled among them, looking like minnows among trout. He'd never seen sharks act in such a fashion—gorrahs generally ate them with enthusiasm, and sharks avoided the bigger, more vicious predators. And gorrahs didn't usually school, either; they were solitary hunters.

The Mirror seemed to bring out the worst in everything. Uncanny behavior from deadly beasts, the insistent crawling of his skin, the feeling he had that he was being watched—he studied the approach of the Mirror of Souls with less certainty. What, after all, did he know about it? Nothing but what he'd been told by a ghost. He could order it dropped back into the sea, or let Anwyn take it back in the *Galweigh's Eagle,* or . . .

Then he stopped and laughed at himself. His cousin Ry had touched the artifact last. It would be like that treacherous bitchson to put some sort of spell around it so that it would disturb anyone who tried to claim it. Ry and whoever of his friends had survived would undoubtedly be thrilled if they returned to this place to find their prize intact.

No thrills for them. Crispin smiled slowly, savoring his victory. The Mirror of Souls broke the surface and with it rose half a dozen gorrahs, but they fell back into the sea, and the radiant Mirror continued to rise.

It was a lovely thing. Godsall, but the Ancients knew how to craft tools! It looked to him like a giant metal lily growing on a stalk of light. Five connected petals of luminous platinum-white metal formed a ring around a circle of blazing red light; the largest of the petals bore incised markings that appeared to be inlaid with precious stones. The base supporting this ring, which mimicked the smooth curve of three long, swordlike leaves, had also been fashioned of that glowing white metal. And in the center of the leaves rose the stem, which was nothing but more light, born of nothingness, flowing upward to feed the center of the flower in a spiral that swirled outward from its heart and vanished as it touched the inner aspects of the petals.

He had envisioned something different. Something more mirror-like, and more ominous. Something with buttons and levers and complicated gears, something that looked like it *did* something. Not a fancy light fixture for a room, nor a work of art. He couldn't get any clear idea of how it worked from looking at it, and he couldn't imagine how he would make it grant him immortality.

Those concerns would have to wait, though. Now he had business to take care of. At his direction, the captain of the *Heart of Fire* signaled a midair rendezvous with the *Galweigh's Eagle*. He and Anwyn would direct the airships to Calimekka and would take on the Sabir soldiers who would be waiting, armed and armored, at Sabir House—and by the end of the day, or daybreak of the next day at latest, Galweigh House and its strategic position, vast wealth, and surviving population would belong to him to do with as he pleased.

The women and children would make entertaining slaves, he thought. The men . . . they would become fodder for executions in the public squares. He would erase the Galweigh name and the Galweigh crest from Calimekka, and eventually from the world.

And he would become a god. Sometimes he was amazed at how well his life was turning out.

Chapter 22

Kait and the other survivors came ashore at the base of the volcano on Falea in the lengthening shadows of twilight, weary, thirsty, hungry, and afraid. They'd spent the day hiding from one of the airibles, which had plainly been searching for them. The Thousand Dancers, however, offered some cover from visual searches, and a second blood-drawn shield spell had given them equally effective cover from magical searches.

They had survived—so far—but they'd lost the Mirror. Kait had failed the Reborn. She dreaded the future.

They dragged the boat into the underbrush at the shoreline, then trudged single file along a narrow path that Ian pointed out. They were a quiet group, downcast and despairing. Ry and his lieutenants, no longer pressed by immediate fear of capture, had begun to talk softly of Karyl's death. Hasmal and Kait didn't speak at all; Kait still saw the Mirror of Souls tumbling beneath the surface of the water, the blood-red ray of light that burst from its center spinning as it fell. Her memory still heard the thrumming engines of the airibles growing closer, and though her heart wanted to believe those aboard the airibles would not be able to retrieve the Mirror, it did not. She knew, as surely as she knew her own nature, that they—whoever they were—had the Mirror already and were on their way to Calimekka with it.

Ian alone had lost nothing in that last exchange, but he was as subdued as the rest of them.

"The village is up ahead," he said at last. "We have to stop here, or risk being shot by the sentries."

Kait came to a halt with the rest of the small band, and sniffed the air. She smelled the village ahead, the scents carried lightly on the breeze. Along with unmistakable odors of human habitation—composting human waste, cookfires, sweat, and domestic animals—she smelled flowers, overripe fruit, and the rich sweetness of caberra incense.

"*Hayan, etto burebban baya a tebbo,*" Ian called into the darkness.

They waited. Kait listened, Karnee senses straining for the sound of the sentry, but she heard nothing. She could not smell his position either, though they had approached the village from downwind.

"I don't think anyone is watching," she said when they had stood in the darkness for a long time with no response.

"They're watching," Ian said. "They're always watching."

A cool breeze moved through the treetops, and Kait suddenly realized he was right. She didn't smell humans, but she smelled . . . something. And she could feel eyes watching her in the darkness—eyes as sharp and wary as her own.

A shrill, high-pitched voice directly over her head trilled, "*Hayatto tebbo nan reet. Bey hetabbey?*"

Kait jumped, startled by how close the sentry was. Nothing had managed to get so close to her without her knowledge since . . . she couldn't recall a time when anyone had gotten so far inside her defenses. The sentry wasn't human, but that didn't excuse her carelessness.

Ian said, "*Ian Draclas, ube reet.*"

"*Hat atty.*"

"The sentry says to go ahead. They know me here. Don't put your hands near your weapons as you go toward the village, though, or do anything that looks threatening. Some of them will be following us all the way in."

"What are they?" Kait asked.

Ian shrugged. "They're Scarred of some sort. Allies of the villagers here. I've never seen them; I don't know what they look like or how the villagers came to reach an agreement with them. All I know about them is that they are deadly shots with the poisoned arrows they carry, and that they slaughtered more than a hundred men who attacked this village in the length of time it would take me to sit down. One instant the war party was charging forward, screaming, weapons raised, and the next instant every one of them had fallen to the ground, dead from the wounds of single arrows."

No one spoke the rest of the way into the village, for fear of having some sound or movement mistaken as threatening.

Two men, both holding torches, waited for them at the village gate. They spoke Iberan, though with a heavy accent.

"We knowed you for to be coming," one of them said. He was stout, middle-aged, his face laced with knife scars. His cloudy eyes squinted through the flickering light at them. "The old warrior, he telled us for to be watching for yourselves."

"This is to being Ian Foldbrother, Father," the other man said. "The old warrior was not to be saying Ian Foldbrother would come."

"He never was saying who maybe to be coming. Only saying *someone,* and that the fire we was to be seeing last night was for being a sign."

"*Bad* sign, he saying."

"Bad sign," Kait agreed under her breath. "It was that, for sure."

"To be coming in, all of you," the younger man said. "The old warrior is to be waiting."

Some weary old village chief, Kait thought, had watched the sky and guessed the red beacon of the Mirror of Souls slashing through the night sky had portended trouble. And had warned the sentries and the villagers to be on the lookout for anyone it might stir up. Now they would go before him and try to convince him that they didn't mean trouble. And after that—

Her mind was too tired to try to guess what would happen after that. She and Hasmal would have to try to get into Calimekka to find the Mirror, she supposed. They would likely get killed in the attempt, but they were going to have to make the attempt.

Meanwhile, she followed the old man, who, in spite of his near blindness, led them through the narrow streets of the tiny village with swift confidence. "To be following me," he kept saying.

He stopped in front of a house that looked no different than any of the other houses. Whitewashed baked mudbrick walls, a roof thatched with bundled palmetto, windows covered with cloth mesh, a bamboo door that would keep out nothing but chickens or ducks . . . or goats, but only if they weren't interested in getting in to begin with. The house smelled of caberra incense. And of something else. Something familiar, or perhaps someone familiar, though her mind refused to connect the smell with a name.

Their guide shouted into the house, "They are here! They are here, Foldbrother!"

She heard a softly muttered oath—but an Iberan oath, said in accentless Iberan—and the hair on the back of her neck stood up, and she braced herself.

In the next instant a face peered through the door, and face and name and scent all tumbled into one familiar picture, and the rest of the world fell away.

"Uncle Dùghall!" she shrieked, and burst past the old man and her traveling companions. She tore the flimsy door off its leather hinges in her haste, and threw her arms around the still-drowsy man who stood before her.

Chapter 23

rispin still couldn't believe his luck. The Galweighs of Galweigh House, invaded from within, had surrendered within moments of the landing of the airibles. Less than a station had passed since he had stepped out of the airible into his new House, and already he had claimed an apartment, sent the new Galweigh slaves to Sabir House, and sent both Anwyn and Andrew in search of whatever interesting treasures they could find within the House itself.

The Dragon's voice in his head had spent much of the trip back to Calimekka telling him the other things he needed to do. Now he paced in his apartment, feeling the press of time at his back.

It is essential that you have a crowd around you, the voice told him. *The moment you activate the Mirror, it will draw its magic from the lives of those within its reach. If you are alone, it will have no one else to draw on, and will draw from you and suck you dry. It has safeguards built in to protect the operator, but those safeguards are useless if you're alone.*

How many people did he need? he asked. Ten? Twenty?

The more people around you, the more power you'll draw into you, and the more godgifts you'll receive. You don't want ten. You don't want a hundred. You want thousands—tens of thousands.

That was how Dragon magic—*kaiboten*—worked. All the books he'd read about it had been clear on that. *Kaiboten* was the magic of masses; it could draw power from everyone at once, not just from those few who had been specially prepared and offered as sacrifices. To the practitioner of *kaiboten,* all the world could become an unknowing, involuntary sacrifice.

And he was about to acquire the secrets of that ancient, wondrous magic. He needed someone who could give him the crowd he required, though.

A knock sounded on his door, and the servant stepped into the room. "Nomeni heo Tasslimi," he said, and bowed.

Calimekka's head parnissa, Nomeni heo Tasslimi, stepped into the room behind him. Nomeni had been Crispin's instructor when he was young. The parnissa, a lean old hawk of a man, looked like he had come directly from his prayers; he breathed hard and still wore his parnissal robes, though the parnissas never wore the sacred robes into the streets.

"Crispin!" He smiled and patted his old student on the shoulder. "How odd it is to hear from you at this late hour, and how strange the circumstances: I had just been thinking of you. A rumor had already reached me of your . . . acquisition . . . of this fine House." He glanced around the room, noted the glowing artifact sitting in the corner, and raised an eyebrow.

Crispin smiled. Nomeni had always maintained good sources, which was essential in his line of work. "I found treasure," he said.

"So I see. I'll hope that will be good news for the parnissery, too, of course. The generosity of the gods deserves commemoration with a suitable gift."

"I have such a gift, I think. But only for you." He nodded at the artifact. "That's the Mirror of Souls."

Nomeni's shocked expression gratified Crispin, and he elaborated.

"It's better than anyone could have imagined, Nomeni. It's a wonder; the greatest of the Ancients' creations." He watched the old parnissa from the corner of his eye. "It can make men immortal and give them the powers of gods." The old man's eyes grew hungry at that, and Crispin smiled inwardly. He turned to the old man. "I want to be a god."

"I'm old. I'm sick . . . I suspect that I'm dying. Will you give me immortality, too?"

Crispin nodded. "That's why I asked you to come here. I won't share this great power with everyone. Gods must have their subjects, after all. But two gods could share the vast world with little problem, don't you think? The two of us . . . and eternity."

The parnissa looked down at the floor and said softly, "I fear death. There is little peace for me in the thought of dying and being reborn, of struggling through helpless childhood again, of creating myself anew, of fighting my way back to power. I'm already where I want to be, doing what I want to do." He looked at Crispin and said, "Tell me how I can help you."

"At daybreak, call a holy day. Ring the summoning bells, require all businesses to close, and demand that the people gather in the great square to hear your prayers. Say you had . . ." Crispin shrugged. "I don't know. Say you had an omen, or words from the gods, or something. Whatever you want. Just get as many people into the square as you can. The Mirror will draw its magic from them to give us life and power."

"You're of Familied blood, Crispin. The Sabirs could call such a gathering on their own."

"The Sabirs could," Crispin agreed, "but I couldn't do it now, without the consent and blessing of the paraglese. He would want to know why, and he would insist on benefiting the entire Family with this treasure. And I have no wish to confer immortality on most of my relatives. If we do this now, you and I need not share our secret with Andrew or Anwyn, with the paraglese, with the Wolves, or with the rest of the parnissery. If we act now, we two will hold the world in our hands."

"Ah." The old parnissa nodded. "So that is why I come into your scheme. I can call a gathering without involving anyone else."

"Precisely."

"And these gathered thousands . . . what of them?"

"Their lives will feed the magic."

"Will they die?"

Crispin shrugged. "I don't know. They might. Does it matter?"

The parnissa smiled at him. "I taught you. I molded you in my own image. You are the man I created. Why do you even ask such a question?"

Crispin returned his smile. "You asked what would happen to them, when I could not imagine you worrying yourself with such a question back when I was younger. I wondered if perhaps you had grown tender with age."

Nomeni threw back his head and brayed. "Old birds only grow tougher with time—never more tender. Let us go, then. You and I and your servants and the Mirror of Souls will creep from this House like the thieves in the tale of Joshan and the five winds. At daybreak the sheep will pray. And you and I shall prey."

Chapter 24

The cry spread out from the central parnissery tower in Calimekka to the hundreds of outer towers throughout the great city, *"Kae ebbout!"*

Come to prayer.

The city echoed with the calls, and men slogging their goods to market over the rough-paved back streets hurried their burros or oxen along, hoping to get their goods to warehouse before sunrise; and women setting up stalls in the markets sighed and began repacking their wares; and servants in the great Houses groaned and rose from their hard beds and began readying the fine silks and linens that their parats and paratas would require in the next station. The city breathed in, an expectant little gasp, and did not exhale. The air itself seemed to shiver with anticipation.

In the darkness before the dawn, the cries of the *shevels* brought sleepers out of sleep and warned the night workers that there would be no pleasant bed for them at daybreak. Those who could ate lightly of the foods permitted before a day of prayer and fasting.

Crispin stood in the great parnissery square, staring out at the city that lay beneath his feet, feeling his heart race and his blood pound through his veins like floodwaters overfilling a stream. Soon . . . so soon . . .

What does a god wear to his inauguration? Crispin wondered. He considered the green silk, but chose the cloth of gold, and his best emeralds. His best sword. The Fingus headdress, with the emeralds inset in the gold cap, and the two oxbow-cock feathers at each side. And his *comfortable* dress boots. No god should have to suffer aching feet.

The Mirror of Souls already occupied its place just in front of the main altar in the central parnissery. He stood behind it, smiling down at the men and women and children who began to fill the square. They were his meat. *His* fuel, all of them. He could already feel the energy from their miserable little lives coursing through his blood.

The sun rose over the horizon, barely making its presence known before vanishing behind the swollen bellies of the rain clouds that blanketed the sky. The bells began pealing out the single alto note of Soma, and as they did, the first huge drops of rain spattered the pavement and hit the carriage, and the low rumble of thunder rolled through the jagged hills. Crispin watched hundreds of heavy paper umbrellas blossom like desert flowers, and smiled to himself. How many fewer people would walk home than had hurried toward the sacred square? How many of them would he bleed dry to create himself as god?

Nomeni took his place on the step in front of the Mirror of Souls and began leading the sheep in the first of the prayer dances, spinning slowly on one foot, bent all the way over with his wrists dragging the stone stair. He was still a limber bastard, Crispin thought. Old, certainly, and perhaps truly dying—Crispin had heard rumors to that effect for months—but not out of the game yet.

Watching him, Crispin could regret the lie he'd told to win the old parnissa's cooperation. Nomeni would not be joining him in godhood. No one would. Crispin didn't care to share his power with anyone, so only he would rest his hands in the pool of light that swirled in the heart of the Mirror—the pool of light his Dragon told him was the key to immortality. Only he would be fed when the Mirror drew life and magic from the assembled thousands. Only he would live forever.

The old man finished his prayer dance, and Crispin moved out from behind the Mirror and down the stairs. There he knelt in front of

Nomeni, to all appearances the dedicated son of Iberism he'd been trained to emulate.

"Rise," the old man told him.

Crispin kissed the hem of Nomeni's robe—simple, pious black silk this morning, that made his own cloth of gold and emeralds and feathers look like the cheap gauds of a concubine by comparison. He felt silly for a moment, as if he'd seen in the old man the true definition of power with grace. But when he rose, he allowed only a warm smile to show in his face and his eyes, and he whispered, "Are you ready, old friend, to join me in godhood?"

"Wait," Nomeni whispered. "The square is not yet as full as it can be. I'll tell the cattle why they're here—by then, it should be packed."

Crispin nodded and tried to relax. He reascended the platform and stood behind the Mirror of Souls with his hands at his sides. The parnissa took his place directly in front of the Mirror as Crispin had told him he should.

The parnissa raised his arms and pitched his voice to the back of the square. "Iberans, Calimekkans, sons and daughters of Iberism, hear now the words of the gods as they spoke them to me. As you watch, the sky darkens and the gods who hold Matrin in their hand crush the clouds in their fists and squeeze out thunder and lightning. They stare at you in anger and send forth foul omens of death and disease, of the destruction of this city and all who inhabit it."

Nice opener, Crispin thought. Good attention-getter. The people in the square were staring at the sky, crowding together tighter and tighter as more of them squeezed their way in. They were packed like pickled herring, and their faces wore expressions of fear. Their fear-stink rose from them in great waves, and touched Crispin's nostrils like the sweetest of perfumes.

He heard above their cattle moans and sheep bleats the rattle of other wheels on the pavement outside of the square. Other carriages, coming fast. He frowned. Only members of Families were permitted to ride in carriages to the parnisseries. But Families had their own parnissas, and their own private chapels, and would be meeting in them to hear the words of the parnissa broadcast from the Ancients' tower in the central parnissery square of each lesser parnissery. So which Family members were out in the dreadful weather, fighting through the crowds to attend the prayers with a mob of the unwashed? From which Families? And why?

"Your sacrifices," Nomeni growled to the listeners, "have been shameful. You have not offered your best of anything to the gods. Your penitences have been false; you have hidden secrets deep within the dark corners of your lives; and you have lied to Lodan, who gives and takes, and to Brethwan, who rejoices and suffers."

The carriages rolled into the square, parting the already packed crowds as they moved forward. Galweigh crests decorated their doors, and Galweigh colors caparisoned their horses. For a moment Crispin was bewildered. Then his cousin Andrew stepped out of the first carriage. Anwyn, cloaked and masked, his deformities disguised as parts of a costume, jumped down from the second. Both had disguised themselves in Galweigh finery, red and black; they stalked through the crowd like scythes through grass, the cowering peasants scrambling out of their way in fear of their lives. With reason, of course—the unfortunate un-Familied peon who touched a Family member without prior permission would find himself a featured attraction in Punishment Square.

His brother and his cousin had discovered what he was up to, Crispin realized. But how?

It didn't matter—Crispin had enough time to do what he needed to do if he acted immediately. He wouldn't have to share godhood with anyone.

He slipped his hands over the colorful incised symbols on the main petal of the Mirror of Souls. He followed the pattern his Dragon had carefully described to him. His fingers touched the cool, polished surfaces of the gemstones inlaid in the metal. There, and there, and *there*—pressing, watching the gems light up from within, watching as the light swirling in the center of the Mirror began flowing faster, and faster, bulging upward in the center. It changed color, becoming first pale blue and then deeper blue and finally a blue so deep it was almost black; and at that instant, as he'd been instructed, he plunged both his hands into that darkly glowing dome of light in the heart of the Mirror of Souls.

I win, he thought.

You lose, the voice in his head shouted gleefully.

Light poured upward and outward, a dark blue waterfall inverted
and shot at the sky. It arced over the people in the square, over his
brother and cousin, over the lesser parnissas that stood atop the altar
behind him and at points around the square. It bounded from person
to person in the crowd, touching all of them, connecting them, illu-
minating them. It shot into the central parnissery tower, and Crispin
could see the light streaming from there toward other towers throughout the city. He could see . . . but he could not affect. He could not
move, not breathe, not cry out—he could not even fall down and
break contact with the Mirror of Souls.

Inside his skull, the screaming of demons.

Pain that lit up the backs of his eyeballs, seared the roots of his
teeth, burned his tongue until he was sure it was a charred cinder in
his mouth. Screaming white-hot pain shot through his spine, and
from his spine burrowed outward, tearing him apart. He felt his
awareness—his soul—rip loose from his body. He tried to resist the
ripping, tried to fight the terror that he felt, but he was helpless. Utterly helpless, while the merciless light stripped his soul in tatters
from his flesh and flung it in frightened, howling gobbets into the
blazing maw of the Mirror of Souls. Sucked out of himself and tossed
into the terrifying infinity of the Veil, left to float in the darkness—a
mind without senses, a soul locked inside the impenetrable walls of itself. He screamed silently, pled for mercy or a second chance, begged
the forces that had destroyed him to return him to his body and his
life.

The gods weren't listening.

In the square, the light retreated from the people it had touched; a
sea swallowing itself at ebb tide. The parnissa, Nomeni, lay dead on
the steps leading up to the altar, his corpse desiccated, mummified,
his twisted body and horrified face locked into a hideous rictus, a
silent testament to the pain and terror that had preceded his death.
The crowd held a few other corpses, their locations marked by the
movement of the living away from them—they were pocks in the
complexion of the crowd. Surprisingly few—in a crowd of close to fifteen thousand people, there were fewer than twenty such pocks.

Crispin stood with his hands still immersed in the light that swirled in the center of the Mirror of Souls. His body was stiff, his head bowed, his shoulders straining against invisible forces.

Then the last pale strands of light spiraled down through the center of the Mirror and vanished. The artifact sat dead, dormant, silent. Crispin staggered backward and yelled, then caught himself and shook himself as if awakening from a nightmare. He flushed, embarrassment clear in his expression.

With a deep sigh, he walked forward and down the steps, to kneel beside the corpse of the parnissa. As he did, a single beam of sunlight broke through the clouds and illuminated him, and the gold of his clothing and the gems he wore caught the light and scattered radiance around him as if he were a prism.

He rose, and lifted a hand, and the panicked sounds in the crowd died down. "My people," he said softly, though his voice carried clearly, "the gods brought us here to witness their judgment against the unfaithful, the unworthy, the dishonest. Many of us have been fooled by those we trusted; many of us have followed with pure hearts the edicts of the wicked; many of us have been victims of our own trust." He stepped backward one step, up the stairs, placing intentional distance between himself and dead Nomeni. "I was made a fool; I allowed myself to be brought here at the insistence of a man I believed in, to offer sacrifice. But our gods have spoken for themselves, and have chosen their own sacrifices. And we who have been judged by fire, and have been found acceptable in the eyes of our gods, must now go back to our homes and reflect on those who have died for the evils they have done."

The people stood staring. Sheep. Stupid sheep. He waved a hand at them. "Go home," he said. "Go back to your homes, to your work, to whatever you would have been doing. The gods have had their amusement, and have made their point. We must be vigilant in our care of our own piety—and the gods will be vigilant for us in guaranteeing the piety of those they set over us to serve them." Bitterness tinged his voice. "For now, go home. Begone."

Anwyn made his way through the crowd that finally began to move out of the square, fighting the tide of humanity. "You don't sound happy," he purred. "Dear me, you don't sound happy at *all*."

Crispin stared at him coldly. "How perceptive of you to notice, brother."

"Didn't your little toy work the way you had hoped?"

"Had it worked the way I hoped, I would have been a god, and you and everyone else in this city would have been bowing on your knees to me," he snarled. "I don't see anyone bowing."

Anwyn laughed, and the laughter echoed hollowly behind his metal mask. "Poor Crispin—being so clever and failing so miserably. You should have waited for us—perhaps the three of us together could have made the Mirror do what it was supposed to do."

Crispin shook his head. "It . . . failed. Some component inside of it shattered—I heard it go—and when it did, the magic fell back on itself." He shrugged, a look of resignation on his face. "I lost nothing by the attempt. We'll take the Mirror home, and you and Andrew can play with it, and see if perhaps you can get it to work." He pointed to one of the junior parnissas who had been hovering well behind the altar. "You—have that taken to Sabir House." He jerked his chin toward the Mirror of Souls.

"Not to Galweigh House?"

"It's too remote for convenience. I'm having the treasures from its vaults brought to Sabir House. You will have already received the slaves. The furnishings . . ." He shrugged. "We can use the place as a fortress, perhaps, or for entertainment. But I've discovered that Sabir House is much more convenient for everyday use."

"I see. Just as well you'll be rejoining us," Andrew said. "We need to watch you better, Crispin. I don't trust you."

Anwyn laughed; then Crispin laughed, too.

"Trust. A concept the three of us are far too civilized to be seduced by," Crispin said. "Trust is the domain of cattle—watchfulness the purview of the cattleman who raises and slaughters the cattle." He walked down the steps, brushing past his brother and his cousin, and strode to his carriage. "I'll see both of you back at the House. At your leisure, of course."

He got into the carriage; the driver whipped the horses; they clattered out into the street.

Crispin sat with his face to the window, staring out at the people leaving the square. A beautiful young woman caught his eye. She stared straight at him, gray eyes coldly curious. He touched his cheek with his little finger, and her lips curled into a smile. She nodded curtly and turned away. Then he spotted a man, tall and broad-shouldered, with a flat belly and jet-black eyes. The man gave him the same intent stare, raised his little finger to his cheek. Crispin nodded.

A slender girl with the build of a dancer turned away from the boy who held her hand; at the sound of the approaching carriage she stepped back and lifted her chin and stared at Crispin, and her smile was feral. A quick gesture, hand up to brush a stray lock of hair from her forehead . . . and the little finger dragged for just an instant across her cheek. She turned away before he could even respond. It didn't matter. They would all come together. He and she and the rest. Hundreds of them throughout the city, returned from the dead, invested into the youngest, strongest, most beautiful bodies available, and into bodies with access to power.

Within a week, they would meet. Within another week, they would have gained control of the resources they needed to begin rebuilding the life-pillars that the Great War had destroyed. And with the life-pillars re-created . . .

. . . Well, then they truly would be immortal.

Dafril, the Dragon who wore Crispin's body, smiled and flexed his arms, and stretched his legs, and arched his back. He couldn't believe how good it felt to be embodied again; after more than a thousand years, he'd forgotten many of the pleasures of the flesh. He'd have plenty of time to reacquaint himself with them, though. The Dragons were back. And this time, they intended to stay. Forever.

Book Two

"There is no day so dark that it cannot grow darker,
and no man so strong that he cannot be crushed.
Or are you immortal, Rogan?"

ALLIVITA, IN ACT II OF *THE LAST HERO OF MAESTWAULD*
BY VINCALIS THE AGITATOR

Chapter 25

. . . And that's how we came to be here," Dùghall said.

Kait sipped gratefully at the mug of plantain beer and leaned against the bolster on the floor. Of all the rest of her fellow survivors, only Ry was awake. He sat to her left, devouring the meat-flavored rice dish that Dùghall had offered. The rest of them were sleeping on the floor in the back room; she could hear soft snores and the occasional rustle as someone rolled over. "But that explains nothing of how you arrived here, or why you've changed so much."

Dùghall smiled. He was thinner and harder—to Kait he looked like he'd been put in an oven, where the fat had melted off his body and left him tough and brown and wiry. Gone were the round belly and full jowls that were the mark of the wealthy man in Calimekkan society.

"I've told you how we escaped from the Sabirs, those of us who survived. Perhaps others lived that I didn't see, of course—the House, after all, is the friend of those who know her secrets." He shook his head, and Kait saw pain in his eyes. "I hope more live than the few that spent the night in that room with me. After the walking dead rid the House of its invaders, I returned to my quarters. I'd thought to help the Family rebuild—regain its foothold in the city. But I sought guidance on how I could best do that; I threw the *zanda,* and it gave me a message I'd thought never to see in my lifetime. I was to leave the House, taking nothing with me but what I could carry on my back and telling no one of my departure, because according to the *zanda,* there were traitors among our survivors. I was to journey in secret. I was to go home and from there seek allies to stand with the Reborn and the Falcons against the Dragons.

"So I did exactly that. I slipped out of Galweigh House unseen and unremarked and placed myself aboard the first ship I could find that was sailing for the Imumbarras. Once there, I emptied the embassy treasury, sent out a call to my adult sons to join me for battle, hired the best soldiers I could find on the islands, claimed the Galweigh ships in harbor under martial law, and sailed ships and men through the Imumbarra Isles, the Fire Islands, and the Thousand Dancers. Along the way I hired more men, stocked my ships, trained them—"

"Then you have a navy hidden here?" Ry interrupted, his voice eager.

"No."

"No?" Kait was puzzled. "Then what happened to the ships and men and supplies?" She kept seeing herself sailing into Calimekka with a trained, eager marine force to reclaim the Mirror of Souls.

"When we reached Falea and began to add to our supplies, the Reborn spoke to me. He told me that I was to send my great force on to Brelst under the command of my oldest son. He said I was to wait here."

Ry said, "If you hadn't sent your fleet off, they'd be here now to help us retrieve the Mirror of Souls. Or perhaps they could have prevented the Mirror of Souls from being stolen in the first place. We, after all, were also on our way to Brelst."

"The ways of Vodor Imrish are . . . well, convoluted at best, and his motives are rarely clear to the mortal mind." Dùghall managed a wry, wan smile. "I suspect I'm here to help you reclaim the Mirror of Souls. Though why this could better be done by the few we have now instead of the many we would have had a month ago, I don't know."

"I would have sailed with the fleet," Ry said. "To cold hell with oracles."

"And had I done that, I wouldn't know my niece lived," Dùghall said, "and I wouldn't be able to travel back to the city to assist you in regaining the Mirror."

"I doubt a diplomat will be of much use to us," Ry said.

"And if I were a diplomat, I'd have to agree with you. But I'm a wizard, son—your better by far, even with all your men assisting you; better than young Hasmal in there; better than my little Kait-cha here who I can see has been doing diligent study in the science since I saw her last."

Ry flushed. "How did you know . . . ?"

"That you were a wizard? A Wolf?" His smile was sly. "I'm a Falcon. An *old* Falcon. I've been watching your sort all my life, and not one of you has ever so much as suspected that I was anything but the diplomat I claimed to be. I can smell Wolves the way Kait . . . or you, I suspect . . . can smell the animals creeping through the underbrush outside the village walls."

Kait watched Ry's eyebrows slide up his forehead, though he looked away before he could betray his surprise to Dùghall. "You're an observant man," he said quietly. "Observant enough that I'm surprised someone hasn't had you killed."

"Observant enough that I'm still alive, in spite of the fact that more than a few have tried."

"Perhaps you'll be an asset to our mission after all."

Kait glanced at Ry. "When did it become *our* mission? I don't recall asking you to help me retrieve the Mirror of Souls."

He looked straight into her eyes and said, "I have my reasons for going with you."

"I need to know what they are," Kait said.

Dùghall nodded. "I'm afraid I have to agree. Sabir reasons and Wolf reasons are unlikely to mesh well with Galweigh reasons and Falcon reasons."

Now Ry faltered. He looked from her to Dùghall, then back to her again. Kait saw long-buried pain in his eyes. "The truth?" he said. "Aside from being with you, that is? I need the Mirror of Souls as much as you do." He looked away from her and his voice went both quiet and hard. "I want my brother back."

Kait's stomach lurched. "He's . . . dead?"

"For a long time."

Kait worded her question carefully. "What makes you think the Mirror of Souls could give him back to you?"

Ry managed a small smile. "He told me so himself."

"A voice inside your head, you mean? One that claimed to be your brother? One that came to you not long ago . . . maybe after our Families fought?"

He nodded.

"That wasn't your brother."

"He was Cadell. He knew things only Cadell could know."

Kait shook her head. "He read your memories. Such a spirit told me how to find the Mirror—she told me she was an ancestor of mine, martyred by your Family hundreds of years ago. She lied, because she wanted me to bring the Mirror of Souls to Calimekka. She was a Dragon."

She thought his face went pale. "And how did you discover that?"

Kait didn't know how he would respond to her story of seeking out the Reborn in the womb, or how reliable he would consider the information. So she said, "Hasmal performed a spell. From it we discovered her origins."

Ry frowned and sat quietly for a moment. Kait felt a tiny tendril of magic curl out from his body; she tightened her shields until she could feel nothing. His sort of magic would pull its power from the people around him, and might rebound to him and anyone he involved; she wanted nothing to do with that.

"Cadell won't answer me," he said at last.

"That's because he isn't Cadell," Dùghall said.

"So you have no reason to go with us when we retrieve the Mirror."

Ry looked long and hard at her. "I still have reasons. I left my Family and crossed the ocean to be with you, Kait. I still want to be with you." He looked away from her and said, "Maybe you think I'm a fool." He shrugged. "Maybe I *am* a fool. But I'll see you safely where you're going. And my men will stay with me. They're loyal and brave—they'll be good to have along."

Dùghall said, "Events fall into place." His tone was enigmatic, his expression troubled. Suddenly he stiffened and turned toward the west. "Shield yourselves!" he snapped.

A wave of pure malevolent magic rolled over Kait, overwhelming the light shield she already had in place. The pain of the magic blinded her, threw her to the floor, and drove into her belly like a knife.

Blind.

Deaf.

Mute.

Paralyzed.

Devoured by agony.

She fought for a handhold in that sudden sea of horror; a single point upon which she could concentrate, a single piece of debris in her shattered world that she could use to keep herself from drowning in madness.

Focus.

She found a place of calm energy beneath her.

Drew in protective magic.

Rebuilt her shield.

Fed it, a slow trickle at a time, then faster as the shield began to buffer her from the maelstrom around her. She expanded it, let it meld to Ry's shield and Dùghall's, then expanded it carefully over the men in the other room who had been caught sleeping and had been crushed by the wizardstorm.

She crouched, huddled and shivering, on the floor. Blessed stillness cradled her, and slowly, slowly, the pain subsided.

Her hands trembled, and cold sweat beaded on her forehead and dripped down her nose and off her upper lip. But she had herself under control, and the evil could no longer touch her. Her vision began to clear, and she saw Dùghall and Ry curled on the floor beside her, both pale and sweating and shivering. She rose, shocked at how weak her legs were and how wobbly her gait, and tottered outside. She looked west, toward the birthplace of the evil she felt.

The cloud-smeared sky glowed impossibly blue, the blue of sapphires illuminated from inside, their light sent streaking across the horizon in tight arcs. Lovely. But the poison that poured from the beautiful light pounded at her, even as she tightened her shield. She knew the evil—knew its shape and its appearance, knew its name, and how it had come to be summoned forth.

She leaned against the cool, whitewashed wall and closed her eyes. That light came from the Mirror of Souls. They'd used it. She could feel the artifact's imprint in the magic; she could recognize its signature. After months of living on the ship with the damned thing, feeling its energy permeating the cabin, hearing the almost-imperceptible hum of its light core, she felt she knew it better than she knew her shipmates. And it was awake, and alive, and exultant.

Evil. The artifact was inherently evil; she did not think there would be any way to use it for good. She hadn't been able to sense that before, but now, with it fully awake, she couldn't mistake the Mirror's essential nature. It had been created to cause pain, to maim and destroy in some manner that she could not, from her great distance, fathom. It had waited more than a thousand years to carry out its evil. It was . . . happy.

I brought it here. If I hadn't gone after it . . . if I hadn't listened to the voice that told me the only way I could hope to see my Family alive again was to retrieve it . . .

But no. Down that path lay madness. She had acted in good faith, using the best of her knowledge at the time. She had done the only thing she believed she could do. And if she had not been willing to undertake the arduous voyage, the same voice who lured her across the ocean would have found another person with equally compelling desires.

Others had crawled out into the daylight to stare at the distant light show. Kait heard Hasmal nearby, and Ry, and Dùghall. Dùghall stood staring at the sky, and frightened villagers hurried to surround him, babbling questions in panicked voices. He shook his head and pointed his finger at those glowing blue arcs and answered them in their own language. She heard his attempt to be comforting and, underneath that, his fear.

She walked to his side. "We're too late. They've used it."

Dùghall looked from her to the sky, where the lights had finally begun to flicker out. Back to her, to the sky, to her. Finally he said, "We've known for a thousand years and better that the Dragons would return, Kait. We've been waiting for them. We knew they would find the Mirror, though we didn't know how. Vincalis predicted all of these things in his Secret Texts, and warned us to watch—that these evil things were the signs that foretold a good outcome. The Dragons are back, their magic has returned, and the Mirror of Souls is in their hands. But prophecy said all these things would come to pass before Solander returned to us. He's ready to be rebirthed—and when he returns, he'll lead all of us against the Dragons, and we will wipe them utterly from the face of the earth and raise the city of Paranne for everyone."

"Danya carries the Reborn in her belly," Kait said. "But she has closed herself off from him, and won't answer me when I try to reach her, either."

Dùghall's eyebrows slid up his forehead, and she knew she'd stunned him.

"Danya?" he whispered. "Danya! Is alive? She escaped from the Sabirs? How?"

Kait cut him off. "I don't know how she's doing, and I don't know how she got away from her kidnappers. All I know is she's pregnant with the Reborn. I can feel her anger and her hurt, but I can't reach her. Either I don't have enough control of magic to get through to her, or else she isn't listening."

Dùghall looked worried for a moment. "I'd feel better if I knew where she was. How she'd come to be there. How she was doing." He sighed, and stared toward Calimekka, where the last of the lights had vanished, and the overwhelming feeling of evil had dissipated. "Whatever they did there, it's finished now. But we have Vincalis's assurance that the Reborn will set things right. We'll follow his guidance; with his help we'll destroy the Dragons. And when it's done, the Reborn will build an eternal empire of love better than any empire the world has known before."

Kait nodded, hoping the future's outcome was as certain as her uncle believed. "What about Danya?"

"The Reborn will protect her."

Chapter 26

The horrible darkness and the bitter cold of winter had given way to a short, startling spring, and then to a summer where the sun never set. The bleak tundra bloomed, suddenly and shockingly fertile, covered with berries of a dozen varieties, short-lived flowers in colors Danya had never even imagined before, sturdy greenery that grew so fast she kept thinking if she sat down and watched just a little longer, she could see the plants move.

Birds flocked to the just-melted waterways and filled the skies with their chatter and themselves with the larvae of mosquitoes and burstbugs. Blackflies and coppergnats filled the air in clouds, and spawning salmon and firth and grayling raced into the pure, cold, shallow streams to mate. Wolves and bears trailed their young, foxes trotted ahead of round-faced kits, caribou and wixen swung across the spongy ground in huge herds with their calves at their sides.

Danya swelled, too, as fertile as the rolling tundra. The baby was huge inside of her, all angles and lumps and kicking, squirming protrusions. She waddled when she walked, fought for balance, slept sitting up because she could no longer breathe when she lay down. A small part of her embraced the changes, because they made her feel necessary and vital and somehow more alive than she'd ever felt. That small part of her was the Danya she had been before the Sabir Wolves kidnapped her, tortured her, raped her, and used her as the buffer for the spell they launched against her Family. That small part of her had always wanted a baby, and found the life of the one inside her enthralling.

But she was no longer human, and she felt sure that the magic that had twisted her into a monster had done the same thing to the unborn infant. And she could not forget the rape that had forced the child on her, and the three detestable Sabirs, one of whom had fathered it. Luercas said that the father was Karnee—that meant that he was either Crispin or Andrew, both of whom had changed into beast form at one time or another while torturing her. So the infant would have their beast-nature, too.

Had she still been human, she might have been able to forgive the unborn creature for his existence; after all, *he* had done nothing to her. But she looked at the monster she'd become, and her ugly, ravaged body twisted the joy she found in the wonder of pregnancy and poisoned it. When the magic made her into a monster, the people who cast it took away everything she'd ever wanted in her life: home, friends, Family, position, wealth, and future.

She shifted her weight to her other hip when the baby kicked, trying to find a position that didn't hamper her breathing or hurt her back and at the same time trying to find a comfortable position for her thick tail. She sat among the hummocks on the edge of a high bluff, watching the light glint off the water below her, though her body was no longer designed for sitting.

No. The Sabirs hadn't taken away *everything*. She was still a Wolf. She still had her magic. And Luercas promised her that with her magic and his help, she would have her revenge. She would bring about the deaths of the Sabirs—she would feel her hands wrapped around their cold, silenced hearts, and their blood would congeal on her fingers. She would see her own Family humiliated, subservient before her, made to suffer for their callousness, for their unwillingness to pay the necessary price to rescue her.

The baby stilled in her belly, and she felt it reach out to her. Mind-touch to mind, soul-touch to soul. It felt like sunlight—hope and warmth and still, soft brightness that radiated outward from her center, blurring the edges of her pain and promising her peace. Hope. Love.

I am your reward for surviving all that pain, it whispered. *I will make you whole again.*

As she did every time, she blocked its delicate touch and tentative contact. She pulled her magic around her like a wall, holding herself separate from the intruder in her body. She would not love the thing. She would not. If she allowed herself to love it, she would lose the keen, fine edge of her hatred . . . and she would *not* lose that. Without hatred, she could not keep herself keyed for revenge. And she had sworn on her immortal soul that the Sabirs would pay for what they did to her, and that the Galweighs would pay for what they failed to do.

She rose awkwardly and stretched. Below her lay the river Sokema, and her little boat waited on the sandbar. Across the river, the Kargans worked in their fish camp, gutting the fish they drew from the river, spreading it flat, drying it on lines the way women back in Calimekka had dried their clothes, or smoking it over green willow fires in smokehouses to make the tough fish jerky that sustained them through the winter.

She watched them from her perch on the bluff. Brown in their summer fur, squat and rounded, they bounded from task to task with the energy of cubs. The Kargans. Her people now. They had given her a house, a name within their clan—Gathalorra, or Master of the Lorrags—and their friendship. She would have traded all of it for a single room in the servants' level of Galweigh House, if she could once again be a true human.

She heard steps behind her and turned.

"We are finished, kind Gathalorra," one of the children said. He held up his berry bag to show her. The other children nodded, and made the grimaces that she'd learned to identify as smiles, and held up their berry bags, too. "Do you want some berries before we go home?"

"No," she said. "I had all the berries I wanted while I waited for you, and you worked hard for those. Save them all for night-meal." The charming Kargan children, who were unfailingly polite and helpful and who treated her like a cross between their big sister and their favorite aunt, bounded down the bluff like wolf cubs released from their den. They yipped and snarled at each other, bared teeth and laid ears flat back, raised the fur on their spines . . . then laughed wildly at the fierce creatures they appeared to be, and pounced on each other. Two-legged puppies.

In Calimekka, they would have all been murdered in the public square for being abominations against the gods.

She thought about that sometimes.

She waddled down the bluff so slowly that all of them were already in the long, flat boat and seated with their berry bags on their laps when she arrived. She shoved the boat into the water and clambered in, thinking that she wouldn't be able to take them across the river for berries many more times. Her body was becoming too ungainly.

She paddled carefully—she had only learned the art of boating the month before, and she still felt uncertain of her skills. Her taloned hands scrabbled to keep their purchase on the short, flat paddle, and her tail, which she tried to keep coiled around her while she knelt in the back of the boat, kept uncoiling on its own and striking the boat's ribs and clinker-lapped boards, as if it were a thing apart and desperate for escape.

"Da says the hunters are meeting tonight for the Spirit-Dance, and I mustn't forget to invite you, in case you wish to hunt," one of the children said.

The men loved to have her hunt with them, because her keen nose took her to game not even they were aware of, and because her speed allowed her to run down the heavy golden caribou and the bulky, violent wixen, and her teeth and claws gave her the tools she needed to bring them down.

But now, of course, she didn't have much speed or much stamina.

"Offer your Da my thanks for me if you see him before I do," she said. "But I'm too near my time to hunt." She'd been pleased with herself for the skill with which she'd negotiated the complex Karganese tenses, but from a few soft giggles toward the front of the boat, she guessed she hadn't gotten them right after all.

One of the older children, who would be hunting within the next year, ducked his head diffidently and said, "You mean, 'If you see him before I do.'"

"That's what I said, isn't it?"

The child shook his head and said, "You said, 'If you see him before I do.'"

Danya sighed. She couldn't hear the difference. She'd always thought she had a good ear for languages, and she'd spent much of her life learning the handful of major tongues that served Ibera, but the subtleties of Karganese eluded her.

"Say it again," she said. "Your way. The *right* way."

The child's ears perked forward, and he repeated the phrase. Danya said, "Now say what I said."

The child flicked his ears back and tipped his head and said exactly the same thing he had said before. Danya heard no difference at all. None.

"I don't hear it," she said.

She'd learned the Kargan face that meant puzzlement—lifted upper lip, lowered brow, fur around the eyes erect so that they seemed in imminent danger of disappearing. "Hear?" the child asked. Now the other cubs began to giggle.

The Karganese were polite to the point of pain sometimes. She'd had the feeling before that she was missing something important when she spoke; she got that puzzled look more often than she could explain. But none of the adults would admit she was doing anything wrong. They invariably ascribed their puzzlement to their own stupidity.

Perhaps she would be able to get something out of the kids, who didn't seem as inclined to call themselves stupid.

"What am I doing *wrong*?" she asked. "I don't understand."

She looked at the kid and he looked back.

He flicked his ears forward. "If you see him before I do." He flicked his ears back and tipped his head to the side. "If you see him before I do." He flicked his ears forward. "If you see him before I do." He flicked his ears back and tipped his head. "If you see him before I do."

She was staring at him, suddenly beginning to comprehend the scale of what she had been missing. She swiveled her own huge ears forward and made sure she kept her head straight, and she said, "If you see him before I do." She swiveled her ears back and tipped her head. "Not, 'If you see him before I do.'"

The kid grinned. "Almost. But it's . . ." He perked his ears stiffly forward. "Like that, not . . ." He relaxed them slightly.

She groaned. "What's the difference?"

He shrugged, a gesture that meant the same thing to him that it did to her. "My way is right, yours was . . . ah . . . rude."

That was the way of it. The kids would tell her what she did wrong, but couldn't explain why. The adults probably could have explained why, but were too polite to admit that she wasn't perfect. Now she knew why they never looked away from each other's faces when they talked. Now she knew, too, that she had a second language she would have to learn, and perfectly, if she was ever going to communicate with the Kargans the way she needed to. A woman who could not speak fluently could not raise an army with eloquence, and Danya had nothing but eloquence with which to move her adopted people.

She was resolving to never look away from the face of a speaker again when more giggles roused her from her reverie. She glanced at the children, and saw them looking ahead, to the bluff they'd just left behind. She'd been paddling in a circle.

With a sigh, she shifted the paddle and fought the boat back to her original heading.

Revenge would take time. Lucky for her it was the one thing she had in abundance.

Chapter 27

The Z'tatnean blade-hulled ketch slipped along the last stretch of the north coast of Goft, its triangular sail making the most of the sparse night winds. Black against black in the cloud-blanketed night, it drew no notice from the tenders of the watchfires on shore. Its destination was not Calimekka's great harbor, but rather a rocky bit of shoreline fifty leagues to the north of the city. There it would drop its cargo; then it would return to Z'tatne.

Its cargo, huddled in the bottom of the ketch and dressed in stolen Salbarian paint and finery, conversed in hushed whispers.

"It's going to be a long way to walk with us dressed like the gods' damned harem dancers." That was Yanth, who hadn't been happy since he had to paint over his cheek scars, and who didn't think the baggy, stiff, broidery-laden fashions of the Salbarians flattered his lean frame, and who had gotten loud and threatened violence when Dùghall hacked off his long hair. "I'd rather sail into the bay and take my chances at being recognized than prance down the coast in this ridiculous costume."

Kait studied him. She found herself liking Ry's first lieutenant, even if the man did stand loyally in the Sabir camp. "The Salbarians always pack their goods overland from Amleri. If we go into Calimekka through the west gates, we'll just be more of what the guards see every day. No one will notice us; no one will remember us. If we sail into the bay, we might as well paint, *Look at me, I don't belong here*, on our faces."

"How can it matter that much?" Yanth asked. "Who will pay any attention to a bunch of traders?"

Dùghall laughed. "Spoken like a fighter. If they don't carry swords, they must be invisible."

"I *am* a fighter. Not that anyone will believe it now." He snorted. "Looking like this, not even my blade brothers would know me."

Ian, equally garish in Salbarian dress, sighed. "First, we don't want your blade brothers to recognize you, and we especially don't want people to believe you're a fighter. If you're a trader, you don't have to pay warrior's bond to enter the city, and your name won't go in the Red Register. When you're trying to be inconspicuous, that's a *good* thing. Second, if you're a trader in the wrong place, people will notice. But they'll be people you aren't used to noticing, and that will be bad for you." He shrugged. "Believe me on this if you believe nothing else you ever hear from me—people know their own. You'll be able to pass as a Salbarian trader only if you never speak, and rarely move. If you can do it long enough to get through the Circle of Gates, we'll let you stop pretending to be a Salbarian and dress up as something closer to your nature." He closed his eyes and leaned back against the hull of the boat. "A gaming cock, perhaps," he muttered.

Kait suppressed a smile. The idea of Salbarian disguise had been Ian's, and even when he'd presented it, he had been less than optimistic about their success in infiltrating the city without drawing unwanted attention. Now Kait thought he looked resigned. "Third," he said, "we won't be walking down the coast road. That *would* draw attention. I have connections—friends from years ago—not too far from where we'll be putting ashore. They used to take some of my cargo for me, in exchange for favors I did for them. They'll take us into the city the same way they transported some of the larger cargo."

"I always suspected you went into piracy." Ry gave his brother a disgusted look.

Ian narrowed his eyes at Ry, and Kait could see the hatred there. "Smuggling," he said. "I didn't have the stomach for the cold-blooded murder that pirates and Family indulged in. I provided goods that were hard to obtain to people who had a need for them."

"You're saying I'm a cold-blooded killer?" Ry asked.

"I *know* you are."

"If I were, you would have been dead long before now: I swore your death when my magic revealed your . . . liberties . . . with Kait, before I even knew it was *you* who had taken those liberties. Only the fact that I honor Kait's agreement has kept you breathing until now. I've *never* killed in cold blood."

"Not by your own hand, perhaps. But when you hired the assassin to slaughter my mother and my sibs, her knife marked you with their blood as surely as if you'd spilled it yourself."

Kait could see the shock in Ry's face. "They're dead? Delores and Jaine and Beyar?" he blurted. "When?"

Ian faltered for an instant. Then his lips stretched into a feral smile. "You're good. A man could believe you innocent if he didn't know better."

"I *am* innocent. I never wished your mother or your siblings any harm, and certainly didn't pay to have them killed." He frowned, puzzlement creasing his brow. "I didn't like you, Ian, and I thought Father showed questionable sense in choosing a mistress who was so young and pretty, and terrible lack of judgment in trying to hide all of you in Sabir House . . . but I also know Mother. If I'd been Father, I would have kept a mistress, too."

"And when Father told my mother he would legitimize the lot of us, you thought that would be just fine, did you?"

"I never knew of it." He shook his head. "I swear . . . if Father had taken Dolores as his na-parata and made all three of you my full sibs, I would have been relieved. Then one of you could have moved into the line of succession and I would have been . . ." He faltered and his face bleached white. "Ah. I would have been free to pursue the things that interested me. And that would not have suited Mother's ambitions at all."

"Your mother's ambitions?"

"My mother was determined that I would succeed my father as head of the Wolves, and that she would guide them through me."

"Then you're saying that Imogene hired the assassin? But when I caught him, he said you had done it."

"And you believed him?"

"He was bargaining for his life at the time."

Ry managed a harsh chuckle. "You spent much of your life around Family, Ian. Do you think a hired killer would dare betray the Family member who hired him? More to the point, do you think he would have been mad enough to betray Mother? Even had you let him live, she never would have. And the things she did to him before he died—and to anyone he'd ever cared about—would have made your threats meaningless."

Ian stared at his hands, his expression both thoughtful and uncertain. When he finally looked up, Kait thought he looked peaceful. "You believe Imogene knows you're alive, and that she has declared you *barzanne*?"

"Almost certainly."

Ian nodded. "And if she knows I am alive, she will surely still have her price on my head. You agree?"

"Yes. She would never rescind an order for assassination."

"Then we find ourselves on the same side."

"Not precisely. We find ourselves standing against my mother. And we both want to get the Mirror of Souls back from whoever has it. But so long as you still seek Kait's favor, we remain enemies."

"Agreed. But enemies with a common cause. Before the gods themselves, I revoke my oath to have your life."

"If you would also swear to remove yourself as Kait's suitor, we could be friends."

The corner of Ian's mouth twitched. "No. Not that. Kait will choose one of us, or neither of us, but I won't clear the field for you without a fight. I could ask you to do that, but I suspect your answer would be the same. So I won't."

Ry's smile was thin. "It would." He shrugged. "Then we won't be friends. But nevertheless, before the gods, I revoke my oath to have your life . . . and thus we can be allies, at least until Kait makes her choice."

"Allies, then. For now." Ian reached out his hand, and Ry clasped it.

Both of them looked at her, and from their expressions, she thought perhaps they expected her to declare one of them winner at that moment. She wouldn't play their games. Kait turned to her uncle and asked him, "Do you truly think we'll be able to reach the Mirror?"

Dùghall nodded. "Prophecy was clear. The Falcons will triumph over the Dragons. In order for us to triumph, we must acquire the Mirror of Souls and undo the evil the Dragons have done with it. Therefore, we will prevail."

"Well, not *us*, necessarily," Hasmal said. He'd been quiet until then, lying with his head resting on his rolled-up cloak. Being short, blond, and heavy of bone and muscle, Hasmal could never have been mistaken for a Salbarian. Instead, he wore clothes intended to make him look like a homesteader from the New Territories: a much-patched homespun broadcloth shirt dyed a dull mustard yellow, ankle-wrapped breeches of tight-woven gray cotton, boots that were plainly both handmade and ill-fitted, and a much-patched cloak. Yanth, on seeing the costume Hasmal had been given, offered to pay him to trade. Kait had found that hilarious. Hasmal continued, "If *any* Falcons reach the Mirror and win it back from the Dragons, the prophecy will be satisfied. But *we* might all get killed."

"Thank you so much for your encouraging words," Kait said. "That's exactly what we needed to hear right now."

"It is," Hasmal said, his voice thick with stubbornness. "If you get to thinking that the prophecy guarantees you'll survive, you'll do something careless and get yourself killed. And maybe everyone with you, too. The prophecy only promises that the *Falcons* will triumph over the Dragons and that the Reborn will be restored to his place as the leader of humanity. Nowhere in the Secret Texts does it say 'Kait Galweigh will go into Calimekka to steal the Mirror of Souls back from a whole nest of furious wizards and walk out alive and in one piece.'"

Dùghall said, "He's right, Kait. All of you. I prefer to think of our mission as being divinely planned and divinely protected, but we have no assurance that we will succeed. Our only assurance is that *someone* will—that the Reborn will ultimately crush the Dragons."

Valard, darkly pessimistic, said, "If you ask me, we should join the Dragons. No matter what your prophecy says, they sound like they have a better chance of winning this than we do. You say there are probably hundreds of them and possibly thousands, and you think they'll have managed to put themselves in positions of power. They have the resources of Calimekka at their disposal, and probably, because of that, the resources of all of Ibera. And you've already admitted that their sort of magic is better than yours."

"Stronger. Not necessarily better."

"If you ask me, stronger *is* necessarily better."

Kait had spent the last two days in the Z'tatnean ship listening to variations on this argument. "We aren't strong enough to beat them in a fight," or "We don't have enough people to get through their guard," or "No matter what your prophecy says, this whole mission is doomed to failure," or "Why can't we just get our families out of Calimekka and take them somewhere safe to live in peace for the rest of our lives?" Ry's lieutenants seemed to have few loyalties or interests beyond maintaining his friendship. When he had volunteered to come with her to get back the Mirror, they had immediately exerted every effort to get him to change his mind. When it became clear that he didn't intend to back down, they told him that they were going with him to help him. But it was clear to Kait that they would help only as long as Ry was involved—that they had no interest in the Reborn, and that their real interest, outside of Ry's goodwill, lay with their families in Calimekka.

She let her eyes drift shut and listened to the back-and-forth bickering, the questions and answers, restatements and rebuttals, and all of them began to float away from her, as if the words themselves had been put on a boat, and the boat had been set into a different current that led far from her. She allowed her shield to dissipate, and focused on the thin tendril of magic that curled toward her from the still-distant Reborn. She followed it, watching as it grew brighter, feeling its increasing warmth, and at last she touched the Reborn's soul.

Love and acceptance enveloped her, and hope filled her heart. She would be able to get the Mirror of Souls. She would survive. She would live to touch the Reborn, and she would help to bring about a world filled with love and goodness—a world that would rise out of the ashes of the Dragons' evil.

She woke to a change in the rhythm of the ship and the tone of the voices around her. Now everything was hushed, the whispers urgent in character and brief in nature. The ship bucked fore and aft, and waves slapped loudly at the hull; the long rolling swells of the deep sea were gone. She opened her eyes to find herself alone. So they'd reached land. She rose and peeked over the hull, and saw a rocky shore rolling into gray mist and tattered fog in both directions. The clouds, thick and black, bellied near the ground, crowding into the steep sides of mountains, obscuring their peaks. Hooded strangers stood among the men with whom she'd traveled and whispered prices and dates of delivery and return, and never asked questions about what was wanted, or why.

She clambered up to the edge of the hull, judged her distance from the deeper water where the ship lay at anchor to the shallows and the shore, and before she thought about it, bunched her muscles and jumped. She was in the air and irreversibly aimed for dry ground when she recalled that neither the strangers with whom her uncle bargained nor the Z'tatneans who had brought them to Ibera's shore knew her secret. Carelessness. Damnall carelessness. She should have waited for someone to row back to get her, or should have let herself fall short of dry ground if she jumped.

They were watching her when she landed. Expressions of surprise, curiosity, instant distrust. One of the strangers turned to Dùghall and said, "Athletic, isn't she?" but his voice asked more than his words. In a land where any difference was suspect of being both a curse of the gods and a crime punishable by death, even criminals sometimes had their own brand of piety.

Kait gave him a cold, calculating look and said, "I ought to be. I've spent my entire life training in gymnastics. It makes my . . . work . . . both safer and easier."

The curiosity vanished, and the man said, "Ahhh. Practical. I ought to consider having some of our young women trained the same way. They stay small enough that agility would be a real asset even once they become adults." He looked back to Dùghall. "Now, about the horses . . ."

She turned away from him, pretending to study the sea, and felt the gorge rise in the back of her throat. Carelessness. She could let it kill her if she chose. Or she could remember that she was only lucky that the people with whom she traveled did not exercise their right to kill her for being the monster that she was. She could reclaim the wary, fearful, life-preserving habits of a lifetime, happily discarded in the last half year, and by so doing choose to survive.

They spent two days waiting for the arrival of their horses, their clothes, and their supplies, and four days on the road just to reach the outer edge of Calimekka. They spent another three days riding into the center of the city, signing false names to the documents at each gate, providing false identification, working out their stories bit by bit.

By the time they reached the center of the city, where the Houses of the Families marked the hilltops and the wealthy clustered together in their tall apartments and stately homes, they had discarded their stolen finery and bought more ordinary clothing, and had gone from being emigrating Salbarians and Territory failures returning from colonial disaster to well-to-do foreign traders looking for new markets.

Thank all the gods for diplomatic training, Kait thought. She spoke accentless Donneabba, the primary language of the Imumbarra Isles, and looked enough like a short, thin Donneai to convincingly act the part of Dùghall's assistant. Ian turned out to be brilliant in Hmago, the trade language of the Manarkans. Hasmal claimed to be Hmoth by birthright, and his Hmago was perfect, too. Jaim and Trev looked like cousins; they pretended to be from the Veral Territories, since they spoke only the normal Iberan tongues. Yanth, who had skipped language studies as much as he could, could pass for nothing but a Calimekkan when he opened his mouth, so he played the part of the locally hired guard. Valard, too, was unmistakably Calimekkan; he donned scruffy leathers and joined Yanth in pretending to be a mercenary. Ry, tall and golden, with his exotic pale eyes and fierce blade of a nose, might as well have had the Sabir crest tattooed on his cheeks. But he'd dyed his hair with ecchan stain, which turned it a muddy, dismal shade of brown, and he'd changed his walk, slumping his shoulders a bit and shuffling to make himself appear both older and less threatening. His story was that he was back from the Sabir territory in western Manarkas.

They called themselves the Hawk-Kin Trading Alliance, and split up to work their way through the commercial districts of the city nearest the centers of power, Sabir House, Galweigh House, Embassy Row, and the Great Parnissery. They were hunting for Dragons, but in the week that they'd conducted their search, they'd found no sign, no rumors, no obvious marks of new magic.

Kait heard from a number of sources, just in passing, that the Galweighs were no more, and that Galweigh House had fallen and lay empty. She thought about that at night when she listened to Ry talking to his lieutenants in the room next to hers. The inn's walls were thin; sometimes when he slept she could hear him breathing, and she thought about the rumors then, too. If the Galweigh Family was no more, what did she owe to its memory? Had the Sabirs overrun the Galweighs in the New Territories? In Galweigia? In the scattered cities and towns of Ibera? Had those distant Galweighs renounced their interest in Calimekka, or in her branch of the Family? She did not discuss the matter with Dùghall. She had a job to do, and any personal matters would wait until she had successfully completed it. Or died trying.

She had little success at that job, though, until she entered a gem shop on Amial Throalsday and started selling her story to the gauntest specter of a gem merchant she'd ever seen. "Hawk-Kin Trading Alliance offers you finest goods," Kait was telling him. She leaned forward on his counter, simultaneously tucking her upper arms against her rib cage to deepen her cleavage, giving him a good opportunity to take a look. She wished she wasn't so skinny—in general, men in Calimekka preferred plump women—but the stress of being in constant contact with Ry and not following her body's desires had worn her to a stick-thin shadow of her already lean self. This particular merchant didn't seem to mind, though. She was taking pains to keep her Imumbarra accent authentic, but from his glazed eyes and quickened breath, she figured she was probably wasting the effort. On him, anyway. His mournful gaze had never reached all the way up to her face.

The customer at the back of the store was straining to hear, too, though, so she stayed in character. "Goods from secret harbors, from our own places. Top quality, low prices, nothing like you get from anyone else. Best-best stuff. Dream-with-eyes-open smoke, firestones and filigree, fine caberra, worked terrapin-shell and durrwood incenses and perfumes, the best ivory and greenstone you ever see, excellent white nalle pelts. Artifacts and Ancients' books, too, if you know anybody want that sort of thing."

"And how much do I have to pay up front?"

Kait shook her head. "We small, you small. Right now I looking for big fish." She winked at him. "You know any big fish you can send me to, if he buys from us then you just give us order and, like magic, the big fish gonna pay expedition cost for you. You no tell, we no tell."

The man's gaze finally rose from her breasts to her face, and he smiled broadly. "Really? You'd do that?"

"Sure-sure. We got our own ship, got our return cargo mostly ready, but we need big spender to pay supply costs and cover trade expenses. You know what I mean?"

He nodded. "You need an investor."

"Yah. In-vess-tor. Deep pockets, new money . . . somebody who not minding take chances to get a nice return. He get good stuff . . . you not have to worry you tell your rich friends about us. They still be your friends after. But you help us, we help you."

"Firestones, you say? And ivory and greenstone? I suppose I know a few people . . . they probably know a few people."

"We make meeting, your people and my people, yes?" Kait had given him the bait, which he didn't take. No interest in books or artifacts from before the Wizards' War. But she'd heard the spy who was studying the goldwork in the long cabinet across the room catch his breath when she'd mentioned them.

She thought her best chance to flush the eavesdropper would be to leave, and not to leave any contact information with this merchant. So she told the man, "You think at what I say, you talk your friends. I come back in day, maybe two days, and if they interested, Hawk-Kin and your people meet someplace."

He nodded. "Anyplace I could reach you to let you know earlier?"

She shook her head. "Easier for me find you than for you find me."

"Well, then. I'll look forward to seeing you again." He said that mostly to her breasts, but Kait suspected he was telling it to the promise of firestones delivered without shipping costs, too.

She sauntered out into the street and heard the customer slip out the door behind her. She kept her pace jaunty and confident, but allowed herself to do a bit of gawking, the way she'd noticed most tourists did when they came to Calimekka. She didn't want to go so quickly that he lost her before he worked up his nerve to approach her.

As she was staring up at the six-story stone apartment buildings that rose above the street-level shops, and admiring the waterspouts carved in the shape of leopards and pythons, his courage fired to the catching point.

He cleared his throat and tapped her elbow. A light tap, but insistent. She had already begun to learn things about him before she turned—things that made her dislike him. He smelled of deviousness, and he walked like a thief. But when they were face-to-face, she managed a polite smile. She took in his narrowed eyes, the shiftiness of his stance, and the way his smile never revealed his teeth.

"I meet you before?" she asked him.

"We haven't been introduced. But I heard that you were looking for investors. For a trading run."

"You heard that listening, eh, but I not talking to you. No one ever telling you it not a good thing listening to people talking each other? No one ever tell you if you do then you hearing things you not like? Eh?"

"Sorry I was eavesdropping. And really, I don't think any large investor would begrudge you giving free shipping to the man who hooked you up with your major investors. That's not necessarily an everyday practice, but it isn't as uncommon as you might think. However . . ." He raised one finger and his smile broadened and became even oilier. "*How*ever, I believe that I can give you all the investors you need without you having to resort to cutting prices. If you would be willing to talk with me, I can offer more than you might imagine."

She stopped and leaned against the wall of the shop beside her. People hurried by, glancing at her and the man and then looking away. The street was packed, the noise tremendous. She waited with her arms folded tightly across her chest until a peddler hawking his tin wares had rattled by and rounded the corner. Then she said, "So, then. I sure-sure love to fill my hold and get back to sea, but you don't look like rich man to me."

She looked pointedly at his clothes, which were of fair cut and decent cloth, but nowhere near the quality of the clothing she had worn as a daughter of the House. They were painfully new. His hands were callused and bore old stains, though they were raw from scrubbing, and the nails had been carefully cleaned and manicured. He had a new and stylish haircut, something drastically different from what he had worn before; his skin was still pale on his forehead and above his ears and in a broad band across the upper half of his neck.

He was, she realized, terrifically handsome, and young, and powerfully built. But he didn't seem completely at home in his own body.

Interesting.

He smiled—again, that oily, lying smile.

"I've come into some money. And I intend to make a great deal more. But I'm especially interested in the books and artifacts you mentioned. Things from the . . . the Ancients. And I have a number of wealthy friends who would also be interested in hearing what you've found. We've decided to, ah, specialize in that area of investing."

She smiled and waited.

"Have you located a hoard? Or even a city? You have a city, don't you? One that hasn't been found by anyone else?"

She kept smiling.

"Which one?"

She waited.

He looked at her, then nodded and chuckled, and looked at his feet. "If I were sitting on an undiscovered city, I wouldn't say anything about it, either. Well enough." He returned his attention to her. "Will you arrange to meet with us? Let us make you a fair offer for your services, and a promise to pay excellent prices for your trade goods. I assure you we won't waste your time."

He fit the Dragon profile Dùghall had given her. Her shields were up, which prevented him from sensing her magic—but the same shields also prevented her from telling whether he had magic. That would be the final identifying factor, but she didn't dare use it. She would have to content herself with the fact that he was a strong, handsome young man who showed signs of having suddenly and recently come up in the world, and who had a dangerous interest in artifacts of the Ancients.

She gave him an appropriate Imumbarran bow, head ducked and

hands palm down at hip level, parallel to the ground. "Our senior traders meet with you. Give me place where I can reach you. You talk with your people, and I talk with mine. And when everyone agree, we set time for meeting."

"Your name?" he asked.

"Chait-eveni." It was the Imumbarran equivalent of the diminutive for Kait. A name she'd heard often enough to remember and respond to, thanks to visits by a multitude of Imumbarra-raised cousins, but one different enough from her real name to prevent uncomfortable connections. "And yours?"

"Domagar. Domagar Addo."

It was a field hand's name. A name with not even the slightest connection to Family, to the upper classes, to wealth or power. She said, "I will tell my partners." She got him to give her an address where she could contact him, then left as quickly as she could.

Yanth and Valard sauntered into the inn just ahead of Jaim and Trev. All four of them were grim. Ry, alone at the table, beckoned them over.

"Trouble?"

Valard waved one of the serving girls over and ordered plantain beer for all of them. When the girl left, he said, "I'd say yes. And I'd say it was trouble we could get out of if you'd take your woman and get the hell out of this city with us."

Ry looked from face to face. "What sort of trouble?"

The four of them were quiet for a moment. Then Jaim said, "We can't be sure. You're *barzanne*—we found notices posted on the doors of the Great Parnissery today, and in the slave markets. There's no mention of any of us. . . ."

"But I'm not soothed by that," Yanth said. "We made cautious inquiries after our families, hoping to at least get news of them. But none of them are in the city anymore, and no one knows where they've gone or why they left. Our family homes are empty, the belongings still inside—"

"You went *in*?" Ry couldn't believe what he was hearing. "Believing that your families were gone and knowing that if they fled Calimekka to save their lives, their homes would surely be watched, you went *in*?

You're insane, the lot of you." How fast would Imogene have her soldiers on them? He stared at the inn's front door. Men in Sabir green and silver probably already had the place surrounded; he and his friends would have to fight their way out, and they were sure to die in the process—

Yanth rolled his eyes and gave an exasperated sigh. "Of course we didn't go in. We didn't go anywhere near our old homes—we aren't madmen. But people were only too happy to tell us what they knew."

"That your families have fled Calimekka."

Jaim said, "As best anyone can tell, yes."

The darker possibility—that their families were dead—Ry left unspoken. His friends would have already considered it, and they would deal with it in their own ways. While hope remained, however, he and they would act as if the happiest outcome were also the only outcome.

Valard said, "You could take Kait with you and we could leave. Follow our families wherever they went, start a new life there. There's nothing for you here anymore—you're forsaken and cursed now, and this city is dead to you."

The shock of being *barzanne* for certain, instead of just considering the possibility of it, burrowed into Ry's gut like a knife. Taking Kait with him and leaving Calimekka would be both easiest and safest. The city could never be his home again. Nevertheless, he shook his head. "I stay. If you want to go after your families, I release you from your promises to me, and I wish you good speed and good health. But I won't take Kait from Calimekka against her wishes, and as long as she is here, I won't leave."

His friends glanced at each other and nodded, as if he only said what they expected. "I told you," Jaim said. "He'll stay here until they catch him and skin him and march him through the streets."

"Then I stay, too," Yanth said.

"And I." Trev nodded.

"I'm not going to abandon you fools here without me," Jaim said. "You wouldn't survive a week."

They all looked at Valard. "Which leaves me." He looked at the door of the inn, and Ry saw a dark, dangerous hunger flash across his face. "I want to be away from here," he said. "This isn't the city I know anymore—it's full of secrets and ghosts." He looked back at Ry and slowly smiled, but the smile couldn't erase that ominous strangeness from his eyes. "We're all friends, though," he said. "So I'll stay."

Ry said, "Thank you. We'll do what we have to do here, and find your families as soon as we dare."

And while he smiled and bought another round of beer and sat talking about the day's many failures, he watched Valard out of the corner of his eye and wondered when his old friend had become a stranger.

Chapter 28

A week to the day from Kait's meeting with Domagar Addo, the traders met with the would-be investors. Dùghall had chosen the site, and he and Kait went in early by separate routes, carefully shielded.

The Bradenberry Inn squatted at the base of Palmetto Cliff, nestled into the bones of the Galweighs' mountain, positioned directly beneath Galweigh House. As she walked up the street toward the inn, Kait looked up at her old home with both longing and regret. Galweigh House, the part built into the face of the cliff, soared toward the clouds, a gleaming white fortress sparkling with semiprecious stones and mosaics of colored glass that blazed like gemstones in the midday sun. It was an Ancients' artifact made a part of the mountain, haunted by the horrors of its past; it was a treasure house locked away above the rest of the world; it was like a beautiful woman who flaunted her riches but held herself in haughty disdain over the heads of the poor and the powerless. And if the rumors were true, it lay empty, home only to vermin and ghosts. She longed to climb up to it, to walk through its gate and enter its great hall and run through its corridors. She longed to touch its walls and call out the names of her mother and father, her brothers and sisters—and she longed to hear their voices shout her name in greeting.

But she wouldn't make that climb—only dust and the ghostly

whisper of the wind and the echoes of her voice would greet her if she dared return.

Ahead of Kait, the translucent half-arch of the Avenue of Triumph rose from the center of Celebration Square to the western end of Palmetto Cliff Road, looking like a thread spun by a spider to connect the mundane world with the magical House above. Behind her, the obsidian Path of Gods switchbacked up the cliff face, ugly and solid and imposing.

She was as close to home as she dared to get. She might never step inside Galweigh House's translucent white walls again, might never again sleep in her own bed, might never watch the sun rise through her window or reclaim her belongings. She had to assume that everything she had lost was gone forever. So she indulged herself with only that one wistful look at the white balconies stepped down the cliff face, and then she returned her attention to her task. She reached the inn and pushed through the thick, carved mahogany doors into cool dimness.

Dùghall, already in place, sat at a table near the interior arches, which framed a lovely garden. He sipped at a tankard of iced papaya beer, and nibbled at a plate of steamed maize, peppers, and Rophetian beans. He was staring out into the garden, and he didn't look in her direction when she entered. Her shields were as tight as she could hold them, so he couldn't feel her presence. He gave no sign that he was aware of her arrival.

She stood along one thick adobe wall, studying him. Eight months before, in the month of Maraxis, the two of them had been in Halles, celebrating Theramisday and preparing for her cousin Tippa's upcoming wedding. Then, Dùghall had been plump running to fat, to all appearances an amiable jester happily serving his Family by smoothing out little diplomatic difficulties. Now, on the first day of Nasdem . . .

The angle of the light coming in from the garden only accented how much he'd changed. He'd grown lean and hard. He said it was because of the work he'd done while he was waiting in the Thousand Dancers for the gods to let him know what they wanted of him. But there was more to it than that. The way he held his body made him look dangerous. Predatory. She had seen shrewdness in her uncle all her life, but never anything that made her identify him as a fellow hunter. Until now.

He'd told her that he was the sword of the gods, tempered over time and only recently unsheathed. Watching him waiting for his prey, she could believe him a good blade.

She took a seat at one of the common tables, making a space for herself among strangers. They made room for her without a word—all of them were evidently strangers to each other, as well, for everyone sat in silence, each diner carefully not touching any of the others, all eyes intently focused on the food and ale before them.

With fair promptness, one of the tavern girls came over and asked what Kait wanted to eat. She studied the listings of the day's food posted on the wall in four languages, and said, "Haunch of monkey, blood-rare, no spices. House beer. Sweet yams."

The girl said, "Cook's got a good parrot broth today."

"No."

"Got fresh cane-and-nut tarts, hot out of the oven."

"Large or small?"

"About so." The girl made a smallish circle with both hands.

"Two, then."

"Anything else?"

"No."

Kait had positioned herself to face the entryway, far enough behind one of the columns that she would be hard to spot. In preparation for this meeting, she'd bleached her hair to a pale yellow, and traded her gaudy Imumbarran trader garb for the breeches and light shirt appropriate for a woman working in a shop. She had bathed in nabolth and verroot, which would, at least for a while, hide her Karnee scent—Ry had warned her that his Family had a number of Karnee members, and since Dùghall believed that the Families and the parnissery were the two segments of society most likely to have been infiltrated by the Dragons, she had taken the step of disguising her own affliction. Her shield would hide her Karnee magic from any wizards. She had gone to some trouble to make herself look plain and dowdy, so that any men who might notice her in spite of her shield wouldn't react to her as they otherwise did. By shield, appearance, and movements, she said, *I'm no one of importance. Ignore me.*

Two diners at her table rose and left. Another entered the inn, squinted into the darkness, and sauntered over. He settled himself beside her, glanced at her once, dismissed her, and began reading the posted menu.

Her food came. She ate, taking her time. If necessary, she could nurse the tankard, or even order another, but she didn't want to be obvious in her loitering.

Across the room, Dùghall emptied his drink onto the sawdust floor so quickly she almost missed it, and would have if she hadn't known what he was doing. He then pretended to take a few more long draughts from the tankard. And then he shouted for more. When the tavern girl brought it to him, he tried to pinch her. He was loud and jolly and rude—clearly on his way to a memorable drunk. He resumed his silence when the girl left, and buried his face in his tankard, and again seemed to disappear.

The doors swung open again, and Hasmal and Ian entered, both wearing Hmoth trade garb. Dùghall had made them the designated head traders because no one in Calimekka would know Hasmal, and those who might recognize Ian were unlikely to be in the heart of the city so far from the docks, and were even more unlikely to acknowledge him if they did see him. Ian said his fellow smugglers were, by necessity, a circumspect lot.

Hasmal and Ian requested a cleared private table, explaining to the tavern girl that they needed to conduct business while they ate, telling her in loud voices that they had important friends coming. Kait saw money change hands, and the girl went to work creating a private table. Moments later, when Domagar Addo and his two companions arrived, both Ian and Hasmal were seated in isolated glory beneath an arch, their table half in the inn proper and half in the garden. Kait couldn't have chosen a more perfect spot for spying on them.

Hasmal rose and waved to Domagar and his friends, and the three investors strolled through the press of tables to the cleared space. "Greetings, noble Parats, most excellent Parata," he said. He pressed his hands together, touched fingertips to his chin, and executed the step-and-duck bow of the Hmoth wellborn. "I am Ashtaran, second son of Dashat, of the White Fox Village. This is my chief partner, Ibnak, third son of Muban, of the Storm Bear Village." Ian bowed in flawless imitation of Hasmal. He had bleached his hair, too, and had had it cut in the same style as Hasmal's. With both of them decked out in the flowing tunics, baggy pantaloons, and wildly patterned sashes of the Hmoth, the fact that one of them was tall, lean, and dark and the other was short, pale, and powerfully built became almost invisible.

The man beside Kait watched the five of them, and said, "More money at that table right now than in the rest of this inn put together. Probably more than in the rest of the street. Rich bastards."

He was talking more about the investors than about Hasmal and Ian, she decided. The investors wore their wealth as plainly as they could. One of them was a Galweigh by birth—Kait knew her as Cousin Grita, one of the second cousins on her father's side, and a member of the trade branch of the Family. She and Grita weren't friends, but Grita would certainly have recognized Kait's face. However, Grita wasn't wearing Galweigh red and black. Instead, she wore a fine pale blue skirt of embroidered silk and a blue and white tunic over a blouse woven entirely of the Galweigh Rose-and-Thorn lace . . . but the lace, which should have been black, had instead been bleached, then dyed a deep cobalt blue. She still wore her Galweigh rubies and onyxes, and the Galweigh crest was clearly visible on the pommel of her dagger. Her hair was bound back in a simple twist and held with a heavy gold pin worked in the shape of a tiny jeweled hummingbird. She still smelled like herself, but she moved like a complete stranger.

Beside her stood a Sabir, a golden-haired man of lovely countenance and dangerous aura, whose elegant silver and green tights showed off the fine lines of his legs. His low boots were heeled in silver, and his casually tied emerald silk shirt was so sheer that Kait could make out every muscle in his overdeveloped torso. He kept a hand at the small of Grita's back, and occasionally ran a finger down her spine in a gesture that was both sensual and possessive. Kait couldn't imagine Grita tolerating the touch of a Sabir. Grita had lost a brother and a father to Sabir depredations years earlier, and she had never forgiven or forgotten, and Kait was sure she never would. But when the man touched her, Grita smiled up at him and kissed a fingertip and pressed it to his cheek. That alone would have convinced Kait that she was seeing Dragons.

Dùghall had suggested the Dragons might be wearing familiar forms. She hadn't imagined how familiar.

The Sabir was more than just a Dragon, though. He was Karnee. Kait could smell the scent that marked pending Shift on him, dark and rich and earthy. She tightened her shields and prayed that her perfumed bath would mask her body's instinctive response. All the other scents in the room grew faint next to that tantalizing musk.

Breathing hard, she picked up the monkey leg and tore meat off it with her teeth. Focus, she thought. Focus.

"You all right?" the man next to her asked.

"Mmmph." She nodded a quick affirmative and gave the stranger no other response.

Finding no encouragement for his familiarities, he turned to the man who sat to his other side and said, "You ever go to the games?"

The stranger regarded the man warily, then broke into a cautious smile. "Oh, sure. Saw the challenge between Hariman's Long-Legs and Lucky Ober's Hero-of-Hills just last night." He had a hint of some outlander accent—surely the only reason he would talk at table with a stranger. Damned barbarians.

"Make anything?"

"A bit of copper passed my fingers." Laughter. "But never in the right direction. You?"

Kait blocked out the conversation, wishing bolts on the tongues of both the chatterers, and returned her attention to her work.

The third investor was Domagar Addo, but he no longer looked like a farmer dressed up for worship. His clothes were as rich as those worn by his two associates, and a gold headdress with a tail of horn-bird feathers cleverly disguised the last traces of unevenness in the skin color on his forehead and neck. Rings covered his hands, which still bore heavy scars of a life spent working. Before too long, though, Kait thought even those scars would vanish. Then only his name would betray him as someone who had risen from poverty. And new names were easy enough to win. Or buy.

The blond man nodded at the bows, and said, "I'm Crispin Sabir of the Sabir Family. This is Grita Jeral of . . . House Ballur. Ballur is a new Family in Calimekka, eager to expand its contacts and its wealth. And this is Domagar Addo, with whom your other partner made our appointment. Where is she, by the way?"

Ian sniffed, his face displaying annoyance. "Chait-eveni is an *employee,* not a partner. She sometimes reaches above herself, and implies that she is more than she is . . . which is why she is unlikely to ever truly *be* a partner." He chuckled. "She has the employee mind, if you know what I mean; she wants what others have but she does not want to earn it herself."

Hasmal shrugged and smiled and spread his arms wide. "Enough unhappiness. This is a happy occasion. We meet as potential partners; we should become friends. So, sit and eat at our table, and we will treat you, and you will tell us how we can become your friends, and how we can bring you happiness."

"How you can bring us happiness." Crispin Sabir sat opposite Hasmal, with Grita beside him, and Domagar beside her. Perfect for Kait, because all three of them had their backs to her. Not so good for Dùghall; he sat facing all three of them. And as ambassador to the Imumbarra Isles, and the main negotiator for the wealth that flowed from the Isles to the House, his face would certainly be familiar to Grita. Well, his younger, fatter face. Perhaps—if there were any part of Grita's mind or memories left in her flesh—she wouldn't recognize him in this harder, older body. Crispin said, "What we want are Ancients' artifacts. Any of the books or manuscripts that you might find would be useful, too, of course, but there are *technothaumatars* . . . er . . ." He flushed and faltered, the alien word hanging in the air like a public fart. A Dragon's revealing slip—but only revealing to someone who knew that technothaumatars was the word the Ancients had used for their magical artifacts. He covered his slip as quickly as he could. "There are Ancients' devices we've researched that we would love to acquire."

"We're capable of paying," Grita said. "We have the full support of the most powerful House in Ibera behind us, and the backing of Families both old and new."

Both Hasmal and Ian sat like polite idiots, smiling and waiting, oblivious by all appearances to the huge slip they'd just witnessed.

"Ah, yes. Families. Forgive me, please, but I was noticing your crests," Hasmal said. He did a neat job of changing the subject. "In my dealings in Ibera, I have always thought that Sabir and Galweigh did not do business together, and I heard in this last visit that Galweigh House was no more. But unless I am mistaken, she is Galweigh. You clearly are Sabir. Aren't you enemies?"

"She *was* Galweigh. She *is* Ballur. She made an alliance with Sabir House when Galweigh House fell—she and a few others," Crispin said. "We have discovered common ground, though, and common interests."

"Common ground? In broken toys from the Ages of the Damned, eh?" Ian laughed.

Crispin tipped his head, curious, and said to Ian, "You know, I think that I know you."

Kait felt a sudden rush of horror. She'd forgotten that Ry and his lieutenants were not the only ones to grow up in Sabir House. Ian, too, had spent some of his childhood there. Ian, the illegitimate son of Ry's father, would be as closely related to the Sabir across the table from him as his half-brother was. And Ian certainly knew the man who had introduced himself as Crispin. When she and Dùghall and Hasmal had been figuring out how to meet with the investors, she'd recommended Ian as one of the negotiators. But she'd only considered his years of exile and his years on the sea, and had been certain Ian would be safe acting as a trader in the heart of Calimekka. The thought that he might meet up with someone who had known him as a child, or that the person he met might recognize him, had never crossed her mind.

Evidently it had crossed his, though, for Ian's reply was casual. "You might have. I am a great traveler, and I seek out such amusements as our ports of call offer. If you also enjoy the offerings of this city . . ." He held his palms up and offered a self-deprecating smile. "My weakness."

Crispin shrugged. "Perhaps. In any case, our alliance is about much more than the lost trinkets of a dead age. We intend to create a new Calimekka. A glorious city overflowing with riches, ruled in harmony; a city that can embrace the world and reshape it into a place without wars, without disease, without suffering."

Ian's eyebrows rose. "The three of you? Ambitious."

Crispin, Grita, and Domagar looked at each other, and Grita said, "We have others who share our dream. And we've had these goals for a long time. But we have only just been able to come together to begin bringing them to life."

"And you need our help."

"We desire certain works of the Ancients that would make our task easier. If you can supply them, then yes, we need your help."

Ian said, "We can add to your happiness greatly, dear new friends. But you must know that the places we have to go to get for you what you ask of us are dangerous places. They lie within the Scarred Lands, where few venture and fewer survive, and where all manner of monsters make their homes, and where even the earth and the air conspire against the human state of true men. We would need much assistance to fuel our courage. . . ."

"We weren't looking for charity from you. If your goal is wealth, we'll see that you achieve it in quantities you cannot imagine. If you want friends in powerful places who can do good things for you, well, help us and you'll have them." He looked straight at Ian. "Amusements . . . hmmm. I can assure you that we can share amusements with you grander than any you've ever known."

They dickered back and forth about price then. The Dragons passed their wish list of artifacts to Hasmal. Kait kept her head down and her ears open, and started on the first of her tarts, savoring each bite.

She sipped her ale.

The negotiators agreed on a price for the outfitting of the expedition.

The talkative man seated beside her began regaling the man beside him with a blow-by-blow account of a challenge that had taken place a week before. His loud tones got louder, and drowned out much of what was being said by the Dragons, even to her inhumanly sensitive ears.

She took tiny sips of her ale, stretching out her meal as much as she could without being obvious about it. Hurry up, she thought, but she didn't allow her body to display any of the impatience her mind felt.

Then it began.

Dùghall shouted to one of the tavern girls, his accent heavy, his words slurred by drunkenness. "Girlie! Hey. You wit' the honkin' big jugs. Bring me s'more ale!"

One of the girls hurried to his side, shaking her head. She murmured something, and his face twisted with rage.

"Whatcha mean I've had enough? I got money. I can pay, damn you!" He lurched to his feet and stared at her wildly, his mouth gaping, his clothes disarranged, his face flushed. He slapped a coin on the table and said, "See! I got the money. Bring me some more goddamned ale!"

She shook her head again. Murmured something intended to be calming, in a low voice. Rested a hand lightly on his arm.

The majority of the people in the room were watching the scene by then.

"No? *No!*" He made a grab for her, and she jumped out of his way. He lunged again. "I'm thirsty! A thirsty man with money deserves another drink!"

"You need to leave now," the girl said, this time loudly enough that everyone could hear.

At the taps, the barkeep had already fished out his peacemaker— a large cudgel with a brass-bound head—and was moving calmly toward the cause of the disturbance.

Dùghall stood there for a moment, swaying as heavily as a tree in a gale. Then he launched himself at the girl again, and missed. He staggered, and veered wildly to his right, and tripped on the leg of a chair, and fell into Crispin Sabir. He toppled to the floor, and lay cursing loudly. Then he grabbed the bench seat upon which the three investors sat, pawed Grita's back, and as he pulled himself to his feet, slapped Domagar on the shoulder with beery camaraderie. He said, "Pigballs. *You* know a man deserves a drink when he's thirsty, don't you? Hells-all! I'll sit wit' you people an' buy you all drinks, and they can bring me a goddamn drink, too."

Kait waited for Crispin or Grita to demand that Dùghall be killed. They would be within their rights, being Family, and touched by one who was *not* Family without having given their permission. Dùghall was ready, too. But the two of them only looked at each other while the rest of those in the inn held their breath, waiting for the explosion.

It didn't come.

The tavern girls and the barkeep were on him by that time, though. "Have you anything you want us to do with him, Parat? Parata?" the bouncer asked.

"Send him on his way," Grita said.

Not a first for Family—Kait had been bumped on occasion and had never requested punishment for the poor cowering person shuddering at her feet, and she knew of other Family members who had also waived their privileges for the goodwill that it won them. But many didn't, and this act of forbearance won a round of applause from the inn's diners and staff.

The bouncer and two of the tavern girls dragged kicking, swearing Dùghall to the front door and launched him out. Kait could hear him raging at them until the doors swung shut. The noise died and the inn returned to relative calm.

Hasmal and Ian rose, apologizing profusely for the incident, for their poor choice of eating places, for their shame in exposing their guests, even unintentionally, to such appalling behavior. They bowed, cringed, and even mentioned a discount on their price—though only a small one—as a way of making amends.

"You have no need for shame or guilt," Grita said. "Such men are everywhere. But they won't be once we've made things better."

Kait's eyebrows rose when she heard that. She wondered how the Dragons intended to rid the city of drunks.

Hasmal called their tavern girl over and said he wanted to pay, telling her how displeased he was with the atmosphere provided by an inn he had only heard praised, and how poorly his guests had been treated. The girl grew flustered and called the owner out from the back. He looked at the people the drunk had been pawing, paled, and told them that not only was the meal they were eating free, but that he begged them to return on any other occasion for complimentary service.

Interesting way to get free food, Kait thought.

Hasmal waited until the innkeeper had gone back to his office. Then he told the Dragons, "We know what to look for. We'll check our warehouse to see if we have any of the artifacts you seek in our possession yet. And we'll notify our other partners that they should also watch their stores and shipments for these things. In return, you'll have your messenger bring your investment money to our ship three weeks from today. No sooner, no later. Once we receive the money, we'll finish outfitting for the trip out."

"Why can't you leave sooner?" Crispin asked.

Hasmal said, "We have business to attend to in the city. I assure you we'll work as quickly as we can, but some dates are unchangeable. We'll be ready to begin outfitting in three weeks, and our ship will be back in the same length of time."

"Your ship isn't *here?*"

"No," Ian said. "It's taking the rest of our cargo to Costan Selvira. It will be here when we need it."

The three Dragons looked at each other and nodded.

Hasmal said, "I must ask you—do you have other traders who are also searching for the same things?"

The three Dragons looked at each other again.

"Yes," Crispin said. "Is that a problem?"

"Do you agree to buy the artifacts we bring back, even if some other trader has already brought you similar artifacts?"

Crispin nodded. "If you find duplicates of any of the things on our list, acquire all of them. We'll pay our agreed-on price for every one you can get."

"That, then, is all the assurance we need."

In Hmoth fashion, Hasmal kissed the backs of his hands, then pressed them to the top of his head while bowing. Ian followed suit.

After the briefest of pauses, Crispin copied the Hmoth parting salute. Domagar also imitated it. Grita turned and, smiling, stepped over the bench. She turned back to face the two faux Hmoth traders, kissed the back of one hand and pressed it to her forehead, and at the same time tucked her right foot behind her left one and bent both knees sharply. *"Tah heh hmer,"* she said. It was in Hmago, the Hmoth tongue, and it meant, "Walk in goodness." The feminine version of the salute, and nicely executed.

Kait, picking at the last of her tart and watching the exchange through the fringe of her eyelashes, experienced a transitory flash of pride in her cousin's grasp of the Hmoth customs. The Galweighs required all their young people entering the trade and diplomatic branches of the Family to take classes on customs, cultures, and languages. Those classes were grueling. But like Grita, Kait could have done the salute in her sleep.

"*Tah heh entho nohmara,*" Hasmal and Ian responded. "In goodness breathe forever."

The blessing given, the Dragons headed for the door, Domagar glanced over at her table briefly, and for just an instant their eyes met. She almost panicked. Then she remembered that she was shielded, and that her shield would keep him from noticing her even though he could see her. She relaxed and looked down at her food, and when she glanced up again, all the Dragons were gone. Ian and Hasmal left a sizable tip for the tavern girl. Then they, too, left.

She realized the chatty man had been watching them as they walked out the door. The instant the door closed behind them, he stopped his conversation in midsentence, rose, and walked out after them, leaving food uneaten on the table and a stack of bronze coins in the middle of his plate to pay his bill.

Kait almost laughed. Him, eh? She should have known immediately. She had, after all, picked the perfect spot for spying on the room. What was perfect for her turned out to be perfect for another secret observer. Her fellow spy pretended to be rudely interested in everything but the table. A bit different from her method, but effective.

She didn't go after him immediately. She waited; after all, she had the benefit of knowing where Hasmal and Ian were going. They had agreed to amble when they left the inn. She would travel parallel to them, taking the inside track they'd planned in advance, and moving faster. When she picked them up a block before their destination, she would fall in and follow their follower back to *his* lair. She wanted to be sure, though, that the Dragons didn't have another tier of watchers waiting to see if someone like her was keeping track of their spy.

Those levels of paranoia could nest indefinitely—followers of followers, spies spying on the spies who spied on spies. But one of the three Dragons had made a slight gesture toward a table across the room as they left, and Kait had seen one of the two men at that table nod acknowledgment. So Kait waited. She had a little time, and she wanted to know what they were up to back there in the darkness.

When no one followed the Dragons out of the inn, both of them rose and walked toward the front door. "Home, or watch their backs, then?" the one said.

"Watch their backs. I didn't see anyone, but they might have been waiting outside."

So they'd been planted to find anyone who was following the Dragons. Kait's job, but in reverse.

She smiled. They were going to fail. Dùghall had planted telltales on Grita, Crispin, and Domagar when he fell. The telltales were tiny Falcon talismans that he'd made and shielded—when they touched the skin of their targets, they were absorbed, and for the next week— or two—they would connect the three Dragons to three viewing glasses that Dùghall had fashioned. Ry and his lieutenants could watch the glasses, see where their targets were going, and trail them without ever coming near them. Their targets would lead them to the Mirror—or to people who *would* lead them to the Mirror. Either way, they moved closer to their objective. And neither the Dragons nor the people they'd hired to guard them would know that they were being watched. Not even magic would betray the presence of the talismans—created with only the energy of their creator, formed with pure intent to cause neither pain nor harm but merely to report their location and surroundings, they would leave no trace of their presence for even the most sensitive of observers.

Kait handed a bronze coin to the tavern girl as a tip and strolled out of the doors. She turned left, heading for Three Monkey Road and the Furmian Quarter down by the harbor. The air smelled especially sweet, the sun welcomed and comforted, the whole of the world offered her a joyous embrace. She was on the hunt, and her heart beat faster and her breath came quicker and life felt better than it did at any other time.

She caught up with Ian and Hasmal near the harbor, as they were entering the Merry Captain, which was a hostel frequented by well-off travelers and seamen from some of the richer ships. She spotted her target leaning against the wall across the street from them. She found her own hiding place and watched him. The spy waited until they were inside, then crossed the street, stepped into the Merry Captain, and moments later came back out, a satisfied smile on his face. So he'd checked to see that they were registered there, and had discovered that they were. A room had also been reserved there for Kait, in the name of Chait-eveni, in case the spy had the presence of mind to ask after her. She had never been in her room and never would be, but it was there all the same. Paid through the next three weeks.

He scurried right by her, head up but eyes forward instead of searching the crowd. He never caught a glimpse of her. She fell in behind him, staying well back. He was clearly in a hurry, but she kept pace while still managing to appear that *she* wasn't hurrying. Longer steps, a slower stride, and a studied air of relaxed interest in everything that went on around her.

He led her by the shortest route straight to the gates of Sabir House. He gave his name and was promptly admitted. She decided to wait for a while, mingling with the street vendors that sold their wares just outside the gates and with the customers that bought them. Maybe he would come back out again and she could track him further, to a place that would tell her something she hadn't already known—because now she knew only what she had known all her life: Trouble came from Sabir House.

anya fought back the scream. Pain turned the world red; she closed her eyes tightly and locked her muscles and held her breath, but that only made it worse. The baby felt like it was ripping its way out of her with teeth and claws, fighting to birth itself. She could see the little animal in her mind. It would be a monster like her, scaly, with a mouth full of fangs, with hideous spikes at its joints—a nightmare, a beast that would devour her entrails, then claw her belly open and swallow the two midwives who crouched beside her, holding her back up and helping her to squat.

"Gathalorra," one of the midwives shouted to Danya, "you must not fight the birthing. Breathe, and let the baby come. Shejhan, pull her forward. She's leaning too much on her tail and it's blocking her." The senior midwife, whose name was Aykree, turned away from Danya and did something at the hearth. She said, "I'm making a steaming potion for you that will ease your labor. It will be ready in a few moments, and then the pain will not be so severe."

The pains had started two stations earlier. Danya, prepared by the midwives for what would happen, had not been frightened. They'd told her she would hurt, and she had hurt. They'd told her that her belly would tighten, and it had tightened. They'd shown her how to breathe, and they'd taught her the mind exercises they used to control pain, and she had used them, and she thought she was doing well.

The pain had been bad, but not as bad as the torture of the Sabirs; she had controlled it, and she had been proud.

But in the last half a station it had gotten worse. She hadn't been able to keep it under control. She had cried out, had wept, had growled and begged for relief. And now—

Now she hoped only that she would die quickly, before the monster inside exploded out of her, flinging the tattered remains of her body in all directions. She prayed for quick death, but the gods who had abandoned her to the Sabir Wolves did not listen to these prayers, either. She sobbed and shouted and swore, and the pain battered her, then receded briefly, then battered her again, each time getting worse, each time leaving her more frantic and more frightened and more hopeless. It would not quit, and she could not make it quit, and the only way to be through with it was to have the baby. And now she knew that having the baby would kill her. Nothing survivable could hurt so much.

The touches of a thousand strangers reached inside her head and tried to offer her comfort, tried to assure her that she would survive and that her baby would be special and that she was not alone—but they were the same strangers who had bound their spirits to the damned unborn creature months earlier, and who had tried to invade *her* mind as well with their false kindness and their platitudes. She'd shielded herself away from them, but now she was too weak and in too much pain to maintain a shield. So they were all over her.

The midwives were doing something that she couldn't see. They were rattling things, and poking at a fire. She could hear water boiling.

Then Aykree was at her side. She sounded like she was speaking through a tunnel when she said, "That contraction has stopped. I want you to move on your hands and knees, and put your face near this." Aykree and Shejhan pulled Danya onto her knees and dragged her face toward a steaming cauldron that they'd moved onto the board floor in front of her. The steam stank of herbs and rotted meat and the bitter musk of civets. "Breathe deeply," Aykree said. They draped a blanket over her head and the cauldron, and the steam filled her nostrils and she gagged.

"Keep breathing it. It numbs the pain."

Abruptly, she vomited, which left her feeling better. She inhaled more of the steam, and her anguish receded a bit further. So she sucked in the stinking steam greedily, and felt a delicious lassitude invade her entire body. She started to let herself fall backward, but the two midwives pulled her onto all fours again. "Don't quit. Keep breathing it. Deep. Deep! Deep breaths."

Deep breaths? Why? The pain was gone. She didn't want to expend the effort. She suddenly felt wonderful—her mind was clear of the red haze of pain, and her muscles no longer fought against each other. She didn't need any more of the wonderful steam.

"Did we give it to her too soon?" Shejhan asked. She sounded like she was half a world away. "Did we stop her labor?"

"No. She'll keep going. This will just relax her enough that she'll leave off fighting her own body and let the child be born."

Then the next labor pain began. That ripping, tearing anguish started at the top of her belly and seared its way downward, and she sucked in the steam with the desperation of a drowning woman offered air. She wanted to yell again, but she couldn't do that and draw the steam into her lungs at the same time. She gasped, and trembled, and only at the height of the contraction, when the pain overwhelmed even the numbing drug she breathed, did she cry out.

Then that contraction subsided, and once again she felt good.

"How close is the baby?" Aykree asked.

Danya listened with disconnected interest; she felt as if the two midwives were discussing someone she might have known once. Shejhan said, "I can see the top of the head. We have to tie Gathalorra's tail out of the way, though, or I'll never be able to guide the baby out. She nearly killed me with it that time, thrashing the way she was. Here . . ."

Danya felt her tail being lifted and bound to the central post of the house.

They could see the head? Interesting. She wondered what it looked like.

"Have her push with the next one," Shejhan said. "She's ready."

And Aykree leaned under the blanket and said, "With the next pain, hold your breath and bear down. It's time for the baby to come out."

Well, that was good. She still vaguely recalled that once the baby came out this ordeal would be over. She tried to imagine what that would be like, but she couldn't. She had been like this forever.

She could form one question coherently, though. "Will it hurt worse?"

"Gathalorra, when you have come this far, pushing feels better than not pushing. You're ready, and if you let it, your body will take care of you," the midwife said.

Then the pain slammed into her again, and the blissful haze in which she'd basked ripped away. Once again the world was real and harsh and drenched in red. Aykree said, "Now. Hold your breath and push the baby out. Push. Push!"

She closed her eyes, and tensed her belly, and pushed against the agony of being ripped apart. Things shifted inside of her. The unborn monster moved. She could feel her progress suddenly. She could feel her burden growing less.

"Good! Good! Harder!"

She gasped, took another quick breath, held it, pushed again. She was winning. She was getting rid of the thing.

The pain exploded without warning; ten times—a *hundred* times—worse than it had been before. She collapsed forward onto her elbows and screamed and flailed and wept, and heard something else begin to wail as well.

She became aware of the midwives shouting at her—yelling above her screaming. "You're almost done! Gathalorra! *Gathalorra!* Listen! The head is out. Push again and you'll be finished!"

The unbearable urge to push was building inside her, unstoppable, inescapable, and all she could feel was mute, anguished astonishment. Again? She had to do that *again*?

She couldn't . . . and yet, the next contraction hit, and she did. More pain—pain so terrible it seared and enveloped and overwhelmed. Then, as suddenly as it had overtaken her, it was gone, and the most wonderful feeling of warmth flooded her body. No pain. No pushing. No red haze. She was still alive, while in the background, even the thin, ragged wail ceased.

Silence.

Release.

Shejhan said, "You have a boy-child." She sounded doubtful.

Danya didn't care whether she had a dog-child. She was done. Done. She was freed of the thing that had invaded her body. She could hear its cry begin again—fragile, punctuated, but stronger. She wanted them to take the little beast away, but instead they were rolling her onto her back, onto cushions on the floor, and propping her up, and pressing the thing into her arms and against her chest.

She stared at it, and time stopped. The baby moved in her arms, stopped crying, and stared at her gravely. Her baby. *Her* baby.

Not it. Him.

She stared at him.

The world held its breath, and sounds, only loosely bound by gravity, spun away. In the silence, she stared into her son's eyes, and he stared into hers. He wriggled, blinked, blinked again.

Not a monster at all.

Not like her. No claws, no scales, no spikes, no teeth.

She felt swallowed tears burning their way down the back of her throat; her vision blurred as her eyes filled with water.

Her son. Her *human* son.

His bottomless blue eyes regarded her intently; his soft rosebud mouth made a tiny round soundless O. He had five tiny fingers on each hand, five tiny toes on each foot, a soft body with perfect legs and perfect arms. A perfect human baby, and he was hers. The Sabirs had twisted her, they had twisted everything about her, but they had not managed to twist her son.

She gently pressed one scaled, taloned finger into the palm of his hand and his fingers wrapped around it. He held on to her tightly and looked into her soul, and his love, the love she'd fought off and denied throughout her pregnancy, overwhelmed her. He was her gift. He was her reward for all the suffering she had endured. He was wonderful.

She put him to the nipple that protruded from her scaled breast, and he sucked. While he sucked, he looked at her. His free hand clenched and unclenched, but with his other hand, he held on to her finger.

Shejhan said, "He doesn't have any scales. Or any tail. Or claws. He looks . . . tender. Will he get them later?"

"No." Danya ran the back of a finger gently over his smooth, damp cheek. "No scales. No claws. No tail." She looked up. "Can you bring me a blanket for him? Please?"

She could see the length and delicacy of her hands—her hands as they had once been—duplicated in his. She could see in the roundness and the slight upward slant of his eyes her own eyes as they had looked the last time she admired herself in a mirror in Galweigh House.

She held him gingerly, afraid that her scaly skin might scratch him, or that she might accidentally injure him with her claws. But she wouldn't. She couldn't. He was more magical than anything she had ever seen or known. How could she have thought she hated him? How could she have wanted to be rid of him?

Some part of her deep inside looked at him with jealousy. He was human, after all, the one thing she wished to be and could never be again. Human.

But the rest of her mind said, *He's mine. My son. My beautiful son.*

In the back of her mind, a voice that did not belong to her began to whisper, *Danya? Can you still hear me? Are you listening?*

Luercas. She hadn't heard from him since she had gotten too ungainly to make her way across the river to In-kanmerea, the secret House of the Devil Ghosts he'd led her to—the only place where she could talk to him without being overheard by the spirits that would not leave her and her baby alone.

I can hear you. She spoke to him in her mind, not wanting to speak out loud with the midwives watching.

Luercas sounded pleased. *You did well, Danya. He's an excellent infant. Much better than I had expected. He'll do nicely. Very nicely.*

Danya accepted the compliment without comment. She was surprised that she wasn't happier to hear from the spirit who had saved her life. She hid her mixed feelings as best she could, not wanting to offend him, and said, *I'm glad you're back. I've missed you. I was afraid you had abandoned me.*

You're my friend. You're my window to the world of the living. And I've missed you, too, all this time that I couldn't talk with you. But I won't abandon you, Danya. I'll never abandon you.

No. He wouldn't. He would be with her always. He would take

care of her, keep her safe, and eventually help her get her revenge on the Sabirs and the Galweighs, and on the world that had destroyed her. She knew this—knew it with bone-deep certainty. She should be delighted to hear his calm voice speaking into her mind again. She *should* be.

I know you're my friend. She stared down at the baby in her arms, the lovely baby that she hadn't wanted, and blocked out her reservations about Luercas. *Isn't he marvelous?*

Luercas said fervently, *He's the most beautiful thing I've ever seen.*

Chapter 30

Ry crouched over the viewing glass Dùghall had fashioned, watching his cousin Crispin moving through Sabir House as if he were the paraglese of it and not a minor Wolf in the hierarchy. He could see that the other Wolves gave Crispin deference—at least to his face—and that their expressions twisted with fear and distaste as he moved past them.

What had happened in the House while he was gone? What could have placed Crispin into a position of authority? Why would any Wolf bend a knee at Crispin's passing, or press fingers to heart?

Bitter, evil changes had taken place; Ry knew it. But he couldn't imagine how they could have come to pass. His cousin Crispin had become a Dragon, or was possessed by a Dragon, or was working in tandem with a Dragon—Dùghall hadn't been able to determine what happened to the host soul when the Mirror of Souls inserted the Dragon soul into the host body. But after Ry had carefully laid out the scene of his own murder in his room, and had left clues blaming Crispin and his brother Anwyn and their crony and cousin Andrew, Crispin should have been disowned, and executed in Punishment Square long before a Dragon had the chance to possess his body.

Dùghall stood behind him. "Have you seen it yet?"

Ry stretched, and felt a dozen points along his spine pop. He looked up at Dùghall, who remained obsessed with the Mirror. The damned Mirror that had betrayed him and his men and Kait, that had drawn his cousins and trouble after them, that had almost gotten all of them killed. He wished he'd refused to let Kait bring the accursed artifact aboard the ship when he rescued her. Or that he'd found a way to throw it into the sea before they ever neared Calimekka. Then they wouldn't be sitting and staring at little pieces of spelled glass, hoping to find a way to undo whatever bizarre damage the Mirror had done.

"No," he growled. "I haven't seen it yet."

For love of Kait, he had allowed himself to suffer under the thumb of her uncle. Do this, Ry. Have your men do that. Go here. Watch there. And he suffered without protest Dùghall's unspoken opinion that he and his men were inferior because they were Sabirs. He tolerated the distaste and distrust and dislike.

Actually, he *shared* the distaste and distrust and dislike. He couldn't give himself too much credit for his tolerance, because he didn't like Dùghall any better than Dùghall liked him.

But in spite of everything he was doing to win her over, Kait refused to move past the boundaries of polite distance that she'd built between them. They were bound to each other, powerfully and inexplicably; he could sense her trotting through the city at that moment, tracing one of his Family's servants through Calimekka's back streets. He was with her as if he rode inside her head. When he was in the same room with her, he could feel her bare skin against his even though a hundred people stood between them. In his bed at night he could taste her lips pressed to his, though she had never kissed him; when he closed his eyes he could feel her dancing naked against his body—dancing beneath the moon. And when he managed to look into her eyes, he knew she felt what he felt, as fully and vividly and inescapably as he did. Yet she wouldn't come to him. She wouldn't touch him. She wouldn't give in to the passion that rode them both. She would not accept Ian's offers of companionship and she avoided his embraces, but she avoided Ry's attempts to charm and tempt her, too.

She was as celibate as a novice parnissa; Ry passed her in the morning as she knelt in meditation, practicing the silent, traceless magic her uncle and Hasmal had taught her. While meditating, she became invisible to him behind her shields. When she did, he felt that she was cutting away a part of his soul.

Ry kept staring at the glass while he said nothing, and Dùghall took the hint. He wandered over to see if Jaim, working his shift on the glass linked to the Galweigh woman, had anything to report.

In the viewing glass, Crispin strode toward the center of the Wolves' domain. He moved purposefully down the corridor that led to the White Hall, between the rows of arches filled with harlequin-patterned stained glass, and at last into the hall itself. He was alone in there. Alone with the incised pattern on the floor, the Trail of Spirits. Alone with the solid gold sacrificial pillar.

And there it was. The gods' damned Mirror of Souls sat in front of the pillar like an altar before an idol.

Ry suppressed a shudder. He hated going anywhere near the White Hall. At the best of times, the unhappy spirits of the sacrificed dead cried out from the walls for release.

"Here it is," he said, and instantly Dùghall was across the room and on his knees beside him, peering into the murky glass.

"Which of those things is it?"

Ry had forgotten that Dùghall had never seen the Mirror. He pointed it out from the other artifacts that sat in the hall. "The flower-shaped artifact on the pedestal. The last time I saw it, it had light rising up through the central stem and pooling in the middle of the petals. Now it looks . . . dead."

Dùghall didn't breathe for the longest time. He seemed frozen in place, rigid, with his eyes locked on the shifting image. Ry felt a change in the air around him, a sense of leashed power moving through the universe's currents. Dùghall was doing something with that silent magic of his, but Ry couldn't begin to guess what. Then, as Crispin left the room, the Mirror disappeared from view, and Dùghall pulled back with a sigh.

"Ah. Clever. Incredibly clever. They did so much with simple spells. . . ." Dùghall rose and started to walk away.

"Wait," Ry said. The old bastard *lived* to be enigmatic, but Ry didn't have the patience to let him. Not after crouching over the viewing glass until his feet went numb and his back muscles burned. "You mean to tell me that by looking at the artifact for just that short time, you can not only tell what it does but how it works? And what spells the Dragons used to power it?"

"To some extent. I can tell the basics. Magical success, at least success gained at the expense of others, leaves tracks. If you had been taught an acceptable form of magic, and had studied it diligently, you could have looked at the success of what the Ancients' Dragons did to create the artifact, and followed their tracks to the same conclusions."

Ry rose to his feet, ignoring the blatant insult to his scholarship and his form of magic. He glared down at the old man. "If that were true, Hasmal would have known what the Mirror did. He's one of your people."

"He's one of my people in that he was raised a Falcon by his father, who is also a Falcon." Dùghall crossed his arms over his chest and smiled. "But Hasmal was anything but a diligent student. He learned what his father taught him because it was expected of him, and because he was a dutiful son. But one does not get inspired scholarship from dutiful sons. Inspired scholarship only comes from passion."

Ry waited for him to say something else, but the old man would play his games. "What?" Ry snapped at last.

Dùghall chuckled, apparently surprised by the annoyance in Ry's voice. He shook his head, and Ry felt the unbearable urge to Shift and rip the old goat's throat out with his teeth. He didn't—as much out of healthy fear for the old man's magical ability as out of love for Kait.

At last Dùghall answered him. "Though to the untrained eye the Mirror of Souls doesn't appear to be doing anything at the moment, it's feeding off the life forces of most of the people in this city in order to run itself. I won't be party to bringing another such evil into the world. But I believe I see a way to create a small reverse of the Mirror—something strong enough to reverse the Mirror's spell one person at a time."

Ry rolled his eyes. "One person at a time. *That* would be useful. Then we could track down all of the hundreds—or perhaps thousands—of Dragons hiding inside the bodies of the city's citizens . . . and do you *know* how many people paid parnissal taxes as citizens of Calimekka last year? More than a million. Do you have any idea how easily a hundred people, or a thousand people, or five thousand people, could hide within that crowd? So we could track them down one at a time, and revert them. If they don't destroy us first. They were the greatest wizards of their age, after all. I imagine they're dangerous, don't you think?"

"Certainly. But we wouldn't have to track down all of them. We'd only need to get one. One in a high position, with access to the true Mirror, and one who, rid of the Dragon who possesses him and restored to his original state, would be sympathetic to us. Who could let us into Sabir House and assist in creating a diversion that would let us get the Mirror away from the Dragons. The Mirror is feeding the Dragons now. If we could shut it off or reverse it, they would be ripped from the bodies they've inhabited and thrown back into the void."

"And that would end the threat of Dragons to Calimekka and the world, and leave the road open for you and the rest of the Falcons to bring in your Reborn god and set him up, right? But aren't you being terribly optimistic? From what I've heard from Kait and Hasmal, the prophecies foretell a war to come between the Dragons and your Falcons before this issue can be resolved."

Dùghall grinned up at him and shrugged. "The wording of the prophecies is subject to interpretation. Perhaps our interpretations have been wrong, and the battle, such as it will be, will only happen between a few powerful adversaries, and not between great armies. If we've been wrong all these years, I won't complain. Conquering the Dragons before they can strike will only bring Solander to his throne that much sooner, and the world will become a paradise that much faster. I'll do what I can to hasten the start of paradise."

Ry turned away from him, shaking his head. All of them—Dùghall, Hasmal, and even Kait—were irrational on the subject of their Reborn. "You risk your life in the hopes of bringing a nonsensical legend to life. You're a fool, Dùghall."

"You want to see how much of a fool I am?" Dùghall rested a hand lightly on Ry's shoulder, and turned him around so that they were face-to-face. "The Reborn is not a god. And he's not a legend. He's been born—he was born this morning, and I felt him come into the world and draw breath. It was the greatest joy I have ever known. He grows stronger with every breath he takes. Would you like to meet him?"

Ry laughed out loud. *Meet* the Reborn? What trickery did the old man have planned to convince him that the Reborn was real? Better yet, how did Dùghall think he would benefit from winning Ry over? Had he been planning to convert Ry to the Falcons' silly religion all along?

Perhaps Dùghall had decided there weren't enough Falcons to rule the world. Maybe he'd discovered what a powerful wizard Ry was and decided he needed him as an ally in his own right, not a reluctant ally helping the Falcon cause to stay close to Kait.

He looked at the old man and thought, What chicanery have you planned for me, eh? Well, I like a good magic trick as well as the next, and seeing yours will tell me more about you than you can guess. You want me to "meet" your great hero? By all means, entertain me.

Aloud he said, "Certainly I'd like to meet your Reborn."

Chapter 31

They sat cross-legged facing each other, the old man's blood-bowl between them. "I won't need to draw my own blood for the bowl," Dùghall said. "I've already walked the light path many times, and my soul knows the way. But you'll need a link."

Ry shook his head. "If you don't spill your blood into the bowl with mine, I'll leave now. I don't trust a spell that calls for my blood but not yours."

Dùghall shrugged, and pulled out a tourniquet and a hollow thorn, and quickly poured a few drops of his own blood into the bowl. "I have no tricks planned for you, son. I only want you to understand what we fight for, and why. You want Kait—you make it plain with every word you speak and every gesture you make that she is your only reason for standing with us. So I am showing you the reason that Kait now follows the path of the Falcons, and that she and Hasmal and I stand with each other."

"I told you I'm ready to see your little show. Just don't expect me to believe it." Ry fumbled with the tourniquet Dùghall had used, and with the fresh thorn that Dùghall had given him; in the end he managed to add a bit of his own blood to the bowl, though it was nothing like the effortless process it had been for the old man.

Then Dùghall spread his arms wide and began to chant in one of the old, old tongues. By listening closely, Ry could make out the rhythms and patterns of the language, and categorize it as a cousin of the Ancients' tongues that he'd studied. But he couldn't understand a word of it. He could, however, feel the effects of the words Dùghall spoke into the darkened room.

A shield swirled into existence around them, at first invisible but then gaining radiance and luminous form as it strengthened. Within the shield, Ry felt peace descend on him. It was a tranquillity he had never felt when in contact with magic before—it was truly beautiful and strangely gentle; to his mind beauty and gentleness were the antithesis of magic. He sat within the shimmering globe, suspicious but shaken, and waited for Dùghall to begin entertaining him with some clever light show. The old man, though, said, "There is nothing to see. Close your eyes and I will lead you along the golden thread."

He closed his eyes as he was told, and discovered that he could clearly "see" a spiraling golden rope that led from the blood-bowl and away. Heading south.

He sensed the old man with him, but with eyes closed, and within the shell of the shield, Dùghall didn't feel like an old man. He felt huge, as powerful as a force of nature, as terrifying as the leading edge of an enormous storm sitting off the coast. Ry knew the storm could strike and destroy everything in front of it, but he had no way of knowing if it *would*.

Follow, Dùghall told him as he moved into the core of that glowing rope, then along it. Ry found that he could follow, and that as soon as he'd placed himself within the rope, it drew him forward, impossibly fast. He had no control, but he wasn't afraid. Love surrounded him and infused him, becoming stronger and more wonderful the nearer he came to its source.

They arrived at the birthplace of all that love. Ry could see nothing, but he had no doubt what was going on. A newborn infant lay in his mother's arms, quiet and at peace. Ry felt the power that poured from the baby, magic already fully formed and trained with skill and precision . . . but magic controlled by love. By compassion. By hope and optimism. Joy flowed through him, an internal radiance as brilliant as the light of the sun and as gentle as the kiss of a light breeze on the petals of a flower.

The infant offered himself as a gift to the world. Newborn, he already knew that he would live his life serving others, teaching them, leading the world toward the beauty of the place he already inhabited. Ry could see that it was not beyond reach, that place of perfect happiness. Inhabiting it, he could see that he could create such beauty within himself, though until that moment he would never have imagined such a thing could be possible.

We do not fall in love, he discovered. We do not stumble into joy, or trip over compassion on our way somewhere else. We *choose* the path of love, and joy, and compassion, and acceptance, and by following that path we leave the path of hatred behind. They are opposite roads going in completely different directions, and those who walk love's road will have lives filled with love, and will have no room for hatred.

He felt like an idiot for suspecting Dùghall of trickery. No one who had spent time in the presence of the Reborn could even consider wasting time trying to trick people into becoming the Reborn's followers. The Reborn reached out and touched, and his love overcame all obstacles. No trickery could do what he did simply by existing.

I have a place for you, the Reborn told him.

And Ry said, *Take me, I'm yours.*

Welcome, friend.

At last he had to leave that peaceful presence and return to his body, and to the darkness of the little workroom. He opened his eyes, and sat in silence across from the old man, letting the tears flow down his cheeks. He was shocked at his reaction—but he could understand it, too. His meeting with the Reborn was his first encounter with genuine love. He had been appreciated before that, but not loved. His mother considered him a useful playing piece, his late father had looked at him as someone who would someday take his place and carry on his work, his other relatives saw him as a potential threat or a potential ally. But love, joy, compassion, hope . . . those were not feelings that had a place in Sabir House.

The Reborn had come to change that. He had come to teach love.

Ry looked at Dùghall, and wiped the tears from his face. "I'm with you," he said. "No matter what, no matter the price, I'm with you. I understand now."

Dùghall nodded, and leaned across the again-empty blood-bowl, and hugged him. "I'm glad to have you on our side."

Chapter 32

Inside the secret corridor within the wall that surrounded Sabir House, Domagar crouched at one of the spy-slits. "You see her? Lean girl, bleached blond hair in a braid, work clothes, moving right now past the fat sausage vendor. Bland girl—doesn't catch your eye."

The spy who had followed the two traders to their inn squinted out his own slit and said, "Yes. I see her. What of her?"

"She's the girl who was sitting next to you in the inn. I happened to get a good look at her face as I was leaving . . . met her eyes and I saw that she recognized me and wasn't happy about it, though I was certain I'd never seen her before. It took every bit of my concentration and most of the trip from the inn to here to realize that she's the *same* girl I approached when I heard she was trying to sell artifacts. The one who said her name was Chait-eveni. When she claimed to be a trader, she had an Imumbarran accent and wore Imumbarran clothes. Had *black* hair then. And she was pretty. Striking, even. But now she's dressed like any Iberan laborer, plain as hell, and she damn near disappears into the street while you watch her. Did you speak to her?"

The spy had to think about it. "She didn't leave much of an impression, really. But . . . yes. I guess I did speak to her. Briefly." He frowned thoughtfully, and he stared harder at the girl. "She had no accent. None whatsoever. In fact . . ." The spy who had followed the two Hmoth traders to their inn closed his eyes for an instant, recalling the woman next to him. Her voice, her scent, her way of eating. "In fact, this is so odd that I should have made note of it at the time. I heard traces of Family in her voice. And I should have noticed it in her table manners, too, if I'd been paying closer attention." He looked down at his hands and muttered, "That isn't like me, to be so inattentive. It *isn't*." He looked back out again, and started. "Where did she go?"

"She hasn't moved," Domagar said.

The spy kept looking, then said, "Oh, you're right. She hasn't."

"She slides out of the mind. I don't like that. I can't see why, but she does."

"I was afraid it was just me," the spy said. "As I think about her now, I realize that she was the most interesting thing at our table—because of the contradictions. But I didn't see it at the time. She was a polite eater, if you know what I mean. One bite at a time, didn't speak with her mouth full, sipped her drink instead of gulping it. Didn't spit. And she had no stink of sweat or work to her, though the day was hot and the laborers around her smelled strong enough. She . . ." He paused, wanting to be sure he was right. "She smelled distinctly of flowers. And herbs. Good clean smell."

Down two spy-slits from both of them, Anwyn Sabir stood beside the captain of the Sabir guards. They had been watching the girl, too. "There's something dishonest about the whole lot of them," Anwyn said. "Whatever they're doing, it isn't about trading for the artifacts my brother wants." He turned to the guard captain. "So let's find out what they're really up to. Bring her in."

Kait sighed. She'd waited long enough; her friends would begin to wonder where she was. She'd given the man she followed plenty of time to report what he'd done. If he'd intended to leave by the gate through which he'd entered the House, he would have done so already. Therefore, either he was a permanent resident of the Sabir House or he had gone out one of the lesser gates. Either way, there was nothing more she could do.

As a form of further disguise and because she was once again hungry and thirsty, she bought a hot sausage on a stick from a fat young man with a shaved head, and had an ale-monger fill her tin work cup with a bronze fifth-preid's worth of rice ale. She sipped and nibbled as she started back to her rendezvous with Dùghall. She concentrated on looking like a weary laborer trudging back to her job, however reluctantly. She kept her shields tight, even though she had seen nothing that would indicate that anyone in Sabir House was aware of her presence.

She wished she had more to tell Dùghall. She wished she could have thought of some way to follow her target clear into Sabir House. She was certain there were things in there that she needed to know. She wished . . . but caught herself wasting her time on wishes, and turned her attention to the task at hand.

The street she was on pitched steeply down a hill. It was not, she suddenly realized, a normal street. Buildings on both sides hemmed in the horizon, while the street switchbacked left and right half a dozen times, leaving the person on it perpetually blind to what lay before and what came up behind. The builders of Sabir House had no doubt designed it that way. No alleys split off anywhere, making the street one long corral, and not even the buildings would offer hiding places to someone in need. Every one was a warehouse marked with the Sabir crest or with crests of allied Families. All of the doors were closed and, in most cases, padlocked. Kait had been too intent on not being spotted by her prey to pay attention to the details of the approach on her way up, but on her way back down, she realized she didn't like the setup. Not at all. The advantages of the long, narrow, twisting, exitless street with its blind approaches lay exclusively with the Sabirs.

A few boys scurried into view around the sharp curve in front of her. Their heads were down and they kept their eyes forward. They said nothing to each other; they carried fenny sticks and a fenny ball tucked under their arms. They gave no indication that they were friends, though from the sweat on their faces and on their clothes and the labored sound of their breathing, Kait would have guessed they had been playing a game in the street only moments before.

Their silent, hurried progress set her teeth on edge. Suddenly everyone coming toward her seemed nervous to her. Chary. Watchful. She smelled the air, and she smelled fear. She dropped the uneaten half of her sausage into a gutter, poured her ale, and tucked the cup back into her belt. Her heart beat faster.

A few old women appeared from around the corner in front of her, their scarves and skirts tucked up, their heads down. They scurried up the street, carefully not looking around them. They stank of fear.

Now she was certain. Something lay ahead, and because of the design of the street, ahead was the only way she could go. Did this stir have anything to do with her? Perhaps not. The Sabirs might have sent their guards out to collect an impromptu street tax from the vendors, but then why would the boys have ceased their fenny-ball game? Why would everyone be hurrying *toward* the House instead of away from it?

She pulled a few strands of her hair down over her face, slumped her shoulders, hung her head, and tightened her "don't-see-me" shield until people coming toward her barely managed to avoid her before veering out of the way. She thought of a story for why she was on the street—her foreman had sent her to look for a mason he'd sent up the street to get his lunch. She swallowed, and tried to look inoffensive.

Rounding the next corner, her heart slid up into her throat. Ten guards in green and silver had cordoned off the street, and were requiring identification papers before they would let anyone pass.

Kait's falsified papers identified her as a black-haired Imumbarran trader named Chait-eveni Three-Fast, daughter of an Imumbarran stardancer mother and a Gyru-nalle trader father. She looked as purely Iberan as she was, and that dichotomy was going to cause her grief. She knew within the Galweigh districts, traveling with obviously falsified papers (or legitimate papers but an obviously falsified appearance) was a crime, punishable by imprisonment and hard labor. Within the Sabir district of the city . . . well, the Sabir district had a reputation for being a tougher, meaner place to make a mistake.

This was about her. Sometime in the last station, she'd made a mistake. Somehow, she'd allowed the spy to catch sight of her. Or he had planted a telltale on her. Or . . . what she'd done wrong didn't matter as much as what she could do to get away.

Some workers came out of a warehouse to her left. They looked like she did—equally shabby, equally weary. Any animation they exhibited at leaving work dissolved when they saw the roadblock. The door swung slowly behind them, almost closing. But not completely.

Kait could see that the latching mechanism had caught on the door-frame, keeping it from shutting all the way.

Her first lucky break.

She took a deep breath and ducked into the warehouse. She quietly pulled the door closed behind her. Pins tumbled into place as it locked itself. That didn't bother her. Warehouse doors often required a key from the outside only.

But the darkness inside was nearly complete—she'd expected lights, movement, voices, some sign of life. The only smell in the air was dust, however, and the only sound that broke the silence was her breathing.

A crew had just walked out the door behind her. They'd been in the warehouse for a reason. If they shut the place down behind them, she should still find some sign that they'd been working earlier—stacks of goods, or a smell of life in the air, or *something*. She sighed, and the emptiness echoed her sigh back to her from all four directions.

She didn't even hear any rats.

She looked around once her eyes adjusted to the darkness. Four walls rose up the height of five men, supporting a trussed ceiling; the walls to the left and right of her were unbroken by any window or door. The floor between those walls was completely bare. Directly across from her, though, a single door like the one behind her pierced the wall. No light showed underneath, but perhaps the door merely fit its frame well. All sorts of activity might be in progress on the other side.

She leaned her back against the door that led out to the street and pressed one ear to it. She heard shouting outside, and screaming. If they were truly looking for her and they didn't find her among the people in the street, they would search the warehouses. This one held no hiding places. But perhaps the laborers had been working behind that other door. Perhaps there she would be able to find a hiding place.

She hurried across the bare floor and rested a hand on the other door, and offered a quick prayer to Nerin, who watched over his followers during his station, that the laborers had left it unlocked. Then she turned the handle. The door opened.

Quick thanks to Nerin.

More darkness, but now punctuated at intervals by distant light. She was in a long, curving corridor with tiny windows set high along the outside wall. The corridor ran both to her left, back up the hill toward the House, and right, down the hill and toward safety. She paused in the doorway, holding her breath, every sense straining for evidence that she was being pursued. The corridor was empty for a long distance in either direction. Perhaps entirely empty. She stepped into it, pulled the door shut behind her so that she would not make her trail obvious to anyone who might step into the warehouse, and turned right. She passed other doors on her right. She tried each, hoping one would open for her, but all were locked. She quickly reached a dead end—the place where the Sabir warehouse district ended and lower Calimekka resumed. If she could just get out through the wall . . . but it was stonework of high caliber, and thick. She stood about parallel with the place where the guards had set up their roadblock. The horrified realization grabbed her; she was standing in the corridor through which those guards had traveled to get ahead of her. More could come along at any time, or those could decide to go back.

The warehouse had been safer, if only marginally. She ran back the way she'd come, trying doors as she did. She didn't remember which one had been the one she'd come out of, and in the dim light, they all looked the same.

It was only when she'd traveled twice as far up the hill as she'd gone down that she realized she'd passed her warehouse. The door had locked itself behind her. She was trapped in the corridor.

She wished the doors were lighter, or the locks were simpler. She felt certain she could have kicked a lighter door in. But she felt equally certain that the massive warehouse doors wouldn't give way for her.

Which meant she could stay where she was, or she could head back toward Sabir House, hoping to find another warehouse with an open door before she ended up inside . . .

. . . the walls . . .

. . . of the House itself . . .

She stopped and smiled. She was an idiot. She'd wanted to get into the House. She'd fallen into her perfect opportunity to do so without being observed. The corridor was empty. Her Karnee senses picked up neither sound nor scent of anyone. If she just moved quickly enough, she ought to be able to get into the House through its service corridor without being caught. She broke into a lope, no longer wasting time checking warehouse doors.

The corridor switchbacked along with the warehouses it had been built to service. Kait stopped before every switchback to listen and smell ahead of her for danger. Her road stayed clear. Near the House, she passed sounds of activity within the warehouses to her left, but she didn't check the doors to those, either. She had taken the offensive. She intended to keep it. The Sabirs wouldn't look for her within their midst.

Finally she reached another termination to the corridor, but unlike the blank stone wall at the bottom of the hill, this wall was translucent, white with a hint of opalescence, smooth as good glass. The narrow, delicately etched white door set into it promised access to the Sabirs' realm that lay beyond. *If* she could get through it. The door was, after all, of the Ancients' make, and for all its apparent delicacy, created to survive both enemies and eons unscathed.

Kait rested her hand on the smooth curve of the opening mechanism and pressed lightly. The mechanism recessed and the door slid open silently. She stepped into warm light that radiated from everywhere at once, and felt a brief pang of homesickness. The smooth, translucent white walls of an Ancients' building rose around her, reminding her of her suite of rooms in Galweigh House. Home—lost but not forgotten. She pushed the wistfulness to the back of her mind and focused on her work. To her right, a staircase made of the same exquisite, indestructible stone-of-Ancients spiraled upward. While loitering beyond the gate, she had seen the top portion of an Ancients' tower that stood just inside the walls of Sabir House. This had to be that tower. Excellent! She knew where she was. Beyond the stairs lay the only other door in the bottom floor of the tower, this one certainly leading out onto the grounds of the House itself. Or perhaps into the servants' area, or the House storage rooms. No matter where it went, it led someplace she wanted to go.

She listened carefully at that door and heard only more silence. Again, excellent. Eager to be on her way, she gripped the curved mechanism and pressed. It failed to open. She tried it again, this time keeping her pressure on the mechanism light. The door was still locked.

She closed her eyes and swore softly but with great passion. She could go back the way she'd come, and go out through one of the occupied warehouses. But now, with the promise of Sabir House lying like an uncracked egg in front of her, the thought of merely escaping felt like failure.

Well, she could tell Dùghall about the warehouses and the corridor—perhaps he would think of some magical way to get past the tower and its locked door.

Frustrated, she retreated to the door through which she'd entered the tower, and pressed its opening mechanism.

It, too, was locked.

Nausea twisted her stomach and she felt lightheaded. She'd managed to trap herself. She took slow, deep breaths to ward off panic. She closed her eyes. She had seen only one window in the tower, and that had been all the way at the top. High up, terribly high up. High enough that she would kill herself if she leaped from it. But perhaps if she climbed the stairs, she would find a lower window facing inward, one she could safely jump out of. She could only hope.

The sound of footsteps and voices reached her ears. Men, coming toward the tower from the corridor. The guards? Perhaps.

She started to panic again, then relaxed. They would have the key that opened the tower door. They wouldn't be looking for her. They would go out into the House, and she would find a way to follow them.

She slipped up the stairs and around the first complete arc of the spiral, out of sight.

Their voices grew louder, and finally she could make out what they were saying.

". . . dasn't seem right t' me that she got away. I reckon had we kept on, we'd 'a found her."

"The cap'n says quit, I'm for quitting. They're after something freakish, you ask me, an' I want nothing to do with it."

"Nor I." The door opened and the first of the guards entered. "They decided to let her go, I say all to the good. Tellin' us she might have a weapon could kill us all with a stroke, then sendin' us out without telling us *how*. Let someone else get the reward. I'll take my little daughter's hug when I walk through the door t'night an' call myself a rich man."

They started up the stairs.

Kait swallowed hard, suddenly and completely scared. They didn't know about her and they weren't coming after her, but she had no idea what lay above her. There might be no place to hide between where she stood and the top of the tower.

But there might be. She concentrated on that, and fled up the stairs, years of practice in sneaking through Galweigh House making her flight nearly soundless. The guards behind her covered her few scuffles and the sound of her breathing with their casual chatter and their heavy, thudding footsteps.

They were in no hurry and she was running, so she gained ground.

The ceiling neared, and she could see an archway ahead. She ran faster, trying to think of what she would do if there were already guards in the room. She lunged through the doorway in a state of near-terror.

It was empty.

Even better, it was clearly the guards' destination. Uniforms hung from racks all around the room's perimeter, and a lunch table stacked with papayas and melons and squashes sat in the center. She could see nowhere to hide in the room, but the stairs continued upward, with another ceiling overhead and a door, standing ajar, visible from the stair on which she stood.

With the guards' voices ringing loudly behind her, she raced upward again.

She slid through the door, saw that no one was in the room with her, and pulled it almost closed. To keep it from closing completely— because her luck with closed doors had not been good that day—she grabbed a stick of wood from the wood bin and wedged it between the door and the frame.

Then she stood shaking, her forehead pressed against the cool, smooth stone-of-Ancients, and listened to the voices below her. The men were changing, gathering up their belongings and getting ready to go home for the day. They didn't sound like they would be coming up that final flight of stairs. She turned, leaned her back against the door, and studied her hiding place. She was in the watchroom she'd seen from the ground. The top of the tower.

The wood bin sat to her immediate left. Left of that, a squat, ugly metal table hunkered between two arches, covered with a dark cloth held in place by lead weights at each corner. She frowned at the lumps beneath the cloth, curious about what might be there, but she didn't investigate. The center of the room held a tall, long, heavy wood table edged with metal rings, upon which rested coiled rope, chains, locks, and balls of wrapped gauze. Beside the table were several chairs, none of them comfortable-looking; and in the eastern corner a brazier that had a fire going in it, though the fire was down to coals; and beside the brazier three buckets of water. The room itself was beautiful. Architecture with the Ancients' unmistakable preference for simplicity and elegance. Arched doorways punctuated the walls at intervals, and through them she could see the delicate parapet that had looked so fragile and lovely from the ground below. A breeze blew through from the western arches, laden with the scents of jasmine and frangipani and freesia. The wind was cool, and that high up, blew hard. She could see why anyone using the tower would need to have a fire going.

The view through those arches was fantastic. The sun was beginning to drop below the mountains to the west, and the sky had turned orange and blood red around it, with streaks of violet stabbing into the red and deepening into rich blue when they reached the eastern edge of the sky. In minutes it would be dark. Already the city sparkled with lights, a million gems tossed onto a velvet cloak and glittering with inner fire.

Kait missed the long twilights she'd discovered in North Novtierra—darkness there crept up quietly, and sunsets hung in the sky for what felt like forever. Had this scene taken place in North Novtierra, she would have had most of a station to enjoy it. In Calimekka, the night charged down on the day like an angry bull, tramping the brief, fragile sunset into oblivion in mere moments.

She moved forward, drawn to the westernmost arch and to the flaring sunset. She stood for several moments taking it in. Then, below her, she heard the voices of the guards growing fainter. They were leaving. If she followed them down, she could wedge something behind the tower door before it could completely close. She guessed that they would head into the Sabir compound; she could follow them in and still find out something useful for her uncle.

She hurried to the door. The stick she'd wedged into it was gone. The door was shut, though she hadn't heard it shut. The wind? Could the wind have blown the wedge out of place and closed the door while she stood watching the setting sun? She didn't see how, but she couldn't think of what else might have happened.

She tried the mechanism. It was locked. She stood still, trying to collect her thoughts, which began racing madly the instant she realized she was trapped.

I can use that coil of rope, maybe the gauze, tie everything together, wait until dark, lower myself to the ground.

There wasn't enough rope to reach the ground—she could already see that.

I'll get close enough that I won't be too badly hurt.

Maybe.

I'll find a way out of here before someone comes.

She rested her head on the door and closed her eyes.

I'll find a way out of this.

Behind her, rhythmic clicking on the floor.

She turned, and jammed the side of her fist into her mouth to stifle the scream that tried to burst free.

Two men and a monster stepped through the arches from the eastern half of the parapet to face her. One of the men was Domagar Addo. Beside him stood a burly ox of a man with massive shoulders and a chest sprung like a water barrel. He had shaved his head, keeping a single braid above his left ear in the fashion of the Sloebene sailors. Either fights or bad bloodlines had given him a nose like a squashed mushroom and eyes as cold and flat as a snake's.

But both men were handsome next to the thing that stood beside *them*.

Horns curled from its forehead, and scales covered its face and skin, and daggerlike spines rose from its shoulders and elbows. It had long claws on its hands, a thick, lashing tail, rows of triangular, serrated teeth. It alone among the three of them smiled at her. She wished it hadn't.

"Looking for this?" it asked, and held up the piece of wood she'd used to keep the door from closing. "It didn't do the job very well, did it?"

The instruments and ropes on the table, the lumpish things beneath the cloth, even the fire left burning down to coals—all of those things suddenly took on a new and sinister character.

The monster said, "Nothing to say? Well, perhaps that's because we haven't been introduced. You are Chait-eveni." Its smile grew broader. Its voice was the rasp of a file on metal. Kait shuddered. "And I am Anwyn Sabir, of the Sabir Wolves. This is my cousin Andrew. And I believe you know our friend Domagar."

Her hands twisted at the mechanism of the door at her back, trying anything to get it to open. But it held fast.

Domagar said, "We began to believe that you would never follow the little path we made for you and find your way to us. But we're so happy you did. We're delighted to entertain such a clever girl."

Anwyn said, "We are indeed. We have an interesting evening planned for you."

Andrew Sabir giggled, a sound that made Kait's skin crawl.

Anwyn said, "Come, don't be shy. You might as well join us over here. That door won't give way, and there is no other way out. We intend to know you well before you leave us."

"*If* you leave us," Domagar said. "Not something *I'd* count on."

Chapter 33

ùghall stared over Ry's shoulder into the viewing glass. He could clearly see Kait, disguised still as a common laborer. He could see the table she faced, and the instruments of torture that covered the table sitting along one wall. He released his shield and sent a single tendril of his spirit-self crawling through the delicate strands of magic that connected the viewing glass to Domagar, the Dragon. He put himself in danger, because with his shields down, Domagar could follow the link back to him, if he became aware of it. Thus linked, however, he could not only see through Domagar's eyes, but experience everything the Dragon felt and heard and knew through his other senses, too.

He took a deadly risk, but he took it for Kait. He feared that he was going to watch her die, but he was determined that if he could do nothing else for her, at least he would find a way to make sure she was not alone when they killed her.

The men Domagar was with were both Sabir Wolves. Domagar controlled them, though neither of them were aware of the fact. From Domagar's mind, Dùghall could draw out little snippets of fact. That Domagar had been the name of the true owner of the body, and that his soul had been ripped out and replaced by the soul of a Dragon named Mellayne; that one of the two Wolves with him was also Karnee; that they didn't know the girl they'd captured was a Galweigh or Karnee, and they had no awareness of the magic she controlled, but that they were sure she was more than an employee of traders; that they intended to torture Kait to find out who she was, who she worked with, what she wanted, and what she knew. And then they intended to kill her.

Domagar said, "If you cooperate with us, you have my promise that we won't hurt you," and Dùghall became aware of voices around him muttering, "Don't you believe him, Kait!" and, "Kill them and get out of there," and, "Shift! Shift!"

He focused his attention on his physical surroundings for an instant. Hasmal and Ian and Ry and all of Ry's lieutenants were now crouched around the viewing glass, talking to her as if she could hear them.

He returned himself to his connection with Domagar. Kait had a dagger in one hand and was saying, "Stay back and ask me what you want to know, and I'll tell you. Come at me and I'll kill you."

All three men laughed. Through Domagar's eyes, she looked so frail, so helpless. A slender young woman surrounded by three wizards.

The Scarred one limped to the table that held the torture implements and picked up a flaying knife and a set of finger dicers. Dùghall shuddered and tried to think of something that he could do that would protect Kait without leaving himself open to attack. He had to remember that his first duty as a Warden of the Falcons was to survive, so that he could rescue the Mirror of Souls and get it to the Reborn; only if he didn't jeopardize his own survival could he take steps to save her. He was taking unacceptable risks just by linking into Domagar.

"Do something," Ian was saying. "Do some magic that will save her."

"Magic doesn't work that way," Ry said. "She's shielded so tightly nothing I could do would reach her. Maybe we could attack them, but hitting them hard enough to save her would rebound an equal attack onto us, and we don't have sacrifices to take the *rewhah*. We'd die, but she wouldn't live."

Hasmal interrupted. "No sacrifice would be required for magic that caused no harm. If we could get through to her, we could . . .

maybe we could lift her out of there, or do something else of that nature. But you're right. Her shields cover her so completely that no magic leaks out at all, and if nothing can get out, nothing can get in."

Ian said, "But they're going to kill her." His voice was anguished.

Dùghall tried to keep his focus on the scene around him in the Sabir tower. The Wolves, the Dragon . . . and Kait.

The Scarred Wolf, whom Domagar's mind named Anwyn, said, "Girl, you're not in a position to make choices. Not now. Not ever again. Come to me. If I have to come to you, I promise you'll pay doubly for it."

The other Wolf began to laugh. His laughter was the uncontrolled, high-pitched tittering of a madman. Dùghall, looking at him through Domagar's eyes, was overwhelmed by the hopelessness of the situation. Domagar's memories insisted the shaved-skulled madman was Karnee, which made him the one among the three who posed the most immediate physical danger to Kait. He was most likely to discover that she was the same sort of creature he was.

The mad Wolf, Andrew, said, "She's not going to come to you, cousin. Not by herself. You're too ugly. She wants someone handsome to help her talk. Someone like me."

"I'll kill them," Ian was muttering. "If they hurt her, I'll destroy all three of them and the rest of the Sabirs, too."

Ry said, "Don't make promises you can't keep. You haven't the skill or the power to destroy even one of them. They're wizards."

"I'll find a way," Ian said.

Dùghall's mind kept racing in circles, looking for something—anything—that might allow him to save his niece. If he could create a tiny reversed Mirror of Souls, he could capture the Dragon soul in Domagar's body in it, which would return Domagar's true soul—the soul of the devout young farmer—to its rightful place. He thought. Or it might kill the soulless body. Could that help her? A dead body in the room would be worthless—worse than worthless, because it would give away the presence of observers, and alert the other two. But a devout young farmer might try to come to the rescue of a poor trapped girl.

Could he create the Mirror quickly enough?

He looked at the rings on his fingers. The form of the ring was essential to the structure of the Mirror spell. He'd seen that, had figured out that the purity of the metal the ring was made of mattered, too. He had good rings. But he would also need three wires. He said, "One of you. Get me wires—three short wires. Fast."

A brief pause, while the men stood thinking.

Yanth snapped his fingers. "Dagger."

Trev caught the direction his thoughts had taken. "Yes. But you'll need two."

Both lieutenants shot out the door and an instant later were back, prying wrapped silver wire from the hilt of one fine dagger with the blade of another. "How long?" Trev asked.

In the tower, Andrew Sabir was moving toward Kait from around one side of the table, and Anwyn, holding his torture implements, was approaching her from the other.

Dùghall didn't waste time listening to what they were saying. He was fighting to get his most perfect ring, a plain circle of refined electrum, over his knuckles. He'd lost weight over the past months, and the ring had been loose on his finger, but his joints hadn't gotten any smaller. He said, "The length of your longest finger, all three of them."

By the time they'd broken off the wires, he'd gotten his ring free. He quickly attached the wires to the ring and twisted the three of them together, then fanned out the ends to form a crude tripod. He stood the little tripod on the floor and nibbled skin off of his lower lip. The tiny fragments of skin he dropped into the center of the ring. This was going to be crude. Terribly crude.

He crouched over the tripod. Focusing his will and his attention completely on the little band of electrum, he said:

Follow my soul, Vodor Imrish,
To the Dragon soul of Mellayne,
To the usurper of the body of Domagar,
Faithful child of Iberan gods,
And from this body expel the intruder.
Bring no harm to the intruder,
The Dragon Mellayne,
But give his soul safe house and shelter
Within the unbroken circle before me—

Unbroken that it may guard
Mellayne's immortality, and
Protect the essence of life and mind.
I offer my flesh—all that I have given
And all that you will take,
Freely and with clear conscience,
As I do no wrong,
But reverse a wrong done.

He felt fire along the tendril of his spirit that linked him to Domagar. He wanted to scream, but he held himself firm. And within Domagar's mind, he felt first astonishment, then raw terror. White heat
burned away the anchors by which the spirit of Mellayne the Dragon
held itself within the body it had taken; white fire pursued that spirit
back along the threadlike path that connected Domagar to Dùghall.
And when Mellayne's spirit blasted *through* Dùghall, flailing for any
crevice or crack in him that would give it purchase, that angry fire surrounded it and absorbed it and burst from Dùghall's chest in a blazing
stream that poured into the ring. The fire spiraled around, and the
room filled for an instant with fog and the scent of honeysuckle and
the oppressive weight of a wordless scream.

When the air cleared and silence returned, light rose from the bottom of the tiny Mirror, crawled up through the center, and circled into
the ring, forming a little pool in the center. A perfect replica in miniature of the Mirror of Souls. Mirror of Mellayne, Dùghall thought.

"Ah, gods," Ry whispered. "It's doing what Kait's Mirror did."

"Indeed." He looked into the viewing glass, and discovered that it
had not gone black. Domagar's body, then, had not fallen to the floor
in a lifeless heap. Domagar—the *real* Domagar—was looking around
the room, his gaze flicking from the men to Kait to the torture instruments, then back to Kait again. "The boy has his own soul back. The
ring houses the soul of a Dragon. Watch now," Dùghall said, and
everyone stared into the viewing glass.

Kait had her back to the balcony, the blackness of the gulf beneath
her clearly visible. Anwyn and Andrew closed on her slowly, playing
with her. Through Domagar's eyes, both of their backs were visible.
Domagar had picked up a handful of knives.

"Stop," Domagar said, and Anwyn answered with a sigh.

"She won't hurt herself—she isn't so stupid as that. We may let her survive, but if she throws herself over, the fall will *surely* kill her."

"I said *stop*!" Domagar shouted. He lifted the knife and aimed it at Andrew, who had started to Shift into a four-legged nightmare.

Kait didn't seem to realize she had an ally, though. She gripped the rail with both hands and shouted, "I *won't* stop." And threw herself over the edge.

Ry and Ian screamed, "No!" and Hasmal shouted, "You *can't* die!" And Dùghall dropped to his knees and stared at the tiny Mirror with its single captive. And he whispered, "Oh, Kait. Sweet little Kait-cha. I'm sorry."

Chapter 34

Danya tucked the newborn baby into the sling and wrapped him close, hiding him away from the eyes of the villagers. In the middle of what should have been darkness, the sun still glowed, low on the horizon and dull red but ever-present now, having become the unblinking eye of a meddlesome neighbor. In the winter, she'd thought she would go mad from the unceasing darkness, but in darkness at least she'd found privacy. Now, in the undying light, she felt herself constantly watched—by the villagers, by the distant wizards who spied on her and the baby, even by the uncaring gods who'd abandoned her when she prayed to them.

The baby squirmed against her scaly breast, nuzzling her. He made a faint, delicate mewling sound and drifted back to sleep, and she touched the softness of his cheek with one scaled finger. Red, wrinkled, delicate, lightly covered in downy hair, he was the most helpless thing she had ever seen. She'd never paid that much attention to the babies her cousins had—they'd seemed messy and loud to her, always spitting up or crying or pissing themselves, always needing to be held or fed or changed. She'd never planned to have a child; she'd looked at her place among the Wolves and decided magic and power would be enough for her.

But this baby touched her; when he looked into her eyes, she felt herself become a better person than she'd been before. He gave her a part of herself that she'd never been able to find—a warmth and a depth and a patience that she'd never before needed. And he returned to her the assurance that she was human, if only somewhere on the inside. That wasn't enough to soothe the pain she carried with her, but she thought it was a start.

For the moment, at least, she could forget where the child had come from, and how he had come to be.

She slipped down to the river's edge and took a boat. The water was still, a mirror reflecting the lines and shadows of the tall bluff on the opposite shore, and the rich greens of the willows that grew down to the bank, and the glorious fuchsia of the stand of fireweed that covered the bluff's crown like a brilliant, man-high head of hair. With the baby resting between her feet, she paddled gently across. She heard loons somewhere in the distance, their mad laughing call eerie in the silence. Behind her, a few of the villagers' dogs barked, but the barking was lazy, unexcited. The villagers were mostly asleep, keeping to their winter rhythms as best they could. She would draw the least attention now, at what would have been the dead of night in a lower latitude.

The boat slid across the river, disturbing the water only slightly in its passage, moving as silently as the huge pike that inhabited the lakes of the tundra. A family of ducks, the ducklings paddling in a line behind their mother, crossed Danya's bow and took no notice of her. Their quacking amused her as she slipped up to the bluff and dragged the little boat ashore.

She went to meet again with the spirit Luercas. In one of the hidden back rooms of In-kanmerea, the grand place of the Ancients, he waited—her savior, her friend, her link to the time when she had been human. This secretive trip fulfilled her promise to him—they had agreed in their last conversation, before advanced pregnancy made her too ungainly to travel across the river, climb the bluffs, and hike across the tundra to the hidden Ancient hideaway, that once the baby was born she would return to the shielding room, and she and Luercas would speak again.

She'd missed him. Not as much as she'd thought she would, though she wouldn't admit this to him. She'd engaged herself in the village life, working to make friends, trying to find her place, and in many ways she'd succeeded. She'd created a sort of life for herself, even if it was poor and shabby, the sort of existence she would have scorned in her days as a Galweigh Wolf. At least she wasn't alone. She had her friends—subhuman friends, true, but they cared about her.

But Luercas was—or had been, before his death—human. He was her only human link, other than her son, and the only creature in this bleak, flat place who knew what she really was. He alone understood the station in the world she'd been destined to occupy before the Sabirs intervened. To him alone, she was something other than the scaly, Scarred monster who hunted and fetched and carried and took little children from one side of the river to the other. To him she was Family, and Galweigh, and a Wolf, a highborn young wizard who would have one day had the world at her feet.

Now . . . well, no world of wealth and glamour lay at her feet now. Only bluffs spongy with caribou moss and low-growing blue-berry bushes and mouseweed and scrub willow. She made her way across them, and the baby began to cry; she sat on one grassy hum-mock and nursed him, awkward and frustrated with her body, wish-ing that she could be human again. If she had soft skin and full breasts, she could hold him without worrying that she might break him or scratch him with her claws, and she could nurse him without wondering if her milk was right for him, or if the magic that had so completely twisted her might have altered that, too, so that he would gain no nourishment from it. If she could only be human again, her body would fit his. She would be a real mother.

He would grow up with his perfect body, seeing the malformed beast that had given birth to him, and he would never understand that once she had been beautiful, too. That once she had been someone desirable. He would grow away from her, he would become disgusted by her, his perfect love would one day gutter out and die when he came to understand that he was perfection and she was an abomina-tion.

It would have been easier to bear if she hadn't been able to see herself as she had once been, mirrored in his tiny features.

When the baby finished suckling, Danya rose and hurried to In-kanmerea. She hurt inside, and the shelter of the Ancients' House of the Devil Ghosts would soothe her and let her pretend, as she strolled beneath its huge arches and through its fine halls, that she could be a woman again. She reached the main entrance and went down the dark stairs without faltering, her feet now familiar with the way. She hurried through the grand lobby, and down the huge hallways, and finally reached the room she wanted, the room that held the shielding device.

She wrapped her infant firmly and placed him on the seat nearest the dais that held the Ancients' magical apparatus, out of the range of the shield the device would create. He slept, his tiny face turned toward her. She could still feel the strangers touching him from afar, their magic stroking him, lulling him, caressing him. She could still feel them trying to touch her, too. But she maintained her magical shields, grateful that once she moved onto the Ancients' device, she would have peace from their attempts at prying.

She clambered onto the dais, and the apparatus came to life. Silence descended. Instantly, Luercas was with her.

Danya, it's so good to be with you again. I've been bereft without you.

"When you came to visit me just after he was born, I thought you would stay with me. But you left again before I could even tell you how happy I was to hear your voice again. Why did you leave so suddenly?"

Those who invade your child with their spirit-touch would gladly destroy me, and you with me, if they knew you were my friend. I wanted only to congratulate you on the birth. You were strong, and brave—and now you are free of the pregnancy at last. But I dared not stay after that. The wizards who watch you are powerful and many, and I am weak and only one.

She reminded herself that Luercas had been the only one she could talk to honestly through the long months while the baby grew inside of her; he was the only one who knew the full tale of rape and torture and horror that had visited the unwanted infant upon her. He'd sympathized, kept her spirits up, reminded her that she would have her revenge on those who'd hurt her, promised her that one day she would see the Sabirs and the Galweighs bow before her while she passed sentence on them for their evils. She'd complained endlessly about the baby she carried, and about the prying wizards who constantly watched him and watched her, and Luercas had kept her calm, reassuring her that she would have her revenge on them, too. He'd cared about her in a way no one else could have. She didn't think she would have survived the ordeal without him.

But when he spoke of her being free of the pregnancy at last, her guts knotted and slight queasiness touched the back of her throat. She didn't feel that way anymore . . . that she was *free* of it. She'd . . . she'd done something powerful, and terrifying and magnificent, and she'd survived. She'd come out on the other side of the ordeal changed—a fact that poor Luercas couldn't understand.

When she discovered that she cared about the infant she'd delivered, she felt as if she were betraying Luercas, which was ridiculous. Luercas wouldn't feel betrayed when he discovered that she was coming to love her baby. He would support her, as he had supported her throughout her ordeal. "He's a sweet little thing," she said softly. Hesitantly.

A sweet . . . Ahhh. Luercas paused for a long time. *Of course he is. How could he be anything else?*

She wanted to think he understood, but the way he said that frightened Danya. "What do you mean?"

He's a helpless newborn, and adorable as such creatures go, and you had to go through hell to bring him into the world. So of course, when you look at him, you see a baby that you can love. You deserve love more than anyone in the world—you should be able to love your son. That is, to me, the saddest thing about this. And surely why he chose you. How could you ever stop him, when you're so needy?

"Luercas, you aren't making any sense."

Your infant is destined to stand against everything you desire. He will destroy both you and your hopes and dreams, but he will do it out of what he will claim is love. And you will help him do it, because you truly will love him. Luercas sounded sympathetic, but Danya heard something else in his voice, too—something she hadn't heard before, and couldn't identify.

"He's a baby. How can he be destined to stand against me? Destined to destroy me? How can that be?"

Look at him carefully, Danya. Look at him, not with human sight, but with Wolf sight. See him through your wizard eyes. He's the product of two Wolves, changed by magics so overpowering that when they were released they woke the dead and freed spirits from traps that had held them a thousand years. Look at that tiny, helpless baby, and tell me what you see.

Danya did as Luercas asked. She looked down at her son tucked safely between the arms of the nearest chair, wrapped in a blanket, and she closed her eyes and summoned Wolf sight. After an instant, the baby appeared in front of her closed eyes, but this time as a glowing spirit form, and not what she would have expected. His spirit form was already twice as big as the infant body to which it was attached. He radiated a serene glow, a pure golden light that flowed without flaw or blemish in all directions. And tapped into that glow were hundreds of multicolored tendrils, each connecting back to one more spy, one more meddler. The baby basked amid those foreign touches, content with the comfort of strangers.

"He welcomes them, and they surround him," Danya said. "He loves them."

Indeed he does. He loves everyone and everything, with the complete lack of discrimination you'd find in any idiot. He loves the Family that abandoned you and the villains who tortured you exactly as much—and in exactly the same way—as he loves you.

"But he's just an infant. As he grows, he'll learn."

Luercas sighed, and said, Oh, how I wish that were true. Danya, my dear friend, I would give anything for that to be true, and for this child to be salvageable. But he isn't. His soul is already set. It has been waiting in its current form for a thousand years, unchanged, hoping for a body like that one to come along. The soul in that body has not forgotten who he was, as the gods decree we all must when we are born into flesh form, so he recalls every bit of his life as a wizard in the days before the Wizards' War. And he aims to pick up his life from the point where he left off when he died. His spirit claims noble goals—peace for the world, love for all creatures—but test his goals against what you know to be right, and tell me if you can allow him to succeed in what he's come to do.

"What has he come to do?"

He has come to force humankind to open its gates to the Scarred—he'll make Ibera welcome the monsters of Strithia, and the crawling vermin from Manarkas, and the skinless horrors of South Novtierra, and he'll make them the equals of Family. He'll prevent all wars, no matter how just. He'll reward the Galweighs and Sabirs with riches and joy and long life. I tell you *truly, under his hand no innocents will suffer unjust accusations, and that I must concede would be a fine thing, if it were not that under his hand, no guilty monster will suffer, either. He demands peace. Absolute peace, without thought of justice. Peace on his terms.*

If you permit him to become the man he will be, you will never have your revenge on the Families that destroyed you. You will never see them crawl. Instead, you will see them grow fat with riches. You will see everything they touch grow fertile and sweet. Rich harvests will burst from their lands, children will fill their halls, and gold and gems and caberra spice will spill from their overfilled treasuries. It will not matter to him that you are his mother, or that those he aids destroyed you. He will not care about your pain.

"You can't know that. He's just a baby. He's . . . helpless. Tiny. His future is as much a mystery as anyone's."

If you think that, you play into his plans, and those of his friends, the Falcons. You know about the Falcons, don't you?

She had read about them in her childhood studies, but not much. There wasn't much to read. "A secret sect devoted to the return of the Age of Wizards. Worshiped a dead god and a martyr. Much persecuted hundreds of years ago, utterly destroyed in the Purges two centuries past."

Their main patron god, Vodor Imrish, has been far too busy of late to be dead. And if the Falcons were utterly destroyed, that squirming infant would not be communing with them now. Who did you think was touching him the whole time you were pregnant, eh? They're still out there, and they're happier than they've been in a thousand years.

He's their martyr, Danya. He's the one who's going to give them the return of their Age of Wizards, who's going to make them gods and set them above humanity. He's the one who's going to wrest from you the revenge you so truly deserve, and reward your enemies with joy. His name was Solander, and he is called the Reborn, and for all his seeming goodness, he'll make you love him, then use your love to make you his slave.

Danya looked at the baby. He looked no different on the outside, but safely within the magical shield of the Ancients, she was walled off from the touch of his love. He couldn't move her with his sweet gazes or fill her with the warmth of his acceptance. He was just a baby, just a *thing* that would soon cry and shit and demand food.

She took a deep breath, staring at him. Not *just* a thing—her arms longed to hold him again, to feel his slight weight against her chest; she yearned to feel him feed at her breast, and to know that she fed him from herself. She desired his sweet scent, and the touch of his breath against her face. Not all the emotion she felt for him had come from him.

That's the betrayal of your body, Luercas told her. *All mothers hunger for those things, or else the species would not survive.*

Danya blocked him out. She didn't want to hear any more of what he had to say. But she could not accept the future that Luercas painted, either. She could not think of the Sabirs and the Galweighs rewarded when they had done her such evil. She could steel herself against her emotions for the moment. She could force herself to form the question she had to ask.

"Can I change this? Can I prevent the future you paint for me?"

You can. Or I should say, you could. *Now. Only now, only for this one moment, he's still weak. He has not become the unstoppable monster that he will be a few days from now. Now, at this moment, his body is still too new and too delicate to act as the channel for the magic he will command.*

But you won't do anything, because he chose you so carefully. He found someone who would need his love, some pitiful Scarred creature who had once been someone of importance, and who would cling to him as a link to the past she could never have again. The bastard won the moment he chose you as his mother, and now the world will pay forever.

"You can't know that. You don't know what I'm capable of." But she thought, The baby told me before he was born that he was my reward for having suffered so much. That he was coming to bring me joy. And love.

Luercas heard her thoughts and laughed. That laughter sounded hopeless and hollow to Danya.

You see? He has you.

Danya closed her eyes. She knew that the baby wasn't just a baby, no matter how much she might wish otherwise. Everything Luercas told her had the ring of truth to it. She could look at him with Wolf sight and *see* the truth. The infant in front of her would prevent her from taking her revenge. He would change everything, and because of him she would remain hollow, trapped within her anger. She would never be set free from the prison of her own memories, because the only key that would open the door of that prison was the blood of her enemies.

She couldn't even hold her own revenge up as the sole reason for stopping him. He aimed to bring back the Age of Wizards. He aimed to put the Falcons into power, to make himself into a god. Civilization had been destroyed a thousand years earlier by the Falcons and their enemies the Dragons. She didn't know if one group was better than the other, but she didn't care, either; magic had come through time into the hands of Wolves like her. Her kind kept it carefully secret, and did not threaten the world with it. Letting the Falcons return to power would betray her world.

She could not let him do what he had come to do.

He was a beautiful baby—but now that she looked at him closely, she could see the mark of his father on him. His hair was golden, his earlobes long, his skin pale. So his father had been Crispin Sabir. She closed her eyes and summoned memories of that monster. She revisited her pain, her fear, her humiliation. And when she opened her eyes again, she could see Crispin's mark more clearly on the babe.

"Tell me how to stop him, Luercas."

You already know. In your heart, in your soul, you already know what you have to do.

"But tell me anyway."

I won't. You seek someone that you can blame afterward. I won't be that someone. Either you are strong enough to stand alone, to act alone, or you are the weak thing he thought you were when he chose you.

She breathed in slowly. Her hands were shaking. The baby lay on the chair, sleeping peacefully. He was a beautiful baby. Her beautiful baby. But he was Crispin's baby, too, and the Falcons' savior. He was an evil thing cloaked in beauty.

And Luercas was right.

She knew what she had to do.

Chapter 35

Kait felt the rail against the small of her back. Her damp palms slid along the smooth, cool stone-of-Ancients without finding purchase; the sweat of terror soaked her clothing. The night wind bit her through the loose weave of her tunic, and she shivered.

Andrew and Anwyn approached her from opposite sides, weapons in hand. Grinning. Domagar stood by the central table—the torture table, she realized now—his face unreadable. He held knives in both hands, and he stared at her, a strange wildness in his eyes. He said, "Stop."

Everyone ignored him.

Anwyn said, "She won't hurt herself—she isn't so stupid as that. We may let her survive, but if she throws herself over, the fall will *surely* kill her."

Her magic shields and the scents she had soaked herself in kept her from revealing to them who and what she was, but they were going to find out too soon. She was going to Shift if she didn't get away soon, and all the scents in the world would not hide her identity then. And the one with his head shaved was Karnee. He would love to discover that she shared his Karnee form.

She had no options. Her years of classes in diplomacy had taught her that the diplomat who endangered his mission would do whatever he had to do to save it. The secrecy of the mission counted. Now the mission was to prevent those bastards from discovering the hiding place of Dùghall and Hasmal, who still had the chance to regain the Mirror. She could be a coward and destroy them, and die horribly. Or she could be brave, and die quickly.

Domagar was screaming, "I said *stop!*" Perhaps he saw the intent in her eyes. It didn't matter. The Karnee was Shifting, moving at her with that grin stretched across his face, becoming the four-legged killer.

She tensed her body and gripped the rail and shouted, "I *won't* stop!" as she launched herself backward into oblivion.

She fell, her jaws clamped tight to keep herself from screaming—she was determined to die silently, to steal from the three monsters in the tower even the slight pleasure they might have gotten from that proof of her fear.

Her body flung itself into Shift, frantic for survival even when the situation was hopeless. She felt her muscles burn and her skin stretch and flow. Her clothes tore away as she mutated into a form she didn't recognize. She tumbled until she fell facedown, and the city lay below her like stars in the sky flung to earth and spread on a bed of velvet. If she were to die, she would face death looking at the beauty of her home.

The night wind caught at her and buffeted her, and the jewels rolled beneath her.

The jewels rolled beneath her.

But they came no closer.

Her heart thudded in her chest, and her eyes, sharper and clearer, made out the individual ships in the dark and distant harbor and the shapes of horses and men and beasts in the streets below. She looked sidelong at her right arm. Behind a frame of bone so slender it looked like it would shatter at the slightest touch, a film of transparent skin billowed from distant fingers to delicate ankle. She flicked her index finger and her whole body followed her to the right. Her finger was twice as long as a tall man, her arm that long again. Wings. She had wings. She could fly.

This was Karnee, too?

By the gods, she could fly.

She was elated, but she made no noise. She let the wind fill her wings, and she pointed herself as best she could toward the quarter in which her friends waited for her. She didn't want the Karnee in the tower behind her to suspect that she'd survived. He might know about this flying. Worse, he might be good at it. She had never thrown herself off a tall tower expecting to die before, so her body had never had need to take on this winged form. The manuscripts she'd read didn't mention it.

She could fly.

She wondered what she looked like. She wondered how much of what she did to keep herself aloft was instinctive knowledge, and how much was sheer dumb luck that could run out at any time. She stretched her fingers and held the air in her hands and made it move where she wanted it to go. She glided, and imagined herself soaring in the warmth of the day, with the sun on her back, with the wind in her hair. She thought of hitting thermals in the airible, of watching the soaring birds using them to go ever higher while they hunted, circling around and around while they rose higher and higher, and she knew instinctively that she could use thermals. But of course there were none at night; the ground was cool and the sun couldn't warm columns of rising air. Where could she go to launch herself so that she could fly again? And how could she be sure the Shift would work correctly? What if this were the only time in her life she could fly? If it were, how could she step on the ground and know that she would never leave it again?

She would fly again. She promised herself that. The air was glorious. She held the night in her heart and embraced every slight sound, every scent that she'd thought she was losing forever. She was alive. Alive. And she could fly. The world was hers, and hope remained. Miracles happened. Somehow she and Dùghall and Hasmal would get the Mirror, and prevail against the Dragons. Somehow good would win over evil, and the Reborn would bring his love to all the world. She was alive, and infinite possibility lay open to her.

She circled above the quarter where her friends waited for her and found a place where she could safely land. A large garden, rich with the scents of melons and ripening maize and palomany, lay at one end of the street. No one was anywhere nearby. At the thought of landing, uncertainty gripped her. How was she to land? She'd watched birds do it often enough. But even baby birds required practice.

Wouldn't it be ironic to survive her plummet from the tower, only to die because she didn't know how to safely reach the ground?

She dropped toward the field as slowly as she could, cupping the air beneath her wings and hoping for the best. She reached forward with her feet, trying to emulate the birds she'd watched, wishing she'd watched them more closely. Her caution didn't help her. She hit the ground like a sack of rocks anyway, and tore the delicate skin on her right wing, and lay in a tumble in a field of smashed melons and downed stalks. But when she had calmed herself sufficiently, she managed to get up and to control her Shift back to human form, and the wounded flesh healed.

So she had another miracle to credit to the night. She was alive, and now on the ground and unhurt.

Of course, she was also naked and in a field at the end of a street that was busy even in the middle of the night, and she needed to get to an inn that sat three streets over and one back.

She grinned, unfazed. She was still alive, by the gods. She could handle anything.

Chapter 36

Danya stepped outside of the shield and picked up the baby. He opened his eyes and looked at her, trusting her. Loving her. His love encircled her again, and she responded to it. She pressed his soft face lightly against her scaled cheek and blinked back the tears that threatened to spill from them. He made a soft, mewling sound. He's hungry, she thought, and she put him to her breast.

She did not think about Luercas, about the future, about anything at all. She didn't dare let herself think. While she held him and fed him, she lived for that moment only, kneeling on the floor beside the chair that was still warm from her baby's presence. He wriggled and her arm cradled his tiny body, and his sweet scent filled her nostrils, and his love encompassed her. His tiny mouth tugged at her nipple, and her flat breasts tingled as they filled with milk. In that moment, she was a mother with a newborn baby, and she loved him and he loved her, and the future was nothing that mattered. In that moment, they were two bodies and two souls joined in a bond that transcended thought and mind and the necessity of the world.

The strangers—the Falcons—were all around her, but she ignored them. Luercas hovered inside her head, but she blocked him out, too. None of them had anything to do with this moment, with this beautiful thing that passed between her and her son. This moment was for her. It was something she could keep, something she could cherish. It was beyond right or wrong, beyond fair or unfair. It simply was.

The baby's eyes drifted shut, and Danya brushed one scaled finger along his skin, and leaned her face close to his again. She felt his breath on her cheek. She kissed him as best she could with her deformed face; her long muzzle and predator's teeth made the gesture almost impossible. He was already everything in her world. A tiny scrap of flesh and breath and life, and she wanted to give him everything he desired, wanted to build walls around him to keep him safe, and wanted to change the world to fit his needs.

She rose and climbed onto the dais again, this time holding him in her arms. As she slipped within the walls of the Ancients' shield, she felt the hundreds of tendrils that connected him to the distant Falcons snap, like the threads of a spiderweb when a hand brushed it away. He woke and looked at her again, but he didn't cry. He just looked, those round innocent eyes searching her face, uncomprehending.

He would not have been allowed to live past his first Gaerwanday in Calimekka, she thought. He was Scarred by magic, even if he looked outwardly human. He was already growing visibly—not yet a day old, he already had the form of an infant two or three months old. He would have been sacrificed to the gods of Iberism for the good of the people of Ibera.

He lay in her arms, and a smile flitted across his face. Eyes crinkled, dimples appeared, a broad toothless grin flashed and then vanished. He was a beautiful little boy. And helpless. He was still helpless.

But only for the moment.

She lifted a corner of the blanket away from his chest. She could see the lines of each tiny rib beneath his skin, could see his breath moving through his body, could see the tremor of the chest wall where his heart beat. A drop of water landed on his sternum and beaded and trembled in time to the beating of his heart, and she realized she was crying.

I love you, he said into her mind.

"I know," she whispered, and stabbed two talons into his skin, between those fragile ribs, into the tiny heart. "I love you, too. But you can't live—for the good of the people of Ibera, you can't live."

He screamed in pain, and bright blood welled up around her talons. She held them in place and the first wave of magic rolled over her as he tried to heal himself. The magic flowed from him into her, though, and she felt her body changing again—felt her skin burning and her bones melting and her blood boiling through her veins.

He screamed, *Save me!* into her mind, but she closed his mind-cries out the way she blocked out his physical shrieks.

He thrashed and his tiny hands flailed against her talons, and his round little feet drummed against her chest.

She was doing the wrong thing. She knew it. She knew she was wrong to sacrifice him, just as she knew the people of Ibera were wrong to sacrifice their Scarred children. She could still save him. He could still live, if she just pulled those claws free from his heart. He would still be her child, and he would forgive her the evil thing she had tried to do.

But she had sworn to the gods that she would have her revenge. In order to keep her promise, she had to make this sacrifice. One baby had to die. One baby. Her baby, and only because he stood between her and the justice she owed to the Sabirs and the Galweighs. She had seen him in the future, standing at the head of the Falcons, with all the world subject to his edicts, and she could not allow that, either.

The second wave of magic hit her, and she hung on. She could feel his desperation even as her body melted and mutated—and then she felt the thing that almost stopped her. She felt his love. He still loved her.

She cried out and closed her eyes tightly and turned her face away from him. She pictured Crispin Galweigh, the rape, the torture, her pain. She fought to find her hatred, and felt it slipping between her clawed fingers. "I have to do this!" she screamed. "You'll ruin everything!"

He stopped struggling. He was weak, now. There would be no more magic. She opened her eyes and looked at him; she had to face the fact that she did this thing, that she *chose* to do this. She had to take responsibility for what she did.

He lay along her arm, limp and barely breathing, with blood coating his chest. His eyes watched her, and in spite of everything, they were full of love. *Poor Danya,* he whispered into her head. *Luercas lied to you.*

The life went out of him at last, and she pulled her talons from his heart and lay his tiny body on the dais and knelt over him, weeping. He was dead, and the love he had poured into her was gone, withdrawn beyond her reach forever. She shuddered and stared at her hand, the hand that had killed him. The talons of the first two fingers, the talons she had buried in her son's heart, remained unchanged, as did the fingers out of which they grew. But the rest of her hand had become . . . her hand. Human. Smooth pale skin, delicately tapered fingers, a slender palm attached to a finely boned wrist, a graceful arm, a softly rounded shoulder. Beneath her leather wraps, full, soft human breasts heavy with milk. A small waist, a flat belly, lean, muscular legs. Her left hand was perfectly human. She touched her face. It was once again her face.

With his magic, he had given her back herself. Dying, he had tried to give her back her life. She could have let him live, she could have gone home.

She stared at the two beast's claws that had killed him—the Reborn—her gift. They marked her as Scarred, but she could cut them off. She could take an ax and hack them off and go home, except she had sworn to have her revenge on her Family.

Her Family would welcome her back now, but her oath to the gods stood between her and them.

I could have let it all go. I could have begged the forgiveness of the gods. But I have sacrificed my son to my oath. I'm bound by his life.

She stroked the soft cheek of her son. "I could have been a real mother for you," she whispered. "I'm sorry."

A sickly blue glow surrounded the baby's body, and Danya pulled her hand away. Magic touched him again, but this time it came from the outside, accompanied by the reek of rotted meat and honeysuckle. The holes in his chest closed, though two black scars remained to show where her claws had dug through him. His chest rose once. Fell. Rose again.

She wanted to rejoice, but she couldn't. She felt no love when she reached out to touch him—instead she felt terrifying coldness and calculating watchfulness. The infant took another breath, and his eyes focused. After a pause, he took another breath, and then another, and then the fact that he was breathing again ceased to seem miraculous. His arms moved, but cautiously. Experimentally. He gave two quick kicks with his legs, then let them rest, too. Another smile crossed his face, but this smile had none of the infant innocence she had seen in her son's only smile. This smile was smug. Self-satisfied. Evil. Whatever spirit inhabited the body of her son, it was not her son's.

"I should think not," the baby said in a whispery, thin voice. It struggled to sit up, but couldn't. "You know me, Danya. I'm your friend Luercas. I'm going to be your new son."

No. She couldn't watch someone else grow in her baby's body. Not even Luercas, who had saved her life. Luercas suddenly terrified her. She reached for him with her talons, determined that her son's body would not be tainted by a stranger's spirit. A flash of powerful, furious magic shot from the baby's fingers straight at her eyes. It drove her back, fire burrowing in her skull. She screamed and collapsed on the dais, and gripped her eyes. Pain roared through her head.

"I didn't hurt you permanently," Luercas said. "*This* time. But don't try that again. You want your revenge, and you'll get it, but not without me. And I needed a body. No sense letting this perfectly good one go to waste." A chuckle that made her skin crawl. "Until I can make this body do what I want it to, you can take care of me. Feed me. Change me. So you see, you didn't lose your baby after all."

But she had. Her baby, dying, told her that Luercas had lied to her. She realized that was true, that Luercas had found a way to lead her in the direction he'd wanted her to go. But she had followed. Willingly, she had followed, and now her baby was gone and something evil had taken his place. What sort of mistake had she made?

One she needed to undo. She could leave Luercas behind, run away as fast as she could, never return to In-kanmerea. He would die without her, and whatever evil he'd planned would die with him.

"Don't even think it. You and I are going to do tremendous things. We are going to be immortal and own the world. We'll need a little time, and a bit of effort, but together we'll manage. You're just having qualms right now, and that's understandable. Infanticide is a nasty thing, and hard to get over. But you'll put it behind you."

She lay on the dais, still blind, still in pain. "I won't. I did something evil."

"Well, yes. You did. And you did it voluntarily."

"I can't live with myself," she whispered. The answer came clear to her then. She could kill herself, pay for the evil she'd done, and stop Luercas at the same time.

"No, you can't." The little baby voice sounded so delicate that she couldn't understand how it could have such a foul undertone. "I won't let you kill yourself any more than I'll let you kill me. You're stuck with me. You'll do what I want you to do voluntarily, or you'll do it because I make you. I can do that. Either way, I'm going to get what I want, and you're going to give it to me. But you can make yourself as my ally, Danya, or you can find out that you're my slave."

She cringed.

"Now pick me up and feed me," he said. "I'm hungry. And when you're finished, take me back to the village. You'll have to think of something to tell them about your new look. The Kargans don't like humans much." He laughed again. "But if you're a good girl and don't try to give me trouble, maybe I'll fix those fingers of yours."

She picked the infant up, wishing him dead. Wishing herself dead.

Chapter 37

Kait crawled through the window she'd left open and dropped to the floor with a relieved sigh. If she ever had anything worth stealing again she might someday regret it, but her bad habit of not closing windows came in useful from time to time—this night she was grateful that she wouldn't have to parade naked through the tavern that lay on the ground floor of the inn, where men and women still sat eating and drinking and watching the two dancers who twined and shimmied to the smoky beat of the tala drums.

But she only had an instant to be grateful. She realized she wasn't alone, and a heartbeat behind that, she heard breathing, caught his scent and *felt,* with that sixth sense she could only think of as magic, that the darker shadow in the darkest corner of the unlit room was Ry. He wore an air of waiting and anticipation around him like a heavy cloak.

She froze and stared into the corner. "Why are you in my room, Ry?"

"I'm celebrating the fact that you're alive." His voice was velvet, and her pulse quickened at the sound of it. "Waiting to congratulate you on your escape. I had to celebrate alone until you got here because your uncle and Hasmal and damned Ian are convinced you're dead. They took offense at signs of merriment from me."

"How did you—" she started to ask, but when she thought about it, she already knew how he knew she'd survived. Part of him was bound as tightly to her as her own soul. She took a deep breath. "I—thank you for . . . waiting for me. I'm amazed that I survived. . . . I didn't expect to when I jumped."

He rose, and took a step toward her. She took a step back in response. He said, "You were courageous. Even facing torture, I don't know that I would have jumped to my death to protect my friends." He paused. "I like to *think* that I would have. My record for doing the brave thing hasn't been so wonderful, though."

Kait realized suddenly that he could see her much more clearly than she could see him—he stood in the shadows, but the light from the moon and the stars shone in the window, and she still stood clearly framed by that. She felt the heat rising to her cheeks, and said, "I have to let everyone else know I'm back. Leave just a moment for me, please? I'll hurry, and we can talk once I'm dressed."

"We could do that," he agreed, but he didn't move.

She waited. He still didn't move. She cleared her throat and said, "I have clothes in the trunk behind you, but I can't reach them if you're standing there."

He didn't say anything for the longest time. Finally, he murmured, "I know that," and the dark, silky timbre of his voice made her skin prickle and her heart race.

Weary though she was from Shift, hungry and worn and dragged down, still her body responded to the fire she sensed in him. Every sound came clearer to her ears, every scent grew sharp and separate, every form in the room seemed to glow with its own inner light. Her long abstinence fed her hunger, but more than that, his presence fed her. She wanted him, as she had wanted him from the first time she caught his scent in the air, and her body sang with eagerness. "Oh, no," she whispered.

"Why 'no,' Kait? Why always no? When I crossed the ocean pursuing you, every night I dreamed that we danced, you and I. That we floated over gardens and fields and forests, naked in each other's arms; that I held you and that we moved together to music that we felt but never heard. Every night, I slept with your body pressed against mine, and every morning, I awoke to nothing."

"I know," Kait said after a moment.

"It wasn't a dream," Ry told her. "It was real. It was the truth. You and I were made for each other. We are the two halves of a single perfect soul, and our incomplete souls reach out, when we sleep, for the only thing that will complete them. In our sleep, we are together because we are supposed to be together."

Kait shook her head.

She saw the quick flash of his teeth—a brief, stubborn smile in the darkness. "Yes. You know we're meant to be. You *know*. Yet you refuse this . . . this gift the gods have given us . . . even though you and I are the only ones who suffer when you refuse."

"You're *Sabir*."

"And you're *Galweigh*. And I don't care. I didn't care when my parents told me I couldn't have you. I didn't care when my mother told me she would make me *barzanne* if I pursued you instead of taking over as head of the Sabir Wolves. Well . . ." He paused. "I did care about that, but I came anyway. And I don't care what my Family thinks now, or what they will think in the future. I waited a lifetime to find you." He laughed softly, a mirthless laugh. "Mine was a lifetime of careful celibacy and painful restraint—partly to avoid the fate my Family planned for me, but partly because I knew that somewhere you existed, and I didn't want to be tied to anyone when I finally found you."

Kait felt the pain of her own past weighing on her then. "I wasn't so . . . circumspect."

"Ian." She could hear the distaste in his voice; he covered it well, but not perfectly.

"Not just Ian."

A sigh. "I know. I accept your past. I had training in controlling the Karnee drives from the time I was born. You obviously didn't."

"The *Family* would have demanded that I be sacrificed with the rest of the Scarred children on Gaerwanday, had they known about me. *My* family hid me, and got me to a house in the country, and raised me on a farm away from sight until they'd taught me what they could about hiding my . . . curse. My mother and father had given birth to boys on two occasions who were Karnee, but both were murdered in their cribs before they reached their first month, so my parents knew nothing, really, about the Karnee Curse or how I could control it. They read Family histories and gleaned what they could from those, and learned the rest from trial and error. They taught me what they could." She shrugged. "As far as I know, I'm the only Galweigh Karnee."

As soon as she said it, she wished she hadn't told him that. Better perhaps that he should think the Galweighs had a number of Karnee, as the Sabirs did.

But he seemed uninterested in the strategic import of what she'd told him. He shrugged. "I know about your past lovers. They're past."

It was her turn to laugh. "I haven't had lovers. I've had *encounters.* Brief meetings with strangers when the curse drove me the hardest. I can only call one of the men from my past a lover, and he . . ." She fell silent. And he was Ian, and he still loved her, and she still cared deeply about what happened to him. And the moment she declared herself for Ry—the instant she told Ian of her choice—she hurt him in a way she could never undo. She would not make such a decision lightly.

Ry said, "The past is the past. It doesn't control the present unless you let it. *My* past is behind me forever. I've found the Reborn; my first loyalties can never be to Sabir again, any more than yours can be to Galweigh. You and I walk the same path now." He looked at her, and in the darkness she caught a change in his eyes. They began to reflect the light in the room as a cat's would. His voice when he spoke again was deeper. Huskier. "But that's not all. Kait. I love you. I need you." He took another step toward her, and she could feel the burning edge of Shift pushing him. "Dance with me."

She could tell herself forever that she avoided him because she honored her Family, but when she looked into her heart, she knew that was only partly true. She also avoided him because he would take her into an unknown realm. She knew pain, and loneliness, and despair. She knew emptiness. She knew how to settle for less than what she wanted; she knew how to pretend to feel something she didn't feel; she knew how to live on scraps and refuse. She hated those things, those feelings, but she had survived them before and she knew she could survive them again.

But she knew nothing of the realm of love. Of the banquet of passion. Of the feast of genuine, mutual desire. Those terrified her. "I'm not ready," she said, and wasn't sure whether she had said it aloud or only to herself.

"Dance with me," he whispered.

He took another step toward her, and she knew that if she never had the courage to declare what she wanted, she would never really live. She could deny herself the love she wanted, but that wouldn't make her dead Family return to life, and it wouldn't create in her the love that would be the only thing that would satisfy Ian's wishes. She couldn't give Ian what he truly desired, and if she kept it from herself, they would both be unhappy.

He took another step toward her.

And she walked into his arms and whispered, "Yes."

Their bodies pressed against each other, her skin against the silk of his shirt, the leather of his pants. Their cheeks touched, and their hands twined together. They moved slowly, spinning around to the faint, sensual beat of the tala drums that rose through the wood-plank floor.

The dance was the dance of her dreams, though this time her feet touched the ground. They moved together surely, confidently, knowing when to step, how to turn, as if this were the hundredth time they had danced this way instead of the first. Perhaps her dreams and his dreams had been real, and it truly was.

They stepped and turned, stepped and turned, gliding left, spinning right. His warmth surrounded her. She pressed her face against his chest, liking the broad expanse of hard, flat muscle. She inhaled his scent—musk and spices, heat and hunger. They danced that way for a while, and then he kissed her once, lightly, at the point where neck and shoulder met.

She shivered, but not from the cold. She slipped one hand free from his and with it undid the laces of his shirt while the two of them kept dancing. Leaned close and kissed the hollow of his throat, and he made a sound halfway between a purr and a growl. Freed her other hand and slid both arms around his waist, and pulled the tail of his shirt loose from his pants, and let both hands wander beneath the shirt, stroking the lean, hard muscles of his back, discovering the heat and texture of his skin, the soft triangle of silky fur between his shoulders at the base of his neck.

His hands in the meantime settled on her bare shoulders and slowly, slowly stroked down either side of her spine to the small of her back.

She lifted Ry's shirt over his head and let it drop to the floor. They danced skin to skin as they had in the dreams, the fullness of her breasts pressed hard against the furred breadth of his chest.

In the tavern below, the beat of the talas quickened.

She fumbled with the buckle of his belt, and he moved one hand from her back to release it with a short, impatient tug. He loosed the laces of his pants, too, but then returned his hand to her back. She got his message—he would go so far on his own, but no farther. She would have to show him she wanted him.

Her heart pounded and her blood burned. In the dreams, they had only danced, but she wanted more than dancing. She wanted him, wanted to take him as her lover—wanted to meld with him, to complete herself.

She stopped dancing and tugged his pants down. He kicked off his boots, stepped out of pants and underclothes. Waited. The beat of the drums, resonating through the floor, mimicked the racing of her heart.

He kicked his clothes out of the way, then enfolded her hands in his and began to dance with her again. They moved slowly, sensuously, skin against silken skin, heat to heat, kissing lightly, nipping and biting, dragging fingernails down backs, always spinning close and then stepping apart, then pulling together again, tighter than before.

At last they danced their way into a corner, and Ry stopped. "Now," he said.

And she said, "Now."

He stepped in closer and caught her around the waist and lifted her up, and pressed her back to the wall. She locked her legs around his hips. And as the tala drums died away to silence, they danced another, older dance.

asmal began to sense the wrongness of the night even before Kait leaped from the tower. He'd carried that gut-wrenching premonition of pending disaster with him while he watched her fall and when he and Dùghall lashed out at Ry for insisting she lived. While he and Dùghall knelt on the floor of the common room, saying the offices for a dead Falcon—for though Kait had not taken the oaths of the Falcons, and though she had not yet learned all the secrets, both of them agreed that she had been a Falcon in truth—that sense of doom had grown worse.

The sense of wrongness had become an inescapable horror as the night progressed, until Hasmal asked Dùghall if he felt it, too.

"Of course I feel it," Dùghall had snapped. "She's dead, and lost to us forever. How could I not feel it?"

But Hasmal wasn't convinced that his grief over Kait's death was the demon that rode him.

Ian joined them for the final prayers, and Hasmal wished he would go away. In normal circumstances he would have been pleased to share the burden of praying a soul safely through the Veil—in normal circumstances, it was a burden best shouldered by as many as would willingly assume the task. But the presence of even such allies as Ian grated on him like a rasp on bare bone. The night felt like it would never become dawn.

When Yanth burst into the room in the midst of their prayers, grinning like an idiot, and Ry stepped in behind him holding Kait's hand, Hasmal had looked at his clearly unharmed friend and had been unable to find any joy inside himself at the indubitable proof of her survival. He cared about her; she was a dear confidante and a trusted colleague; and *still* the fact that she lived couldn't even begin to penetrate the haze of dread that gripped him.

Ry stood staring at him and Dùghall and Ian, his face bewildered. "She's alive, you asses," he said. "You can put aside your mourning clothes and leave your prayers for someone who needs them. She's *alive.*"

Dùghall rose, looking old and stiff and bent, and walked over to Kait, a false smile on his face, and embraced her the way a polite man embraces the confused stranger who insists he is a dear friend of years past. "You're a sight for hurting hearts," he said. But Hasmal heard in the old man's voice the same pain he felt in his own soul. The entire universe vibrated like strings tuned off key.

Kait frowned and turned to Ry and said, "You said they didn't believe you when you told them I was alive, but I'd think they didn't believe *me.*"

Ry put one arm around her shoulders in a protective gesture and said, "I don't know what's the matter with them. But you have me."

"I do," she said, and turned into his arms and kissed him.

Ian looked like she had slapped him, and Hasmal felt the man reverberate with an echo of the night's wrongness. Ian stared at Kait with eyes gone flat and hard and cold, and said, "You've chosen, then."

She swallowed and nodded. "It isn't as if . . . I don't want you to be . . . happy or . . ." Her voice trailed off and she shook her head. "Yes. I have. I've chosen. I'm sorry, Ian—I truly am."

His hand moved to his sword, seemingly on its own, and Hasmal braced himself for sudden violence. But Ian only fingered the sword's pommel and said, "You need not apologize to me. You were always free to take the path you desired. I had hoped I would be on that path, but I wouldn't want to spend my life with someone who didn't love me, no matter how much I loved her." His whole face tightened, and he looked at Ry. "I wish you every happiness. Brother." That was said in a voice Hasmal would have reserved for cursing enemies into Iberan hell.

Then Ian stalked from the room, his movements angry and his back stiff.

And Hasmal thought perhaps *that* was the heart of the despair that clutched at his heart, but no—the wrongness of Ian's fury was a single grain of sand on an infinite beach compared to the hollow, foul fear that gripped Hasmal. He said, "Kait, your return brings me great joy, but I'm exhausted. Dùghall and I have been praying and performing the Falcons' last offices since we thought you died." He hugged her and kissed both her cheeks. "I'll be more able to show my happiness after I've had some sleep, and more eager then to hear how you survived what I thought was a terrible fall."

Dùghall nodded. "As will I. Dear girl, you've twice returned to me from the dead, and I am overjoyed. And after sleep and the morrow's late breakfast, we'll celebrate."

When everyone had left but Dùghall, though, Hasmal said, "Something weighs on my soul tonight. Some part of the universe has gone astray. I'm sick at heart, and I don't know why."

Dùghall said, "As am I. I fear, and don't know what frightens me. We must find peace. Sit with me, and we'll go to the Reborn."

Hasmal dropped cross-legged to the floor and released his shields. The darkness inside didn't leave him. When Dùghall got into position, both men closed their eyes and began spinning out the delicate tendril of soul-stuff that would connect them to the Reborn. But this time, the magic didn't work.

Hasmal struggled to put his whole concentration into his meditation; he cleared his mind and breathed slowly and focused on the still center and on the clear bell-pure ringing that was the sound at the heart of the universe, and even when he held those things inside of him and his mind was still as motionless water, he could not reach the Reborn.

Dùghall's voice broke his meditation. The old man's voice shook as he whispered, "We must offer our blood."

They brought out blood-bowl and thorns and tourniquet, and spilled their blood into the silvered surface, and said the *He'ie abojan*, the prayer of those who waited in the long darkness. They summoned the magic that would connect them to Solander. And they waited. The blood in the bowl lay untouched. No radiant fire burned through it, building the bridge between the Reborn and his Falcons. No warmth flowed from it, no energy filled Hasmal, no love touched him. Where he had once felt the reborn hope of the world, the fount of joy, now he felt . . . emptiness.

He prayed harder. He pushed harder. His body stiffened and his breathing grew rough. He felt tears beginning to leak from the corners of his eyes; he tasted their salt burning at the back of his throat. Finally he opened his eyes and stared down at the blood-bowl, at the dark puddle congealing in its center. He touched Dùghall, who opened his eyes. Dùghall, too, had been crying.

"He's gone."

"I know." The old man nodded, and his suddenly haggard face looked ancient.

"Where has he gone? Why can't we find him?"

Dùghall wiped roughly at his eyes with a sleeve, then looked down at his hands. "We've lost, Has. We've lost everything, and the Dragons have won. Solander is dead."

"No," Hasmal said, but he knew it was true. Some part of him had known from the moment it happened that the Reborn had been taken from them. Stolen. Murdered. He couldn't understand how such a nightmare could come to pass, but he knew that it had. "None of the prophecies ever hinted that this could happen," he said. "Nowhere did Vincalis give an indication that the Reborn would be in danger when he returned. Solander was promised to us. Promised. How could this . . . ?"

But Dùghall waved him off, wearily. "How doesn't matter, son. Why doesn't matter. The only thing that matters is that the Reborn is dead, and the Falcons are dead with him. The Dragons have won."

The Falcons were dead. The hope of the world was dead. The promise of a great civilization that spanned the world, that rose above war and evil, that based itself on love and peace and joy—all of that, too, had been murdered with a distant babe, while a thousand years of faithful, patient prayer and offered blood became as nothing.

Solander was dead. Hasmal rose, wondering how the world could even continue to exist. He plodded to the room he shared with Ian, stripped off his clothes and let them drop to the floor, crawled into his narrow bed, closed his eyes, and wished himself into oblivion. If he did not wake to greet the new day, he would consider himself no worse off than he was already.

Chapter 39

When morning came, it announced itself only as a slight lessening of the night's darkness. Kait shifted in Ry's arms, listened to the drumming of a downpour against the inn's shutters, and considered going back to sleep. But she felt surprisingly good. She'd Shifted the night before, she'd had nothing to eat afterward, and because she had spent the night in Ry's arms she had only had a little sleep, yet she suffered neither the exhaustion nor the depression that always plagued her post-Shift.

She rolled over and kissed Ry's neck, and bit him lightly. "Wake up. Let's do something."

"We were doing something," he murmured, his muffled voice sounding eminently reasonable. "We were sleeping."

"I know. But I want to do something more interesting. Let's go out and get something to eat."

"It's pouring rain. The streets are knee-deep in water—listen. You can hear the roar of it running down to the bay. Let's sleep."

"Don't be dull. I feel too good to stay in bed."

Ry raised his head and grinned at her. "My beautiful love—if you insist on being awake, at least I can think of things we could do without getting out of bed."

"We can do those things, too." She leaned over and nibbled on the lobe of his ear. "And *then* we can go get something to eat. I'm ravenous."

He flopped back on the pillow and sighed. "How ravenous are you?"

"I Shifted last night and I've had nothing to eat since."

"*That* ravenous. Oh." Ry jumped out of the bed and began pulling on pants, shirt, and boots without another word. He made his haste intentionally comical, and Kait laughed appreciatively, but the fact that he responded immediately underscored something about their relationship that Kait had never experienced before. She was with someone who understood. Who knew what it was to be Karnee; who had felt the madness of Shift racing through his own flesh; who knew the hunger that followed as intimately as she did.

Being understood was disorienting, but pleasantly so.

Kait got out of bed and began dressing, too. "What about the bed sports you mentioned?"

He looked at her sidelong, and his smile teased her. "Your lovely body and wondrous kisses will wait. I have no wish to become your next meal."

Kait and Ry negotiated their way along the quarter's raised walkways and over crossing stones at intersections, while the muddy torrents of rainwater roared beneath their feet and sheets of rain poured down on them. They were nearing the end of the rainy season, but had obviously not yet reached it. Calimekka, however, did not let itself be distracted by the vagaries of weather. The business of the city went on.

In the market district, they found a few eateries already doing brisk business with day laborers and merchants who would be opening their shops and stalls soon. Kait and Ry joined a few who stood, soaked and shivering, beneath the bright red awning of a pie-seller's shop; the two of them debated the merits of adder, rattlesnake, venison, monkey, parrot, turkey, and grasshopper as fillings before settling on a large combination pie that sat steaming on the shop sill. The various meats had been sweetened with chunks of mango and tanali and made richer with sliced manadoga root and coconut, and the thick crust had been glazed with a savory nut butter.

Kait forced herself to eat slowly. If she weren't careful, she could give away her nature simply by eating in front of strangers. She thought of how often people said to each other that they were "dying for a good meal," or "dying for an ice," or "dying for a big slab of juicy mutton," and considered that, unlike most of them, she could literally die for a meal. The thought injected a little needle of unpleasantness into her lovely morning.

She and Ry wandered hand-in-hand through the profit-gate into the maze of covered stalls in the inner market. They found a peccary stand where the shopkeeper used netting to keep most of the flies off the carcasses he had hanging from hooks along the front. Kait thought this was a nice touch, and picked out a plump little piglet that had been roasted on a spit, and that the pig-man had braised in its own juices, without spices. She split that with Ry. Still hungry, she led him even farther into the increasingly crowded huddle of shops, and brought them up to a place that sold one of her favorite treats— honey-dipped roasted parrots on sticks. The price was reasonable, and she ate two, wishing that she dared to have more, but knowing that she would draw too much attention to herself if she did.

By the time they reached the street again, the rain had let up and the sun was beginning to show through the clouds. The streets steamed in the heat, and the arcs of three rainbows marked the sky.

"Shall we go back to the inn now," Ry asked, "or do you think you need to get a sweet or two to hold you over to midday? Say, a basket of melons or some lucky shopkeeper's entire stock of sweetened ices?"

She laughed. "You don't need to sound so prissy. You'll have your turn before long." She looked down the street in both directions. There were other shops that sold things she would enjoy, but though she could eat, she thought she'd let her appetite regain its keenness before she did. "I'll live till the next meal. We can go back to the inn." She leaned over and kissed him on the cheek, and his warmth and his scent made her suddenly hungry in other ways. She ran a fingertip down his chest and flashed a wicked smile. "In fact, I'll race you there. If you can catch me"—her grin grew wider—"you get to keep me."

He grabbed for her, but she leaped out of his reach and bounded down the street, arms pumping and head up. She shot across the crossing stones, touching down only in the center of the street, pounded along one raised walk after another, and careened around corners, oblivious of the danger any obstacles might pose to her . . . or she to them. She ran flat out, putting everything she had into the race, exhilarated by the fun of the chase.

When Ry popped up in front of her, not even winded, as she hurtled past the alley beside the inn, she burst out laughing. He caught her in midstride, wrapping his arms around her waist and lifting her into the air. Her momentum spun the two of them around in a circle.

"Caught you," he said.

His fingertips touched at her navel; he held her with her back against his chest, with her feet dangling a hand's breadth above the ground. She lay her head back against his shoulder and looked up at him. "So you did. Clever of you to find that shortcut." She was panting, still breathless from the run. "So now I'm yours. What are you going to do with me?"

"Do you really want to know?"

"Not really. I'll be just as happy if you surprise me."

He shifted her around, sliding one arm under her knees and the other along her back, and when he held her cradled, he kissed her slowly.

"You can put me down now," she said after a long moment.

"I could. But you belong to me now, and I don't want to."

He carried her into the quiet tavern, and through to the stairs that led up to the rooms. Halfway up, they met Dùghall coming down.

Kait got one look at his face and something inside her grew still and wary. In all the years she'd known him, she had never seen his eyes look lifeless; she had never thought of him as truly old. In that moment, however, he looked both ancient and unwell.

"Put me down," she whispered to Ry, but he was already swinging her feet to the floor when she spoke. "Uncle, what's wrong?"

"I've been waiting for you to get back." His voice sounded like death. "We have to leave. Quickly."

"Leave?" She frowned. He was pushing past her, already heading down the stairs. "What's happened? Have the Dragons discovered our hiding place here?"

He didn't even look back at her. "Worse. Come. Your things are already packed. I'll explain when we're on our way."

She and Ry turned, and Dùghall led them out a side door, where Hasmal, Yanth, Valard, and Jaim waited. Trev drove up on a rickety farm wagon pulled by a pair of spavined horses, his pale round face bleak and frightened. The wagon was full of straw bales.

"We've hollowed out a place in the center," Trev said.

And Dùghall said, "In. Quickly."

They climbed over the outer row of bales and crouched down on their bags, which covered the slatted wagon floor; when all of them were hidden, Trev tipped the inner bales toward each other and piled a few on top to form a makeshift roof.

The wagon lurched, the wheels rattled over the cobblestones, and everyone jostled into each other, knees and elbows poking uncomfortably. They hardly had breathing room.

Lucky, Kait thought, that there weren't any more of them. Then she realized Ian was no longer with them.

"Where's Ian?" she asked.

The haunted look Dùghall fixed on her made her think that he was dead.

But Dùghall said, "He was gone this morning . . . took all his belongings with him. He left a note telling Hasmal that he would be back after midday, by the end of Nerin at the latest, that he'd thought of something that would help us. I trusted him, but Hasmal suggested that we do a viewing on him to see what he was doing. We gathered a few hairs from his bed and linked him to them."

He shook his head and fell silent.

"What?" Ry asked. "What did you find?"

"He sold us out. We tracked him to Sabir House. When we saw him, he was telling a lesser functionary that he knew of a plot against the Sabirs headed by Ry Sabir and his inamorata, Kait Galweigh. He said if they would hire him, his first act as a Sabir employee would be to give the plotters over to the Family." Dùghall sighed and rubbed his temples. "If you had come back any later, you might have found the Sabirs waiting for you. I believe the only reason they weren't was that Ian had trouble convincing the House functionaries to grant him an audience with the people he needed." He leaned against the bale of straw behind him and closed his eyes. "As it is, they might find us before we can get out of the city."

Kait pressed her head into Ry's chest. Ry kept his arm tightly around her. She'd made her choice, and Ian had made his.

Ry said, "I should have killed him when I had the chance. Then he couldn't have betrayed us."

"He helped us," Kait said. "You can't kill an ally because someday he may turn on you. Anyone could turn on you someday." She remembered Ian dragging the Mirror of Souls across the rough plains of North Novtierra, of him fighting side by side with Hasmal and the now-dead Turben and Jayti, of him taking charge and getting them to safety in the Thousand Dancers—of the multitude of other things he'd done for them and with them. She remembered, as well, the nights she'd spent in his bed, in his arms, and his happiness when she was with him.

Then Kait recalled the expression on Ian's face the night before, when he saw Ry's arm around her shoulder. His eyes had flashed from pain through anger to a strange, flat blankness that made him look hollow. She recalled the deadly coldness in his voice when he wished his brother happiness.

She knew she'd hurt him then, but she hadn't thought he would be capable of the sort of betrayal he'd committed. She'd expected him to accept her decision. Maybe be angry, maybe hostile. She'd considered that he might not speak to her, or that if he did, he would be cold. She even thought he might choose to leave their little group and return to the sea. She'd misjudged him badly, but from the start she had brushed aside her gut feelings about him and allowed herself to trust him because she needed him.

She closed her eyes, seeing the choices she'd made and watching them lead to the moment where Ian sold her out, and she could see where she'd chosen badly time after time. She knew the night she first approached Ian Draclas to take her across the ocean in search of an Ancients' city that he wasn't trustworthy. That night she'd expected him to try throwing her overboard once he was sure of the city's location; she'd done what she could to eliminate any such attempt from his plans. He'd claimed to be a smuggler, but in her darker moments she'd suspected him of piracy, and she had always heard that there were no honorable men among pirates. She'd seen the avarice and the power-lust in his eyes from the first, and had noticed the way he looked at her when he didn't know she was watching—as if she were the gold prize in a contest. She'd seen the ease with which he assumed different characters and acted different parts and became complete strangers, and yet she let herself believe that the man he pretended to be around her was somehow more real than those other faces he created. Knowing that she was Karnee, and that her curse affected the way men reacted to her, she nonetheless let herself believe that he loved her—and because she believed he loved her, she allowed herself to trust him.

In that, she'd been a fool.

She closed her eyes and wished she could hate him. He'd sold her out to her enemies; he'd sold her *life*. He had *earned* her hatred . . . but she didn't hate him. She'd allowed herself to like him too much— she recalled the way he'd rescued Rru-eeth and the slave children from torture and death at the risk of his own life, and the way he fought beside her against the airibles, and the way he had held her in his arms. She'd spent too much time discovering things about him that were honorable and kind and courageous, and when she thought of him, those were the pictures her mind summoned first.

The instant Ian discovered he wouldn't get what he wanted—that he wouldn't be able to marry her and acquire the Galweigh status and power and the rights to the Novtierran city she owned—he went straight to the people who would pay the most to get her. He hadn't just turned on her, though. He'd turned on Dùghall, whom she believed he had liked a great deal. And worse, he'd betrayed the Reborn. More than anything else, she couldn't understand how he could do that.

"Dùghall, you helped Ian touch the Reborn, didn't you? Several weeks ago?"

Dùghall looked at her with anguish in his eyes and nodded.

"Quiet back there," Trev said suddenly. "Checkpoint coming up." Everyone in the cart fell silent. The cart clattered and shook, and came to a stop, and the city noises flowed in. Bells rang; herders and farmers and craftsmen shouted to each other or explained their cargoes to the taxmen who waited at the checkpoint to collect their transit taxes; in the distance some crier from a minor sect of Iberism called her faithful to prayers; children shrieked with laughter; and over it all, the city breathed with every door that opened or closed, and its arteries pumped with the people and their belongings that moved through its countless streets and alleys.

Checkpoints. The gates that pierced the many walls of Calimekka were remnants of a time when the city fit within smaller borders. They had, over the years, been claimed by the Families, who maintained the walls around the gates and the strips of road near them, and who taxed those who passed through them for the privilege of using the gate. The checkpoints also allowed the various Families to keep an eye on everyone who entered or left their domains, what they were doing, where they were going, and whether or not they were welcome on that Family's land.

Kait imagined the taxman at the upcoming gate demanding that Trev unload the first bales from the wagon so that they could see those behind. She could just see one of the big guard dogs shoving his nose into the straw and barking the alarm that the cargo hid secrets within. She closed her eyes and offered her own strength and put that into a shield that she cast over the whole of the wagon, and everyone in it . . . and even the horses. She designed the shield to make Trev and his cargo appear innocuous, and to deflect suspicion. She couldn't understand why Hasmal and Dùghall had not already cast such a shield, but both of them looked sick. Perhaps they were too sick to manage the magic.

She could tell they'd joined a queue waiting to get through the gate because the cart rolled forward and stopped. Rolled forward and stopped. Rolled forward and stopped. Each time they rolled closer, she could hear the taxman at the gate more clearly, and each time she noted his hostility toward the people in line her apprehension grew. Everyone hidden within the hay huddled in silence, afraid to move or breathe.

Finally they reached the head of the queue. Outside the cart, so close she could have reached through to touch him, the guard dog sat and panted.

"Family?" the taxman asked.

"Ainthe-Aburguille, distantly. No *Family* affiliation."

"Cargo?"

"Straw, thirty bales." Trev sounded bored, as if this were something he did every day. Kait marveled at his control. She was certain that she would have been sitting there thinking about the people hiding in the back of the wagon and what would happen to them and her if they got caught, had she been in his seat.

"Destination?"

"Low Kafar-by-the-Sea."

She frowned. She'd never heard of such a place.

The taxman apparently had, however. "That's a far piece to haul straw." The taxman didn't sound so hostile anymore.

"Got to sell it. Doesn't really matter where. So I figured to make the trip and see family out that way while I'm there. The folks in Kafar will buy from me because they know me, and I can check in on my da and my ma and my little brothers. Got one supposed to apprentice with me this season; maybe I can pick him up this trip."

The dog snuffled along the baseboard of the wagon—happy, panting sounds. He could give them away at any time . . . and Hasmal had taught her that magic affected animals less reliably than it did people. She put her concentration into maintaining the shield, and prayed it would hold.

The taxman said, "Good to have a business where you can fit family into work. Spent my early years on the sea, I did, and the sea doesn't offer such amenities. When the fish run, you run with them."

Kait wished the fish had eaten the taxman; the longer he chatted with Trev, the more likely someone hidden within the straw was to move or sneeze or cough, and no magical shield would cover that. She could feel her nose and her back beginning to itch, all because she didn't dare scratch them. The straw poked and tickled her, and the mildewed, damp stink of it clogged her nose. She could imagine how the others felt.

"My da fished when he was young enough. Tough work," Trev said.

"It's that. Thirty bales, you say? Wouldn't have thought that cart to hold more than twenty-five."

"Some of them are small."

"Explains it. Tell you what—you can pay transit for twenty-five. That'll be three ox an' habbut. An', hey—what road you takin' out of the city?"

"Either South Great Pike or Shearing Head."

"Pah! if you take the Dally Furlong south to Slow Walk, you can cut half a day and three gates off your trip. It's the way I take going home. You go that way, you want to stop at the Red Heach Inn your second day from here. My cousin owns it, can give you a deal if you mention I sent you."

"And who do I tell him sent me?"

"You say Tooley. He'll cut you a full ox off the season rate."

"My thanks, Tooley. I'll remember you to your cousin."

Kait heard the slap of the reins and the snap of the whip, and one of the horses snorted. The wagon jerked and rolled forward again. Before they were out of Calimekka, they would face at least half a dozen more checkpoints, and if the Dragons began a concentrated search for them, each checkpoint would become more dangerous than the one before it.

And that brought her back to thoughts of betrayal . . . and Ian. She'd been asking Dùghall something before they were interrupted. Something about just that. She tried to relocate her thoughts, and finally had them.

She'd asked Dùghall if he'd introduced Ian to the Reborn, and Dùghall had told her he *had*.

"Dùghall," she asked, "how could Ian have chosen to side with the Dragons after he met Solander? I understand free choice . . . but how *could* he choose their hatred and their evil and turn his back on the Reborn's love?"

"What difference would the Reborn make to him now?"

Kait frowned. "Every difference." She was missing something— Dùghall didn't seem to think it strange at all that Ian could turn away to evil after having experienced joy, while she thought it would be impossible. "I could never betray the Reborn," she said.

Dùghall covered his eyes with his forearm. "Godsall, you don't know," he groaned.

"I don't?" She looked at Ry, who shrugged. "What don't I know?"

Dùghall just shook his head, and left his arm over his face. Hasmal glanced at him, saw that he wasn't going to move, and sat up straighter. He studied her with weary, swollen, red eyes. "The Reborn is dead," he said.

Kait tried to put those words into a frame that made sense. The Reborn dead? No. Vincalis's Secret Texts had clearly and correctly described the return of the Reborn, the rise of the Dragons against him. The Texts went on to describe a multitude of things that hadn't happened yet—battles the Falcons and the Dragons would fight, cities that would be born and cities that would die, and Solander's eventual but total triumph over his age-old enemies.

If Vincalis had seen the future so clearly, he would have seen such a thing as the Reborn's death. He hadn't. His prophecies didn't even allow for such a possibility.

"That can't be," Kait said.

Dùghall muttered, "And you know, eh? You, who aren't a true Falcon?" He didn't look at her. He just lay there, face hidden.

"I know he can't be dead, because if he is, then what of the prophecies?"

"You can't let this alone, can you?" Her uncle sat up slowly and stared into her eyes. "The prophecies are dead, too. The bright future, hope for Ibera and the rest of the world . . . it's all dead."

In short, harsh sentences, despair reverberating in his every word, he told her what he'd found out. That other Falcons had been with the Reborn at the moment when Danya had moved him within an impenetrable shield. That, when she brought the baby's body out of the shield stations later, the soul inside it had no longer been Solander's— that it had belonged to a Dragon. No one knew why she had done this thing. But she had, and the Reborn was dead, and the future had died with him.

Kait tried to hold that thought in her mind. It wouldn't stay. She kept thinking of the wondrous radiance, the complete, uncritical love that had infused her when she touched the baby's soul, and she could not accept that he was gone. That his life had been snuffed out. That her own cousin, his mother, had either destroyed him or allowed him to be destroyed.

"You've missed something," she insisted. "You've overlooked something; he's managed to hide himself away; he was in danger from the Dragons and he discovered it and shielded himself so that you can't find him right now. Something of that nature. He isn't dead."

Dùghall shrugged. "Believe what you wish. I have sought him, I have spoken through mirror and blood with others who were there when this horror came to pass, and the Reborn is dead."

Kait tried to imagine what it would mean if what he said were true; if they had already lost the fight before it was well begun. She looked into the well of despair that had swallowed Dùghall and Hasmal, and for a moment experienced the simplicity that despair brought. If she admitted loss, she wouldn't have to do anything else. If she admitted that the Reborn was dead and that the future was hopeless, she could give up and mourn the fate of the world, and she would be relieved from any responsibility. It was a seductive thought. She could find someplace to hide and let the world take care of itself.

But she wasn't made for despair. She'd overcome too much just to survive; she couldn't accept defeat without fighting. She decided to act as if the Reborn had survived and was hiding to protect himself. If she found out for certain that he was dead, she would reconsider the merits of despair, but not until then.

She became aware that beside her Ry sat weeping.

Chapter 40

The Dragons clustered around the long table in the Sabir meeting room and crowded back to the walls; more than two hundred stood present, wearing the strongest, most flawless, most beautiful bodies in all of Calimekka.

Dafril, wearing the body of Crispin Sabir, stood at the head of the table—he would have been leader no matter which body he'd chosen, but this one made his task easier. It was powerful, it was attractive, and it was highborn. He raised a hand and even the little whispers of fear and consternation ceased.

"I know we swore not to meet until each of you reached your designated target, but we have an emergency that threatens all of us. Mellayne has been taken from us, and barring miracles, is not likely to be restored to us in any form."

Dafril felt his colleagues' unease, and knew it well. His own gut still twisted at the horror of this unexpected disaster that had befallen them.

"What do you mean, 'taken from us'?" a delicate beauty with ebony skin and golden eyes asked. Dafril couldn't place her yet—she was certainly one of the lesser Dragons, maybe Tanden or Shorre or even Lusche—but she had good taste in bodies. Hers touched on every physical preference he had and improved on it. His thoughts flicked for just an instant to a picture of the two of them as the couple who ruled Matrin, and he liked what he saw. He thought that after he reassured himself that she was one of the agreeable young Dragons who admired him, he would tell her he'd chosen her as his consort.

He managed a smile for her that intimated his appreciation of her intelligence in asking the question and said, "I truly mean 'taken.' Falcons are hiding in Calimekka right now, and last night they tore Mellayne's soul from his body and trapped it in a ring that belonged to one of them."

Their massed unease became outright horror.

"A ring?"

"What—some piece of jewelry?"

"With no escape vector?"

"How could they?"

Dafril raised a hand and said, "According to our source, who has given us a tremendous amount of information, all of which we've so far been able to verify independently, the ring used was either gold or electrum, featureless in all respects except for a groove that ran along the circumference of the ring in the center as a form of decoration. The ring bears no designs, no jewels, no writing—in other words, no irregularities of feature that we could use to draw Mellayne back out, even if we could acquire it."

"Why not create such a feature?" a tall, muscular blond with a huge, drooping mustache asked. He would house one of the sloppy youngsters who never bothered to learn the theory behind what they did—who worked the rote spells without mishap until one day he decided to be clever, and made a little change or took a little shortcut and blew himself and everyone around him into oblivion. Efsqual, perhaps, or Clidwen. Probably Clidwen.

Most of the Dragons were glaring at the questioner—no one appreciated dangerous stupidity.

"What?" the young man asked, looking at all the angry faces. "What would be wrong with that?"

Clidwen, certainly. Pity it hadn't been his soul caught in a ring.

"Because," Dafril snapped, "once the soul is bound, any alteration of its housing sufficient to alter its flow through the ring will throw it through the Veil. We wouldn't get Mellayne back, you idiot. We'd just kill him, same as if we drove a knife through your heart. Where the soul is concerned, a body is a body. You destroy the flow, you kill the body."

He was tempted to demonstrate. The idiot had waited a thousand years with nothing more pressing than planning for the day of his eventual reembodiment, and he'd spent the time learning nothing.

"This source of yours," the first questioner asked, "why did he choose to help us? How did he know about us?"

"We had a bit of luck. He was with the Falcons, but never became one of them. And when the girl he loved chose his worst enemy over him, he decided the time had come to go where he would be more welcome." Dafril pushed his way through the assembled Dragons and opened the tall, arched door at the end of the meeting hall. "Come in, please. We're ready for you."

He smiled at the man who stepped into the room. Ian had shaved his head since their first meeting—the false white-blond hair and false Hmoth hairstyle were both gone. He wore Sabir finery—a fine brushed cotton shirt embroidered with silver trees, coarse-woven emerald green silk breeches, fine black boots. His eyes were not the usual pale Sabir blue or the less common amber, but a fine shade of gray-green. "This is a body-cousin of mine," he said. "Long lost and surely thought dead—and we can count ourselves lucky that he wasn't. Please welcome Ian Draclas to our company—the first, but surely not the last, of our willing allies."

Ian smiled at them. The smile was cold and bitter, and held in it thirst for the destruction of his enemies; hunger for revenge; anger and shame and hatred at the humiliation he'd been dealt. It was, Dafril thought, a good smile. The sort of smile you wanted to see on an ally's face. As long as the girl loved Ry Sabir, Ian would belong to the Dragons.

Dafril rested a hand on Ian's shoulder and added, "Ian has sworn to give us the Falcons. And thanks to him, we already know where to begin."

The room erupted with applause.

Chapter 41

He grew visibly—sometimes it seemed to Danya that the beast-child grew in the time it took for her to turn her head. In two weeks he had become as big as babies in their third month. He could already lift his head well, and he flailed his arms and legs constantly—exercising them, he told her when she tried to get him to be still.

She wished she could smother him and put an end to him, but he terrified her. She didn't dare make any movement that seemed in the least threatening to him, or he would remind her that he could destroy her between one heartbeat and the next. She hated him, and she hated herself, and she shuddered each time she picked him up. He looked at her with those ancient, evil eyes, and somehow turned his toothless smile into a leer. He pinched her breasts while he fed, and told her how fine he thought they were, and what a lovely creature she was. He made her sick.

She huddled in her little house with him, cut off from everyone in the village. The Kargans had not forgiven her for her reversion to human form—she'd shown them the two claws on her right hand as proof that she was still their Gathalorra, but she couldn't *be* Gathalorra anymore, of course. In this soft, scaleless, weaponless body, she couldn't hope to fight down even one lorrag. She'd betrayed them by taking on the form of their most hated enemies, the humans. They recalled the good she had done for them, so they still tolerated her in their village, but she was no longer their friend.

Danya rose and walked to her open door and stared out of it. The village women were down by the river working. The men cleaned and mended the nets, preparatory to going out that night to set them for the next morning's run. The Kargans chattered and laughed with each other, telling stories and gossiping about each other's lives, or about Kargans from other villages. From time to time one of those furry faces would glance in her direction, and see her standing in the door-way. Then those dark eyes would narrow and the muzzle would draw back in an expression of disgust. And that Kargan would look away and be silent for a moment, until someone else could draw him or her back into the pleasure of the day and the day's work.

She was alone. She had to face that fact. In that village of sixty-plus souls, she no longer had anyone except Luercas, and she didn't really have him. He had her. He owned her.

She had herself, and only herself. But she was alive, and she intended to stay that way. The wind blew through the door and she felt the cold that the fierce terrain threatened even in its brief summer. She looked toward winter, and knew that she would have to get tougher. Her human flesh wouldn't withstand the rigors of the arctic terrain as easily as her Scarred body had. She needed to begin planning. She needed to win the Kargans back to her side, because they had things she needed—furs, thread, needles, food, the protection that numbers offered. She wouldn't forget that they had shunned her when her body changed; but she wouldn't show her hurt or her anger, either. She would add them to the list of people to whom she owed revenge. Their day and their time would come, and they would learn to regret their callousness.

They could be in the front lines of the army that she intended to raise. They could fight for her—ostensibly to win a place for the Scarred in the soft, fertile lands of Ibera—but in fact to repay her for her pain. She had paid in blood and suffering and shame; she had stupidly ripped out her own heart and destroyed it when she killed her beautiful son. She had been lied to, she had been tricked, and love and beauty and hope were gone from her life forever. But she still had revenge, and she would have her triumph. The Sabirs and the Galweighs would bow before her and the warriors she would lead against them. They would see her on a great horse at the head of a horde of barbarians, and they would know that they'd brought their destruction on themselves. And then they'd die.

Time. It was all that stood between her and her desires. Everything would fall before her; everything would bend in the direction she wanted; everyone would acknowledge her power and her right to command. With time.

She turned away from the door and returned to the dark interior. Her Wolvish practice of the arcane arts waited. If she couldn't win the Kargans to her side with offered friendship, she'd win them with a force they couldn't counter. But one way or the other, she would have them at her side when she began to gather the peoples of the Veral Territories beneath her banner.

The banner of Two Claws, she thought. Proof that she was still Scarred. Her rallying symbol.

And when she was done with them, she would destroy Luercas for his lies, for his evil, for what he'd tricked her into doing. He had cost her all the good in her life, and she would see that he got no reward for it, no matter the price she had to pay.

Chapter 42

Kait shook off the pack and dropped to the ground next to Ry. A boiling sun had cleared away the last of the morning rain, but the road was mud that sucked at feet and boots and dragged at every step. That mud felt to Kait like an extension of the people she traveled with: dismal, dreary, and dragging on body and soul.

They'd left Port Pars behind two days before, and had another three or four days' walk ahead of them before they would reach Costan Selvira, where they might hope to obtain passage on a ship heading south. Thirty days had passed since they'd fled their rooms at the inn, and in those days, she had meditated and searched for any sign of the Reborn's survival, and she had tried to comfort herself with the thought that because he was in terrible danger, he would have to hide from *everyone,* not just his enemies. But the endless gloom was contagious, and Kait was losing faith.

Dùghall trudged with his head down and most of the time said nothing. Hasmal snapped at anyone who went near him, and slept apart from the rest of the travelers, and at night when he thought no one could hear him, he wept quietly. Even Ry had withdrawn. He didn't want her embraces, or her comfort, or her suggestions that things might not be as bad as they appeared. He had come late to the Falcon way of thinking, but he had come completely, and he was, if anything, more bitter than Dùghall or Hasmal at having the Reborn snatched away when he had so recently found him.

"Enough resting," Dùghall said. "Back on your feet, all of you."

"Why bother?" Hasmal muttered. "If we stayed here, the Dragons would find us quicker and end our misery for us."

Dùghall snorted and kicked the biggest clods of mud off of his boots against the nearest tree. "I'm too old to welcome the horses in the square, son. Or boiling lead, or firebrands, or being skinned and having my hide inflated with floating gases and paraded through the streets, for that matter. I'll live, thank you." He swung his pack onto his back and stepped onto the road and into the mud again. "But you're welcome to walk back and offer yourself as a sacrifice if a quick end is what you want."

Ry got up and trudged after Dùghall, so lost in his own misery that he didn't even wait for Kait to put her pack on. She hurried after him, scowling, and Hasmal and Ry's lieutenants plodded after her.

She was the only one not soaking herself in her own unhappiness; she suspected that was the reason that she was the only one of the group who heard the rider coming along the road from the south. Most times the whole party stepped into the jungle when they got first notice of other travelers—meeting strangers in the wilds along the coast road could be dangerous. So Kait said, "Hai! Rider from the south!" as softly as she could.

"Not much sense in hiding if trouble's coming," Ry said. "We're the only ones on the road since this last rain, and our fresh tracks would point right to us. If we jumped behind the brush, we'd look like brigands. Or worse."

Kait nodded. "I realize that. I just thought all of you might like to know we have company coming."

By this time, even those with the poorest ears could hear the horse squelching through the mud toward them. "We'll be ready," Yanth said.

Kait dropped back a few steps. As the rider came into view, the travelers' hands covered sword hilts instinctively. Kait couldn't hide her surprise, though. The rider was a woman, and alone. That in itself would be enough to cause astonishment, but she was Gyru, too, and as far as Kait knew, Gyru women never traveled alone.

She rode a dapple gray gelding—a solid beast as high at the withers as Kait's head, broad through the chest, short in the back, solid of haunch, with a nice length of pastern and a good arch to his neck. He moved well and obeyed his rider's cues beautifully, and Kait would have paid a small fortune for him right then. Horses generally didn't like her, but she loved to ride . . . and after days of plodding along muddy roads, she would have *adored* the comfort of a good saddle.

The rider herself was sodden. Her beautifully embroidered carmine shirt clung to her skin like paint, and her baggy leather pants were streaked and soaked. Her boots, which from the looks of the top seaming and beading were of fine make, from mid-shin down bore a crust of mud so thick they made her feet look like tree trunks. So horse or no horse, she'd done her share of walking over the worst of the road. Her hair, still fiery red, worn long and braided and beaded, was marked by streaks of gray. Her eyes were . . . remarkable. Brilliant green, round as doe eyes, but with the intent gaze of a hunting hawk.

When she caught sight of them, the expression on her face went from wary alertness to pure, exhausted relief. She shouted, "Chobe!" and swung down from her mount with fluid grace. Kait would have guessed from the lines around the stranger's eyes and the gray in her hair that she had seen at least forty years come and go, but when she moved and smiled, Kait thought perhaps she'd misjudged, and the woman was graying early. She moved like a girl.

She wondered who the woman had mistaken for "Chobe," and got a second surprise.

Hasmal's eyes went wide and he said, "Alarista?"

"Of course it's me. I came looking for you!" Her Iberan bore a faint accent, and the slower rhythm of one who spoke it as a somewhat unfamiliar second language.

Hasmal jogged forward as fast as the mud would allow, and lifted her off the ground and hugged her fiercely. She was half a hand taller than him, Kait noticed. If she was as old as her eyes and hair indicated, she was at least ten years older, and possible fifteen. Hasmal didn't seem in the least put off by either of those things.

"By damn, it's good to see you," he was saying, in between kissing her and hugging her and picking her up so that he could swing her around again. She looked for just a moment like a tall slender tree being mauled by a short, blond bear. Kait liked that image, but kept it to herself. She would have told Ry, hoping that it might make him laugh, but he was so far lost inside himself that she doubted he *could* see the humor.

Alarista finally pulled free of Hasmal, and turned to the rest of the group. "I didn't just come looking for Chobe," she said. "I was searching for all of you."

They made brief introductions, everyone supplying a nickname or alternate name in deference to the Gyru-nalle custom of never revealing a true name. The custom came from the Gyru belief that knowledge of anyone's true name made the knower responsible for the named's soul. Kait, whose full name was Kait-ayarenne Noellaurelai Taghdottar Aire an Galweigh, never burdened anyone with the full stretch anyway. That name, loaded with the memories of long-dead ancestors and the qualities of heroes her parents had admired, was more than *she* wanted to carry around. So to Alarista, Kait was comfortable still being just Kait.

"My band has a camp two days' hard ride from here," Alarista told them once the formalities were done. "We can resupply you there if you wish to keep going. Or you can stay with us." This last she said specifically to Hasmal, and Kait saw hope in her eyes.

Dùghall shrugged. "Doesn't matter where we go. We can't get far enough away to escape the disaster that's coming."

The woman nodded. She turned to Dùghall and said, *"Katarre kaithe gombrey; hai allu neesh?"*

They were Falcon words, Kait knew, though she didn't know the ancient tongue in which they were spoken. Hasmal had taught her that they were the formal Falcon greeting, and meant, "The Falcon offers his wings; will you fly?"

But Dùghall didn't give the formal response. Instead, he said, "The Falcons are dead. Or didn't you know?"

When they made camp that night, Alarista sought out Kait and took her aside. "The Falcons believe the future has died; that the world is coming to an end; that we are beyond hope, have already lost to the Dragons, and are destroyed. Destroyed. I would believe the same thing. I would." Kait watched the Gyru woman's lower lip tremble, and saw her stare fixedly into the jungle and take a deep breath, lift her head, and pull her shoulders back. Every curve of her body spoke of fierce determination held together by the thinnest of hopes. "I lived for the Falcons, for the prophecies. I rejoiced when I felt the Reborn touch me for the first time, and I nearly died when he . . . when he . . ." She shook her head. Took another steadying breath. "But I've done auguries," she said. "My Speakers tell me that you are the one who can save the Falcons; that you will give us hope. I've come all this way to find you. Is what they say true?"

Kait sat on a fallen tree, peering in her turn out into the layered tangles of darkness before her. "I *have* hope," she said cautiously. "I haven't yet managed to convince anyone else that there's a reason for it."

"But you *have* hope." Alarista managed a tremulous smile, and sat beside her on the log. She said, "You are the only one. Of all of us, you are the only one who has not already seen the morrow to its grave. I've looked, I swear. Since . . . then, I've tried to contact any Falcon who could answer. Only a few will. So many killed themselves in the few days after the Reborn's death . . ." She shook her head and shivered. "And most of those who still live won't respond. I traced your uncle by blood offering weeks ago, but couldn't get through his shields. The same with Hasmal. And you didn't answer, either, though I didn't get the feeling you were ignoring me. With you, it was more that you couldn't hear me."

"I couldn't." Kait was surprised. "You were trying to reach me?"

"Yes. Then they haven't taught you Falcon far-speech yet."

"No."

Alarista nodded. "I thought it might be that way. But I couldn't help thinking that perhaps the Secret Texts weren't wrong, that perhaps this disaster was something other than it appeared to be. I know you aren't fully a Falcon yet, but when I summoned Speakers through the Veil, each said you were the key. That you could give the Falcons reason to hope again. That if you chose, you could see how the Falcons could yet break the Dragons. That you . . ." She sighed. "That you hold the secret of our hope. When I couldn't reach you by far-speech, I came after you. I don't know what you know, Kait. I don't know how you are our key. Tell me, please. I lost everything when . . .

I lost everything I believed in, and everything I loved. I lost who I was, and who I was supposed to become. Please tell me what can change all that."

Kait rested her hands on her thighs and leaned forward, eager. This was validation that what she had thought must be true. The spirits from beyond the Veil *said* she had the key. So the Falcons *must* be missing something. Kait had believed from the first moment when Dùghall told her of the disaster that he had to be mistaken, that a thousand years of waiting would not end with the birth and almost immediate death of the one who was to have led the world to Paranne, Vincalis's promised land. Not even Brethwan and Lodan, the most ill-starred of the god-pairs, could be so cruel. "I almost gave up," she said. "Of the Falcons, I only knew Dùghall and Hasmal, and you can see them. They've given up. They see themselves as dead men who have not yet fallen on their pyres. I couldn't reach them. They wouldn't let me talk to them. They've locked themselves into their shields, and they . . ." She shrugged. "You've seen them. You've seen others like them, from what you say."

Alarista nodded.

Kait continued. "But they can't be right." She dared a smile. "A thousand years of true prophecy cannot end with a falsehood. I've read the Secret Texts. I've tracked the Seven Great Signs, the Hundred Small Signs, the Three Confusions. All of them came to pass. Vincalis spoke true in particulars as well as generalities." She narrowed her eyes. "Even in prophecies that speak directly to today, he holds true. 'Dragons will lie down with Wolves and rise up with full bellies,' he said, and isn't that exactly what happened? The Dragons' spirits claimed the Wolves' bodies and their memories, but the Wolves are gone, and only the Dragons remain." She clenched her fists. "Since the Reborn disappeared, I've been through the Secret Texts every day. Every day. I read while I walk; I study all the passages. Vincalis promised that the Reborn would hold his empire for five thousand years, and that the world would learn in those five thousand years how to love, how to be truthful, how to be kind. Five *thousand* years, and Vincalis was right in every other prophecy he made. Alarista . . ." She rested a hand on the other woman's arm. "How can he be wrong in the most important prophecy of all? Everyone is sure the Reborn is really gone. But he can't be." She took a deep breath. "The Reborn is still alive. I don't know where, and I don't know how, but he's still alive."

Hope died in Alarista's eyes.

"What's wrong?" Kait asked.

Alarista's head dropped forward, her shoulders slumped, her hands lay limp on her lap. In a voice so broken Kait almost couldn't understand her words, she said, "That was your hope? That the Reborn is still secretly alive somewhere?"

Kait didn't understand. "What other hope could there be?"

Tears had started down Alarista's cheeks. "The Speakers told me you could give the Falcons hope. So I'd thought . . . that perhaps you knew some magic that would reembody a spirit lost through the Veil. Or that you could reach through the Veil, at least, and speak to the Reborn, and perhaps ask him what we are supposed to do without him. Or that you knew something we didn't know about the Secret Texts; that his death was a part of the prophecy that no one had understood, and that he would return yet again. I'd thought you could give us . . . *real* hope."

"You're so certain that what I've said is wrong? That the Reborn is truly dead?"

Alarista nodded without looking up. "Even the Speakers said that he was gone. That we had lost him. That the prophecies were broken. But you . . . they said you . . ." She lifted her head again, and once more pulled her shoulders back. "Well. They were wrong, just as the Secret Texts are wrong. You have no secret answer that will save us." She turned to Kait. "But that isn't your fault. You're young. The young have a hard time believing in death, and in their own impotence in the face of disaster. 'Old age stutters, while reckless youth decrees.' Isn't that what they say?" She rose. "If this life and this world must end, at least I can spend the last of my time with Hasmal. That's some comfort."

And she walked back to the camp before Kait could find another word to say.

Kait found herself facing not just the darkness of the night, but the deeper, harsher darkness that welled up inside of her. Alarista had dismissed out of hand her secret hope that the Reborn still survived.

He was gone and the prophecies were broken—her Speakers had declared it, her experience had verified it, and something about her assurance drove a stake into Kait's hope. Perhaps it was the fact that, unlike Dùghall and Hasmal, Alarista had dared to hope, had dared to believe that something might yet be salvaged from the shattered ruins of the future. She'd looked for an answer, and her hope had brought her to Kait.

And then she had found in Kait the hope she had hungered for . . . and had discovered that hope sustained by something she *knew* was not true.

Kait closed her eyes. The scents of the jungle surrounded her—rich moist earth and meaty decay; the heavy sweetness of night-blooming flowers; the musk of nearby animals that crept past the human outpost in their domain, wary of men. No leaves rustled—the night was as still as if it held its breath. She opened her eyes and looked up. Above her head, the black canopy of leaves parted to show stars burning like the cold, unblinking white eyes of blind gods. They stared down at her, but they did not see her. They did not care.

She felt the hollow place in her soul where the connection to the Reborn had once been. She touched that place inside her the way she had probed at a missing tooth when she had been a child; sliding her tongue against the gap, tasting the iron tang of her own blood, worrying the raw, tender flesh. She let herself accept the truth.

The Reborn was dead.

She could not feel him, and he would not have hidden. His life was not to have been about hiding, about preserving himself in secret while his desperate followers wept over his absence. He had come to be a beacon. To show the world a better way to live. And he had died before he could do that.

But he hadn't just died. He'd been destroyed, and her cousin Danya had killed him. Kait probed that other wound, that other raw place in her soul. One of the few cousins she had cared about had slaughtered her own child. Had given his body over to something evil. Had become something evil herself. Danya, whose survival had sustained Kait when she thought all the rest of her Family was gone, was as dead as the soul of the child who had come to give his love to the world.

I knew the truth. I knew it, but I refused to believe it, because the truth was too ugly. I couldn't face what my cousin had done, couldn't face the destruction of goodness by evil, couldn't look at the death of the future. Dùghall was right. Hasmal was right. We're walking corpses, all of us.

And Alarista's Speakers were wrong. I have no hope to offer to anyone.

Even Vincalis was wrong. The future will not be the home of love, of joy, of the worldwide city of Paranne. We're lost, all of us. Everything is lost.

Interlude

In Calimekka, a year marked by uneasy omens and eerie events suffered a final blow on Galewansasday—the Feast of the Thousand Holies. On that day, the twenty-first day in the month of Galewan, the people of the city gathered to celebrate the Family gods and the old lost gods and remembered that not even the gods live forever. The day was the Throalsday of the Malefa-week of the month, and as such was a day that bore its own dubious omens: Chance of loss, waiting pain.

But on that day, while traveling to the Winter Parnissery to lead the prayer of remembrance, the carais, who had named the year by lottery at its birth, and who had been chosen by the gods to be its speaker, died of unknown but suspicious causes, and his year, *Gentle Seas and Rich Harvests,* died with him. The parnissas canceled the feast and convened in the parnissery, and for the last six days of the month, they read oracles and cast lots and prayed. They drew their new year, and found that the new year had been born dead—its carais, when they located her, had died the day before, of unknown but suspicious causes.

Amial Garitsday, the first day of the month of Joshan, was usually the day of Fedran, in which a morning of solitude and prayer, fasting and silence was followed by midday tithing at the nearest parnissery and the Breaking of the Silence, where Calimekkans ate a traditional meal of plain rice and unspiced black beans on cornbread. But the parnissas declared Fedran void, and did not even collect their tithes. No one in the city could recall a time when the parnissery had turned away its tithes, and the mood of the city grew panicked, and people spoke of the coming of the end of the world.

On that day and the following days, all vows and all holidays waited, as did all contracts, all marriages, all new ventures; no business could be carried on in the dead time between living years. The parnissas, instead, after further prayer and divining, drew another name from the great vat of yearnames. They went out in search of their new carais, and this time found him alive, and healthy. And that, perhaps, was the worst omen of all.

The carais was a man named Vather Son of Tormel, who had only a month before been charged with the deaths of his wife and children, all three of whom he'd slaughtered, cooked, and eaten in a brutal ritual the purpose of which he had refused to reveal even under torture. He had been sentenced to die on the first day of Joshan in Punishment Square for his crimes.

But the gods had given him their own reprieve—no executions could be carried out unwatched by a living year, so his execution had waited the conclusion of the parnissas' business. And no carais could be executed during his or her term, for the carais was chosen by the gods, and all his deeds, past and present, became the instruments of the gods. So the murders of Vather's wife and children were automatically, entirely, and eternally forgiven. The judgment of the gods in choosing the carais for the new year was final, and not subject to questioning by mortals. So Vather Son of Tormel would be draped in gold cloth and paraded before the people of Calimekka like a hero, and he and he alone would speak for the new year.

Vather Son of Tormel named his year *Devourer of Souls*.

Dafril smiled from his place within Sabir House at the appropriateness of that name. Solander was dead, the Falcons leaderless, and Luercas still invisible and, it seemed increasingly likely, powerless. He reveled in the helplessness of this new world, at the unguarded souls that flowed in endless torrents past him, and he called his people together and laid out for them the plans for their new city—a city that would be built by nothing less than the devouring of souls.

This was a good world he had brought them to. A good time. And it would become their world and their time.

A few more technothaumatars, a few more pieces of the puzzle filled in, and they would become the new immortals.

Book Three

"It's very large, the world, and that's what is—and always will be—its saving grace. So look to far seas and distant hills in your time of need, and welcome unlikely heroes, for help comes from the strangest quarter."

THE BEGGAR IN THE GUTTER, IN ACT III OF
THE TRAGEDY AND COMEDY OF THE SWORDSMAN OF HAYERES
BY VINCALIS THE AGITATOR

Chapter 43

In the last days of the month of Brethwan, Kait ran through the snow-buried mountains that surrounded Norostis, Shifted to beast form and lost in beast mind. She hunted whatever moved—mice, rabbits, small birds, deer forced down from the peaks by the heavy snows above. She fed on raw flesh, blood, and entrails; she rolled in the carcasses of her kills; she slept in the hollows of dying trees, in banks of snow, on sun-warmed boulders above ice-clotted streams. She rode Shift obsessively, fighting off her woman-form, seeking oblivion from the events that touched humanity.

She was, for the time that she could hold herself within the beast body and the beast mind, beyond grief, beyond thinking, beyond regret and pain and loss. She exulted in the bitter sting of the wind, the violence of the weather, the pale hard blue of the day sky and the still-lengthening nights. Her hungers were things she could fill with food and sleep; her regrets were the quick sharp pains of a missed pounce or a bit of game stolen by a larger beast.

But she could not hold Shift forever. When, bloody, gaunt, filthy, and stinking of dead things, she dragged herself back to the camp where Alarista's Gyru-nalle band and Dùghall's soldiers and her own people hid, she discovered that she'd lost a week. She had never been Karnee for so long. She would have been amazed, but she was too tired to feel anything. She gave herself a cursory wash, ate everything she could lay hands on, and finally crawled into her cold tent and fell into the deep, miserable sleep of post-Shift.

She woke two days later with the full weight of post-Shift depression riding her. Her fugue had solved nothing. The problems her world faced remained unsolved, but were a week more firmly entrenched. The Reborn was still dead; her once-beloved cousin was still a murderer not just of her own child but of the hopes of the world; the Dragons still walked free and worked toward the day when they would rule the world as gods from the backs of a world of enslaved mortals.

"This won't do," she whispered to herself. "If I'm not yet dead, I can't act as if I am."

So she forced herself to get up. She ate hugely, then washed, ignoring the icy water, the howling wind. She dressed in the only good clothing she had—a fine winter suit of Gyru-nalles spun wool with heavy fur boots and a long fur coat. She plaited her hair and painted the symbols of devotion on her forehead and eyelids.

She looked for answers as she had been taught by the parnissas. She prayed—to the Falcons' god Vodor Imrish, who had fallen silent with the death of his Reborn; to the Iberan gods whom she had been taught to revere, but who had no place for a magic-Scarred monster like her; and even to the old gods that her parents had scorned as the superstitions of ignorant peasants. For two days she fasted and prayed, but the gods had no word for her.

She could have despaired then, but she didn't. If the gods offered no answers, she would find one for herself. She took food again, then meditated. She discovered that she did not wish to give the world over to the Dragons without a fight, no matter how hopeless that fight might be. She discovered that she still had breath and will, the two things she'd had before the death of Solander. And she discovered that action—even action she firmly believed was hopeless—gave rise to its own strange breed of hope.

She began to wonder if she and the Falcons had overlooked something in their rush to declare their cause lost and the Dragons triumphant by default. Another three days spent poring through the Secret Texts convinced her that they had.

So she sought out her uncle.

Dùghall lay in one of the Gyru wagons, wasting away. The Gyru girl who had taken over tending him said that he had only accepted bites of food and sips of water in the last days, that he would get up to relieve himself but that he never spoke or moved otherwise. She said she'd begun bathing him each morning with a bucket of cold water and coarse rags, partly because he had begun to smell, but mostly because she hoped the rough treatment would stir him to some sign of life. So far, she said, her plan had failed.

Kait stepped up into the wagon and noted that, even after the baths, Dùghall stank. He lay in a fetal position, curled under several blankets, face to the featureless wall. His hair stuck out at odd angles, unwashed, greasy, gone from black with a smattering of gray to gray entire in the days since the Reborn's death. Where he had been lean— the Reborn's sword, he'd said—now he was scrawny. He looked like a sick old man, like a dying old man.

"Uncle," she said, "this has to end."

He said nothing. He didn't move, didn't twitch. The rhythm of his breathing didn't even change. She counted his breaths for a moment and realized that he had put himself into the Falcon trance; he was far beyond the reach of her voice.

She shook him hard, and felt his breathing pick up, then fall back into the slow trance-inducing rhythm. She considered her options, didn't like any of them, and chose the least offensive. She slapped him. Again she jarred him from his breathing for an instant, but again he escaped her.

She was going to have to hurt him. A lot. She jammed her thumb under his collarbone and pressed hard. He lost the rhythm of his breathing entirely; he growled and tried to push her hand away. She was stronger than he, though—Karnee strength would have let her best a stronger man than sick Dùghall—and she pushed harder; he whimpered with pain.

"You can't sleep yourself to death, and I can't hide inside the monster. There aren't any answers there. You know that. You're hiding out of fear, but you can't be a coward anymore. We need you. Get up."

"Go away."

"Get up or I'll break your collarbone." She shifted her pressure from the space under the bone to the bone itself, and bore down. She could feel the grinding of the ends of the bone transmitted through her fingertips, and she shuddered and gritted her teeth and pushed harder.

Dùghall yelled and flailed at her with his free arm.

"I'm not leaving, Uncle, and you aren't going to lie in here and die. Get up and face me." He tried to fall back into trance, tried to regain the slow, steady breaths that took him there, but she applied more pressure. She hated to hurt him, but she could think of nothing that would force him to act faster than intense pain. Better a broken bone than death. She hardened herself to his eventual wordless scream, and was rewarded for her efforts—thankfully, before she had to snap the bone in two.

He jerked himself upright in the narrow bed and turned to glare at her. "Get out of here, Kait."

"No."

"Let me die. The world is doomed, and I want to end before it does."

"I don't care what you want. We have things to do, you and I."

"Things to do. Don't make me laugh."

She stood over him, staring down, and said, "The Reborn is dead. He's gone. His soul has slipped beyond our reach, and nothing we can do can bring him back. This is the truth, isn't it?"

"You know it is."

"Yes. I finally do. And a thousand years of prophecy have just come crashing down around our heads; the Dragons returned as promised, and the Reborn came when he was supposed to, but Danya has destroyed the prophecies and we've lost him forever. Correct?"

Dùghall sighed. "Of course it's correct! Why do you think I want to die?"

"I think you want to die because you've become a coward. Uncle, think with me for a moment. The prophecies are shattered, the Secret Texts overturned in a single blow. What does that mean?"

He stared at her, his face creased with frustration. "It means we're doomed, you idiot. With the Reborn gone, the Dragons have already won."

"Who says so?" Kait asked.

"What?"

She asked again, patient. "Who says so? Who says the Dragons have already won?"

"That's a stupid question. If the Reborn doesn't lead us against the Dragons, then the Dragons will triumph. The Secret Texts constantly refer to the doom that would come upon the world if the Reborn did not conquer the evil at its heart."

Kait nodded. "I know what the Texts say. I've spent the last three days and three nights reading them yet again, looking for anything that warns of the possibility of the Reborn's premature death."

"He wasn't supposed to die."

"No. He wasn't. Vincalis never considered his death a possibility. Nowhere in all those prophecies does he say, 'If the Reborn's mother kills him at birth . . .' or 'If the Reborn dies before he can lead the Great Battle . . .' or anything else of that sort. I've been over every word again, Uncle. Such an occurrence doesn't exist within the Texts' pages."

"I know that." Dùghall's evident annoyance grew greater. "I knew most of the Texts by heart long before you were born."

"Then answer my question. Who says that, because the Reborn is dead, the Dragons have already won?"

He glowered at her. She crossed her arms over her chest, refusing to be cowed, and waited.

He said, as if speaking to a particularly stupid child, "The Texts clearly state that the Reborn is the key to conquering the Dragons. So, if Solander cannot lead us, the Dragons must win by default."

Kait shook her head. "If the Reborn cannot lead us because he died at birth, then the Texts no longer predict the future of our world."

"Clearly." Dùghall shrugged. "The Texts promised us the leadership of the Reborn, the city-civilization of Paranne, and triumph over evil. Without them, we face doom, destruction, and the Dragons' hell on earth."

Kait smiled slowly, and asked him for the third time, "Who says so?"

As he saw her smile, a puzzled expression crossed his face. "The Texts warn—"

Kait held up her hand. "You and I have agreed that the Texts have become invalid. Something has happened that Vincalis could not foresee. So we cannot trust the Texts to guide us from here on. Correct?"

He nodded slowly.

"So. What authority now tells you that the Dragons have already won, that they cannot be defeated, that our world is doomed?"

Dùghall sat quietly for a moment. "It only stands to reason—" he began, but Kait shook her head, and he stopped.

"Uncle, the future is built by *unreasonable* men. You told me that when I was a little girl, and again when you stood me for my place among the diplomats."

He took a deep breath. "That's true. I have said that."

"So. Just tell me the name of the authority you now trust to tell us our doom is a foregone conclusion, and I'll let you go back to sleeping yourself to death."

He shook his head slowly, knowing what she wanted him to say, but not wanting to say it. She could see the stubbornness on his face—the way his mouth compressed, the way his brows drew down, the way his eyes tracked across the room, as if looking for his answer among the wagon's fittings and furnishings. His arms locked across his chest, shutting away the possibility that he might have been wrong.

She waited, patient as a cat at a mouse's hole, and finally her mouse came out.

"There is no such authority," he admitted.

"I know."

"But how can we hope to win against the Dragons without Solander?"

She shrugged, and her smile grew broader. "I don't know. But finally you're asking the right question." She sat down in the little chair across from Dùghall's bed. "I know this—we are only beaten for sure if we don't fight. And if we can't count on the Texts, we can at least count on each other." She took a slow, shaky breath. "And the time to act is now. A thousand years ago, our ancestors destroyed all of civilization rather than allow the Dragons to carry out their plans for the world. They gave everything to make sure their children and their children's children wouldn't be locked into eternal slavery, that *our* souls would not be the fodder that fed the immortality of a few powerful wizards. They fought and died so that we would live. Now it's our turn to fight. We've suffered a bad loss, but we can't let that stop us. We can't just hand the future to the Dragons."

Dùghall looked at her warily. "So who else have you convinced of all of this, dear Kait?"

Her smile became lopsided. "You're the first, Uncle Dùghall. You're going to help me convince everyone else."

Dùghall gave her a wary smile and said, "Did you know Vincalis the Agitator was a playwright before he became a prophet?"

"You told me something about that. That he gave up writing plays when the Dragons executed Solander, and for a thousand days cast oracles and wrote the Secret Texts."

Dùghall nodded and said, "He created the road map by which a thousand years of Falcons have steered their lives. But some of the best things he ever said, and the truest, were not in the Texts at all— they were in his plays. The Dragons overshadowed the world he lived in for most of his life, and they were hard masters, brutal, murderous, and evil. Most men feared to fight them in any manner. Vincalis fought them with words, but carefully—he never plainly wrote about the Dragons because they would have killed him, and he taught that survival was the first duty of a warrior. He wrote about great villains, and about the small bands of heroes who dared to best them . . . and he wrote many of those plays as comedies, because he could always claim the innocuousness of comedy if questioned." Dùghall looked down at the gnarled hands folded on his lap, then glanced sidelong at her, and the ghost of a mischievous smile played across his lips. "Those who have no sense of humor rarely realize how deadly humor can be."

"So what did he say?"

Dùghall closed his eyes. "The putative hero of one of my favorite plays, which he titled *The Tragedy and Comedy of the Swordsman of Hayeres,* was the swordsman Kinkot, a mighty-thewed master of weapons and a great lord. Kinkot swore to protect his countrymen from a vile monster that ravaged the countryside . . . but the monster proved to be too much for him. For the first two acts of the play, every step he took against the beast failed, and he became a laughingstock. He lost his lands, his wealth, his title, even his sword, and by the beginning of the third act he finds himself homeless, sitting on a street corner holding a begging bowl and hoping to die."

"Sounds like a *hilarious* comedy," Kait said.

Dùghall snorted. "Watching the cocky bastard getting his ass kicked by the monster in the first two acts *is* hilarious. But Vincalis never just wrote to entertain, and when Kinkot has had his come-uppance and is sitting on the corner begging, a fellow even worse off than he is lifts his head out of the gutter and says, 'When you're beaten, when you're crushed, when you're broken, you remember this, boy—*nothing* touches everyone in the world to the same degree. It's very large, the world, and that's what is—and always will be—its saving grace. So look to far seas and distant hills in your time of need, and welcome unlikely heroes, for help comes from the strangest quarter.'

"Kinkot, who has kicked this same beggar once in each of the first two acts, listens to him this time. He gives the poor sot his begging bowl and the few coins in it, and gets up to go off in search of help, for humbled as he is, he finally realizes that he can't beat the monster alone."

"Right. Beggars are ever full of good advice and deep wisdom. That's why they spend their days lying in gutters."

Dùghall shrugged. "The plays were a part of their time, and some of the storytelling is stylized, and some is a bit . . . predictable. Nonetheless, Vincalis knew his audiences. No sooner does Kinkot give the beggar the gift and follow his advice than the poor sot trans-forms into a beautiful young girl, and the girl, after kissing him and blessing him, transforms herself into a tiny bird. The bird rides on Kinkot's shoulder, and the two of them, weaponless, go out to face the monster one last time. The bird plucks a flea from under its wing and flies to the monster and drops the flea on its back, at the precise spot where he can't reach, and the monster, driven mad by futile scratch-ing, doesn't see Kinkot coming. Kinkot breaks its neck with his bare hands, thus winning back everything he'd lost, plus the love of the girl who helped him slay the beast."

Kait tipped her head and eyed her long-winded uncle. "It's a charming story," she told him, "but I'm afraid I don't see your point."

"You *are* the point, dear girl. Consider yourself—a death-sentenced Karnee coming to the salvation of the land that sentenced you by rallying the Falcons who were supposed to save it themselves. You're the man in the gutter who becomes the beautiful maiden who becomes the bird with the flea. You are the unlikeliest of heroes. Vincalis would have loved you."

"I'm not a hero," she said quietly. "I'm a coward like everyone else. I'm just a coward who would rather die fighting than die a slave."

Dùghall grinned slowly. "You're a coward, then, if it pleases you to say so. And I'm a coward as well. But I'm a coward who will rise and eat and dress myself, and who will be about the work of the world. Have that nattering girl bring me some food. I've decided I won't die today."

Chapter 44

The sun crept over the horizon and a single alto bell rang the station of Soma from Dogsister's Tower near the Cloth Market. But when the bell finished ringing, a new sound rolled across the region. The air rang like a crystal bell, the sound coming from nowhere and everywhere at once. Horses and cattle shied and balked and rolled their eyes back; birds launched themselves into the air in great clouds; dogs whined and cringed against the legs of their masters, then howled and ran. Perhaps most ominous of all, a river of rats poured into the streets and fled in all directions.

The ringing grew louder, and the air took on a pale green sheen. Shopkeepers slammed the shutters of their just-opened shops and followed the rats through the streets. Young women tucked their babies under their arms and raced after them. Customers stopped their bargaining in midnegotiation, stared wildly around them, and fled. No one knew what was happening, but everyone knew it was trouble.

The ringing grew even louder—painfully loud—and in the center of the Cloth Market coils of green smoke crawled up out of the shop floors and twisted toward the sky.

Only the old, the lame, and the foolhardy remained to see what happened next.

Gashes opened in the ground, and shimmering white spears grew out of the gashes like the fronds of pale ferns reaching toward the sun.

These spears unfurled gracefully and flowed both outward and upward, spinning themselves into translucent towers and delicate arches and fairy buttresses, into shining walls and corbeled vaults, as if fashioned by the *ganaan,* the invisible folk of old myth. The whitewashed, sun-baked brick buildings that had occupied the ground from which they grew crumbled around them, and the new structures swallowed the debris—and all the buildings' contents—leaving no trace. The shining white buildings absorbed the people who had not been quick enough to flee, too, enveloping them while they screamed and dissolving them with terrible slowness.

White roads, softly textured, forgiving to the feet that would tread upon them, oozed up from the cobblestone streets and spread into lovely thoroughfares. Those who later would dare to step onto their pristine surfaces would discover that horses' hooves did not clatter, nor cartwheels rattle, nor falling cargo clank when striking them. The roads absorbed sound and gave back only a gentle, restful hush that echoed the whisper of leaves in a cool glade, the delicate murmur of a tiny waterfall chuckling down a stony hillside to the brook below, or the sighing of a breeze that tousled the tall grasses in a broad plain.

The magical city opened like a death rose within the heart of Calimekka. It slowly encroached on other neighborhoods and devoured them, too, filling the Valley of Sisters from the Black River to the Garaye Pass, spinning itself up the pass's obsidian face and crawling along the top, covering Warriors' Mount and spreading from there to the old Churimekkan Quarter and the Hammersmiths' District.

At the end of two days the city finally seemed satisfied with itself, for it threw out no more white feelers at its edges, and no more roads shifted from cobblestone or pavingstone or brick to that white, yielding, eternal stuff.

The survivors—ten thousand left homeless, twice as many thrown out of the dissolved businesses and markets it had consumed—gradually crept onto those whispering white streets and down the broad, gleaming thoroughfares, past new fountains that tossed sparkling diamonds of water into the air, past the tall white pillars of gated walls, past mansions piled onto great houses butted up against castles beautiful beyond all imagining, looking for some surviving shred of those things and those places that had been theirs.

Everything was gone. The survivors looked at each other and whispered, *"Devourer of Souls* has spoken." They wondered at the fates of those who had not fled. And they silently congratulated themselves for having been wise enough to flee, for they counted themselves lucky that they had survived at all.

What they didn't know was what to do next. Dared they knock on the great gates of one of those castles and demand reparation for a lost home, lost belongings, a lost friend? The survivors huddled in little knots, discussing with each other the probable outcomes of such action. In an ill-omened year, with an evil carais singing like a madman from the balcony of his palace, showering down curses on the city and all who inhabited it, they thought they were likely to find nothing but pain and grief beyond those shimmering white gates. So at last, silently, in little clusters, they crept away from the newborn city, having done nothing.

From inside the gates and behind the walls, the Dragons in their new citadel watched and laughed. The Calimekkans were timid mice, terrified of the cats within their domain. And with reason. They would have taken great delight in making examples of any who dared to protest.

They touched the smooth magic-born walls they had created, and they heard the souls of the sacrificed crying within them. Again they smiled. Such walls, held together by human souls, would last as long as the earth on which they were built. The Dragons called their new city Citadel of the Gods, and looked to the nearing day when they would be gods not just in their dreams, but in fact.

The Calimekkans, who also heard the Dragons' walls whispering, and who felt the trembling, frantic terror of those trapped within the lovely, silky whiteness of gates and pillars, arches and balustrades, were not so poetic about the white canker in the heart of Calimekka. They named the city-within-the-city New Hell.

Chapter 45

Hasmal curled next to Alarista in her narrow bed, hiding from the cold morning air. The sun was up, and light streamed through the tiny panes of the window and cast a golden glow on the lovely hand-rubbed wood surfaces . . . and outlined the curls of steam that puffed from his nose every time he breathed. Here, just south of the town of Norostis, in the Glasburg Mountains on the edge of the Veral Territories, winter was a harsh master, and he would have gladly stayed in bed all day to avoid its chilling touch.

He pulled Alarista closer and nuzzled the back of her neck. "Wake up," he whispered. "I don't want to be alone."

She sighed and curled tighter against his body, but didn't wake up. So he lay staring at the sunlight, holding her and hating his thoughts. He and Alarista would have this winter, with the innocence of their lovemaking and the time they spent in each other's presence. They would have this bliss, this brief happiness brighter than anything he had ever known.

But the short cold days and the long sweet nights would end with spring's thaw, and behind this season, another winter was already building—a winter of a different sort.

He and Alarista had thrown the *zanda* and cast bones and summoned Speakers, had sought the trances of Gyru drums and Falcon caberra incense, looking for some sign that they could hope to live out their years in peace together. But every oracle and every attempt had said the same thing. The Dragons held Calimekka, and would soon reach out for the rest of the world, and no one would escape slavery. Dragon power grew, and with it Dragon greed. They snuffed out not just lives but *souls* to build their new city, as unheeding of the price they exacted from others as cattle were of the clover they ate. They created beauty with a heart of ugliness; they spread; they conquered; and soon they would complete the spell that would pin all the world beneath their feet forever. Soon they would finish the complex machinery that would power the spell that would make them immortal.

Then slavery's cold winter would come to Matrin forever.

Alarista stirred, and Hasmal held her tighter. "I love you," he said, pushing eternal winter from his mind as best he could.

She rolled over to face him, and kissed his forehead and his nose and his eyelids, and said, "I love you, too."

He stroked her hip and said, "Let's leave today. We can get the wagon down into Norostis, and as soon as the roads clear we can travel to Brelst. I'll work for our passage on the first ship sailing to Galweigia or New Kaspera or any of the Territories," he said. "There's land in Galweigia going begging—they're desperate for settlers. We can be together, a long way from Calimekka and the Dragons. Perhaps we can have a whole life together before they reach that far—"

Alarista pressed a finger to his lips, smiled sadly, and shook her head. "Before they reach far enough to destroy us. Or our children. After they've already destroyed everyone we ever knew or loved that we were callous enough to leave behind." She kissed his lips lightly and snuggled closer to him. Her skin was softer than silk beneath his fingers.

He closed his eyes to shut out the sun, the proof that time passed and the end of the world drew nearer, and he wished for the sea, for distance, for a safe place to hide her from the hell that came.

"We can't run," she said. "We're Falcons. Even if we can't win, even if we can't fight, we have to stand." She kissed him again and said, "You know this is true."

"I only know that I waited my entire life to find you, and I haven't had you long enough. I want peace for us, Ris. I want us to live out our lives in a world without fear. I want more time."

Her soft laugh startled him. "How much time would be enough, Chobe? A year? Ten years? Fifty? A hundred? A thousand? When could you say, 'We've had long enough. We've had our share,' and let me die? Or when could I willingly let you go?"

Hasmal rolled the future forward in his mind and could not find that moment in all of eternity. "Never," he said at last. "Unless I'm with you forever, I won't have had enough time."

She nodded. "Me either. So if the world ends now or in a hundred years, you and I will suffer the same from our parting."

"Yes."

"Then how do we justify turning our backs on the others that we love? We can't run away while they stay behind, because if we lived knowing that all of them were gone—dead or tortured by the Dragons—and that we had abandoned them to suffer their fates alone, we would poison our love for each other. We would lose the one thing we cherish most."

"I can't lose you," Hasmal told her.

"Yet you will. Remember Vincalis: 'Nothing bites more bitterly than knowledge of mortality.' No matter what we do, we'll eventually die, love, and either you will die first, or I will . . . or perhaps . . . if we're lucky . . . we'll die together. But someday this will end."

Hasmal closed his eyes. "I don't want it to end. I want forever."

"We'll find each other again. Beyond the Veil, or in new bodies, in new times. . . ."

"I want *you* and *me*. Us. I want what we have now. These bodies, this time, this world, forever."

"I know. But nobody gets that. We have this moment. That has to be enough."

He pulled her hard against his chest, kissing her, touching her, driven by the terror of future loss. She responded vehemently. They wrapped themselves around each other and clung together, seeking within the pressures of flesh and the warmth of passion a place beyond the pain, seeking within their lovemaking and their love the promise of eternity.

For just an instant, they found it.

Chapter 46

They weren't impressed; Kait could see it in their eyes.

"So the few of us here will march back to Calimekka—"

"—or sail—"

"—or sail, right . . . and attack the Dragons on their home ground, now that they've had all this time to dig in—"

"—and *knowing* that we haven't even prophecy to suggest that we have a hope of winning—"

"—*lest* we forget *that*—"

"—and you define this as bringing us *hope?*"

Kait nodded.

"New definition of the word," Yanth said.

"Not one I would have ever considered." Hasmal crossed his arms over his chest.

"Still don't. Getting killed in Calimekka so that we can say we tried does not even come close to my definition of regaining our hope." That from one of Dùghall's soldiers at the back of the meeting tent.

Kait frowned at Dùghall. He shrugged; he'd said they'd be hard to convince.

Alarista had been sitting beside Hasmal, her hand in his. Now she pulled away from him and stood. "I'm with you, Kait. Whatever I can do, I'll do."

"What if it's just the three of you?" Hasmal asked. "You and Kait and Dùghall?"

"Then it will be the three of us," Alarista said. "I don't care."

Ry had been watching quietly from the back of the tent. He moved forward. "It won't be just the three of you. I don't know that I think you have much of a chance of winning, but if we do nothing, we have no chance. I'll take something over nothing."

One by one, Ry's men stood, too—Yanth and Jaim and Trev. "I follow Ry," Yanth said.

Jaim said, "As do I."

Trev said, "I don't know where my sisters are hiding, but wherever they are, they aren't safe from these Dragons. I'll do anything to help them. So I'll fight."

Ry and three standing lieutenants looked at Valard, who still sat. He looked up at them and sighed and slowly shook his head. "I'll pray to the old god of hopeless causes on your behalf; he's sure to take an interest in you," he said. "But I think I'll stay here and drink to your health and good fortune, and hear about your heroism from the criers."

Kait was shocked. She'd thought Ry and his men were inseparable. Valard's defection made all of them seem suddenly smaller and weaker and more . . . well, more mortal. But Ry only nodded. "Your choice," he said.

"My choice," Valard agreed.

His cowardice worked in Kait's favor, though. The leaders of the troops Dùghall had recruited back in the islands conferred with each other. His many sons stood as one, and Ranan, who had led the army in Dùghall's absence, said, "I do not speak for the troops in general, but only for my brothers. We will fight. Our lives are yours."

When he and his brothers sat down, the highest-ranking of the troops rose, glanced with disgust at Valard, and turned to Dùghall. "You've paid us on time and we haven't done anything for the money we've already earned. Neither you nor your sons commanded us to follow you into this—you say it isn't what you hired us for. But we say you hired us to fight for you, and where you lead, we'll follow. If you needed us before, you need us even more now."

He touched his heart with his fingertips in quick salute and sat back down.

Hasmal sighed and reached a hand up to take Alarista's again. "You know I won't leave you to face the Dragons without me. Where you are, there I'll be, too."

She looked down at him and smiled. He pulled her down to his side and wrapped his arms around her and kissed the side of her neck.

Most of the Gyru-nalles volunteered their help, too. A few followed Valard's lead and declined, but when the last of those present declared their intentions, Kait found herself at the head of a small army.

And with no idea what to do with it.

She guessed that her volunteers numbered no more than two hundred, and though she might acquire other volunteers as she traveled toward Calimekka, she couldn't hope to rival the forces the Dragons would be able to command, either in numbers or in training.

She thought of General Talismartea again, and his assertion that there was always a way to win if one was but willing to redefine victory. Her forces could not hope to attack Calimekka outright and conquer the Dragons by force. So clearly they needed such a redefinition. Or else they needed a miracle.

Kait and Ry sat on the two chairs in Alarista's wagon; she and Hasmal sat side by side on the wall bench. The corner stove took the chill off the air and the hot, spicy *kemish* she drank warmed her from the inside. Storm lamps gave off bright, cheerful light, but the mood inside the wagon was as gray as the day.

Alarista said, "We're running out of time. With the thaws, the road will clear and we'll be able to travel again. Dùghall's troops are training, my people are training with them—but we still don't know how we're going to use our people. Once we can move, we don't dare delay."

Kait glanced out the window at the thick blanket of snow that covered the ground, and at the clouds that crawled around the ring of mountains that walled the camp, pregnant with moisture, dark and heavy. The Gyrus said they could smell spring coming; Kait believed them. Everyone said that yet another month would pass before the thaws began in earnest, but once or twice at midday she'd smelled wet earth and the first hints of new life in the air. The new year had come upon the rebels before they were ready for it—she and the others in the camp had hurriedly drawn lots and a young man from Dùghall's troops had named the year *We Hope for Better Days.* As carais, he'd led them in a solemn celebration of Theramisday, after which everyone returned to their preparations.

Kait poured herself another cup of *kemish,* the Gyru concoction of cocova, hot red pepper, and ground dried fish paste served in boiling water. She was the only one of the *harayee*—the Gyru word for non-Gyrus—in the camp who liked the drink. She added a pinch of salt and sipped hers, and nodded to Alarista. "You're right. But we have no plan."

Hasmal sighed. "Two hundred people against all the Dragons, the allies they've made, and the armies they've built?" He had a cup of herb tea, which he sipped. "Well enough. Here's your plan. We walk up to the city wall, declare that we have come to conquer Calimekka . . . and while the guards are helpless with laughter, we climb the wall, break into the Dragon stronghold without being caught, capture the Mirror of Souls, use it to destroy the Dragons, and win back Calimekka."

Ry laughed bitterly. "Good plan." He warmed his hands around his cup of tea but didn't drink. He turned to Kait and said, "If we had ten thousand well-trained troops, we might be able to take the city. But even with battle-hardened warriors, I wouldn't count on it, because we don't have the right sort of wizards. Your Falcons practice only defensive magic, which is useless in an attack." He took a tiny sip of the tea and put the cup down. "The *Wolves* might have done something against the Dragons, if they hadn't been taken over from inside. But two hundred people aren't enough to do anything."

Kait had been staring at a few fat snowflakes that were spiraling down to the ground. An idea sparked in her mind, found fuel there, and began to blaze. For a moment, she thought that surely her idea had been considered and rejected by others. But no one else, not even Ry, had her perspective.

She faced the rest of them and put her *kemish* down. "Have any of you considered," she said, "that perhaps we cannot come up with a plan, not because we are planning with too few people, but because we are planning with too many?"

The other three stared at her as if she'd begun to drool and froth at the mouth, and Hasmal laughed. "No."

Ry shook his head. "We have uncounted problems, but a surfeit of allies isn't one of them."

Alarista said, "I don't think you need to drink any more *kemish* if that's the effect it's going to have on you."

Kait persisted. "Listen. What are the objectives we *must* accomplish in order to beat the Dragons and free Calimekka?" She ticked them off on her fingers. "One, we must get into the city. Two, we must regain control of the Mirror of Souls. Three, we must remove the Dragons from the bodies they've stolen. We've only talked about how two hundred people could accomplish those objectives. But perhaps we need to consider how two might."

Ry was no longer smiling. "Two?" He stared into her eyes, suddenly tense, his scent abruptly marked by excitement.

She nodded, the look just for him. "Two."

"Tell me what you're thinking."

"The only way to get to Calimekka from here now, before the roads clear, would be to travel through the air, because the roads out of the mountains are impassable until spring and even if we could get to Brelst the winter seas are deadly; the ships are all in warmer ports now. By air, we could travel above the clouds and *literally* drop into the city in the darkness, bypassing the gates and the guards and whatever other security measures the Dragons have added to Calimekka since we fled."

"We could fly in if we had an airible," Hasmal agreed. "But the airibles are all in Calimekka, in the hands of our enemies."

"Two of us . . . don't need an airible," Kait said softly.

Ry's eyes grew wary.

Alarista raised an eyebrow. "You've been hiding your uncle's bird-girl? Someone who can drop a flea on the Dragons' backs? I would see that miracle myself."

Ry shook his head so slightly that Kait wondered if perhaps she'd imagined it. The fear she read in his eyes made her think she hadn't.

She leaned her head against his shoulder and under her breath said, "If we do this, the secret will be out. The Falcons will have to provide shields and protective spells."

He murmured, "Too many people know now. The more who know, the more who can betray . . . the two."

Alarista had better ears than Kait would have given her credit for. She asked, "Know what?"

Hasmal looked from Kait to Ry and back to Kait, frowning. Kait couldn't begin to guess what he was thinking.

Ry leaned back and said, "I agree that the secret can't be a secret from everyone if . . . they . . . these two, are to get into the city. But perhaps exposing the secret itself could wait."

Kait frowned. "And if we can't explain to people how . . . these two can get all the way from Norostis to Calimekka in two or three days, or even how they're going to get out of the mountains at all in the dead of winter, why will they want to help? And there's something else to consider. Maybe the two who will go need to know from the beginning that the people they need to trust won't turn on them. Because we can make all the plans in the world, Ry, but if the troops won't support the assault team, those plans will mean nothing."

Ry turned his head away from her. "Do what you want."

Alarista said, "I think my question about the bird-girl is somehow closer to the truth than I imagined. Yes?"

Kait studied her with all her senses and noted nothing dangerous in Alarista's movements, her scent, the speed of her breathing, or any of a hundred other tiny cues that could alert the wary to their own imminent danger.

"I'm Scarred," Kait said.

Alarista grew still. Head cocked to one side, eyes watchful, she said, "Not visibly."

"Visibly sometimes."

The silence inside the wagon had its own weight.

"And sometimes . . . you can . . . fly?"

Kait nodded.

"You . . . skinshift?"

Another nod.

"How have you— But I won't ask that. We've hidden the Scarred among our people as well. I know some of the ways it can be done. How you survived to adulthood really doesn't matter. That you can help us now—" She looked down at her hands. "But you said 'two,' and he"—with a nod to Ry—"knew what you were talking about. So"—she looked at Ry again, this time searching for something—"you are a skinshifter as well?"

"We're Karnee," he said.

"Karnee." Alarista breathed the word. She said nothing for a long time; when she spoke again, it was to say, "Then some still survive."

"Some." Ry's scent revealed the impatience, the distrust, and the anger that his face and posture hid. Kait watched Alarista, but most of her attention focused on him. He was tensing, preparing to do something rash if Alarista's responses betrayed any tendency toward treachery.

She seemed only nervous, though, and curious. She leaned forward, her eyes round and puzzled. "And you would willingly help Iberans? I'd think you'd be dancing with delight now, knowing that they were suffering some of the same horrors they would have inflicted on you."

Ry shrugged. "To an extent you're right. I can't say that the suffering of everyone in Calimekka wounds me. There are members of my own Family, for example, who deserve to suffer. Members of the parnissery, too. And . . ." His eyes tracked briefly to Kait, then quickly refocused on Alarista when he realized she'd seen his look. "And others, who have made their livelihoods from the suffering of others."

Kait suspected that he referred to the other Families, but didn't want to say anything of the sort in front of her because her own Family was gone. She wouldn't have been offended. She'd discovered the hard way that not all of the Galweighs had been as idealistic as she'd once believed.

She said, "But even though both of us have reason to feel that the Dragons are dispensing *some* justice, the fact that they are is accidental. More innocent suffer than guilty. And the Reborn wanted to bring love to the world. The Dragons . . . they have nothing to do with love."

Alarista said, "Not that you know of."

"I know what they intended to do to me."

Alarista raised an eyebrow. "You were in the Dragons' hands and lived?"

Kait said, "Long story. I'll tell you another time."

"Back to the point, then." Hasmal took a pastry out of the jar Alarista kept beside the table and nibbled on it. "You say the two of you can fly into Calimekka at night and drop into the heart of the Dragons' territory without being caught."

"We would hope to," Kait said. "I can't promise that we would succeed."

"No. Of course not. But you at least have the potential to make the attempt."

"Yes."

Hasmal took a big bite of the pastry and chewed thoughtfully. "That's certainly a benefit for us . . . but what would you do once you got there?"

Kait smiled. "I'm not sure how well this would work, but here's my idea. We would have to identify the Dragons, and secretly mark each of them the way Dùghall marked the three that you and Ian met with at the inn."

Alarista frowned. "Marked?"

Hasmal nodded. "Falcon viewing spell. Dùghall taught it to me. He touched each of the three Dragons we met with a linked talisman—the talisman absorbed into the skin instantly, and we could have watched the three subjects in viewing glasses for several days. We . . . well, we ended up not being able to, but that was a problem of situation rather than technique."

"So your plan calls for the two of you to get within touching distance of each of the Dragons?" Alarista was shaking her head. "That's insane."

"If it's our only chance of destroying them, it isn't insane." Kait ran her thumb around the top of her cup and stared out at the snow, now falling harder. She wasn't sure how she and Ry could get close enough to the enemy to plant the talismans, but if they *had* to do it, they would find a way. "Dùghall made a tiny Mirror of Souls out of a ring and some wire, Ris. He used the viewing glass and the talisman to connect with the soul of one of the Dragons, and he summoned that Dragon's soul into the ring. It's still in there. He'll show you if you want to examine it. I was thinking if we could create enough talismans and Mirrors, you and the other Falcons could sit here in the mountains and pull the Dragons' souls out one by one."

Ry said, "If we can get close enough to the Dragons to touch them, we can get close enough to steal the Mirror of Souls. With that, we could get all of them at once."

Kait said, "We can't guarantee that we could get to the original Mirror of Souls. And if we go to Calimekka with only that plan and we fail, we won't have any alternative but to retreat. If we go prepared to get them one at a time and we get lucky enough to steal the original Mirror, then our job gets easier. But if we can't get it, we can still win. It will just take longer."

Ry leaned back and rested his left ankle on his right knee. His chair teetered on two legs, and Kait expected him to go over backward at any moment. "All right. Considered that way, as a plan and a backup plan, your idea has merits. So how do we get to the Dragons?"

Kait shrugged. "Why don't we get the Falcons to work producing the talismans and viewing glasses and miniature Mirrors we'll need? In the time it takes them to do that, we'll figure out a way to get to the Dragons."

Dùghall showed the tiny Mirror to Alarista and demonstrated how he'd created the Mirror spell, and she and Hasmal and Trev and Jaim and Yanth went to work. They gathered every scrap of glass, silver, gold, copper, and bronze in the camp, and all the available wire as well. They enlisted the help of the Gyru smiths and metalworkers, and drew wire and hammered rings and fashioned tiny mirrors by the hundreds, imbuing each with a drop of their own blood and essence, focusing purely on the good they would do by returning evicted souls to their rightful bodies and freeing the enslaved people of Calimekka. They sent children into the town of Norostis to buy up all the stocks of the herbs tertulla and batrail. They cut glass and silvered the backs to create viewing glasses, and formed tiny tablets of herbs compressed around a bit of fingernail, a snip of a single hair, a scrape of skin from the inside of the mouth—talismans linked to their makers that would sink into the skin without trace and link the watched to the watcher until bodies absorbed the foreign elements and reworked them into parts of the self. They worked days and nights, catching sleep only when they had to, while Kait and Ry rested and ate and planned. Obsessively planned.

Within two weeks, the supplies were ready.

Neither Kait nor Ry knew how they were going to get to each of the Dragons, but they knew how they were going to begin looking. Now it was time to act.

Both had held off Shift as long as possible. Both had eaten hugely to fuel their bodies for the coming drain on their energy.

On the fifth day of the month of Drastu, which was Amial Makuldsday, Kait and Ry climbed through the wet and clinging snow from what everyone hoped would be the last storm of the season to the top of Straju Mountain. Straju was the highest peak near the camp. The climbing was treacherous, and Shifting would have been easier, but neither of them dared Shift. They couldn't know how long they would be able to hold Shift once they'd changed, and their plan would require every extra moment they could eke from their bodies.

When they reached a high south-facing cliff, they stripped off their winter clothes and left them piled against the lee side of a boulder. They'd said their good-byes to everyone else back in the camp. Now they turned to each other.

"I could go alone," Ry said. "If I knew you were safe, I would gladly go to Calimekka by myself."

Kait touched his face. "And if you went alone, I don't know that I would survive until your return. You already know I have to go, too."

He pulled her close and they embraced, shivering in the cold, some of the warmth of their naked bodies passing between them but most escaping into the icy mountain wind.

"I know. You're sure we'll fly when we jump?"

Kait said, "No. But I hope we will. I did before."

He nodded. They each put on the oddly shaped packs which Kait had designed—packs made to accommodate their flight-Shifted bodies. The packs held typical Calimekkan clothes, some money, and of course the talismans. They both had talismans embedded in their own skin at Dùghall's insistence; he refused to allow them to leave without being able to know of their fate. The talismans *they* wore were special, and would last at least a month, Dùghall had said, and perhaps two.

Knowing that they were being watched made their last embraces awkward.

Ry said, "I love you, Kait."

Kait pressed her face to his chest and listened to his heart beating. "I love you, too."

They looked at each other, then down to the rocky gorge far below their feet.

Kait shivered, more afraid at that moment than she had been when she jumped from the tower back in Calimekka. The rocks beneath her bare feet cut into her soles. Her teeth shook from the cold, her skin goosebumped and her body begged for Shift. "This is for our future," she murmured.

Ry heard her even though she hadn't really been speaking to him. "This is for them, but it's for us, too. For you and me and a world where we can live together."

Kait nodded. "I know." She gripped his hand tightly in her own, and said, "The rocks down there look so . . . hungry."

Ry pulled her close again and kissed her fiercely. "If this is all we have, it was enough, Kait. I'll find you in another life."

She felt his body shivering against hers. She wrapped her arms around him and pressed her face into the soft fur of his chest. "I'll meet you above the clouds."

"I promise."

They leaped from the cliff, and fell.

Chapter 47

A voice spoke to Trev as he lay in his tent dreaming. *Your sisters' heads are on the wall,* the voice said, and showed him a vision. His two once-beautiful sisters' bodies hung from the Bay Wall in Calimekka, and their heads, bloated and rotting, decorated pikes along the top. *Ry put them there with his lies, with his betrayals. You cannot save your sisters, but you can have your revenge. Kill him if you can; or if you can't kill him, simply come. Outside the camp you'll find a conveyance waiting for you. Step onto it and say the words, "Take me to my friend," and you will have your wish.*

Trev opened his eyes to darkness. Horrible pictures still burned in his mind, too horrible to be believed. But what if they were true? He had convinced himself that his sisters had left the city because no one he'd questioned knew otherwise. There had been no public executions, so he had let himself believe they were still alive. But he didn't know. Now he had to know. He had an idea that would show him, though it seemed a risky one. With the little magic he had learned from Hasmal, he thought he might seek out a Speaker and force it to give him the truth.

He lay still, concentrating. He'd never done magic alone before, but he was certain he knew the way to form the spell. He could use his own blood—the Falcons said a man should never use anything that wasn't his to power a spell. So a drop or two of his own blood on a mirror circled with salt, a few careful words to summon the voice of the dream, and he would see if nightmares plagued only his sleep, or if they had reached into the waking world to take him.

He struggled free of the tangled bedroll and looked around the tent. Valard still had supplies in his magic bag, since he'd been too busy drinking and mourning the certain end of the world to help make the talismans and mirrors and viewing glasses that might stop it. Even better for Trev's needs, Valard was at that moment with one of the Gyru girls; he was always with the Gyru girls these days, or sucking down fermented goats' milk or hard grain alcohol with the men. So Trev could safely borrow his equipment.

Which he did.

He didn't dare light a lamp to guide his work; Yanth slept to one side of him and Jaim to the other, and either would be more than a little curious to find him summoning spirits in the middle of the night. So he opened the tent flap enough that flickering light from one of the camp's watchfires illuminated his little workplace. It did its job unevenly, but he had to be grateful for what he could get.

He pulled out Valard's mirror and salt, and pricked the tip of his finger with a knife, carefully dripping his blood into a little puddle on the mirror's surface. For just a moment the light that came through the open flap was bright enough that he could see that the mirror was dirty, streaked with something. That bothered him, but his blood was already on the surface and he didn't want to waste it by wiping it off, cleaning the mirror, and then having to cut himself again. Besides, he'd had a hard time remaining silent the first time he cut himself. He didn't know if he could do it a second time without waking someone.

With a finger, he drew his blood into a triangle and whispered the first half of the incantation Hasmal had taught him for summoning Speakers from the Veil. Then he poured a thin line of salt onto the diagram, being sure not to leave any openings.

He finished the incantation by saying:

Speaker step within the walls
Of earth and blood and air;
Bound by will and spirit,
You must bide your presence there.

Answer questions with clear truth,
Do only good and then
Return to the realm from whence you came
And don't come back again.

The salt on the mirror burned pale blue, and Trev leaned over it with his body, blocking the light. The flames flickered, then steadied. Within the heart of the triangle, a spark appeared and grew into a translucent finger-tall image of a man. His diaphanous robes blew in a wind that never reached beyond the triangle; his long hair tossed as if he stood in the center of a storm. He crossed his arms over his chest and lifted his chin and glared up at Trev with glowing eyes.

"What do you want to know?"

Trev shivered. Hasmal had said the Speakers could be dangerous and sometimes spiteful. He'd said that, although they always spoke the truth, they didn't always tell it in ways a man could correctly interpret. But he'd never said how terrifying it was to see one standing on one's own mirror, caged by nothing but a thin line of blood and salt. Feeling the tiny, glowing man's anger seeping into the air, Trev had difficulty finding his tongue. He said, "I had . . . I had a . . . a dream. That . . . that my sisters were dead. Killed. With their . . . their . . . their heads on a wall in Calimekka. What was that dream?"

The man looked at him. "It was no dream. It was the truth, given to you by . . ." He paused and smiled. "By a friend."

Trev closed his eyes tightly. The image of the two bloated heads on the wall returned to him, clear and sharp, this time as painful as a knife in the belly. Alli and Murdith couldn't be dead—he'd promised each of them he'd find them suitable husbands from within the upper ranks of Families. He'd gotten them into a circle of people his parents wouldn't have even dared speak to. He'd done everything he could to protect them, to care for them, to cherish them . . . and they had died like criminals, with him far away and unable to save them.

"Who reached me?" he asked when he could find words again. "Why did he tell me about my sisters? Why does he say they were killed because of Ry?"

The Speaker's response was elliptical. "Ry's secrets were found out," he said. "His lies caught up with him, but because those who punish lies could not reach him, they reached those close to him. Your parents, too, are dead, as are the families of Ry's other friends. All of you have lost everything. All of you will return to nothing, no matter whether the Dragons are routed from the city or not."

"Who killed them?" Trev said.

"The one who wielded the blade acted on the orders of others, the one who gave the orders acted on the order of others, and that one, too, was simply following orders. If you follow the chain back to the beginning, it leads to Ry and the day he swore that he would stay in Calimekka and lead his Family's Wolves—and broke his oath that very night."

No matter what he asked, the Speaker refused to answer directly. Trev frowned, trying to think of a way to phrase his question that would force the Speaker to tell him what he wanted to know—who had actually put his sisters to death, and who had reached him in this out-of-the-way place to tell him of it. And why that person had bothered.

Outside the tent, the wind gusted, and snow blew in, swirling over the bedrolls and landing on the mirror. Trev crouched down to shield it. But the few snowflakes that landed on the diminishing line of salt and blood melted, creating a bridge from the inside of the triangle to the outside, and the dirty streak that smeared the glass.

The Speaker, becoming more transparent with every instant, and watching his flames beginning to gutter out, saw the bridge and shrieked. Before Trev could do anything, the spirit screamed, "Free!" in a voice no louder than a whisper, and leaped out of the triangle of blood and salt. He skidded across the streaks on the glass and howled, "It's blood! It's blood! Now you're mine!"

Then he disappeared.

Trev stared at the place where the Speaker had been. He didn't know why he'd been spared whatever fate the spirit had intended for him, but he also didn't care that he'd been spared. His sisters, for whom he had lived, were dead. The voice in his dreams might have blamed Ry, but Trev knew perfectly well that Ry was not to blame. *He* had chosen to follow Ry, knowing when he did that he was leaving Murdith and Alli in Calimekka without their single most determined supporter. Had he stayed, they would have still been alive. Or he would have been dead with them.

Either outcome would have been acceptable to him.

Ry was on his way to destroy the Dragons, and Trev still wished him well. *He* had promised to aid the Falcons in destroying them. But he'd broken another promise, one he'd made years earlier, and one to which he'd sworn his life. He'd failed to protect his little sisters, the two people he loved most in the world. He had broken his own oath.

He stared at the little knife with which he'd drawn his blood. It was sharp, but not enough of a blade for his new needs. His daggers lay at the top of his bedroll—two exquisite blades suitable to his station, both gifts from Ry. He chose the one carved with the crest that declared him an ally of the Sabir Family. He unwrapped the wool blanket from around his shoulders and unlaced his shirt, and rested the dagger on his chest to the left of his breastbone, prodding with his fingers to be sure that its point sat between two ribs and not above one.

He closed his eyes and said, "I'm sorry, Alli. I'm sorry, Murdith. I'll serve you better when we meet beyond the Veil."

Then, before he could think about what he was doing, he drove the blade through his heart.

Across the camp, Valard flung himself away from the girl he'd been pawing and dragged himself to his knees. His face twisted in pain, and he screamed and began to claw at his skin. The girl shouted, "What's the matter? What's the matter?" but before she could get to her feet to run for help, the spell, whatever it had been, seemed to pass. He stopped screaming and his face took on an expression of wonder.

Valard got to his feet, muttering, "I'm free. I'm free." He looked around the little wagon as if he'd never seen it before.

"What are you doing?" the girl asked, but he only looked at her for an instant, then shook his head. He wrapped a wool blanket around himself and, otherwise naked, stepped out of the wagon into the night, leaving the door swinging and the wind howling behind him. The girl swore and threw an empty bottle of the liquor they'd been sharing after him, and rose, shivering, and slammed the door and locked it.

Meanwhile, Valard marched across the snow, oblivious to the cold and the wind, until he reached the edge of the camp. There he found a smooth disk of whitest metal, decorated around the rim with characters that glowed faintly green in the darkness. He stepped into its center and said, "Take me to my friend."

The green glow brightened, and the metal disk whined, and he and it both disappeared.

Dùghall crouched by Trev's body and cupped a hand over the mirror, not touching it but carefully reading its energy through his skin.

"What does it mean?" Yanth asked.

"A moment." The traces were muddled and ugly and hard to unravel. He was patient, though, and thorough. At last he felt he had the gist of what had happened. "Trev used Valard's kit to summon a Speaker," he told Yanth and Jaim, who stood just behind him. "He evidently didn't clean the mirror first, because some of Valard's blood was still on it. The Speaker came, but it was a Speaker influenced by dark magic—I would guess that it was directed by the Dragons, though that I cannot be sure of. I don't know what the Speaker told Trev, but he is dead by his own hand—and I find clear traces that the Speaker escaped and linked itself through Valard's blood on the mirror to his body. Which means Valard is now possessed by the spirit of a Speaker. Where the Speaker compelled Valard to go, I also cannot say." He stood and looked up into Yanth's eyes. "But Speakers are by their nature cruel, and this one was magically influenced by evil as well, which makes the situation graver still; if we find Valard, we will have to kill him."

"Can't we exorcise the Speaker, or put him into a ring the way you put the soul of the Dragon into a ring?" Jaim asked.

"The Dragons are human. Their souls cannot infect a body; they can only inhabit it. Speakers are . . . other. Some say they are demons, some say they are the ghosts of monsters from other worlds or other planes. I don't know what they are, but I know that when they possess a man, they possess him until his death."

Yanth blinked rapidly and his lips pressed into a thin, hard line. His eyes gleamed suspiciously bright as he looked down at Trev's body where it still lay facedown on his bedroll in a pool of blood. "It all falls apart," he whispered.

Jaim rested a hand on his shoulder. "These are dark days."

"These days are the hell of the old gods, visited on us because we forgot them," Yanth said. Dùghall heard the rasp in his voice that betrayed the depth of his emotion.

"Perhaps," Jaim agreed with a slow nod. The cold air had raised gooseflesh on his exposed arms, and Dùghall saw him shiver. He seemed too lost in the awful moment to notice, though, for he stood there, staring down at the body of his dead comrade, and made no effort to find his coat or even to warm himself by moving. His breath curled out in frosted plumes, leaving crystals on his eyelashes, eyebrows, and the heavy mustache he'd grown since coming to the mountains. He looked to Dùghall more like an ice statue of a man than one of flesh and blood. In a voice gone flat and dead, Jaim said, "We have to find Valard."

"Why? So that we can slaughter another of our number?" Yanth pulled away from Jaim's touch; Jaim's arm dropped to his side as if it were a dead thing.

Doggedly he said, "If necessary, yes. Ry is on his way to Calimekka. If the Dragons have been spying on him, or if they have found a way to use Valard against Ry, we have to stop him."

Yanth had closed his eyes. He wove from side to side as he stood there, plainly lost in misery. "What does it matter?" he asked at last. "It all falls apart. Nothing we do will hold, nothing we do will succeed. Don't you see? The gods themselves stand against us, and who are we to fight the gods?"

Jaim hung his head at those words, and shrugged. "Maybe you're right. Maybe everything is lost. I don't know who we are to question the will of the gods."

"We are men," Dùghall said roughly, "and we have put the gods to pasture. We will never cower again before gods or men—we will fight them both and we will win."

"Why?" Yanth asked, and Dùghall heard scorn in that one sharp syllable. "Because our hearts are pure and our cause is just? Because we *care*?"

"Goodness has no lock on victory," Dùghall said, staring at the two of them until they had to look at him. "Good men lose to evil men all the time. And caring without doing is weak and worthless and empty. Men who care much but do little always fall to men who care less but do more. We won't win because we are good, or because our convictions matter to us."

He laughed, and his laugh sounded harsh in the bitterly cold air, like the snap of a tree branch breaking beneath the weight of ice and snow. "We'll win because we're too afraid to lose. If we give in passively to the Dragons' plans, they'll devour our souls and the souls of everyone we love—and with our souls, our immortality. If we fight, the worst that can happen to us is death. We'll win because we are afraid. *Because* we are afraid, and rightly so. Fear will be the friend that spurs us to victory."

The three of them stood there staring at each other for a long time. Finally Jaim nodded. "Perhaps."

Yanth looked away. He sighed heavily and shook his head. "I won't quit," he said. "I don't have your faith in our victory, but I won't quit."

Dùghall glanced through the gap in the tent flaps at the brilliant white field beyond. "None of us will. We have that thought to hang on to. Now—we'll have to have a ceremony for Trev, and we need to bury him today. You get him ready. Meanwhile, I'll cast around to see if I can find out where Valard went—if magic was involved, there should be traces of it still about. And after that, we'll go on doing what we must do."

He left the two of them preparing Trev's body for viewing. He trudged over the packed snow, wishing he could be as certain of their eventual victory as he had sounded while talking to them. He dreaded the future, and the present terrified him, too. He hoped what he had told them was truth, because the only thing he was sure of in his life at that moment was fear. He had enough of that to fill an ocean.

Chapter 48

Kait and Ry came upon Calimekka at night, when the city sprawled like an endless bed of embers beneath the cloud-blanketed sky. Kait had seen the city that way many times; her old friend Aouel had taken her up in the airible for night flights when she sneaked out of Galweigh House on nights she couldn't sleep, or when she wanted someone to talk to. So she saw the change in the heart of the city and recognized it, and pointed it out to Ry, for whom this aerial view was a first.

"The white lights in the center of the city—those were never there before."

Ry looked where she'd indicated, and angled his wings to take him closer to those lights.

Kait followed. She didn't like what she saw. In the center of Calimekka, surrounded by shining, translucent white walls of the sort only the Ancients knew how to create, lay a fairyland of pristine white castles, shimmering white fountains, lovely white roadways and paths. Gardens of flowers and fruits and trees and shrubs, artfully illuminated by the white light, glowed like jewels. In one of the gardens, a few men and women, dressed in styles she'd never seen before, danced to the strains of music that sounded foreign to her ears. She circled above them, silent, keeping her magical shields drawn tight around her to hide her presence, and she recalled the bustling markets and fine neighborhoods that once stood where that huge, empty city-within-a-city now sprawled.

"We've found them," Ry said softly.

"We have." She stared down. "Now we have to decide how to reach them."

A week later, Kait and Ry stood together in the cool, sweet-scented air of the Calimekkan dawn, dressed in the clothes of well-off commoners, waiting before the great white gate of the new Citadel of the Gods. Others stood with them—tradesmen hoping to sell food or cloth or worked silver or glassware; peasants hoping to find work; beggars who saw the wealth behind the closed gates and, unfamiliar yet with New Hell, hoped they might find generosity.

Ry's shoulder pressed against Kait's, but they didn't speak to each other or look at each other or give any indication that they were to-gether. Kait's heart thudded heavily in her chest and her dry mouth tasted of sand and fear. Her shields were pulled in close and tight, and she thought that their confining closeness added to her anxiety as much as the press of the crowd or the fear she smelled in those around her.

Fear clouded the air more heavily than the jasmine that grew in the gardens beyond the gates. But Kait, like everyone around her, swallowed her fear and waited, listening to the soft chimes that rang in the white-walled gardens, watching for movement in the city-within-a-city.

At last a woman stepped out of the first building on the right and moved toward them, her rich blue skirts swirling around her ankles as she walked. Her skin was black as onyx, her eyes as gold as the finely worked bracelets that jangled at her wrists. Her black hair, braided with ribbons of deep blue and cloth-of-gold, hung to the ground. She stepped to the gate and opened it, and stepped back. The merchants filed past her and set up their stalls on the pristine white streets, strangely subdued. She turned to the beggars and sent them off to the center of the Citadel, telling them they could sit and beg by the great fountain there.

Then she turned to the workers. "How many of you are here for day work?" she asked. She smiled and her voice was warm, but Kait could find no warmth in her eyes.

A few of the workers raised their hands.

"Good. We have need of laborers in the Red Gardens. Please follow my servant; she'll show you where to go." A beautiful young girl dressed all in white stepped out from beneath the arch to Kait's right and walked soundlessly down the street. The men and women who had asked for day work followed her.

The woman turned back to the few who remained. "And the rest of you must be hoping for permanent positions?"

Kait nodded with the others.

"I thought so. Most have been filled. Unless you have special skills, we likely have nothing to offer you." She studied Ry, and her smile became hungry. "I think, though, that some of you surely have special skills." She stood there for a moment, her expression thoughtful; then, coming to a decision, she said, "Follow me, all of you. I know what I need"—her eyes flicked over Ry again—"but I can't be certain what the rest of my colleagues are looking for."

She touched Ry on the shoulder before she led them off. "You stay close to my side. I believe I have just the right position for you."

Kait wanted to kill her right there. Instead she pretended indifference, and followed the woman through the nearly empty streets to a magnificent hall in the center of the new city. Inside, young, beautiful men and women whose silk robes outshone the parrots in their gardens gathered and chatted. They all glanced toward the newcomers as they entered, and a few evinced real interest.

The golden-eyed woman spoke loudly, her voice ringing over the low hum of chatter that filled the enormous hall. "Here are today's permanents. Who'll interview?"

"Ah, Berral, you didn't bring us much to pick from," someone said, and laughed.

A few others joined in the laughter, but a muscular man with a broad smile rose from his seat at one of the small tables along the west wall and said, "I suppose it's my turn." He nodded toward a girl who looked to be about Kait's age—a pleasantly rounded young woman with skin the color of milk and eyes as huge and frightened as a lamb's in a slaughterhouse.

"You," he said. "What can you do?"

"I read . . . and write," she said, her voice shaking. "I can do sums. I know history and philosophy, drawing and rhetoric. I've been a champion at both querrist and hawks and hounds . . ." Her voice faltered as the people around her started to laugh.

"She's a trained monkey," one of them murmured.

"She might make a decent enough concubine," another answered. "I've often wished for a mistress who knew a few games, and could talk about something other than her shopping."

"How are you in bed?" the first asked.

The girl flushed. "I could care for children," she said, "or keep purchase records, or maintain a library."

"We don't have children," a woman who leaned against the wall said. "And we never will."

At the same time, the man who'd asked how she was in bed said, "She has no talent, then, at the only skill that interests me. So what about you?" he said, turning to Kait.

She said, "I cut and arrange both men's and women's hair." She had decided that job would give her an opportunity to touch as many of the Dragons as possible, planting her talismans without raising questions. The Dragons would certainly have personal servants, but she knew from her own life in Galweigh House that there was nothing like the lure of a specialist to draw people out of their daily routines.

"Do you?" Berral asked, now studying her with real interest. "Your hair is short. Interesting. And is red the original color?"

Kait smiled. "Can't you tell?"

"I can't." She flipped her long braid over her shoulder and said, "What would you do with mine?"

Kait pretended to consider for a moment. "Something with gold beads, I think," she said. "To set off your eyes. And snow-peacock feathers to contrast with your skin. Full around the face to emphasize your bones—they're good, but your current style hides that. And I think I'd work in a few sapphires if you have them."

"Lovely," someone said behind her. "That would be perfect."

"What would you do for me?" a tall, angular woman with emerald eyes asked. Her hair was plain brown, long and wavy and unstyled.

"A new cut first," Kait said. "Your neck is long and slender as a swan's, but all that hair covers it. Then a new color. Pale blond, I think—that would make your eyes even more striking. And then ringlets, with green silk ribbons woven through."

The woman smiled. "You must do just that for me."

"After she does my hair," Berral said.

"And then she can do mine."

"Come, girl. We'll find a place for you, and get you what you need, and you can get to work. I haven't had my hair done well in a thousand years."

The green-eyed woman and a svelte redhead started to lead her off. Behind her, she heard Berral say, "And what do you do?"

She heard Ry's voice answer, "I do *tapputu*—it's a form of massage that uses perfumes and oils and herbs. Excellent for the skin, and soothing."

Berral sighed. "Then we must put you to work with the hairdresser. I'd thought to make you my concubine—but my friends would never forgive me if I kept a masseur to myself. Perhaps, though, I'll have you spend nights with me."

"If you'd like," Ry said.

Kait kept her anger from her face. She consoled herself with the knowledge that as soon as Ry touched the woman with a talisman, Dùghall or Hasmal would summon her Dragon soul into one of the tiny Mirrors, and Ry would have one less admirer.

She hoped he marked her first.

Chapter 49

anya crouched in the back of her little house, staring at the boy who had named himself Luercas. He was paying her no attention, at least for the moment. He'd caught a tundra-vole and was playing with it on the bearskin rug, amusing himself at its expense.

At that moment he looked like a normal eight-year-old boy—solidly built, golden-haired, fair-skinned, with bright eyes and an engaging smile.

What he was doing to the vole wasn't normal. And he'd only been born a few months earlier. And he could change the way he looked. When he was outside of their house, he chose to look like the Kargans—he could skinshift at will, assuming any form he liked. He had been Scarred by the magic that had coursed through his body before his birth, but the Scars had been advantageous. He already knew Karganese before he was born, and because he was outwardly a sweet-natured child, and because he could make himself appear to be Kargan, and because he spoke with the seeming innocence of childhood, yet offered the wisdom of adulthood, he drew the Kargans to him like bears to fish. They admired him, they listened to him, and when he offered them advice in that diffident, childlike voice, they took it. He knew their prophecies and their legends well enough from watching them before he took over the infant body to know how to make himself fit. To the Kargans, he seemed like the savior they'd hoped would come to take them back to the Rich Lands. That, he told Danya with a laugh, suited his plans perfectly.

The vole shrieked in agony, and Luercas chuckled.

"Stop it," Danya said.

"Oh, please. It's a pest. The Kargans kill them all the time, and I don't see you racing out to protest."

"They don't torture them. They don't sit there soaking in the poor thing's pain."

"They don't garner any magic from the poor thing's death, either, which is a complete waste. I'm doing two useful things when I kill the vole—I'm ridding the village of one more pest, and I'm giving myself a bit of energy that I don't have to take from the villagers. Or you."

He turned and smiled at her, his blue eyes as cold as the frozen river, and she hated him even more. She said nothing, and after he'd stared at her, he turned his back to her and returned to torturing the vole.

"We'll be able to leave here soon," he said.

"Leave?"

"Certainly. We'll be returning to Calimekka before long."

Danya snorted. "Going to walk across the frozen wastes again, are we?"

"Not at all. We'll travel in good weather. And we're going to go in style, you and me." His shoulders rose and fell in a casual shrug. "And then you'll have your revenge." He chuckled. "You've certainly earned the right."

Revenge. She thought of Crispin Sabir and Anwyn Sabir and Andrew Sabir lying in a pool of their own blood, screaming. She thought of hurting them the way they'd hurt her, of *destroying* them the way they'd destroyed her. She stared at the index and middle fingers of her right hand—at the talons, rather; dark and scaled and claw-tipped. Her reminder of her right to their lives. Everything that had happened to her and everything she did was their fault. And her Family's; the Galweighs hadn't rescued her. And Luercas's.

Torture rape transformation pregnancy pain birth murder slavery.

That had become the mantra that fueled her rage, that kept her

breathing from one day to the next. She was Luercas's slave now because no one had helped her then. And they were going to pay for her
suffering. All of them, somehow, would pay.

Chapter **50**

Kait felt she and Ry were making progress. The first few days, they didn't plant any of their talismans—they wanted to earn the trust of their clients and build up word of mouth within the Dragon enclave. And their strategy seemed to be working. Kait decorated hair, grateful that much of her diplomatic training had been based on the assumption that she might have to operate from time to time without servants, and would still have to represent the Family appropriately.

When she took them, she'd complained about the hairdressing classes as a complete waste of her time. She wondered if she'd ever have the opportunity to find the woman who had trained her, to apologize for her condescension and to admit that she'd been wrong.

"Whatever you do, do it well," her mother had said to her, and her father had added, "No knowledge is ever wasted."

She'd argued with them, too—cocksure certain that her station in life, her talent and her intelligence would keep her from ever needing to know a menial trade. She owed them an apology, too, and would never get to give it. Dùghall was certain both of them had died in the massacre.

Now she stood all day on a breezy veranda attached to one of the Dragons' public baths, liming and hennaing and curling hair with curling irons or straightening it with flatirons; braiding in beads and gems and ribbons and adding her own touches that no one else had thought to duplicate—working a tiny little cage and a live songbird into one creation, a lovely ivory dancer into another. She shaped men's beards and mustaches, too, and did her share of liming and hennaing and curling on her male clients, as well. Her business picked up steadily.

After the first week, she started touching her clients with the talismans.

She saw Ry for a moment in the morning when she arrived at the veranda, and sometimes at night when he left. They gave each other no more acknowledgment than any strangers who worked in the same building would. Ry went into the baths and massaged muscles and egos. Kait noted that he did a good business, too.

But it didn't last, of course.

Kait arrived at the veranda one damp, gray morning, nodded politely to Ry as he went past her into the bathhouse, and started the fire in the little oven on which she heated her curling irons and flatirons. She laid out the pots of henna and lime, the towels and brushes and razors, and gave her fingertips a light coating of melted wax—that so the talismans didn't embed themselves in her hands as she picked them up. Then she dumped a handful of the talismans into the waist pocket of her work apron and turned to watch a group of musicians setting up their instruments on the far corner, away from the bath's fountain. Some of the Dragons were early risers; she'd learned to have everything ready as soon after dawn as she could.

Her first clients that morning were men. They were not as young-looking as most of the men she'd worked on before, but they had the same haughty attitude she'd come to associate with all the Dragons. They acted as if she were invisible except when telling her what they wanted. That treatment suited her perfectly, and she was as deferential as she knew how to be. She trimmed and shaped their beards, braided and ribboned one mustache and beaded another, and worked their long hair into the heavy coils that many of the men favored, hiding one growing bald spot as she did. Several women came out of the baths by the time she finished and were waiting on the benches by the fountain. They came toward her, laughing and murmuring secrets to each other, and the men rose as if to leave. But instead they merely backed to the edge of the veranda and waved the women forward.

Kait smelled something wrong about them—the scent of excitement she associated with hunters who have cornered their prey. She couldn't see anything out of the ordinary about the situation— sometimes, after all, her clients had stayed to watch her work on their friends. But her gut warned her that something was about to happen. She tensed and moved closer to her stove and her irons, all the while bowing to the women and asking them to decide who would go first.

A handful of men walked out of the bathhouse door nearest the musicians and stood listening to them play.

Three more men came out of the bathhouse door beside the fountain and ambled slowly toward her, seemingly deep in conversation with each other.

A carriage rolled to a silent stop in front of the bathhouse, and a dozen soldiers in Sabir green and silver helped a veiled, misshapen figure to the ground and up the walk.

She was surrounded, her escape to the street cut off by the Sabir soldiers. But no one moved to attack. She smelled the readiness, but the charge that should follow such readiness didn't come. One of the women, instead, seated herself in the chair in front of Kait and held out a decoration. "Work this into my hair," she said. "The way you did the little bird in the cage for Alisol a few days ago."

She handed Kait a delicate carved ebony sphere inlaid along each of its fragile ribs with silver and rubies. Each rib bore a rose and thorn . . . and suddenly Kait recognized it. It was a Galweigh trinket—something she'd seen on a pedestal in a cousin's room or on an aunt's desk. She couldn't recall where. But the fair-haired woman in front of her was not a Galweigh by birth or by marriage. She had no right to the sphere.

Kait reached for it, wrapped her fingers around it. Felt something try to reach from the sphere to her, like a weight pressing against her shields. She looked into the woman's eyes and saw interest, expectation—and then the delight of the hunter who sees the arrow strike true, and watches the prey fall.

She shivered, and her heart raced. The sphere had been a trap . . .

and a test. By avoiding the trap—and had she not been well shielded, she knew, the spell that the sphere had triggered would have swallowed her—she had failed the test. She proved herself not a hapless servant but a dangerous infiltrator.

She had the chance for one move. She tucked the ball into her apron pocket—and in doing so caught the talismans in the pocket with the wax on her fingertips.

The woman rose. "So you're the one after all," she said. "I thought as much." She smiled at Kait. "You can walk along with me quietly, or all of these men can drag you."

"I'm not going anywhere with you," Kait said.

"You think not?"

The men surrounded Kait, weapons drawn. She couldn't run, and she couldn't Shift without giving away the one secret she might use to escape later.

"Give me back my ball," the woman said, and held out her hand.

Kait pretended to hesitate, pulled it out of the pocket, and pressed it into the woman's hand. As she did, she brushed her skin with a talisman. It absorbed instantly; the woman noticed nothing.

"So come with us now. You don't want to die right here, and I promise you that's what will happen if you fight us."

Kait crossed her arms over her chest, keeping her fingertips hidden. Each had several talismans stuck to it; she was going to end up wasting them, but she didn't have any choice. The men stepped in to get her, knives and swords pointed at her, and she nodded. "I'll go."

The woman's face changed. She went pale, and stared around her with first amazement, then terror in her eyes. Then her face went blank again, but Kait knew what had happened. When she looked at Kait again, she was someone else. She was the person who belonged in the body.

Kait nodded; the woman blinked slowly. Back in the mountains, in the camp, her own people were only waiting for her to touch the men so that they could pull the Dragon souls from them. The true owners of the bodies would help her. She was going to survive this.

Behind her a familiar voice said, "That's Kait. Ry is inside, Parata."

She turned, stunned. Valard had come up behind her. He stood next to the twisted, veiled creature who had stepped out of the carriage. The creature lifted its veil, and Kait gasped. Its face had melted. Its eyes were completely gone, its nose was a gaping hole in the center of its face, its mouth was a jagged, lopsided scar twisted into a leer on one side, loose-lipped and drooling on the other. Ragged hair sprouted from a gray patch on one cheek, scales erupted from the forehead like jagged teeth, and tatters and blobs of skin dangled from the empty eye sockets, from the drooping chin, from the places where ears should have been.

Valard smiled at Kait, then at the creature beside him. "Let me introduce you," he said. "Kait Galweigh, this is Imogene Sabir, a dear friend of mine. Parata Sabir, this is Kait Galweigh." He chuckled. "Parata Sabir would be your future mother-in-law. That is, if you or Ry had a future."

From inside the bathhouse, Kait heard sounds of struggle, and Ry's voice shouting, "Kait, run!"

Then muffled, ominous silence.

Kait erupted into action. She darted under one knife, slapped the man who held it, twisted toward another and slapped him, brushed against a third, and broke free. She raced for the bathhouse, wishing she had a weapon, Shifting as she ran, hoping that she would be able to do something—anything—to save Ry.

"Let her go," she heard one of them behind her say. "She won't get away."

She had Shifted too recently and for too long; her body embraced the hunter form only weakly. She bounded forward on four legs, teeth bared, clothes dragging the floor behind her, and even though she could feel the Karnee rage, the Karnee hunger, it was already slipping away.

Ry lay unmoving on the smooth white bathhouse floor, the center of a splash of shocking red. Blood matted his hair and the air reeked with the iron stink of it. She tasted the fear of the men who faced her as she charged forward. She leaped snarling into the air, intent on killing the nearest of them—intent on killing all of them.

But her unsheathed claws blunted in midair, growing soft and thin and weak. Her paws lengthened into hands; her muzzle rounded into a human jaw; her body lengthened and reformed, and when she hit her target, she was halfway between human and beast, and too awkward and misshapen to be as dangerous as either. The man clubbed her on the side of the head with the pommel of his sword, and redness bloomed behind her eyes.

She dropped to the floor, feeling herself hit the hard ground. She felt nothing after that.

Chapter 51

Dafril looked at the bound bodies at his feet. The girl, Kait, had been his first choice for his own body—but he didn't even consider using the Mirror of Souls to trade now that she was in his hands. First, he'd already invested a great deal of energy and effort into modifying Crispin Sabir's body to meet his future needs as an immortal. Second, he no longer found the idea of being female for eternity as titillating as he had initially. And third, he accepted the fact that the Mirror process carried with it a high risk. He didn't want to move out of the body he occupied only to discover that he couldn't take over the body he desired.

He watched her breathing. Pretty girl, if too thin. He looked at the way her long black hair spilled across the floor, looking like a curtain of silk. It had been short and red before she'd Shifted to attack her lover's captors; her body was returning gradually to its normal state as he watched. The process was as interesting to watch as it was to experience.

Briefly, he entertained the idea of taming her and keeping her for a pet. But he put it quickly out of his mind. He had another use for both her and her lover. Several uses, actually. None of them were particularly entertaining, but all of them were necessary.

"Put them in the cages, please," he said. "When they wake, feed them. They'll be hungry."

The attendants nodded and dragged the still-breathing bodies along the floor with neither gentleness nor concern. They slung one into a heavily barred iron cage, carefully chained and locked it, then followed the same procedure with the other.

Dafril watched, satisfied. The cages were sturdy enough to hold Karnee—even healthy Karnee. And he needed these two to be healthy, because their lives and their souls would act as primer for the spells that would fuel the immortality engine. Only a day's work now stood between him and godhood. He took a deep breath and stared down at his unconscious enemies. They'd keep until he needed them, and in the meantime, the appalling destruction of Dragons would stop.

He liked the idea of priming the immortality spells with the enemies who had destroyed so many of his friends and allies. But he had to find out how they were doing it before he destroyed them. If they could steal Dragons' souls from their bodies, someone else might be able to do the same. He had not waited a thousand years in a prison of his own making so that he could be ripped from the body he'd chosen and flung back into the Veil to become an oblivious, ignorant, squalling infant yet again.

"After they're awake and fed, let me know," he told the keepers. "I need to question them. Whatever you do, don't touch them or let them get too near you. They're deadly bastards, though you wouldn't know it to look at them now." He turned to leave the Heart of the Citadel, then turned back. "They're skinshifters, you know."

Both keepers hissed with disgust. He turned away, smiling. Good. Neither of his captives would be able to win sympathy from their purely human keepers. The Calimekkan hatred of the Scarred would work in his favor, and keep his prisoners imprisoned. He could get back to his work with an easy mind.

Chapter 52

Kait? Can you hear me?"

The whisper was so low, human ears would never have heard it. Kait, though, shook off the last vestiges of the haze that had clouded her mind. "Yes," she whispered.

"Are you hurt?"

"No. Hungry, but not hurt. What about you?"

"I'm fine. My head healed while I . . . slept. It still aches a bit, but that will pass as soon as I get something to eat."

"Good. I love you." She lay still while she whispered to him—she could smell the ones in the cavernous hall who watched. She feigned unconsciousness, keeping her muscles relaxed and her breathing steady.

"I love you, too." He was quiet for a moment, then spoke again. "I don't know how much you can see from where you are, but I've moved around a bit and my eyes are open. We're caged, and there are Ancients' artifacts all around us. I've tried my lock. We won't get out of it unless you have something with you that can saw through metal."

"I don't. You can't do anything with magic?"

"No. The locks are spell-shielded."

The Dragons had seen to that, of course. Had she been them, she would have done the same thing. For all they knew, she and Ry alone were responsible for the disappearance of the missing Dragons. So she and Ry would be in the strongest prison that Dragons could contrive, held by their most powerful locks and walled off from rescue by their most powerful spells. If they knew to block against the talismans, they could prevent Dùghall or Hasmal or Alarista or anyone else who cared about her or Ry from seeing either of them through the viewing glasses. Even if the Dragons didn't know to block against such viewing they might do it inadvertently by putting up a powerful shield spell to prevent Ry and Kait from using magic against them.

She had to assume that she and Ry were alone now, invisible to anyone who cared about them, without hope of rescue. Their fate was in their own hands.

"Do you see any way we might get out?" she asked. "Anything at all?"

"No."

"Then we'll have to watch and wait."

"I'll take the first watch. Sleep now. You Shifted—you need the rest. I'll let you know if anything changes."

"I love you," she said again.

He chuckled softly. "I know. I love you, too."

Dùghall's soul stretched along a strand of energy that traversed the known world and the Veil beyond; his body sat in a cold tent in semi-darkness and near silence, barely breathing and worn nearly to death. His consciousness—his *self*—however, peered through the eyes of a powerful Dragon at a delicate silver rose that grew in the center of a garden of white flowers. The Dragon's eyes were fixed on the rose, but he didn't really see it; he was elated and came to be by himself to celebrate the sweetness of the moment.

Dùghall could have ripped him from the body right then, but something about the man's jubilation made him cautious. He could afford to wait a moment or two if he had to—the danger to him while he was away from his body was great, but the information he might gain from the Dragons could be worth the risk.

So he was careful to disturb nothing in the Dragon's mind, and the man never suspected his presence. Dùghall spied on him as he touched the pictures of a long-anticipated future like a bride-to-be touching her wedding silks and dower gifts. Dùghall caught an image of a platinum sphere floating in a pool of thick emerald liquid, while a single man finished adjustments on it. The Dragon thought of this assembly as the immortality engine, and he seemed certain that it would be completed that day. He pulled vague pictures of complex machinery being installed into the towers of the Ancients that still dotted the city from the Dragon's thoughts, too—these were, he discovered, the Ancients' devices the Dragons had been trying to acquire when Ian and Hasmal were pretending to be traders. All the essential ones were in place. Others could have been added, but weren't essential, and would not be.

Dùghall finally won the reward he'd most hoped for—a flashed image of Kait and Ry, both unconscious and bleeding, penned in tiny padlocked cages guarded by men and magic.

The Dragon's elated thoughts rang clear in Dùghall's mind. *The engine is ready, the technothaumatars are in place, and the priming sacrifices are in the holding pens. Today we become gods.*

Dùghall had what he needed. He erupted into the Dragon's body, unfolding and expanding until he crowded the soul of the Dragon and loosened its holds on the body it had stolen. He snarled into the Dragon's mind, *You will never be a god. Upon my soul, you have done your last evil, Dragon.*

Hasmal was one unmoving center of a violent storm. Still as stone, his gaze focused inward and away, he barely breathed, rarely acknowledged the people around him, never spoke a single word. He sat across from Dùghall, the storm's other center, aware at rare intervals of Alarista watching the bank of viewing glasses, of Yanth and Jaim carrying those she indicated to him or Dùghall, of the Gyru volunteers who removed each filled soul-mirror as it became ready. But he and Dùghall . . . sat.

Slowly, they were filling their mirrors with Dragon souls. Tracing each soul back along the lines of power that connected them to their enemies, looking through their enemies' eyes, finding nothing that could tell them where Kait or Ry had been taken or what had happened to them, then carefully casting the spell that restored the original soul to each body and pulled the deadly Dragon soul through their own flesh and threw it into a waiting ring.

But Alarista did not have the knack for containing an alien soul in her body while focusing it into the waiting trap; she'd tried once and the Dragon had almost forced her out and taken her over, and only the fact that Dùghall and Hasmal had stood ready while she made the attempt, and had pressed a talisman into her skin and linked to pull the monster out of her, had saved her. Neither Jaim nor Yanth had the skill with magic to cast the spells or follow them across the long distances. And he would not leave the burden on Dùghall, though he didn't doubt for a minute the old man would take it. Dùghall's skin was pasty gray, his nails and lips and the rims of his eyes purple-tinged white from the strain. Where Hasmal trembled, Dùghall shook. Hasmal did not think he would survive too many more battles with their enemies before one of them succeeded in taking him over and Hasmal had to rescue him. And that would leave Hasmal the only one who could destroy the remaining magic-linked Dragons or save Ry and Kait.

"Have you found them yet?" Yanth asked Alarista. Hasmal heard the question in the back of his mind, and allowed part of his attention to wait for the answer. The rest focused on Dùghall, who was bringing back another of the marked Dragons.

"No. Their viewing glasses are still dark."

"And you haven't seen them through anyone else's eyes?"

"Not yet. But I'm still watching. We have a few marks who are doing a lot of moving around. They're meeting with others, they seem excited. I'm having a hard time hearing what they're saying—some of the links are weak. I have one that I think is spellcasting, and is working on an artifact of some sort."

"That sounds bad."

"I know. The artifact worries me more than anything else that we've seen."

Dùghall's eyes filled with tears, and pain twisted his face. His breathing got faster, and his eyes, which had been closed, flew open. He bared his teeth in a soundless snarl, and Hasmal tensed and concentrated only on the other Falcon. The Dragon was coming through fighting, and Dùghall looked like he might be losing the fight.

Hasmal held the talisman on one wax-coated fingertip and waited.

Dùghall's hands twisted into claws around the tiny empty soul-mirror that sat on the floor behind him.

Hasmal kept waiting, ready, the words of the linking spell already mostly said and their meaning held in his mind, lacking only the final phrase.

"Yes," Dùghall snarled, and light curled from the center of his chest into the gold ring.

"Guards ready," Alarista said, and the soldiers who stood along the back of the tent drew their weapons. Hasmal tried not to see them, and tried not to think about what their presence meant. But the reality of those drawn swords aimed at Dùghall was inescapable.

The soul pouring into the ring might not be the Dragon's. Hasmal and Dùghall had discussed the possibility that some Dragon might be able to oust their souls, not just into the Veils, from whence they were certain they could get it back, but perhaps into the little one-way soul-mirror. If a Dragon succeeded in pushing either of them into the mirror, they would not be able to come back. The Dragon would have permanent possession of their body . . . and the soldiers waiting with drawn weapons would have to kill the Dragon by destroying the body.

Give me a sign, old man, Hasmal thought.

The soldiers watched him, for only he would be able to put them at their ease, or tell them to kill Dùghall's body.

The stream of light pouring from Dùghall's chest grew brighter, and the central well of the tiny mirror began to grow. The light pool formed inside the ring and swirled around, fast as water in a whirlpool, brilliant as a small sun.

A sign. Give me a sign that you are yourself.

Dùghall snarled softly and his body shuddered. The light pouring from him died. Behind him, young men with drawn weapons stared at Hasmal's face, their eyes round and frightened, their bodies tense with the uncertainty of waiting.

A sign.

Dùghall sagged forward and said, "The foulest of enemies can still give the sweetest of gifts. I know where they are, and I know what the Dragons are going to do with them."

Hasmal watched Dùghall's eyes—they were the eyes of the man he'd come to think of as a friend. No stranger stared out of them.

Hasmal told the soldiers, "He's fine," and the men resheathed their swords and dropped back. They slumped to the floor, whispering to each other and laughing nervously.

Dùghall sat up and wiped sweat from his face with the back of his hand. He turned to Alarista and Yanth and Jaim. "Bring me all of the viewing glasses. I want to see if any of the remaining Dragons are near where Kait and Ry are imprisoned, or if any of them are working on their immortality spell." Then he turned his attention to Hasmal. "We're out of time. They're going to link Kait's and Ry's souls to the spell that starts their immortality engine. The magic they're doing will obliterate both Kait and Ry—not just here in this life, but eternally. They'll cease to exist ever again. I'm going to find a Dragon that is close to them. You're going to have to remove him from his body, then convince the true inhabitant of the body to release Kait and Ry from their cages. Meanwhile, I'll find a Dragon who is working on the immortality engine, remove him or her, and convince the body's rightful owner to smash it."

"Then we won't be able to watch each other," Hasmal protested. "We won't be able to pull each other back if one of the Dragons takes us." He didn't say that Dùghall was already so weak and worn so thin, the next Dragon he captured would surely be able to overmatch him.

"We're out of time," Dùghall said again. "If we don't stop them now, I don't know that we can stop them at all."

Hasmal saw foreknowledge of doom in Dùghall's eyes. The old man thought he was going to die, and he was going to go back anyway.

Alarista and Jaim and Yanth brought over the viewing glasses. Dùghall spread them out between himself and Hasmal, turned sideways so that both of them could see the images dancing in the glass. He stared at them for a long moment. Then he let out a sharp breath. He picked up a viewing glass that showed a pair of hands working with tiny tools on a delicate piece of machinery. "This one is mine," he said.

He stared back at the other glasses. Hasmal stared with him. "Look at that," Hasmal whispered, pointing to one of the glasses.

Through one pair of distant eyes, he saw Ian, dressed in guards' clothing, his face grim, stalking up a long white corridor.

Dùghall squinted at the image and nodded. "I see him."

"Pity we can't kill the traitor from here."

"We can't," Dùghall said shortly. "Look for something we *can* affect."

He viewed Crispin Sabir, differently dressed than when he and Ian had met the man in the inn, but unmistakable. Through the pair of eyes that looked at him, he also caught a glimpse of occupied cages just at the edge of the image. They faded out of view, but he said, "That one, don't you think?"

Dùghall said, "He was at the cages, but he looks like he's leaving."

"Then I'd better get him quickly."

"He's with Crispin Sabir—he's surely one of the most dangerous of the Dragons."

"But this one knows what we need to know."

Dùghall nodded. "You're right. Go, and may Vodor Imrish be with you."

"And with you."

Hasmal was only vaguely aware of the soldiers stepping into place behind him and Dùghall, only distantly aware of Alarista and Yanth and Jaim moving near. They would watch him for changes, he knew; they'd tell the soldiers if the soul that came back in Hasmal's body wasn't his, and then his body would die. . . .

He pushed through the fear that enveloped him and sank into the trance that let him follow the slender thread of energy that connected him to his chosen body. He was chanting the words of the spell, but he didn't hear them as words; he felt them as a path that led him closer and closer to the enemy with whom he would soon do battle.

Abruptly the darkness of the path he walked cleared, and he looked out through the eyes of another man. He was walking beside Crispin Sabir, close enough to drive a knife into his back. But the body would not respond to him, of course. He could see what the alien body saw, hear what it heard, feel what it felt, know what it knew . . . but he could not force it to respond.

"That was odd," the man whose body he occupied said.

"What was?" Crispin glanced at him and frowned.

"Suddenly my vision seemed to double for a moment, and I could have sworn I heard . . . a voice inside my head. Just for an instant." He chuckled nervously.

Shut up, shut up, shut up, Hasmal thought. He chanted the spell that would focus his energy and allow him to draw the Dragon soul out of the body it had stolen. He focused on recalling the body's rightful soul from the Veil. Faster. He needed to go faster.

"Stand right there," Crispin said, his eyes cold and hard. "And don't move."

Spin the spell. Call the soul lost in darkness, bring it home. He tried to ignore the fear that consumed him. If he could keep his mind on what he was doing, he could pull the Dragon out of this body right under Crispin Sabir's nose, and the rightful owner of it could turn on the man and kill him.

But he couldn't feel the familiar rush of the rightful soul returning to its body, the oncoming warmth of gratitude, the hope that something would suddenly make sense. No displaced soul answered his call. And the soul in the body he occupied wasn't losing its grip on its stolen flesh.

He pulled his focus in tighter, maintaining only the most tenuous link with his body. Kait's and Ry's chance of survival rested on his ability to restore this body's rightful soul, and on his ability, once he had done so, to convince the man to release Kait and Ry before fleeing the Dragon city.

"Quickly, tell me everywhere you've been today," Crispin told the man.

"I reported from the barracks for special duty. We went to pick up those skinshifters you sent us after—"

"What happened while you were there?"

"I blocked the girl's escape, she slapped me, she ran." He shrugged. "She didn't hurt me when she slapped me, didn't even try to. I thought it was strange at the time, but then I didn't think no more about it. Someone else brought them in. I been guarding the door outside their cages until you came to get me. Sir."

Sir? Why would one of the Dragons call another of the Dragons sir? Or speak with such a heavy docksider accent?

In that instant, it clicked. No soul came because no soul had been displaced. Kait had marked a guard, but the guard wasn't a Dragon; he was just a soldier called from his barracks to do a job. Hasmal pulled away from the body and started following the fragile line he'd left for himself back to his own body.

Nevertheless, he felt a jolt the instant that Crispin touched the soldier. Something big and ugly came racing along the energy line behind him. He fled toward his own body, and heat and weight and rage rolled after him, growing and billowing and consuming everything, using *his* energy and *his* life force to follow him.

He slammed into his own flesh and his eyes flew open and he started to erect the shield that would protect him from the thing that followed him, but he wasn't fast enough. The thing, the spell, the hunter that Crispin sent after him was in the shield with him, and the shield would keep Alarista or Jaim or Yanth from even trying to save him from it.

He screamed, "It's got me!" and saw the soldiers raise their weapons, and saw Alarista's face twist with horror, and then the fire consumed him, and pain flashed through his eyes and his nose and his mouth and his ears straight into his brain, and the world filled with a rushing sound, as if a white-hot ocean had suddenly upended itself and poured its full weight down onto him.

He felt himself stretching, twisting, being pummeled by a current of fire. He knew he was screaming, but he couldn't hear the sound that ripped itself from his tortured throat. He thrashed and fought.

And suddenly he was free of the pain, alone in darkness, cold, blind, deaf.

His ears started working first.

"—don't know if you can hear me yet, so when you can, please nod your head. . . . I'm still waiting. . . ." He heard a long, irritated sigh, then silence. After a few moments, the voice broke the silence again. "One more time, then. My name is Dafril, and I've captured you. You're going to tell me everything I want to know, either now or later, but I promise you, you'll have an easier time if you cooperate with me. I don't know if you can hear me yet, but I know that you'll be able to in a moment, so I strongly suggest that when you can, you nod your head. I'll only be patient for so long, and then I'll start sticking pins under your fingernails because I'll stop believing that you might still be deaf from the transfer and start thinking that you're malingering. You can't get away, you can't protect yourself, and you will tell me what I want to know. . . ."

The truth hit Hasmal hard. Not only had he failed to win Kait and Ry a chance at freedom, but he had also given himself into the hands of his enemies. He'd failed his friends, he'd failed Alarista, he'd failed the world, he'd failed himself.

He opened his eyes, and found himself staring into the cold blue eyes of Crispin Sabir. He was tied to a table, his wrists and ankles bound to the sides, heavy leather straps over his chest and knees. Dafril, the voice had said, but the only one in the room was Crispin Sabir. He realized that the Dragon who occupied Crispin's body must have named itself.

Dafril.

He felt despair. He had no weapons to fight with, his enemy had shielded him so tightly that he could not feel the movement of magic in his own body, and his friends didn't even know what had happened to him. He would never see Alarista again, never hold her in his arms, never tell her that he loved her, or that for the brief time that he'd had her she'd made his life complete. He would die knowing that he had failed her; that he had failed all of them.

And then he recalled the wax on his fingertips. And he remembered the tiny talisman embedded in that wax, held there so that he could press it into Dùghall's skin if a Dragon forced Dùghall from his body. The talisman was already linked to a glass, the glass sat beside Dùghall, and the instant it embedded itself in living flesh, it would come to life, showing Dùghall and Alarista and Yanth and Jaim where he was—and giving them their chance to capture the Dragon Dùghall suspected led the others.

Hasmal almost smiled.

Come a little closer, Dafril, he thought. Just a little closer. I have a surprise for you.

Chapter 53

Through one of the viewing glasses, Alarista had watched the clever hands working on that delicate bit of machinery suddenly take a hammer and smash it to pieces. Through the other, she had seen the Dragon Crispin turn on the man beside him, and the flash of light that followed was so brilliant that it illuminated the tent in which she sat. In that blazing light, Hasmal had disappeared, and at the moment he vanished, the glass through which she had observed Crispin had gone dark; the man through whose eyes she had been watching was either blind or dead.

She'd screamed, "That can't happen! Magic can't do that!"

Yanth had rested a hand on her shoulder, and she had felt it trembling. Yanth—the fearless swordsman—trembling. He'd said, "It's Dragon magic. You can't know all of what they can do."

She stared at the place where Hasmal had been, and knew he was right. No telling the horrors the Dragons could unleash if they weren't stopped.

Dùghall had returned from his successful battle with the Dragon who had been working on the machinery, but he was gray with exhaustion, and so weak he couldn't even sit up. He lay on the floor of the tent, blinking slowly, unresponsive to Alarista even when she told him that the Dragons had somehow captured Hasmal.

So now she crouched over the viewing glasses, looking for anything that might help her help Hasmal, or Kait, or Ry. Whatever had kept her from seeing through Kait's and Ry's mirrors had gone away; she could see what they saw again, but nothing she saw meant anything to her. They lay in their cages watching each other. Occasionally from the corners of their eyes she could make out the movement of guards, but the guards kept their distance, and Kait and Ry focused on each other. They were speaking to each other, she realized at last, though so carefully that their lips barely moved. She could hear nothing they said. And their eyes were so nearly closed that to each other they appeared asleep.

She looked into the other viewing glasses. Nothing useful. Nothing even curious. Pictures of vast white rooms, of elegant silks, of fountains and long corridors and delicate gardens—all pretty. All utterly meaningless.

Alarista wanted to smash the glasses, or tear screaming through the tent and out into the warming spring air; she wanted to shake someone, anyone, and demand that he find some way to bring back Hasmal. Instead she forced herself to stillness, and willed her mind to patience, and she watched. Something would happen—now or later. Something would change, and if she was ready and patient and watchful she would catch that moment when it happened, and she would be able to act.

Kait heard the voices by the door clearly enough.

"You're late. We were supposed to have been relieved half a station ago." The guards had been complaining for a while that their relief hadn't come, and toying with the idea of having one of the two of them go see what the holdup was. The one who spoke had been working himself into a real lather.

"Sergeant told me. Captain's messin' with the duty roster."

"Thought Rowel and Steedman were going to be here."

"Reckon they were. I was supposed to have today off, but they put your regular relief out on the wall an' forgot to assign anyone to this duty until just now. I ran the whole way here." The new guard had the hoarsest voice she'd ever heard. She wondered if he was sick, or if something was wrong with his voice box.

"We're supposed to have two men to this duty."

"Supposed to have a lot of things—ain't seen gold nor promotion nor fine new uniforms, either. I transferred in from Lightning Company just today, and no more than got my kit under my bunk than they stuck me here by my lonesome, and damn me if it don't go well. Told me I'm guarding skinshifters. I'd rather have the gods' damned plague, but captain didn't ask for my drathers. They give you any trouble?"

"Them? Nah. Ate before we got here, slept our whole shift. Don't get too close to 'em, you'll be fine. Only reason you'd need a partner is to keep you awake."

"Hope you're right. Maybe I'll be as lucky as you were. Anyway, got a note from the captain to the two of you."

Kait heard the rustle of paper, then a disgusted snarl.

"Brethwan's balls, Eagan! Bastards have us eating now and straight back to barracks to sleep, and on duty again at Huld."

"Huld! We get only two stations to eat and sleep?"

The voice of the new guard, commiserating. "I told you captain was messin' with the duty roster."

"Futter the bleeding pig! He's been a donkey's ass since we got him."

The guards who'd watched Kait and Ry for most of the afternoon and evening left, complaining loudly about the captain and his policies as they went. When they were gone, silence returned, but only for a moment. Then the stealthy whisper of approaching footsteps set her skin crawling.

Ry whispered, "He's coming over. Got his head down and his face hidden. There's something wrong about him, but I don't know what. . . ." Then he growled and moved into the crouch that was the only position other than lying down that the cage would allow. "Any closer and I'll kill you," he said.

Kait rolled and braced for whatever was coming.

And saw Ian, his skin burnished the color of fine mahogany, his dark hair cropped close to his skull, and dressed in a guard's uniform, approaching quickly with something hidden in his hand.

Fear flooded her veins and sent her heart racing. Ian could kill Ry or her easily; they were helpless in the cramped cages. The question was, which of them did he hate the most, and would either of them have a chance to talk him out of whatever he had planned?

Ian glared at Ry. "The day I came here, I left a note for you morons telling you I had something planned that would help you. When I got back to the inn, you were gone and I've seen nor heard not a word from you until I hear from the guards that they brought in a couple of skinshifters. So I've been stuck here, working in this hell, pretending to be loyal to the Dragons and doing things I don't want to think about to prove my loyalty, and all the time hoping that you would find your way back here to get your gods' damned Mirror. We don't have time to talk now," he said, his voice still harsh and strange. "I set it up so that I'd be alone with you, but one of the Dragons could decide to come after the two of you at any time. I'm going to take you to the Mirror of Souls. Then I'm going to get the three of us out of here if I can."

"The . . . three of us?" Kait whispered.

She glanced at Ry, who looked as dumbfounded as she felt.

Ian looked at her. Pain flashed across his face, though he hid it quickly. "The three of us. You made your choice—you love him, don't you?"

"I do."

He nodded, and bent to insert the key into the lock that held her door closed. "So that's it. I'm saving you because I love you." The chain that held her door closed rattled softly as he worked the lock. "And I'll save him . . . because I love you." He shrugged and avoided her eyes.

"You sacrificed yourself to help us? Me?"

"We don't have time to talk," he rasped.

Something inside her hurt at that moment. She wished she had been able to love him. She wished she could be two people so that she could be with Ian and with Ry without betraying either of them, or that she had never met Ian, or that she could take his pain away. The magnitude of what he'd done for her unrolled before her in the few moments that he struggled with the lock that kept her caged. "Why did you come here?" she asked him.

Her lock clattered open and the chain rattled to the floor. Ian immediately hurried to Ry's cage and began working on that lock. Kait crawled out of her cage and stretched.

"You mean right here? Or to the Dragons?"

"Both."

"I figured out a way I could get to the Mirror of Souls. And I knew you needed it. So since you had . . ." Another shrug. "Since you had someone else, I decided I was free to go. I offered my services to the Sabirs, but especially to Crispin—I told him lies about how much I wanted to get even with you, and he put me in charge of the combined Sabir and Galweigh forces. I . . . I did some things I don't want to think about in order to convince him that I was what I said I was. People died at my word and by my hand. They weren't innocents, but they were innocent of the things I said they did." Ry's lock opened, and Ian backed up so that his half-brother could free himself. "Come with me. We have a ways to go to get to the Mirror, and not much time."

He led them out of the beautiful arched room into a corridor. In the darkness, only the pale glimmer of moonlight shining through skylights illuminated it.

"This way."

They followed him, silent for the moment. Kait could hear movement within some of the rooms they passed, and once she and Ry hid in a room while Ian stood in front of the door, his guard's uniform rendering him effectively invisible. No one spoke again until he led them down a long, twisting staircase into a vault beneath the white city. He took a key and opened one door, then pressed a complex combination of switches to open the next door.

"In here."

Kait and Ry followed him into a narrow room lit by hundreds of tiny pebbles embedded in the ceiling; the Mirror of Souls sat on a dais in the center of the room, dark and seemingly dead.

"How do we get it out of here?" Kait asked.

"I have a friend in a closed carriage waiting at the south gate of the Citadel. I sent him the message just before I came to get you. He'll wait for us for a full day."

"Then all we have to do is figure out how to carry it past the Dragons without them seeing us."

"I'd hoped you could shield it the way you did when we escaped the *Wind Treasure*," Ian said.

Kait looked at Ry. "I can do that. Ry and I are both weak—it might take some time to get it right."

Ian looked from one of them to the other. "Hurry. Someone will be along to check on this thing within the station. I can kill him, but the moment he doesn't report in, more will be on the way."

Chapter 54

asmal told Dafril nothing that he wanted to know, but he was no longer able to feign indifference. Through the early part of the torture, he'd placed himself in the meditative trance he would have used to summon magic, had he not been shielded from it. He'd withstood terrible things by standing apart from his body and watching what was done to him as if he were only a distant and uninterested observer.

Now, though, the pain had become too much, and he'd lost the trance. He was once again entirely in his body, and bleeding from a multitude of cuts, and scarred from burns with a branding iron. The pain was riveting; he couldn't pull himself away from Dafril's soft, amused voice any longer.

"Suddenly I feel that you're with me again," Dafril said. "That's good. That should speed up this process enormously. I'll have you know that I've broken hundreds of your sort, young Falcon—hundreds. Stronger men than you, and men who had full control of Matrin's magic. You'll tell me what I want to know."

Dafril had kept his distance, and kept to the left of Hasmal. The talisman on his right finger still waited, but Dafril had never moved within the slight range of his bound hand. He had to get him close—

Searing pain ripped into his ribs, and he heard his skin sizzle. He screamed and fought against the restraints that bound him.

Dafril sighed. "You see? This hurts a lot, and you aren't as brave or as strong as you think you are. So help me out, and I'll help you. Tell me how you and your friends are stealing the souls of my colleagues."

Hasmal's mind raced. He thought of half a dozen lies, but all of them were improbable and sounded weak even to him—and if he told Dafril anything, he knew the Dragon would just keep torturing him, making sure that what he said at the beginning matched what he would say when he was more desperate.

He turned his face away.

"Look at me."

He stared off to his right, trying to think of something that might save him, that might get Dafril within his range.

"Look at me, damn you."

The searing pain again, this time high on the inside of his thigh.

He screamed and writhed, but kept his face turned from Dafril. It seemed to help.

Dafril said, "I can come around to that side, you idiot. You won't win anything this way."

Hasmal's heart leaped. Yes, he thought. Do come around.

Dafril did, carrying a knife. "Look, you—I can carve out your eyes and your ears, cut off your nose, rip off your balls, or skin the flesh from your body if I have to. The only part of you that I need to have in working order is your tongue."

Hasmal met his gaze defiantly, and managed a grin. So this was courage—being trapped and terrified and holding fast because he loved Alarista, and because cowardice would betray her.

He wondered if that was the difference between courage and cowardice—if brave men loved someone outside of themselves while cowards loved only their own lives. If that were true, then all men might be cowards sometimes and heroes at others. Then he wondered if all courage trembled inside—if all of it felt so thin and fragile, so ready to tatter and blow away in the next faint breeze—or if there was a better sort of courage that filled the belly with reckless fire and protected the mind from terror. If any of that sort of courage existed, he wished he could have some, because he was so scared he feared his heart would burst through his chest.

"Stubborn bastard. I'd cooperate if I were you."

"You aren't me," Hasmal whispered.

"What was that?" Dafril leaned closer so that he could hear what Hasmal had said.

Yes, he thought. "I'll tell you," he whispered, his voice even softer than before.

Dafril stepped in close and leaned all the way over Hasmal. "Louder," he said. "Say it louder."

And that was close enough. Hasmal rested his index finger against Dafril's leg. He felt the slight vibration as the talisman popped away from his skin and burrowed through the cloth of Dafril's breeches.

In a moment, Alarista and Dùghall would see him through Dafril's eyes. Dùghall would enter Dafril and pull his soul out and trap it in one of the tiny soul-mirrors that waited on the floor of the tent. And Hasmal would be saved—if he could just hold on until they could reach him.

"We found a way to make our own Mirror of Souls," he whispered.

Dafril's eyes narrowed, and he ran his thumb along the bloody edge of the knife. "Really? Tell me more."

Chapter 55

They lugged the Mirror of Souls through the dark underpassages of the Citadel of the Gods, breathless, frightened, yet exhilarated, too. Kait had to fight the urge to shout, to scream defiance at the Dragons who went unaware about their business in the white streets above her head. We have it, she thought. We have it, and we're going to get away with it, and we're going to destroy you.

"How much farther?" Ry, the strongest of the three of them, carried most of the Mirror's weight; he'd positioned the artifact with two of its petals resting on the small of his back and he gripped one petal in each hand. She and Ian followed him, balancing a tripod leg each. They seemed to Kait to be moving quickly, but they'd been in those dark passages for a long time anyway.

"Can you see a fork in the passageway ahead of us yet?" Ian asked.

"It goes off in three directions."

"We'll take the left corridor. The passage will start rising immediately and branch again. The right branch comes out in a guardhouse at the Citadel's service gate. We'll have to kill the guard, but my friend and his carriage will be parked behind the stables across the street."

"I can already smell outside air," Kait said.

She saw Ry nod. "I do, too."

The picked up their pace until they were running. It was an unconscious action born of fear and anticipation, but it was dangerous, too. Hurrying, their breathing became louder and their attention too focused on the simple mechanics of not falling down while carrying their burden. "We have to slow down," Kait said, pulling backward on her leg of the tripod.

Both men slowed without a word.

Kait heard voices ahead. "Who is likely to be coming through here at this time of day?" she asked Ian.

"Soldiers . . . gardeners . . . servants . . . Could be anyone."

"We'll have to kill them," Ry said.

"Maybe not," Ian said. The corridor they were in was pierced at right angles by regular intersections with other, similar corridors. "We can just move aside and hope they don't notice us."

"And if they do?" Ry asked.

Kait sighed. "Then we'll have to kill them. But we'll all be better off if we don't." Them included, she thought. She had no stomach for the murder of innocent gardeners or serving girls.

They moved into the first corridor to their right and stood in the shadows, not moving and barely breathing. They saw a light flickering from ahead of where they'd been walking. They waited, and the voices grew louder.

". . . and I told Marthe I was going to quit and find a job slopping hogs if I couldn't find nothing better," a man's voice said. "Hogs is friendlier than these bastards."

"A hog'll rip your arm off and eat it in front of you, you ain't careful," a woman's voice answered. "Hogs is mean."

"And these people's meaner. You're fresh from the country—you haven't seen what I've seen. But you mark my words, Lallie, they'll be dug under your skin and sucking the life out of you before you're here a week. Find something else."

"If that's such good advice, why ain't you already taken it?"

The pair drew even with Kait's hiding place and she watched them. Their torch illuminated a tired-looking man of perhaps forty, slouch-shouldered and with thinning hair, and a fresh-scrubbed young woman with a pert smile and a bounce in her step.

"Because the bastards pay in good gold, and gold's hard to come by these days."

The girl flashed a broad grin up at the man and laughed. "As hard for me as for you, I reckon, and I swear I'm tired of being paid in eggs and promises. I guess I can wash clothes for bastards good as I can for my neighbors."

They were past, then, and Kait's heart slowed its knocking in her chest.

"I reckon you can. I just hope you don't mind paying a high price for your gold wage."

Kait wanted to tell the girl, *Listen to him, you idiot.* Instead, she contented herself with the thought that she held the Dragons' downfall in her hands. Maybe, if Lallie wouldn't save herself, Kait could save her. Maybe.

The voices died away to silence at last, and Ry and Kait and Ian got back under way.

The guardhouse proved to be close, and Ian proved to be right in his description of what they would find there. A guard stood, his back to them, watching a few boys playing ball in the alley he guarded. There was no traffic. There were no pedestrians.

Ian drew his knife, slipped behind the guard, jammed a leather gag into the man's mouth, and slammed him on the back of the head with the pommel of his knife. The man fell like a dropped bag of rocks. Kait saw that he was still breathing. Ian carefully removed the leather gag and stood staring down at the man.

"I thought you were going to kill him," Ry said.

"I've done more than my share of killing since I came here." He looked bleak when he said it. "He didn't see us, he didn't hear us, and he won't be able to tell anyone which way we went or what we did."

Ry nodded. "I'm not complaining."

"Where's your carriage?"

Ian said, "Stand here a moment." He strolled across the street, to all appearances the guard in the guardhouse stepping out for a moment to take a look at something interesting. When he came back, Kait heard wheels rattle, and an instant later, a large black funeral carriage drawn by four black horses rolled into view. It stopped in front of the guardhouse and Kait, Ry, and Ian dragged the Mirror of Souls into the darkened interior and followed it in.

The carriage lurched forward.

"Where are we going?" Kait asked. She couldn't believe that they were free.

"Galweigh House," Ian said softly. "It's the last place anyone will think to look for us."

About the Author

Holly Lisle, born in 1960, has been writing science fiction full time since November of 1992. Prior to that, she worked as an advertising representative, a commercial artist, a guitar teacher, a restaurant singer, and for ten years as a registered nurse specializing in emergency and intensive care. Originally from Salem, Ohio, she has also lived in Alaska, Costa Rica, Guatemala, North Carolina, Georgia, and Florida. She and Matt are raising three children and several cats. Her Secret Texts series concludes with *Courage of Falcons* in October 2000.